Never let me Go

KIANNA ALEXANDER

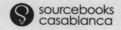

Published by Sourcebooks Casablanca, an imprint of Sourcebooks
P.O. Box 4410, Naperville, Illinois 60567-4410
(630) 961-3900
sourcebooks.com

Printed and bound in Canada.
MBP 10 9 8 7 6 5 4 3 2 1

For Aressa, who helped me look within and find my truest, most radiant self.

Thank you.

CHAPTER 1

CARRYING HIS BLACK LEATHER BRIEFCASE, MAXWELL DEVERS used his free hand to pull open the glass doors at the Hay Street Municipal Building. As the door closed behind him, he enjoyed the feeling of the lobby's heated air warming his frigid fingertips. It was the second week of February, and the cold and blustery weather outside had him wishing he hadn't forgotten his gloves.

After briefly speaking with the receptionist, Maxwell headed for the men's room to check his appearance. He wasn't vain by any stretch, but the importance of today's meeting motivated him to make sure he looked every bit the consummate professional he was. Architecture wasn't just his work, it was also his passion, and he hoped to convey that today.

Two things in his life mattered more than anything: family and architecture. He paused for a moment, pulling out his phone and swiping to a picture of Sasha. *My beautiful baby girl.* Looking at her cherubic face always made him smile and, at the moment, helped quell his nervousness about the upcoming meeting. She'd just turned seven months old, and while his relationship with her mother was less than ideal, he loved his daughter with his whole being. A major part of what drove him to go so hard, to climb toward success at every turn, was his desire to give her a wonderful life. Tucking the phone away, he kept walking.

The restroom's simple white tile walls, gray floors, and chrome fixtures reflected the same modern style as the rest of the building. Tugging off his black trench coat, Maxwell folded it and laid it on the white marble countertop, along with his briefcase. He regarded his reflection in the full-length mirror mounted on the wall, adjusting the lapels of his sports coat. *The black-on-black look suits me.* He smiled, glad he'd chosen the rich black Italian label suit, starched black shirt, black satin tie, and black dress loafers. The splash of color provided by the bright green TDT handkerchief in his breast pocket was just the right accent.

Satisfied, he gathered his things and strode out into the corridor, headed for the conference room upstairs. A short elevator ride delivered him to the third floor, and he entered the conference room a full five minutes before the presentation began. While he moved across the room, he nodded greetings to the men and women present. Taking a seat in an empty chair on the right side of the table, he settled in.

He put his phone on silent, tucking it away, then he took out a pad and pen in case he needed to jot down any notes. This ritual helped him get in the zone, corralling his focus so that he wouldn't miss anything important during the meeting.

A projection screen displayed facts and figures related to the project at hand: a new performing arts center, to be built on the existing Crown Center property in Fayetteville. A smile tugged at Maxwell's lips as he thought of what such a large, high-profile project would mean for his firm and his career. Devers Architectural had handled its share of city and state projects all over North Carolina, including schools, seniors' centers, and shopping centers. They'd never taken on a project of this scale, and the idea of working on the civic center excited Maxwell to no end. DAI was a small firm, and if they were to win the contract, the project would no doubt be a challenge. When it came to his craft, however, Maxwell relished a challenge.

He took a second look at the faces around the room, and when he saw Harold Carmichael there, Maxwell's face immediately folded into a frown. He'd known Harold since college, and they had been locked in competition for architectural contracts for the past seven or eight years. For the life of him, Maxwell couldn't figure out why Harold felt the need to try to beat him at every step. Harold went out of his way to prove he was the better architect, and Maxwell found the man's constant one-upmanship petty and pointless. And while Maxwell didn't subscribe to such childish behavior, he still wanted to win this contract for other, more important reasons. Seeing Harold's tightly pursed lips would only be a bonus. Maxwell had worked hard to get to where he was and had earned his seat in this room.

"Ladies and gentlemen, thank you so much for coming in." Mayor Ravyn Taylor, standing near the projection screen, looked around the room as she spoke. She was a petite woman with bronze skin, brown eyes, and jet-black hair pulled into a bun low on her neck. As the city's youngest ever mayor, she was known for her forward-thinking ways. "We've asked you all here because you're the best and brightest architectural minds in the state. We'd like to have an innovative, green, and aesthetically appealing design for the new civic center, and I'm sure one of you in this room can give us just what we need."

Maxwell noticed the smug look on Harold's face as he glanced around as if sizing up his competition. When Harold's gaze fell on Maxwell, his expression soured.

Maxwell replied with a fake smile and a nod of acknowledgment. *That's right, Carmichael. Your worst nightmare is here.*

Mayor Taylor continued. "Due to the scale of this project, we wanted to give you all as much time as we could to prepare your designs and bids. We'll go over the budget and expectations today in detail. Then, we'd like to see your bids and designs submitted within sixty days."

Maxwell jotted that down on his notepad. Based on the mayor's statement, he and his small, dedicated team would have about two months to come up with a world-class design and reasonable bid. *That should be ample time to get this done.*

For the rest of the meeting, Maxwell continued to take notes, giving his full attention to the mayor. He filled several pages with details about the space requirements, the size and condition of the land parcel, and other general specifications related to the project.

As was generally the case in these types of meetings with city officials, Mayor Taylor left the discussion of the budget for the project as her last topic. "As you go about creating your designs and bids, please be aware that the city is on a tight budget."

Nods and murmurs of understanding came from the people gathered around the table.

Moments later, as the mayor quoted a number, the mood in the room changed significantly. A few snickers went up, and one of the architects simply gathered her things, sighed, and walked out of the room.

Maxwell had to admit, the budget was paltry for a project of this scale and size. Still, after years in this business, he'd come to expect this type of thing with city and state governments. They always seemed to have champagne tastes and ginger ale budgets.

As the meeting adjourned, Maxwell slid his notepad back into his briefcase, then stood and lifted his coat from the back of the chair.

He'd just slipped into the coat when he felt someone enter his personal space.

Turning around, he found Harold standing there, wearing that obviously false, crap-munching grin. "Greetings, Maxwell. How've you been?"

"I'm well, Harold. How are you?" Maxwell fastened the buttons of his coat and picked up his briefcase, hoping his actions would let Harold know he didn't plan to linger.

"Good to hear. You know, Carmichael has been pulling in a lot of big jobs lately. It's been so busy we've had to add some new staff." Harold slipped his hands into the pockets of his slacks, rocking back slightly on his heels, then forward onto his toes.

Maxwell nodded. "Wonderful." He didn't counter with any information about his own business. After all, he had nothing to prove. He looked at Harold, who was a good two or three inches shorter than him, and wondered if the rocking motion was something he did to appear taller.

"No news over at Devers, huh?"

Maxwell shrugged. "Not anything I feel compelled to share with you."

Harold chuckled. "Okay, that's fine. Anyway, I just wanted to let you know, I hope there won't be any hard feelings when I win the civic center project." He reached out to touch Maxwell's shoulder.

Maxwell cut his eyes at Harold's hand. "I wouldn't advise that."

Drawing his hand back, Harold shook his head. "At any rate, there won't be any hard feelings on my part. In fact, I'm throwing a big party to celebrate winning the bid, and I expect to see you there."

Maxwell scoffed. "You're mighty sure of yourself, Harold."

Harold shrugged. "As always."

Maxwell rolled his eyes. Unwilling to waste any more time on this fruitless conversation, he cleared his throat. "Well, it was nice to see you. Have a good day, Harold." Maxwell turned and began walking out of the room.

"See you at the party," Harold called out.

Maxwell ignored him as he left the conference room and took the stairs back to the first floor. If he waited for the elevator, his pesky little buddy might follow him.

Back outside, the chill hit him as he crossed the parking lot to his SUV. Once he and his briefcase were inside the cabin, he started the engine and turned on the heat, including the heated seats. The digital thermometer in the dash showed the temperature in the low forties, but the chilly wind made it feel much colder.

He pulled out into traffic, feeling somewhat jealous of his baby sister, Alexis. While he was here, working hard and bundling up against the cold, Alexis was enjoying the second week of her honeymoon with her new husband, Bryan. Maxwell hadn't been too keen on his baby sister dating his best friend and had made his opinions clear. But when it became obvious that the two of them were in love, he'd apologized for his behavior. Never one to do things by halves, he'd paid for an extra week of honeymoon bliss for them to demonstrate his sincerity.

His cell phone rang, breaking into his thoughts. Navigating the car through the gate of his community, he engaged the hands-free calling to answer it. "Hello?"

"Hey, Max, it's Kelsey."

Hearing his middle sister's voice made him smile. "Hey, Kels. All settled in, I'm guessing?"

"Yes. I promised to call you when everything was moved in, and I'm all set up now." Kelsey's tone was light, indicating that she was in a good mood.

"I'm glad to hear it. Are you sure you don't need anything else from me?"

Kelsey giggled. "Maxwell, you helped me find this apartment, then you helped me move, then you paid my first three months' rent, against my wishes. I think you've done enough, Bro."

"You're my sister, and I love you. I was happy to do all of it."

"I love you, too, Maxwell. And once I get a chance, I'll invite you over for dinner. You can even bring a date," she teased.

He rolled his eyes while pulling his SUV into his driveway. "Fat chance. But I'll be there."

"Tsk, tsk. You've seen how happy your frat brothers are since they got married. Don't you want that for yourself?"

He shook his head, even though he knew she couldn't see him. "Kelsey, you and Lex have got to stop trying to set me up with women. I'm plenty happy just the way I am."

"If you say so." She didn't sound very convinced.

"I definitely *do* say so."

"Okay, I'll let you go. Bye, Maxwell."

Ending the call, he cut the engine, grabbed his briefcase, and took it inside.

It never ceased to amaze him how the women in his life constantly tried to couple him up with someone. As he entered his home, relishing the silence and solitude, he pushed the thoughts aside.

His life was perfect just the way it was. The last thing he needed was for a woman to come into his life.

—⁓—

Yvonne Markham sat in a stiff-backed chair inside the office of Victoria Cross, director of the Wittenmyer Agency. She shifted in the seat, crossing her legs. She was seeking a position that would make her appear calmer and more collected than she felt. Yvonne couldn't remember ever being this nervous during a job interview, but she'd been on edge since the moment she stepped into the building. The décor and air of the place made it seem more like a law firm than a nanny agency. Yvonne felt slightly underdressed, even though she'd donned her best navy-blue blazer and matching skirt, with a fresh white shirt and navy pumps. She'd brushed her short hair into a wavy style and kept her makeup light and professional. Yvonne looked great, and she knew it. But sitting here in the silence as Mrs. Cross read through her résumé made nervous prickles run up and down her spine.

What part is she reading now? What is she thinking? Yvonne didn't dare to peer across the desk to see Mrs. Cross's progress; that would be rude. She could only hope that despite the stoic, blank expression Mrs. Cross wore, she was pleased with what she was reading.

Finally, after what seemed like ages, Mrs. Cross put Yvonne's résumé aside. Looking up to meet Yvonne's eyes, she spoke. "Well, Ms. Markham. I must say, you have an impressive résumé. I do have a question, though."

Yvonne braced for the query, the one she didn't really want to answer but knew she would have to anyway. "Yes, ma'am?"

"What made you quit your last position?"

She drew a deep breath. "In all honesty, Mrs. Cross, I was unhappy with the way management at Avery Child Development treated low-income families and families of color."

Mrs. Cross's brow rose in surprise. "As a woman of color myself, I'm sure you understand why I'd like some clarity here. What do you mean?"

Not one to propagate drama, Yvonne didn't relish elaborating on the situation but knew it was necessary. "Management was very stringent in handling late payments, regardless of the family's situation. I'd seen them dismiss families who were suffering job losses or death in the family and even those who had just fallen on hard times. No provisions were made for these families to catch up on their payments or for them to secure other care."

Tenting her fingers, Mrs. Cross nodded. "I see. And this disturbed you enough that you felt you couldn't continue working there?"

"Yes, ma'am. When I brought up the problems I saw, I was reprimanded and even disrespected. I couldn't accept that, so here I am." Yvonne had put away a small amount of money as a cushion, but with all her responsibilities, the cushion would soon be gone. She needed this job, and she hoped her honesty reflected well on her.

Mrs. Cross was silent for a moment. "Thank you for telling me about your experience, Ms. Markham. I can appreciate your candor. You do understand that at Wittenmyer, we serve a wealthier portion of the population, correct?"

That statement almost made Yvonne want to laugh. If she hadn't known that the Wittenmyer Agency was a high-end operation, she'd have found out the moment she stepped inside the building. "Yes, ma'am, I understand that. I have no problem with people who are well off financially. I just don't like to see those who aren't so fortunate be mistreated." If she could secure the position and get a client or two, Yvonne planned to set aside some funds to open her own childcare center, where less fortunate families wouldn't be treated differently.

"Wonderful. That's just the sort of character we like to see here, so welcome aboard, Ms. Markham." Mrs. Cross stood, extending her perfectly manicured hand.

An excited Yvonne hopped to her feet, smiling broadly as she shook hands with her new boss. "Thank you, Mrs. Cross. I'm going to do my absolute best to be an asset to Wittenmyer."

"I expect nothing less." Mrs. Cross returned to her seat. "Will you be able to start tomorrow?"

"Yes, ma'am. I'll be here bright and early."

"Seven a.m., sharp. We're a busy firm, and I expect you'll be matched to a family within the first week." Mrs. Cross smiled. "I'll see you tomorrow."

"Yes, definitely. Thank you again." Yvonne gathered her things and hurried out of the office.

She slipped into her wool peacoat as she walked down the plush carpeted hallway toward the reception area. She stopped a moment by the chintz sofa in the lobby to pull on her hat and gloves, then stepped outside. The frigid, gray day made her long for the warmth and sunshine of spring.

Downtown Durham buzzed with activity, as was typical of a weekday in the area. Driving past the shops and restaurants, Yvonne thought back on the city she remembered from her youth. It was very different from what she saw before her. The old abandoned tobacco warehouses left behind by the cigarette manufacturers of the late nineteenth and early twentieth centuries had been converted into upscale apartments. New restaurants and businesses were popping up everywhere, and the city had even demolished the old Heart of Durham hotel several years back to build a new transportation hub for the city's residents. Yvonne loved knowing that the city was experiencing so much growth, but she wondered what had happened to the folks who'd once lived in the area, who were largely poor and middle-class people of color. She could only assume that the higher rents on the newer, fancier properties in the area had pushed many of them out.

Yvonne pulled her compact sedan into the driveway at her parents' home a few minutes later. Their small, one-story brick house sat on a hilly road in the Old North Durham neighborhood. She and her sister, Zelda, had grown up in a different house, farther out of the city, but this was the home their parents had downsized to soon after Zelda's high school graduation.

A few minutes later, Yvonne used her key to enter the house. Shutting the door behind her, she stilled for a moment to listen for clues to her parents' whereabouts. She could hear the television playing in the bedroom near the back of the house, so she assumed her parents were back there. Crossing the living room, she went down the hall toward the bedroom.

As she passed the kitchen, her mother, Marissa, called out to her. "Hey, Von. Come here for a minute, baby."

Turning right into the kitchen, Yvonne sidled up to her mother, who sat at the table with an open magazine and a cup of tea. Leaning down, she threw her arms around her mother's shoulders. "Hey, Mommy. How are you feeling today?"

"Not too bad." Marissa smiled up at her daughter. "How'd the interview go?"

Yvonne pulled out the chair next to her mother and sat down, wearing a broad grin. "It went great. I got the job, and I start tomorrow."

Marissa clapped her hands together. "Wonderful, wonderful. I was a little worried when you left the center, but I'm sure you'll do great at this job."

"I really do have a good feeling about this position, Mommy." Yvonne was hoping this position would be her last one where she worked for someone else. "If I can get one or two wealthy clients, I should be able to save up for my childcare center a lot faster."

"Just so long as you don't forget about Daddy and me." Marissa lifted the mug of tea to her lips, taking a slow sip.

Yvonne felt her grin fade. "Of course not, Mommy. I'm always going to make sure you're taken care of. Don't worry, okay?" She'd been supporting her parents ever since she graduated from college, and she wasn't about to stop now. It was the least she could do, to repay them for all the years of sweat and hard work they'd put in to raise her and Zelda.

Setting the mug down again, Marissa sighed. "I wish we didn't have to lean on you girls so much. But with our health being the way it is..." She didn't finish.

Yvonne took her mother's hand in her own. "Mommy, don't worry about it, okay? You and Daddy put in a good thirty years of work already. Zelda and I love you, and it's our honor to take care of you." Her parents both suffered from a host of health conditions that prevented them from working.

"I love you too, baby." Marissa squeezed her daughter's hand. "You know how we are, though. Even though we're both past sixty, your daddy and I would have kept right on working if we could."

"I know." Yvonne had never known anyone with a stronger work ethic than her parents. She could remember times during her childhood when they'd both worked two, even three jobs to make sure she and Zelda had everything they needed. There hadn't been a lot of extras—very few meals out, no long family vacations to exotic destinations. Still, Yvonne and her sister had never gone hungry or lacked for love.

Yvonne released her mother's hand. "Daddy's in the back, I'm guessing."

Marissa nodded. "Yep. Caught up in a marathon of *Gilligan's Island*. You know how he loves that silly old show."

With a chuckle, Yvonne stood. "I'm gonna go check on him, then I'll be back to help you fix something for dinner, okay?"

"Thank you, baby." Marissa made eye contact with her daughter for a long, quiet moment. "For everything."

Blowing her mother a kiss, Yvonne slipped out of the kitchen. A moment later, she stuck her head around the frame of the bedroom door. Her father, Gordon, sat in the old brown recliner next to the bed, eyes glued to the television. "Hey, Daddy!"

His gaze shifted her way, and he smiled. "Hey, sweetheart. Came to watch Gilligan with me?"

She shook her head. "No, not today. I'm gonna help Mommy with dinner. I just wanted to check on you." She kept her eyes on his face, knowing how he hated it when people stared at his prosthetic. Diabetes had taken his lower left leg several years ago.

He grinned. "That's my girl. Always looking out for me."

She entered the room then. The curtains were drawn, as they always were when he watched his shows, leaving the room dim despite the sun's attempts to break through the clouds. Standing next to his chair, she touched his shoulder. "How are you feeling? Do you need anything?"

"I'm feeling okay today, darling. Just a little tired." He stifled a yawn. "Could use a cold drink, though."

"I'll be right back." Yvonne quickly went to the kitchen, returning with a glass of ice water with a lemon wedge.

Gordon frowned as he took the glass. "I was hoping for a diet soda or some juice."

Careful to keep her tone respectful, she said, "Daddy, you know you have to watch your sugar intake."

He sighed. "Yes, yes. I know."

She wanted him to be happy. But more than that, she wanted him to be healthy. While he sometimes railed against the changes he'd had to make in his life since he'd lost his foot, the whole family was behind him. She, Zelda, and their mother did what they could to make the transition smooth for him. When all was said and done, Yvonne knew her father's happiness would come once he accepted things as they were and committed himself to doing what was best for his health.

She leaned down, kissed him on the cheek. "Love you, Daddy."

His smile returned then. "I love you, too."

Leaving him to his drink and his show, she slipped from the room.

Back in the kitchen, she found her mother seated at the table, peeling sweet potatoes. "Did he fuss about the water?"

Yvonne nodded. "A little. But he knows I'm not bringing him anything sweet."

With a shake of her head, Marissa kept up her peeling. "Your daddy's stubborn. Always has been. But he'll come around." A soft smile touched her face as she spoke of her husband. "Thirty-six years with him has certainly been an adventure."

Yvonne reflected on her mother's words. Her parents' love and dedication to each other and to her and Zelda were the model for the life she hoped to share with a special man one day. No matter what life threw at them, Marissa and Gordon Markham always had each other's backs. One of the things she loved most about their relationship was the sense of balance. Her mother, while handling a lot of domestic responsibility, never shrank herself to suit her husband. And her father was a strong man, yet he'd never shied away from displaying his emotions.

Do they even make men like Daddy anymore? I'm not getting any younger, so if such a man exists, I wish he'd make himself known.

Her mother's voice cut into her thoughts. "Now wash your hands, baby, and help me cut up these potatoes."

"Yes, ma'am." Yvonne went to the sink to wash up, pushing aside her fantasies of a tall, dark, and honorable mate in favor of assisting her mother.

CHAPTER 2

MAXWELL STROLLED THROUGH THE MAIN LOBBY OF DEVERS Architectural early Monday, mindful of the potential client walking behind him. He walked at an even pace, his dress loafers making a muffled sound with each impact against the polished dark wood floors. Mary Alice, the receptionist, greeted them as they passed the wood-paneled, curved desk centering the space. Behind the desk, an angled accent wall, made of flat paving stones, provided the focal point for the space. Every time he entered the building, he took a few moments to admire the reception area, which he'd designed himself. He loved the feeling of the space; it was both professional and welcoming. At least he thought so, and he hoped his clients agreed.

Once he reached the end of the hall, he gestured to the open door of his office. "After you, Mrs. Dartmouth."

The petite lady in the navy suit nodded primly to him as she passed him. He followed her inside, keeping a respectable distance between them. In the outer office, they passed the desk of his assistant, who barely looked up from the computer screen as they exchanged greetings. Maxwell didn't mind, because he valued efficiency in his staff over most other qualities.

Inside his private office, Maxwell closed the door before he assisted his visitor into her chair. Soon he and Mrs. Dartmouth were seated on opposite sides of his steel and glass desk. The desk, custom made to Maxwell's specifications, had a top shaped like a crescent moon. His executive chair slid right into the inner curve. Resting his hands on the glass desktop, he looked in her direction. "So, Mrs. Dartmouth. I'd love to hear more about your vision for your summer home."

She smiled, her ice-blue eyes twinkling. For the next ten minutes, she spoke of the retreat she dreamed of. Her ideas were grand and varied, revealing how much thought she'd put into the project.

While she spoke, Maxwell did his best to be attentive.

Finally, she paused. "Look at me, rambling on. You're the designer, and here I am telling you what to do."

Maxwell gave her an easy smile. "It's not a problem. After all, this will be your oasis, not mine."

"It will be so divine when it's done. That stretch of land I own on the lake will be the perfect respite from all the noise and activity of the city."

"It sounds wonderful. And I truly enjoy creating designs for vacation homes, especially when my client is as imaginative as you."

She chuckled. "My generous budget probably doesn't hurt, either."

"No, ma'am. It doesn't hurt at all." Maxwell had been eager to take a meeting with Minerva Dartmouth ever since she'd called him the previous week. Her high six-figure spending limit for the lake house meant he could get very creative with the design, on a level he rarely got the chance to do when designing a private residence.

"Have you designed many vacation homes in the past, Mr. Devers?" Mrs. Dartmouth fixed him with a searching look as she posed the question.

"Call me Maxwell. And yes, ma'am, I've completed several properties of this kind." He slid his chair back, swiveled to open the top drawer of the storage cabinet behind his desk. "Let me show you a few of them." He extracted his hardback, full-color portfolio, then slid it across the desktop to her.

She opened the portfolio and had only flipped a few pages when the intercom went off.

"Excuse me, Mrs. Dartmouth." Annoyed, Maxwell lifted the

receiver of his desk phone. "Carson, I told you I didn't want to be disturbed while I was in this meeting."

Carson Lightner, his young and often overwrought assistant, spoke fast, his words coming out in a jumble. "I'm so sorry, Mr. Devers, but this can't wait."

"Is something on fire?" Maxwell struggled to keep his tone even, mindful of Mrs. Dartmouth.

"Not literally, but there may be something on fire figuratively..."

Maxwell rolled his eyes. "Carson, this is no time to be speaking in riddles. Just say what you mean."

The next voice that spoke over the intercom was Sasha's aunt Bianca. "Maxwell, we're coming in."

Maxwell's brow furrowed, only for a moment, before he realized something might be amiss with Sasha. "Show her in, Carson."

"Yes, sir."

Maxwell sighed. The sooner he knew what had brought Bianca to his office in the middle of the workday, the better. "Pardon the interruption, Mrs. Dartmouth."

She waved him off. "I'm retired. I've got plenty of time, Maxwell."

A few moments later, Bianca flung the door open and strode in. She was dressed in dark denim jeans with a matching jacket, her raven hair swept into a low ponytail. The pink butterfly-print bag that held the baby's belongings was tossed over her left shoulder. Sasha, tucked into her car seat, reached for Maxwell the moment she saw him.

He walked over to meet them, gathering his daughter in his arms. "Hi, sweetheart." Kissing her soft brow, he turned to the woman who'd almost been his sister-in-law. Now that he stood closer to her, he noticed the pale, drawn expression on her face. "Bianca, what's going on?"

"It's Mama." She swallowed. "She's had a stroke."

He frowned. "Oh no. Is she all right?"

"I don't know. The ambulance took her from the house. I need to leave Sasha with you so I can meet her at the hospital." She wrung her hands. "I've never seen Mama look so worn out."

He could feel the stress rolling off of her. "I understand. Go on ahead, and please, let me know about Ines's condition as soon as you can, okay?"

She nodded, her eyes watery. "I will. And just so you'll know… if it's as serious as they think, you might be getting Sasha full-time…at least until Juliana gets back from deployment." That said, she handed him the baby's bag and left.

Standing in the middle of his office with his babbling baby girl and her various necessities, he turned back to Mrs. Dartmouth, who'd watched the whole exchange in intrigued silence. "I'm so sorry about that. This was totally unexpected."

She smiled. "Goodness, don't apologize. What father worth his salt wouldn't take care of his child when there's an emergency?" She shifted in her seat as if to get a better view. "Bring that precious little cherub here."

He paused to take the baby out of her seat. He moved toward his desk, bouncing Sasha against his shoulder as he walked. "Sasha, can you say hi to Mrs. Dartmouth?"

Sasha made a little snorting sound, then focused her big brown eyes on the older woman. After staring for a few seconds, she raised her little hand and gave a backward wave.

"Oh." Mrs. Dartmouth's smile widened. "What a precious little dear. May I hold her?"

He felt his brow hitch. "If you'd like." He gently placed his daughter in her lap, then returned to his seat, placing the diaper bag on the floor beneath his desk.

"Don't look so nervous, Maxwell. I've got eight grandchildren, so I'm an old vet when it comes to little ones." She bounced Sasha on her knee, much to the baby's delight. "Go ahead and slide me your portfolio."

He did as she asked. While she perused the portfolio, he did his best to appear calm and collected. He sat back in his chair, looking at the open pages as she viewed them. Now and again, his eyes would stray to his daughter. The muscles in his neck and shoulders tensed, and he could feel the knots forming. She seemed content for now, gnawing on the liquid-filled teething ring attached to her onesie. But who knew how long that would last? One thing parenting had taught him was that babies were full of surprises.

Mrs. Dartmouth's eyes left the pages of the portfolio, and she turned her head to look at him. Her gaze indicated that she'd sensed the tension rolling off him. "Are you feeling unwell, Maxwell?"

By now, Maxwell could feel the beads of sweat that had begun to form around his temples. "I'm fine, Mrs. Dartmouth."

She continued to watch him, looking unconvinced of his words.

To direct the conversation away from his conundrum and back to the matter at hand, he asked, "Do you see a style of home you like in the portfolio?"

Still looking skeptical, Mrs. Dartmouth pointed to the image on page fifteen. "I think I'd like something like that. Although I'd want a different color for the siding and a stone accent facade around the front door."

Relieved that she'd taken the hint, Maxwell shifted his gaze to the image. "Ah, yes. That's my Merriweather design. With a few modifications to the base plan, I think it will fit well with your needs and desires."

She smiled. "Wonderful. When can we begin the process?"

Sasha smiled a drooling smile.

Mrs. Dartmouth held Sasha against her shoulder for a few moments. By the time he got ready to take her back, he noticed the damp spot of drool on the shoulder of Mrs. Dartmouth's jacket.

He cringed, already fishing in the diaper bag for a burp cloth. "Oh no. I'm so sorry." Standing, he came around to her side of the desk and handed her one cloth to clean herself with. Spreading the other cloth over the shoulder of his own jacket, he picked Sasha up and snuggled her close. "Sorry about that—she's teething."

The chuckling Mrs. Dartmouth dabbed at her shoulder with the cloth. "Heavens, there's no need to apologize. I've been spit up on plenty of times, by my kids and my grandkids."

He could feel the heat of embarrassment in his face. "Yes, but I'm not accustomed to having my daughter...interacting...with my clients."

"Pshaw. Nothing the dry cleaner can't get out, dear." She chuckled as she stood. "Now tell me, when can we get the ball rolling on my little piece of heaven?"

He reached out to shake her hand while keeping a good grip on Sasha. "Two weeks. We'll meet again then, and I'll have your initial plans ready for your approval. How does that sound?"

"That sounds perfect. I look forward to seeing what you come up with, Maxwell."

They exchanged departing pleasantries, and he escorted her back to the main entrance. Once Mrs. Dartmouth's black sedan pulled out of the parking lot, Maxwell returned to his office.

He stood in the open doorway of his inner office for a few moments, shaking his head at his daughter. "What am I gonna do with you, you little rascal?"

Sasha offered only a few hiccups and a drooling smile in response.

Carson approached then. "Is there anything you'd like me to do?"

"Yes. Get in contact with a nanny agency right away. I'm gonna need a hand with Sasha."

Carson nodded, then disappeared.

Releasing a sigh, Maxwell picked up his desk phone and dialed Bianca's phone number.

Bianca answered on the second ring. "Hello, Maxwell. Mama is stable, but she's lost a lot of function on her left side..." Her voice was heavy with emotion. "I don't think she'll be able to look after Sasha, not the way she was before."

"I see. Don't worry. I'll make sure my daughter has everything she needs."

A brief silence came over the line before Bianca spoke again. "When Juliana deployed and left the baby with Mama and me, we never expected things to turn out this way." She paused again. "I know you don't like surprises or being inconvenienced, but it couldn't be helped."

He felt the sting in her words and in her tone. He knew Bianca didn't care much for him. After all, as far as Bianca was concerned, Maxwell had broken her older sister Juliana's heart. "This isn't an inconvenience, Bianca. Sasha is my daughter, and I'm ready to take on my responsibilities for her."

"Mama's stroke has really taken a toll, and I'm not in a position to take care of Sasha. Besides, my sister's instructions were to contact you."

"I understand, and don't worry." Maxwell willed his voice to remain steady despite the emotions inspired by the conversation. "I've got her, and she can stay with me as long as she needs to." He gave his daughter a gentle squeeze. "Besides, this means more father–daughter bonding time for us."

"I'm glad to see you've got a positive outlook about all this."

He took a deep breath, tucking aside his annoyance at the way Bianca had prejudged him. "Things may not have worked out between Juliana and me, but I love Sasha more than anything."

She grew silent for a moment. "Thank you for stepping in, Maxwell."

"It's not a problem at all. Give my best to Ines."

"I will." She disconnected the call.

Several minutes passed in silence as Maxwell looked out his office window. The day outside was beautiful, the blue sky holding only a few wispy clouds that did little to filter the bright sunlight. "Maybe I'll take you to the park, hmm?"

The baby sneezed. Twice. Then she grabbed his ear. "Da-da."

Maxwell winced as he pried her tugging fingers from his lobe, then chuckled as he grabbed a tissue to wipe the damp spray off his face. "You are really something, Sasha."

Carson peeped around the threshold again. "I've got someone coming over from the Wittenmyer Agency. She should be here within the hour."

"Great." Maxwell needed help, and he needed it soon. His lifestyle and home weren't exactly set up for a baby. He shifted his gaze to Carson's face. "What's her name?"

Lifting a bright yellow sticky note into his line of sight, Carson read the name aloud. "Yvonne Markham."

When Carson left again, Maxwell sat down in his chair. With Sasha wriggling in his lap, he turned back toward the window, content to pass the time in reflective silence as he thought on what full-time fatherhood would mean.

—⁓—

Yvonne clutched her black leather purse tightly, the straps crushed between her fists as she crossed the parking lot toward Devers Architectural. The conversation she'd had at the Wittenmyer office with Mrs. Cross thirty minutes prior was still playing in her head.

"You're in luck, Ms. Markham," Mrs. Cross had said. "You've been with us for a very short time, and we already have an assignment for you. I'll need you to be at this address within the hour."

After that, her boss had gone on to give a vague description of the job. A single father had requested someone of the highest skill to care for his baby girl, and the client had offered a generous bonus to get someone over right away. Yvonne's jaw had dropped when she heard the salary, but she'd quickly shut it. Wittenmyer was the top agency in town, and she didn't want to look like a poor country urchin in front of Mrs. Cross or the two coworkers also in the office.

Now, as she approached the beautiful, contemporary building, she wondered why she was meeting the client here instead of at his home. She pushed the thought away, knowing she'd find out the answer soon enough. *For a fifteen-hundred-dollar bonus, we could've met wherever he liked.*

Entering the building, she stopped at the reception desk.

The petite redhead there greeted her right away. "Welcome to Devers Architectural. I'm Mary Alice. Can I help you, miss?"

Feeling her hand begin to cramp, Yvonne finally loosened her grip on the purse straps. "Hello. My name is Yvonne Markham…"

Mary Alice stood. "Oh, from the agency. Just go down the hallway to your right. Carson will be waiting for you."

"Thank you." Yvonne turned and went in the direction she'd indicated, taking in the soft-hued decor, wood paneling, and modern art. The place was immaculately decorated, but then she supposed she should expect no less from an architect.

At the end of the corridor, a rather nervous-looking young man with brown hair and blue eyes stood, tapping his foot. When she approached, he asked, "Are you Yvonne?"

She nodded. "I am. Are you Mr. Devers?"

The tapping stopped, and he seemed less agitated now. "No. I'm his intern, Carson. I'll escort you in. He's waiting for you."

Carson turned and opened the heavy wooden door behind him, gesturing for her to enter.

Yvonne entered the room with Carson close behind her. It was a small office, and by Carson's quick steps, it appeared they were only passing through. They came to another door, this one made of the same wood but with an intricate monogram, *MD*, carved into it.

Carson knocked.

"Come in," called a deep voice from within.

Carson opened the door and stepped away. "Go in, please."

Yvonne took three cautious steps into the room. This inner

office was much darker than the outer one, and looking around, she could see most of the window blinds were shut.

Except for one window, where a man stood, looking out. His back was to her, but she could see his shape clearly. His frame, tall and broad-shouldered, seemed imposing despite the size of the room. Without being able to see his face, she couldn't gauge his mood. The dimness of the room didn't exactly make her feel welcome. This was her first encounter with her very first client, and she didn't want to do or say anything that might offend him. She stood by the door, waiting for him to speak.

After a moment or two of silence, he spoke. "Come in, Ms. Markham. Have a seat."

She eased to the chair by his large, oddly shaped desk and sat down, placing her purse in her lap.

He turned then, and her eyes widened at the sight of the sleeping baby in his arms. Sure, it was the first meeting, and she didn't know exactly what being an architect entailed. Still, she doubted bringing a baby to work was standard practice for professionals in the field. *I suppose that's why I'm here.*

He moved away from the window, circling the room and opening the vertical blinds, all while carefully balancing his slumbering child. As the light began to fill the space, it became far more inviting. Once all the windows were adjusted, he came to stand behind the desk.

As she looked at his face for the first time, a prickling sensation went down her spine. The afternoon sun streaming into the room let her see his smooth, caramel-skinned handsomeness, and she thanked the heavens for the good weather. He had a strong jaw, piercing brown eyes flecked with green, and the most kissable lips she'd ever seen. His suit, a rich shade of royal blue, had obviously been tailored with care to fit his tall, muscular frame. She knew she should say something, but staring at him seemed to be all she could manage.

His lips tilted into a smile.

Her nervous energy melted away instantly. It amazed her how he'd set her at ease. *I bet this brotha never has trouble closing a deal.*

"Thank you for coming in on such short notice, Ms. Markham. I'm Maxwell Devers." He extended his free hand.

She stood, shook hands with him. His large hand enfolded hers, and she could feel the mixture of firmness and restraint. She tried in vain to ignore the tingle that ran up her arm the moment he touched her. When he released her hand, she sat back down.

He spoke again. "I'm not sure how much you know about my situation, but I'll fill you in as we go."

"That sounds fine, Mr. Devers."

"Call me Maxwell." He sat down behind the desk. "If you're going to help me raise my daughter, we may as well be on a first-name basis."

She smiled. "Sure." Listening to the way he'd said that last statement, she concluded that he was a single father. "What's your little one's name?"

He smiled, pride radiating from his face as he looked at his daughter. "Her name is Sasha Lynn. She's seven months old."

"Oh, that sounds wonderful. Developmentally, so many things are happening to an infant at that age. She's developing her fine and gross motor skills, trying new foods..." She paused, seeing the expression on Maxwell's face. She couldn't tell if he was confused or annoyed by her babbling. "I'm sorry. Excuse me for rambling on."

"No, no. Don't apologize. I want someone who's knowledge-able and someone who'll care deeply about Sasha. You just met her and you're already excited, and that's a very good sign." His expression softened into a half smile.

She thought he still looked somewhat unsettled, but it wasn't her place to press. She'd known him for all of twenty minutes. Looking toward the baby, she imagined what her small face would look like. "I'd ask to hold her, but I know she's probably not ready for that."

"Why not?"

"Developmentally, she's at the stage where stranger anxiety starts to kick in." She smiled, moving closer before tracing a gentle finger through the baby's rich dark curls. "It's best to transition her slowly into my care so she won't be uncomfortable with me."

Sasha sneezed, and her little eyes popped open. A moment later, the baby started to wail.

He lifted her on to his shoulder, bouncing her small body and patting her back. "It's okay, honey." He whipped out a portable changing pad, and laying the baby gently on it, he put her in a fresh diaper. After setting her in the car seat briefly so he could sanitize his hands, he produced a jar of turkey and sweet potato baby food and a sippy cup of apple juice.

She looked on, noting how he stayed calm despite his daughter's cries.

"Sorry. She's a little cranky."

"No worries. Let me guess…teething?"

He nodded with a slight roll of his eyes. "For a couple of weeks now. She's got two coming in on the bottom, and she's been quite a little pistol." While he fed her from the jar, Sasha calmed considerably, obviously enjoying her meal.

Yvonne chuckled. "I know what to do to get her through the teething stage."

"Glad to hear it. But what do you know to get me through it?" He followed his words with a wry laugh.

"Patience. It's the only way." She eyed him sympathetically. "Anyway, I think I should spend some time with you and Sasha together before I fully take over her care. It's going to be an adjustment, and we should ease her into this new situation."

"We're already going through an adjustment."

She tilted her head. "How so?"

"Sasha's maternal grandmother has custody of her while Sasha's mother, my ex-girlfriend, is deployed overseas. I usually only have her two weekends out of the month, but now, I may be taking her on full-time until her mother gets home."

"I see." That explained why she'd been called to his workplace instead of his home; there was a family crisis at play.

"How would you normally go about building rapport with a new charge?"

"Basically, we all sit on the floor together and play. Sasha will watch the way you and I relate to each other, and she will follow your lead. If you seem to like and trust me…"

"Sasha will get on board, too."

"Right. So when would you have time for a little free play with your daughter and I?"

He adjusted his grip on Sasha, who wriggled in his arms. "Looks like she's ready for a little playtime right now. Workday's shot anyway."

"If that works for you, I'm ready."

"Let's take her home. That way, you two can get acquainted, and you can learn the lay of the land around my place."

A flicker of anticipation came over her at the thought of seeing the private domain of the drop-dead gorgeous architect slash single dad. Curiosity flared inside her. What kind of place would he live in? A contemporary condo looking down over the city? A modest brick split-level with a fenced yard? A quaint country cottage nestled among the pines? *He's attractive, articulate, well groomed…obviously a consummate professional, accustomed to taking charge and getting things done.* No. The more she thought about it, the more he struck her as a man who lived in a gated community somewhere on the outskirts of town…the "swanky palace in the 'burbs" type. Wherever he lived, she felt a certain eagerness to see it. "Sounds good."

After watching him strap his bouncing baby girl into the car seat in the rear of his SUV, Yvonne got into her car and followed him to his home. Sure enough, they arrived a half hour later in front of a sprawling brick home. A manicured lawn spread out before the house like a splendid tapestry of green, and the towering white columns flanking the front porch added an air of Southern sophistication to the exterior.

She joined him on the porch, watching him put his key in the lock.

Pushing the door open, he gestured her inside. "Come on in." He adjusted Sasha's position on his right hip.

With a nod, she eased past him and into the grand foyer of his home.

CHAPTER 3

SETTLED ONTO THE PATTERNED AREA RUG IN HIS LIVING room, Maxwell watched Sasha scoot around on her bottom. As she reached the edge of the rug and slid onto the polished cherry floor, she picked up a bit of speed.

"Look at her go." Yvonne smiled, her eyes locked on the baby. "She's very mobile, I see."

"Extremely." He shook his head. "Getting her to sit in one place these days is an exercise in futility unless she's strapped down."

She laughed. "Sounds about right for a baby her age."

He watched her in profile as she observed his daughter. The elegant lines of her face and throat captured his attention in a way no other woman ever had. Her hair, while tied back in a bun, looked as dark and rich as a stream of melted chocolate. When he'd sent Carson to find him a nanny on the fly, he never would have anticipated this stunning beauty would be the one to answer the call.

Sasha skidded to a stop near a set of plastic keys under the coffee table. Leaning over, she picked them up and immediately stuck one of the brightly colored keys into her mouth. Smiling and drooling, bouncing up and down on her diapered bottom, she appeared quite content.

His phone vibrated in his pocket, momentarily drawing his attention away from his daughter. Slipping the phone out, he saw Bianca's name on the display. Swiping, he brought it to his ear. "Hi, Bianca. How's Ines?"

Bianca's sigh spoke volumes. "Not too good, Max. The stroke... really took a toll on her." Her voice cracked with emotion.

"I'm sorry to hear that, Bianca." Settling his back against the love seat, he felt his brow creasing. "What are the doctors saying?"

"They say she's lost sensation on her whole left side." Bianca paused, sniffled. "She's having a hard time speaking, and they think she may have sustained some permanent damage to her speech center."

"I know it's not the news you wanted to hear. Do they know how long they're going to keep her?"

"No. At least a week, though." She sniffled again. "And even when she does get home, she's going to need a lot of care."

He scratched his chin. "Sounds like you need me to step up for Sasha."

"We do. Mama can't take care of her, not in this condition. And with my four kids and what's just happened to Mama, I can't add any more responsibility right now."

"Don't worry. Sasha and I will be fine. You just focus on your family."

"Who's going to watch her while you work?"

"I already hired a nanny."

Bianca paused. "What? Really?"

"Yes. After you left, I asked my intern to start searching." He glanced across at Yvonne, who was quietly observing Sasha's play. "Luckily, the agency had someone who could start right away."

"I...wow, Maxwell." She cleared her throat. "I'm glad you were thinking ahead."

"It's just how I am. Speaking of which, will you be able to cover the costs of Ines's care when she comes home?"

Bianca hesitated. "I...probably not. She's covered for home care under her health plan, but there's a pretty sizable deductible we have to pay, and I—"

He stopped her. "When you find out how much it is, call me. I'll do what I can to help you out."

"You don't have to do that, Max."

"I know. But Ines is Sasha's grandmother, and I want them to have as much time together as possible." He smiled at the memory of his own grandmother, with her tight hugs and country cooking. "It's been fifteen years since I lost mine, and I still remember how much fun we had together."

Bianca was silent for a few moments. When she spoke again, her voice was laced with emotion. "Thank you, Max. Thank you so, so much."

"It's no problem. Juliana and I may not be together anymore, but through Sasha, we'll always be family." After exchanging goodbyes with Bianca, he ended the call. When he looked Yvonne's way, he found her watching him intently. "Is there something you need?"

She blinked a few times, her long, dark lashes fluttering. "Hmm?"

"You were staring at me."

"My apologies." Her cheeks reddened, and she looked down for a moment. "Why don't you tell me a little about Sasha?" Yvonne shifted to face him, folding her hands in her lap.

For some reason, the demure gesture fired his blood. Pushing that line of thought aside, he cleared his throat. "Sasha loves squash and sweet potatoes—you know, the sweeter veggies. She won't touch green veggies or peaches though. She's got a little kitchen playset upstairs that she loves to play with. You know the kind. Little plastic pots and pans, a pretend stove, all that."

"Okay. It's good to hear that she's getting some pretend play. That's great for her development. What else?"

"My baby's a big music lover. She's especially fond of Luther Vandross…particularly his recordings from the 'big Luther' era."

Yvonne laughed. "So she's got great taste in music, then."

"Yes, thanks to her daddy. She hates wearing shoes and isn't a fan of pets. She has a little giraffe she loves—" He stood and retrieved the slightly damp stuffed toy from the baby's bag, handing it to Yvonne. "And she won't go to sleep at night without the little butterfly projector nightlight running."

"That's all very good information for me. Thanks." She swiveled her head again, her gaze following Sasha, who was now scooting back in their direction with the keys still hanging out of her mouth.

When she was within range, he scooped the baby into his arms and kissed her on the forehead. "I remember the day this little butterbean was born."

Yvonne turned toward him, resting her elbows on her thighs and her chin on her hands. "I'd love to hear about it."

"Well, Juliana and I weren't on the best terms then, but I wouldn't have missed Sasha's birth for anything in the world. So I was present for the pregnancy, as much as Juliana allowed, and for the entire twenty-six-hour labor. She progressed pretty well, just slowly. Then, during the pushing phase, we discovered the umbilical cord was wrapped around Sasha's neck."

Yvonne frowned. "Oh no."

"They ended up performing an emergency C-section," he recalled, releasing Sasha as she began to squirm in his lap. "I was terrified, because for a while there, I thought we might lose her. But she pulled through. She's got her great-grandmother's warrior spirit, that's for sure."

"Tell me about her. I'd love to hear the origins of Sasha's fierceness."

He smiled, gratified that she wanted to hear about his grandmother. "Willa Mae, my mother's mother, raised six kids in a house no bigger than a postage stamp. She was a librarian and raised her children to love knowledge. She worked hard, baked the world's best homemade coconut cakes, and somehow managed to send all her kids to college. She saw a lot of pain after my grandfather died…but she only grew stronger in adversity. I don't know of anyone else I admire more."

"Sounds like an amazing legacy, and one your daughter is going to carry on."

"Thank you." He could count on one hand the number of people he'd told about his grandmother, because he didn't typically get involved in such deep conversations. Yet Yvonne had proven so easy to talk to, he'd told her without hesitation.

If he'd met her under different circumstances, he'd be planning how to make a move on her.

He pushed the thought away.

After all, this isn't about me.

This is about Sasha.

CHAPTER 4

JUST AFTER EIGHT THE NEXT MORNING, MAXWELL DROPPED into the leather executive chair behind his desk with a sigh. He'd been pacing his office for the past fifteen minutes, and he knew that if he didn't sit down, he'd wear a trench in his floor.

"I'm back with your usual Tuesday coffee and croissant." Carson walked through the open door then, carrying a paper cup and a small paper sack. Setting the items on the desk, he asked, "Are you okay?"

"What makes you ask that?"

Carson tilted his head. "The door's been open this whole time. I could hear you pacing."

Maxwell groaned, reaching for his coffee. After a long draw, he spoke again. "First of all, thanks for the coffee. And to answer your question, it's going to be a bit of a day."

Carson's face folded into a grimace. "I guess that means we won't be working on Mrs. Carmichael's blueprints today, then?"

He shook his head. "Sorry, Carson. I know you're excited about learning the finer points of drafting blueprints, but my head just isn't in the game today. Besides, I'm leaving pretty early, so even if I could focus, we wouldn't have time."

"Understood. I'll keep working on the middle school remodel plans in the meantime." In typical fashion, Carson accepted his words without pressing for more information. That was a large part of the reason Maxwell enjoyed working with him.

After his intern slipped back out into the outer office, Maxwell grabbed his phone from the desk and swiped the screen. A few moments later, he dialed Orion's number.

"Yo, what's up?" Orion yawned. "You don't normally call me this early."

"Sorry about that, but I had something to tell you. I didn't wake you up, did I?"

"Nah. The boys have a photo shoot today for an album cover, so we're already at the studio." Orion's job at Fresh2Deff records kept him quite busy, especially when it came to his flagship act, the rap duo Young-n-Wild. "What's up?"

Maxwell took a deep breath. Out of all his fraternity brothers, he was closest with Orion. Despite their three-year age difference, their personalities had clicked right away when they met in college. "It's been a crazy couple of days, man."

"It has?" Orion yawned again. "How so?"

"First of all, Ines had a stroke."

Orion inhaled sharply. "Sorry to hear that, man. Is she going to be okay?"

"Yes. But with the level of care she'll need for herself, she won't be able to take care of Sasha anymore. And since Bianca already has a house full of kids…"

"You're gonna be taking Sasha on full-time." Orion paused as if the root of the conversation had finally become clear. "Oh, wow. This is gonna take some serious adjustment."

Maxwell chuckled. "You're telling me."

Orion whistled. "Wow. I mean, how are you doing, man? Are you okay with this?"

Massaging his temples, Maxwell said, "It's not as if I have a choice. But yes, I'm okay with it. I've accepted my responsibility to Sasha, and I'm going to do right by her."

"You're a stand-up dude, Max. Of course, I wouldn't expect anything less from my frat brother. Enjoy this extra time with her, man. I hear they grow up fast."

His friend's vote of confidence brought a smile to Maxwell's face. "Thanks, man. The timing isn't the greatest, but we'll make it work."

"Bet." Orion's tone of voice changed. "Bro, how is this going to affect your work? I mean, who's going to watch my li'l niece while you conquer the world of architecture?"

"I hired a nanny."

"Dang, Max. When did you do that?"

"Yesterday, as soon as Bianca dropped her off. I wanted to have someone in place in case things took a turn for the worse."

"Good thinking." Orion's tone communicated his approval. "So what's this new nanny like? Did you hire some older lady, a grandmotherly type who'll knit while the baby naps?"

"Far from it, O. Her name is Yvonne, and she's pretty close to my age." Or at least Maxwell assumed so. He hadn't thought to ask her age, because he'd been far more concerned with her skills when it came to looking after his daughter.

"Oh, really?" Orion's voice took on a mischievous tone. "Since you put it that way...is she fine?"

"What kind of question is that?"

"The kind you should expect from me after knowing me all these years."

Maxwell shook his head, knowing his friend was right. "Orion, I'm not going to do this with you right now."

"I sense you have more to say on this particular topic," Orion teased. "But I won't press you during your work hours."

Maxwell rolled his eyes. "Whatever. I hired her to do a job. She's professional, knowledgeable, experienced..."

"I still wanna know what she looks like."

"Orion—"

"Okay, man. Let me stop aggravating you." Orion cleared his throat. "Anyway, are you still going to pursue the Crown Center project?"

"Of course I am. Why wouldn't I? You know a job this big could really put Devers Architectural in a great position."

"I know. All I'm saying is this job is going to be very involved, and that's if you can survive the bidding process to even get it."

Brow furrowed, Maxwell groused, "Watch it, O."

"Of course, that's no reflection on your talents. I know you've got what it takes. But full-time parenting is going to take a lot out of you in terms of time and energy."

Maxwell scratched his chin. "I've considered that. Why do you think I hired Yvonne? She can take care of Sasha during the day so I can focus on my actual work."

Orion laughed. "Looks like you've got it covered, Max."

"I think so. Either way, I'm going to move forward with things as they are. I have plenty of faith in Yvonne's abilities."

"She sounds like a winner." Orion cleared his throat. "So what does she look like?"

"Really, O?"

"How long have you known me, Max? You knew I was gonna ask."

Maxwell pictured her in his mind's eye and tried to give an accurate, unbiased description. "She's a sistah. Probably about five eight, slender but curvy. Curly brown hair, brown eyes. Nice smile." He stopped himself, knowing that if he went on, he'd start talking about the way she smelled or the way she walked or some other thing that might make Orion start jumping to conclusions.

"Mm-hmm."

"What?"

"After that dry-ass description you just gave, I know two things about her. She's finer than you want to admit to me, and she's single."

Maxwell didn't respond. There were times when Orion was just a little too perceptive for his tastes. This was one of those times.

"Yeah, I know I'm right."

"Fine. You'll meet her eventually, and then you can judge for yourself how she looks."

"Fair enough, I guess." Something clattered, then crashed in the background. "Sorry, Max. I gotta go. These kids are into some shenanigans. Keep me posted."

"I will, O." Maxwell disconnected the call, leaving his friend to deal with the fallout from whatever his young charges had just done in some unlucky photographer's studio.

He checked the time on the screen of his phone. *Eight twenty. She should be here with the baby any minute.* Yvonne had offered to take the baby for a post-breakfast walk so she could get some fresh air. If he were honest with himself, he had to admit he was looking forward to seeing her again. They'd spent the better part of yesterday together, and he could already tell he was going to enjoy being in her company.

Chill out. Remember, she's here for Sasha, not for you.

He stood then, needing to release some of the tension building in his body. Instead of pacing again, he moved to the window behind his desk, looking out on the rest of the office park that extended behind his building. All around him, folks were going about their business. Deals were being brokered, documents getting filed, conference calls taking place.

For them, it's just another weekday.

But my life has been changed in a major way, and there will be no going back to the way things were before.

He'd always considered himself a thoughtful person, one who didn't rush into things or make decisions without careful consideration. But he couldn't remember ever having spent so much time locked inside his own mind, wrestling with his own thoughts. The nature of this whole situation left him with so many uncertainties. And as much as he hated to admit it, his new reality also left him with many doubts.

She seemed to know how I feel. Yvonne's perceptiveness was both impressive and off-putting. How could someone he'd just met be so in tune with him? He told himself she was simply a professional, drawing from her experience working with parents in the past. But something told him there was more to it.

Footsteps sounded behind him, and he turned toward the sound.

Yvonne smiled while she walked toward him, her delicate hands clasped firmly around the handle of Sasha's stroller. "Hello, again."

He let his gaze sweep over her. She'd pulled her hair back into a bun, revealing the elegant lines of her face. She wore a blue button-down shirt, the collar visible beneath her black wool peacoat, and fitted black slacks with low-heeled black pumps and a black purse slung over her shoulder. Her uniform, while professional, could not conceal the feminine curves of her figure. Where she'd looked somewhat hesitant yesterday, her expression today was open and confident. "Hi, Yvonne."

"Sasha was fussy, so I decided to bring her in. She seemed pretty desperate to get out of the car seat."

He chuckled. "Yeah. She's not a fan of the car seat, at least not for long periods." He stooped to his daughter's eye level, giving her a peck on the cheek. "Hello there, sunshine."

Sasha, fully engaged in drinking formula from her sippy cup, emitted a happy gurgle around the spout.

"So I see you have a reflection place, too," Yvonne commented.

He gave her a sidelong glance, his brow furrowing. "What do you mean?"

"In the last childcare center I worked at, the three- and four-year-old classes had what was called the reflection place. When they did something they shouldn't have, they'd be sent there to think things over."

He blinked a few times as he thought about what she'd said. "Oh, I see." He didn't think she was commenting on his choices or the events that had led to his falling-out with his daughter's mother, but he couldn't help drawing that parallel. Both he and Juliana played a role in this, however. "I have been thinking things over quite a bit lately."

She pressed her lips together, dropping her gaze. "Sorry, I hope that didn't come across as judgmental. That's not how I meant it."

He shook his head. "It's fine. That's not how I took it."

"Maxwell, I'm not here to pass judgment on you."

He shrugged, not wanting her to know how much her words had affected him. "It is what it is." That was the truth. Everything happened for a reason, and obviously, a force greater than he had seen fit to increase the role he played in Sasha's life. So he'd roll with it, do the best he could, and forget about the missteps and regrets of the past.

She shifted her weight slightly, then asked, "Ready to go?"

"Sure."

He grabbed his heavy wool-blend trench coat from the coatrack in the corner of the room, slipping into it. They moved through the outer office, passing Carson as he stood at the reception desk, talking to Mary Alice. "Hold my calls. I'll be back in a few hours. And see what you can come up with for the middle school plans while I'm out. I'll look over it when I get back."

Carson gave him a crisp salute. "You've got it, Mr. D."

Sliding on his leather gloves, he held the door open for Yvonne, then walked with her out of the building and into the early morning cold.

—m—

Yvonne rode across town in relative silence, preferring to keep her own counsel from her spot in the plush leather passenger seat of Maxwell's SUV. He hadn't said much, either, and she supposed they were both too busy thinking to talk. As excited and nervous as she felt about getting to take care of little Sasha, she imagined his emotions were a hundred times as high. Life had thrown him quite a curveball, and she could understand why he'd be a bit off-balance because of it. Being a man, though, she didn't expect him to admit to his feelings. She didn't have any brothers, but her interactions with her father, male cousins, and male friends told her that men would do just about anything to avoid talking about their feelings. In a way, she felt sorry for them. Society praised machismo, anger, and bluster as good qualities in men while heralding docility, peacemaking, and cooperation as good qualities only in women. *No wonder men are so screwed up.*

From the back seat came the sounds of Sasha's attempts at speech. Most of it was unintelligible, except for her repeated utterance of the phrase "Da-da." Yvonne felt the smile tugging at her lips. There was something about listening to the voice of a small child that always filled her with a sense of happiness and peace.

They arrived at Words and Wonder, a small independent bookstore located on the north side of the city. He cut the engine, got out, and walked around the car to open the passenger door for her.

"Thank you." She climbed down, aided by his hand. "You're a gentleman, I can see."

"What can I say? Delphinia Devers would expect no less of her only son."

This was the first mention he'd made of his mother, but Yvonne thought both the woman and her colorful name sounded formidable.

After he'd gotten Sasha out of the car seat and into his arms, Yvonne followed him inside the bookstore. The warm, welcoming interior bustled with the activity of booksellers and patrons moving around the space. The walls were decorated with framed candid photos of people reading, as well as blown-up covers of classic novels. The shelves, filled with books of all kinds, were placed in a unique zigzag pattern.

"I see a lot of the other parents and kids are already here for story time." He gestured toward the rear of the store. "The children's area is in the back."

She walked with him into the area, taking in the sight of the brightly colored paint and carpet. A small stage centered the space, where the arrangement of the shelves and a few cleverly placed potted plants created a sort of corral for the youngsters. Flat toss pillows in primary colors were lined up on the floor. Several of the spots were already occupied by adults who were either holding young children or monitoring them with a watchful eye as they explored the section. Looking around, Yvonne could see that this was a baby and toddler event; the oldest child present appeared to be about two years old.

Maxwell took a seat, holding Sasha in his lap. She followed suit, settling onto a yellow cushion next to them.

A young woman walked to the stage, settling into the lone chair and holding up a large picture book. After welcoming everyone, she launched into an impassioned reading of the book, much to the delight of the young audience.

Yvonne observed the way Sasha's face lit up as the story progressed. She even left her father's lap to crawl closer to the storyteller, taking a seat near the edge of the stage along with some of the other children. Watching her, it was easy to see how much she loved being read to. Yvonne filed that little tidbit of information away for later. Turning to Maxwell, she asked, "You have books for her at home, right?"

He nodded. "Loads of them. My mother buys her books constantly. The whole closet shelf in her nursery is full of them."

"Great. I can tell she really enjoys a good story."

"When she's with me, I try to read to her as often as I can." A soft smile came over his face as he shifted his gaze back to his daughter.

Seeing the affection on his face touched Yvonne, and she felt a twinge inside. She'd spent most of her life caring for children, but she wondered if it would ever be time for her to have a child of her own. *All I know is, if I ever do have a child, I want her father to love her as much as Maxwell loves Sasha.*

After the tale ended, story time morphed into playtime as the store employees brought out bins of various age-appropriate toys for the kids to enjoy. Sasha half crawled, half scooted over to a group of tots building a tower out of soft blocks and joined in the construction.

"How often is this story time held?"

"About once a month. I try to bring Sasha as often as my schedule allows." He gestured to where the baby played. "I feel like she needs this interaction with other kids her age, you know?"

She nodded. "You're absolutely right. It's very good that she's developing social skills and early problem-solving skills as well." It was yet another example of how good a father he strove to be. "Not a lot of parents think about things like that, especially not fathers."

"I know. Look around here. There are three mothers to every one father, and that's pretty typical of what I see when I come to kid-focused events like this." He scratched his chin. "I wish more fathers, or father figures, would get involved in this kind of thing. They have no idea of the fun and the memories they're missing out on."

"That would be wonderful, and it would benefit both the children and the parents."

"Right. But you know, maybe some of this is just indicative of societal change." He appeared thoughtful. "Single motherhood is more accepted now than it was in the past. Plus, families look very different now, so there may or may not be a male parent in the picture." He shrugged. "I don't think any of that matters, though, as long as the child is getting what they need."

She blinked a few times, taken aback by his astute observation. It displayed a level of awareness that most people lacked and showed his affinity for intelligent discourse. "What a cogent point, Maxwell."

"Architecture isn't my only area of expertise." He winked.

She melted like ice on a hot sidewalk. She'd never encountered a man like him. Intelligent, self-aware, crazy about his young daughter...and incredibly handsome. Everything about him captivated her, and she sensed that as she got to know him better, her attraction to him would only intensify.

But that simply wouldn't do. If she were to remain focused on her responsibility to her parents and her dream of opening a childcare center, she couldn't get involved in a romantic relationship. And even if she could, it wouldn't be appropriate to do so with a client.

While the tots and their parents enjoyed playtime, she pondered her current situation. *I don't know. Should I go back to Mrs. Cross and ask to be assigned to another client?* That probably wouldn't go over well, since she'd been working for Maxwell for such a short period of time. She could already imagine the agency owner lecturing her about "the Wittenmyer way." No, asking to be reassigned now would only put her job in danger. Aside from that, she had no guarantee that another client would compensate her as well as Maxwell did.

As she and Maxwell were bundling Sasha up to leave the bookstore, Yvonne's phone vibrated. Checking the text, she smiled. According to the commercial Realtor she'd asked to help her find a property for her childcare center, an ideal location had just gone on the market.

Typing a quick response that she'd be around to see the property as soon as she could, she pocketed her phone again. That sealed it. There was no way she could give up such a well-paying position now, because it meant potentially missing out on the perfect property for her center.

Buckling his fussy child into the car seat, Maxwell looked her way, his face etched with concern. "You okay?"

She sighed, knowing he must have caught sight of her "thinking face." Her sister often teased her that when expending a lot of mental effort, her expression became visibly tight. As she endeavored to relax her face, she offered a small smile. "Yes. I'm fine."

Working with Maxwell presented complexities she never would have anticipated. All she could do now was maintain her professionalism and hope her good sense kept her on the right path.

CHAPTER 5

MAXWELL WALKED INTO THE HOUSE THE FOLLOWING EVENING bone-tired. He'd spent most of his day in meetings with clients, both in person and on the phone. He'd been so tied up with work he'd barely left his desk. Carson had taken pity on him and brought him lunch from a nearby deli around one thirty, and if not for that, he probably wouldn't have eaten. It was now close to six thirty, and his stomach was growling.

As he passed through the foyer, he sniffed the air, trying to detect what his housekeeper had made him for dinner. She usually cooked him a hot meal, wrapped it, and left it in the oven for him when her shift ended at five. Most evenings, he could expect to find the lingering aroma of whatever she'd made. Tonight, though, he smelled something else.

Baby powder.

Smiling, he hung his coat in the small closet beneath the staircase, stashing his briefcase on the shelf inside. After closing the closet door, he went into the kitchen to check the oven. Inside, he found a foil-wrapped ceramic plate containing a roasted half chicken, brown rice, and spinach sauté. He removed the foil and slid the plate into the microwave.

He heard the sound of Sasha babbling, and it reminded him again of how much his life had changed in the past week. He looked at his plate, rotating inside the microwave, and sighed. He was tired and hungry. But he supposed fathers all over the world came home each day feeling similarly and didn't let that stop them from greeting their children.

He left the kitchen, making his way to the staircase. As he climbed, he could hear Yvonne speaking in a gentle, lilting voice to Sasha. Following the sound, he went down the hall and stopped outside the nursery.

Yvonne sat on the floor, with her feet tucked beneath her bottom, on the fluffy pink carpet centering the room. Sasha sat there as well, gnawing on a set of plastic baby keys.

Smiling, Yvonne held out a toy purse in Sasha's direction. Sasha stopped nibbling at the keys and dropped them inside. "Good girl!"

Sasha bounced up and down, her smile bright. "Yay yay yay."

"Okay. We've got our keys. What else do we need to put in our bag?" Yvonne reached down, picking up a wooden block. "Do you want to take this with us, Sasha?"

The baby bounced some more as if to indicate her approval.

Watching the scene, Maxwell smiled. The way Yvonne engaged with Sasha touched and impressed him. Where other nannies might be content to do the bare minimum in taking care of their charges, Yvonne seemed genuinely invested in Sasha.

He entered the room then, and Yvonne turned her smile his way. "Hi, Maxwell." She reached for Sasha.

The little one scooted away from Yvonne's hand.

"Don't want me to pick you up yet, huh?"

Sasha blew a huge raspberry in response.

Yvonne laughed. "Look, Daddy's home. Say, 'Hi, Daddy.'"

Sasha bounced up and down on the carpet while looking in Maxwell's direction. Balling her small fist, she curled and uncurled the fingers. "Da-da. Da-da."

He walked over, stooped down, and kissed the baby's soft little forehead. "Hello, there."

The baby laughed, her small tummy shaking inside the confines of her yellow footie pajamas, emblazoned with pink and purple butterflies.

Yvonne remarked, "You look exhausted. Rough day?"

He sighed. "Rough is an understatement."

"Have you eaten yet?"

He shook his head.

She eased over to the white wooden rocker and sat down. "Go on downstairs and eat. I'll look after her."

"Thank you." He looked at his daughter's round, dark eyes once more, then slipped from the room.

As his foot touched the second rung of the stairs, he could hear Yvonne singing. He smiled, knowing her soothing voice and soft delivery of "Beautiful Dreamer" would surely put the baby in a good mood.

Back in the kitchen, he sat down to his meal. The house was mainly quiet, and from this distance, he could no longer hear Yvonne singing. While he savored the well-seasoned food, he contemplated the many changes his life had undergone in less than seventy-two hours. He'd gotten the surprise visit from Bianca on Monday, the same day he'd hired Yvonne and unexpectedly brought the baby home. He'd asked his family to move their usual Wednesday breakfast ahead one day to Thursday. When his mother asked what was so important that he'd want the whole family to rearrange their schedules, he'd simply told them that he wanted to introduce them to someone new in his life. Knowing his mother, she probably thought he was finally bringing home a fiancée, and if he'd been thinking about it, he'd have chosen different wording. He chuckled, wondering how his family would react when they found out who they were actually meeting.

After putting his dishes away, he returned to Sasha's room. Yvonne was still in the rocking chair, keeping a watchful eye on Sasha while the baby busied herself with a pile of wooden blocks.

Maxwell stepped aside just as his daughter hurled a block in his direction. Chuckling, he retrieved the block from the hall, then sat down on the colorful carpet. "Now, Sasha, we talked about this. Blocks are for building, not projectile weapons."

Yvonne laughed. "You know it's normal for her to throw things at this age, right?"

He shrugged. "Maybe so, but somebody's gotta say something. She almost took out my shin with that thing."

Yvonne dissolved into giggles.

A smile tugged at his lips as he realized how much he enjoyed the sound and how much he liked knowing he'd contributed to her amusement.

"It's almost seven. How late are you staying tonight?"

"I wanted to see a little more of Sasha's day so I can plan accordingly. Would you mind walking me through her usual bedtime routine?"

"No problem." He stood then and retrieved Sasha, scooping her up from among the sea of brightly colored blocks. "It's about time for you to get ready for bed, little missy."

Sasha frowned, then stuck her thumb in her mouth.

He shook his head. "She's not the biggest fan of bedtime."

"Most kids aren't. They're so convinced they're going to miss something exciting if they go to sleep." Yvonne stood. "Just go on about the evening as you normally would. I'm just going to observe."

"Okay." He bounced Sasha against his chest. "Ready for bath time?"

Sasha laughed in response.

Shaking his head and not bothering to hide his smile, he carried her out of the room and down the hall to the bathroom. Yvonne walked a few steps behind him.

In the bathroom, he filled the tub with warm water. After testing it to make sure the temperature was right, he undressed his squirming daughter and placed her in the little rubber safety seat in the center of the tub. With a soft cloth and baby wash, he cleaned her up, then stepped back.

Yvonne asked, "Are you done yet?"

He nodded. "Yep. But she loves to splash, so I give her a few extra minutes to play."

She chuckled. "I see."

True to form, Sasha spent the next several minutes laughing and splashing, sending torrents of soapy water into the air. He stood back a bit, avoiding the spray as much as he could while still staying close by.

"All right, little lady. I think you've sufficiently flooded the bathroom." Grabbing a brightly colored hooded towel from the wall-mounted cabinet nearby, he lifted Sasha into his arms while simultaneously wrapping her up. With her secured in the cotton cocoon, he carried her back to the nursery.

Laying her on the soft pad atop the changing table, he massaged the baby with lavender baby lotion. "Helps her wind down," he remarked as he rubbed the lotion into her chubby thighs.

Sasha yawned as he zipped up her small footed pajamas and lifted her into his arms again. "Okay. Now it's story time." He went to the stack of books on top of the dresser and chose a picture book.

"Max, would you mind if I read to her?" Yvonne asked. "I think it will go a long way in building rapport with her."

"Sure."

"Great." She gestured toward the rocker. "You sit in the chair with her, and I'll sit on the floor and read the story."

Once they were in position, Yvonne held up the book for Sasha to see and read the title aloud. "*The People Could Fly*."

As she read through the classic folktale written by Virginia Hamilton, he couldn't help noticing the way she held Sasha's attention. Yvonne read expressively and with enthusiasm. The story, which told of enslaved Africans who tapped into a centuries-old power of flight to escape from bondage, was one he'd heard as a child. Listening to Yvonne read it to his daughter awakened many of the same feelings he'd felt as a youngster, hearing the tale from his own mother. He felt the sadness, the helplessness. The wonder, the power, and the delight.

By the time she closed the book, he realized he'd been holding his breath. "Listen, that was amazing. If Sasha wasn't already drifting off, I'd give you a standing ovation."

Yvonne smiled. "That's one of my favorite stories. Still, I try to infuse some excitement into everything I read aloud. It's how you get kids to be passionate about reading. You have to be passionate yourself."

He looked at Sasha, who was doing her best to keep her heavy-lidded eyes open. "After a performance like that, you deserve a shot at holding her. Want to try putting her to bed?"

Yvonne stood, nodding. After she returned the book to its place, she gently, slowly lifted Sasha from his arms.

They both waited for a few moments to see how Sasha would react.

Sasha took a deep breath…and yawned.

Yvonne's grin widened. Holding Sasha close, she tiptoed to the crib and nestled the baby inside it.

Maxwell joined her, and as they both looked on, Sasha yawned once more and finally gave up the fight, her eyes drifting closed. The two of them slipped from the room, and he closed the door softly behind them.

They stood there in awkward silence for a moment or two before he whispered, "I need to ask you for a favor."

"What do you need?" She sat down on the steps, waiting.

He sat next to her. Being this close to her let him detect the subtle, floral notes of her perfume. The scent, feminine and soft, was a perfect reflection of how Yvonne carried herself. Shaking off that irrelevant observation, he said, "Could you come with me to my parents' house for breakfast tomorrow morning?"

The furrow of her brow gave away her confusion. "Okay, but… may I ask why?"

"I want to let them meet you, and I'll need you along to take care of Sasha. My parents are very particular about who is worthy of being around their precious little granddaughter."

"As they should be. But I'm willing to come to breakfast. Thanks for the invite."

"Thanks for accepting."

Feeling the awareness of her scrutiny, he shifted a bit on the wooden step beneath him. "What is it? Why are you looking at me like that?"

She inhaled. "Excuse me if this comes across as prying, Maxwell. But I feel like there's something you're not telling me."

"It's nothing, really. It's just that...meeting all of them at one time might be a little intense."

"How so?"

"Let's just say they have a certain perception of what parenthood should look like, one that doesn't involve hired help."

She swallowed but kept her expression as calm as she could. "So can you tell me something about your family? You haven't really said much about them."

Over the last couple of days, he'd only mentioned his mother in passing. He'd been so caught up in trying to figure out what Sasha needed, he hadn't really thought much about how his family played into his new situation. "Let's see. My parents are Humphrey and Delphinia. Dad was a civil engineer, and Mom worked as a university librarian. They're both retired now, and when they're not engaged in their various hobbies and travel, they have plenty of time for grandparent duties."

Yvonne smiled. "What about siblings?"

"I have two younger sisters. Kelsey, my middle sister, paints. My baby sister, Alexis, is a fashion designer. I guess we're an artsy bunch."

"Sounds that way." Yvonne chuckled. "I'll be glad to meet them all." She stood, then stretched. "Is there anything else you need from me tonight?"

"No. Can you meet me here around seven-thirty in the morning? They don't live very far from here."

"I'll be here." She took the last three steps to the bottom of the staircase.

As she crossed the foyer, Maxwell couldn't help watching the way she walked. She was grace personified, and he found it difficult to tear his eyes away from the subtle sway of her hips as she walked.

She went to the coatrack, pulled down her coat, and shrugged into it. Pulling down her shoulder bag next, she moved toward the door. "Goodnight, Maxwell."

He hopped up, strode in her direction. "Let me walk you to your car." He opened the door, shivering at the blast of cold air. He gestured, and she walked out ahead of him.

Once she was safely inside her sedan, he closed her in. "I'll see you in the morning, Yvonne."

She smiled. "See you then."

He stepped back, watching as she backed down his driveway and pulled out into the road. He thought about tomorrow and what it might bring. Whatever happened, he hoped his family understood why he'd hired someone to help out with Sasha. He knew having his daughter full-time would be a major change, and he wanted to make sure it would be a change for the better.

He stood there in the driveway for a few moments more until the chill sent him running back into the house.

Yvonne looked out the passenger side window of Maxwell's SUV, her eyes wide. As he pulled up in front of his parents' house, she couldn't help being impressed. Built mostly of stone and nestled on a hill in a gated community, the large home resembled a castle. His house had been beautiful and far too large for a single man, in her opinion. But this home dwarfed even Maxwell's spacious digs.

He pulled the SUV up to the curb, cutting the engine. He climbed out, and as she opened her door, she found him waiting for her with his hand outstretched. With a smile, she accepted his hand and let him help her down. He shut the door behind her, and she opened the back door to retrieve Sasha.

Leaning in, she looked at Sasha's cherubic little face. The baby slept soundly, with her little fingers curled around the edge of her blanket. "No wonder she was so quiet. Look at her."

Maxwell lifted the car seat from its base and looked inside. A smile spread over his handsome face. "She's a cutie, isn't she?" He closed the door, and they began walking toward the front door.

Yvonne patted him on the shoulder. "You get to take at least some of the credit for that. She's got your eyes."

His smile brightened, and knowing she'd contributed to that made her heart flutter in her chest.

Four wide brick steps led to the bright-red front door. Maxwell carried the car seat, and Yvonne had the baby's bag slung over her shoulder. When they reached the door, Yvonne looked to her employer and awaited his next move.

He shifted around a bit. "The door is usually unlocked when we have a family breakfast. Makes things faster."

Yvonne drew her brown trench coat closer around her body and adjusted the hat covering Sasha's head. She'd bundled the baby up well, leaving only her face visible. "Is there a reason we're standing out here in the cold?"

He sighed, his gaze retreating. "I'm nervous. I don't know what to expect."

Yvonne could understand his concern. But she didn't want to stay outside any longer than she had to. The temperature had climbed into the midfifties, but it was still a bit chilly for her tastes. Aside from that, she worried about Sasha being out in the elements for too long. "I'm sure it'll be fine. I stand by my qualifications, and I don't mind answering any questions they might have for me." Yvonne didn't tell him that she'd already started to become attached to Sasha. No use adding another layer to an already complex situation.

"You're probably right." He paused.

Yvonne touched his shoulder again. In the short time she'd been working for Maxwell, she'd picked up on some of his tendencies. He exuded such confidence when he spoke of his work, but that confidence seemed to falter when it came to Sasha and related matters. "Everything will be fine. One way or another, things will turn out as they are meant to be."

"Do you really believe that?"

She nodded. "I do." Her life hadn't always been perfect, but she'd seen enough and gone through enough to know that things eventually settled out. *Maybe happily ever after doesn't exist. But if I'm going to keep my sanity, I have to believe it does.*

He drew a deep breath, then turned the gold knob. As he'd predicted, the door was unlocked, and he pushed it open. A burst of warm air greeted them as they stepped inside.

Yvonne glanced around the entryway, doing her best not to gawk like a country mouse in the big city. The castle feel she'd noted outside continued in the home's interior. The gleaming floors beneath her feet were probably marble. Their footsteps echoed through the space, bouncing off the walls that boasted textured wallpaper in a soft shade of gold. Landscapes in gilded frames, vases with tall, elegant floral arrangements, and a collection of ceramic elephants decorated the space. A grand, curved staircase centered the space, and there were two doors on either side of it.

Maxwell walked toward the closest door on their right, which already stood open. She followed him into an immaculate sitting room. The furnishings were contemporary and included a sofa and two love seats in steel gray. The items were set up in a U formation, with the sofa against the wall and the two love seats facing each other. A large, patterned area rug covered the hardwood floor beneath the furniture grouping. Black bookcases lined one entire wall.

"Nobody's in here," Maxwell commented as they moved into the room. His tone conveyed relief.

Yvonne looked his way. "What should I do?"

"Have a seat." He gestured toward one of the love seats. "Mom and Dad are probably in the kitchen."

She sat down, and he parked the car seat on the cushion next to her before slipping from the room. After he left, she looked inside at the still sleeping baby. Sasha was the picture of innocence, her small lips bowing in time with her breaths as she dreamed. Yvonne removed the child's hat, thinking she might be overheating now that they were inside. Unable to refrain, she stroked her hand over Sasha's crown of soft curls and sighed.

She didn't know if she wanted her own children, though she enjoyed taking care of other people's little ones. Between her work and the time she put in caring for her parents, she didn't know if she wanted to come home to yet another person who depended on her. Despite her uncertainty about motherhood, she saw children as a blessing.

She only hoped Maxwell understood what a gift this child was. Right now, Sasha's presence might be upending his orderly life, but as the baby got older, Yvonne hoped he'd come to see how his life had changed for the better.

She heard talking then, their raised voices indicating that a family discussion was underway. She couldn't make out the words and didn't try, because it wasn't her business. She'd come here to do her job and didn't have any plans on interfering in Maxwell's family matters.

Yvonne looked up at the sound of approaching footsteps and saw Maxwell reenter the room with his parents in tow. His mother, short and dressed in a lavender linen pantsuit, was all smiles. His tall, salt-and-pepper-haired father, clad in khakis and a green polo, wore a much more serious expression. As they approached the love seat, Yvonne stood.

The smiling woman stepped forward first. "My, aren't you lovely. And you are..."

Maxwell cut in. "Sorry, Mom. This is Yvonne, my nanny."

She bristled a bit at the word *nanny* but recovered right away. "I'm Delphinia Devers." She shook hands with Yvonne. "Welcome to our home, dear."

"Thank you, Mrs. Devers. I'm glad to meet you." Yvonne closed her mouth quickly after the pleasantry because she had no idea what would come next.

"I'm Humphrey Devers." On the heels of the rather brusque announcement, Humphrey stuck out his hand. "Nice to meet you."

"Likewise, sir." Yvonne shook his hand, but sensing his ire, she kept the contact brief.

"Please excuse my husband." Delphinia slid into the seat Yvonne had occupied, peering into the car seat. "He's a little... shall we say...shocked right now. I'm sure he'll come around."

The older man harrumphed as he came over and stood near his wife. "Don't worry, dear. I'm not going to make this innocent woman suffer for our son's foolhardy ways."

Yvonne's eyes swung to Maxwell's face, just in time to see his lips tighten. Despite his obvious frustration, Maxwell didn't respond to his father's dig.

"Humphrey, look at our grandbaby." Delphinia clasped her hands together as she took in Sasha's sleeping face. "She's a beauty, isn't she?"

The tight set of the older man's face seemed to relax as he looked the baby over. "You're right, Del. She's a pretty little thing."

Maxwell remained on the other side of the room but seemed to relax a bit.

Watching the scene unfold before her, Yvonne felt at a loss for what to do or say. She wanted to somehow break the tension she sensed between Maxwell and his parents. "Well, Mr. and Mrs. Devers, your granddaughter is one of the most delightful babies I've ever worked with. She's very happy and hardly ever fusses."

Delphinia sounded pleased. "Wonderful. Well-behaved already, I see."

"Unlike her father," Humphrey quipped.

Maxwell rolled his eyes. "Sorry to disappoint you by doing what's best for your grandchild, Dad."

Humphrey stared in his son's direction, eyes flashing. "You listen here! I'll—"

"Hush up, both of you. You'll wake the baby!" Delphinia's harsh whisper put her men on notice that she wasn't having any of it. She grasped her husband's hand and gave it a squeeze. "Darling, take a chill pill. Stop sniping at the boy and just enjoy our little angel."

"I'm going up front to wait for Lex and Kelsey." Maxwell strode from the room.

Left alone with Sasha and her newly minted grandparents, Yvonne stayed behind the love seat. She left a little distance between herself and them so they could get acquainted. When Sasha started to stir, then released a small cry, Yvonne jumped into action. "Excuse me, Mr. and Mrs. Devers. Duty calls."

As the older couple moved aside, Yvonne unfastened the wriggling, fussing Sasha from the restraints and lifted her to her shoulder. Patting the baby's bottom, both to soothe her and to determine if she needed a diaper change, Yvonne felt the telltale swelling in the diaper. "Looks like our little princess needs a change. Where can I take her?"

"I'll show you." Delphinia started toward the door to the foyer, gesturing for Yvonne to follow her.

Grabbing up the diaper bag, Yvonne trailed behind the lady of the house.

They climbed the grand staircase and took a left turn on the landing. Delphinia swung open the door to a bedroom. "You can spread your changing pad out on the bed." She stepped inside the room but moved back to allow Yvonne access.

"Thank you." Yvonne carried Sasha to the bed and fiddled around with the baby's gear while still holding her.

"What on earth are you doing?" Delphinia's expression conveyed her confusion.

"I don't want to get your bedspread wet." The floral bedspread looked expensive, as did most things inside the Deverses' little castle. She rifled around in the bag for the portable changing pad she kept inside, which would protect the surface from any soils.

"That's very considerate. Here, let me hold her while you get your supplies out." Delphinia held out her arms. "I keep telling my husband that Sasha ought to have her own room here. He claims she's not here often enough and that she's too young."

Yvonne placed Sasha gently against her grandmother's chest. "Thank you."

Cradling the baby and looking down into her face, Delphinia looked as serene as a woman could look. "No, thank you. I relish every chance I get to hold my granddaughter." She looked into Sasha's eyes. "We're just gonna ignore Grandpa and fix you up a room anyway, aren't we, sugar?"

Yvonne smiled as she went about her work.

A few minutes later, the two women descended the staircase with a beaming Delphinia carrying her clean, dry grandchild. And when they reentered the sitting room, a surprise awaited.

Yvonne gulped when she saw the two women who'd joined their merry gathering.

Maxwell's sisters. Sasha's aunts.

Yvonne followed Delphinia into the room and offered smiles to the two women. She soon learned that the curvy, shorter woman was the younger sister, Alexis, and the taller woman with the close-cropped hair was the middle sister, Kelsey. "It's nice to meet you both."

Seeing them all assembled, Yvonne took in the sight of her charge's paternal relatives. Alexis resembled their mother, while Kelsey looked more like their father. Maxwell combined his mother's eyes and skin tone with his father's height.

"So," Alexis asked, "when's the wedding?"

Yvonne froze.

CHAPTER 6

MAXWELL STARED AT ALEXIS FOR A MOMENT, WONDERING what the hell his baby sister was about. "Lex, are you high? I just told you, not five minutes ago, that Yvonne was my nanny."

Alexis giggled. "I know, Bro. I'm just kidding. But you should see the expressions on your faces!"

Maxwell rolled his eyes. "You're a regular comedian, Lex." He glanced at Yvonne and saw that she seemed to have recovered from her shock.

Seated on the love seat with the baby in her lap, Delphinia offered, "You two are an absolute mess." She didn't bother looking up from Sasha's tiny face. The baby smiled, laying on the cuteness, and her grandmother seemed to enjoy every second. Maxwell sensed that his mother would be spoiling the baby in no time, but he had better sense than to try and stop her.

Humphrey stood from his seat on the sofa. "Well, I don't see anything funny at all."

Kelsey, stretched out on the love seat opposite where her mother sat, looked toward him. "Dad. Remember what Dr. Morris said about your blood pressure."

"Hush, Kelsey." Humphrey turned his flashing eyes back on his son. "Maxwell, we need to talk. Come to my study."

Maxwell felt the anger rolling off his father, even from a distance. He had no desire to hash this out with him, at least not now. "Dad, couldn't this wait..."

The old man strode right past him. "Now, Maxwell."

Maxwell groaned in his father's wake. He'd known this reaction was possible, but the reality of it still seemed jarring. A quick look around the room let him see the five sets of female eyes trained on him. Even his daughter, resting comfortably against her aunt Kelsey's shoulder, was looking at him.

With a sigh, he trudged out of the room and across the entryway, where he entered the open door of his father's study. Inside the room, he found his father seated in one of his brown leather armchairs, facing the window. Humphrey's gaze seemed focused on something outside.

Maxwell took a seat in the matching chair next to it, settling in for the lecture of the century.

After a few moments of uncomfortable silence, Humphrey spoke. "This isn't about my granddaughter. She's beautiful, Son."

"That's good to know, Dad." Maxwell's eyes swept over the familiar surroundings of the room. As a kid, he'd only ever been called into his father's study when he was in trouble. That had changed over the years as he'd grown into a man and his relationship with his father had evolved. Still, despite all the hands of poker and casual conversations he'd had with his father here for the last twenty years, he couldn't shake the memories of coming here as a boy to be chastised.

"However, I'm extremely disappointed in your actions in this. You've shown irresponsibility and a general lack of commitment in hiring a nanny, Maxwell."

"'Irresponsibility'?" *Dad really has a way with words, doesn't he?* "That seems a little extreme, Dad."

Humphrey turned his way, his lips pursed. "Seriously? You can't see how your unwillingness to make sacrifices will affect that poor innocent child out there?"

Maxwell looked away after the cutting remark. He couldn't take the disappointment he saw in his father's eyes. "That's not true, Dad. I understand the effects of my actions better than anyone."

"How could you do this? I know how much you enjoy your work. And I understand you couldn't work things out with Juliana. But hiring a nanny instead of cutting back at work?" Humphrey shook his head. "I never would have thought you'd do something like this."

"Dad. You're blowing this out of proportion."

"I don't think I am, Maxwell."

He sighed. "You act as if I'm abandoning my daughter. I'm not. I'm simply doing what I have to do for right now."

"That's all fine and dandy, but in case you've forgotten, I was raised by a nanny. And what I longed for most of all was my parents' attention."

Maxwell cringed. "Dad. Seriously. Before you go off the deep end, listen to what I'm about to tell you." He gave a brief recap of Ines's health scare.

Humphrey's expression changed. "Oh no. I'm sorry to hear that."

"So was I. So your granddaughter is with me full-time, at least until Juliana gets back from Afghanistan."

The old man paused, looking a bit deflated. "I see."

Determined not to let his father's rigid opinions make him doubt his own judgment, Maxwell shook off the annoyance he felt. "Listen, I know you don't agree with this. But there's only so much cutting back at work I can do, especially right now. Sasha needs someone responsible to look after her, and Yvonne definitely fills the bill."

Humphrey exhaled slowly. "She does seem very professional."

"She absolutely is. I'm paying her handsomely, and so far, she's been worth every penny." Maxwell slowly moved his head from side to side, hoping to release some of the tension he felt building in his neck and shoulders. This had to be the most awkward, uncomfortable conversation he'd ever had with his father. He only hoped they could hash it all out now so they wouldn't have to revisit the topic later.

Rising from the chair, Humphrey walked to the window and stood by it, gazing out at the gray morning. "Son, I'm not coming down on you because I want to. I'm doing it because I feel I have to. I just want to remind you not to let your work consume you. They're only babies for such a little while, and you can never get this time back."

Maxwell nodded soberly. "I know. And trust me, I'm going to be there for her as much as I can."

"You know I only want what's best for Sasha."

"I know, Dad, and I get that. Believe me, I never intended for any of this to happen. I apologize for disappointing you." Maxwell looked at his father's back, wondering what the old man was thinking. As the eldest child, Maxwell had borne the responsibility of setting a good example for his siblings for most of his life. So he'd tried to be the model child, at least when he was near his family. When left to his own devices, though, he did what he wanted. He kept it legal and sane, but he'd had some pretty wild experiences in his teens and early twenties. Knowing how he'd lived his life, he had more perspective that his father did. *Dad doesn't know about the kinds of stunts I pulled back in the day, and he never will.*

"I never expected perfection from you, Maxwell. I can't. I'm not so perfect myself."

Maxwell's ears perked up. He sensed something in his father's tone, as if he were holding on to some shameful secret. "Something you want to tell me, Dad?"

"Just a little piece of advice. Seeing your child in the arms of a woman, especially one as impressive as your new nanny, can... do something to you. It can cloud your judgment. Make you take actions you normally wouldn't."

Maxwell's brow furrowed. "Dad, are you talking about something specific here? Maybe there's something in your past you want to share?"

Humphrey's back stiffened. "No. A son doesn't need to know everything about his father."

Maxwell wondered what that meant. "Don't you think that's

disingenuous, Dad? To hold me to a higher standard than you held for yourself?"

With his eyes, Humphrey let his son know he wasn't going to discuss that.

Maxwell sighed. "Fine, Dad." While he was still curious about his father's mysterious indiscretion, he knew he wasn't going to get any answers today.

"Son, brace yourself. Fatherhood is going to be the hardest job you ever do. Remember, one bad decision on your part could be the downfall of your whole family." Humphrey turned from the window and looked at him. "And as you can see, the work doesn't end when the kids are grown."

"Yeah, I can see that." Maxwell stood, walked over to his father. "Does this mean you'll give Yvonne a chance?"

Humphrey nodded. "I suppose. But you'd better make sure my granddaughter gets every little thing she needs, or I'm gonna tan your hide."

Maxwell laughed at his father's turn of phrase.

Humphrey looked at him with a lifted eyebrow.

Sobering up, Maxwell said, "Sorry. I'll be good."

Humphrey patted him on the shoulder. "I'll expect nothing less, Son."

Humphrey exited the room then, signaling that the verbal filleting had finally ended, at least for now. A relieved Maxwell remained in the study a few moments longer. He thought about his father's near admission of wrongdoing, then his dogged determination not to discuss the matter further. What was his father hiding? Maxwell had always thought of his father as honorable, a man beyond reproach. For the first time in his life, he now thought his perception of his father might be wrong. But how? He was pretty sure that if Dad had his way, none of the Devers children would ever know his secrets.

Drawing a deep breath, Maxwell savored a few moments of

silence before returning to his newly expanded family in the sitting room.

When he entered, Yvonne turned his way, her eyes meeting his. Sensing her concern, he gave her a slight nod to indicate that everything was fine. His father had taken a seat on the sofa next to his mother, and his two sisters were sitting on the love seat across from Yvonne. Sasha was in Kelsey's lap, gnawing on her brightly colored set of plastic baby keys. Maxwell moved across the room, and Yvonne set the car seat on the floor so he could sit next to her.

Delphinia patted her husband's thigh. "Is everything okay, dear? You two didn't come to blows, did you?"

Humphrey pursed his lips momentarily at his wife's chiding, then smiled. "Everything is fine, Del."

Maxwell said nothing, but inside, he wondered if his mother knew his father's secret. Was she aware of his past, or was the entire Devers family in the dark about the details of Humphrey's life? No matter how curious he was, he knew he couldn't ask the question now, so he kept it to himself. He'd ask his mother another time and would do so with care.

Sasha began fussing, and as Kelsey lifted her up onto her shoulder, the baby segued into a loud, insistent wail. No amount of Aunt Kelsey's bouncing or patting on the back seemed to soothe the baby. Kelsey cast a furtive glance toward Yvonne.

Yvonne reached into the baby's bag and produced a bottle. "It's about time for her to eat." She shook the bottle and removed the cap. Standing, she walked over to Humphrey. "Would you like to feed her?"

Maxwell smiled as all eyes in the room fell on the surprised old man.

He took the bottle from Yvonne. "Sure. May as well start the granddad duties right away."

While Maxwell watched, Yvonne scooped Sasha up from Kelsey's grasp, then laid the baby gently on her grandfather's lap. Sasha continued to fuss but quieted as she saw the bottle in Humphrey's hand. With her tiny head resting in the crook of his arm, Humphrey put the bottle's nipple to the baby's lips, and her crying ceased as she latched on.

The room fell silent, and from what Maxwell could tell, everyone was content to watch Sasha take her bottle. He looked at his daughter, at the soft crown of curls on her head, the brightness shining in her brown eyes, and the way her little lips puckered around the bottle. He could feel the smile stretching his lips. She was a beautiful baby, and the sight of her in his father's lap, looking so content, touched his heart. The situation wasn't ideal; he knew that, and so did everyone else in the room. But now, as he watched the scene unfolding in front of him, he felt hopeful that this newest addition to the family would be seamless and happy for everyone involved.

Juliana's face popped into his mind, and he wondered how she was. He knew her job often placed her in harm's way, and while things hadn't ended well between them, he would never wish her harm. That sentiment echoed even deeper now that he knew she'd mothered his child. Juliana had left him with so many questions. Where was she? Was she safe? When would she be back? Did she know what had happened to Ines and that Sasha was now with him?

But among all the questions he had, one stood out above them all. It was the one that would have the most impact on Sasha's life, his life, and, ultimately, the lives of his family members. It was such a pressing question, yet one he wasn't sure he wanted answered just yet.

Where does Juliana fit into this picture?

―――

Yvonne awoke the next morning with a smile on her face. She enjoyed her new position, partly because her charge was a nanny's dream. Sasha was about as easygoing as a baby her age could be and was cute as a button to boot.

Her thoughts strayed from baby to father, and she felt the heat rising into her cheeks. Last evening, before she'd gone home for the night, she'd stayed long enough to tuck the sleeping infant into her crib. Maxwell had been in the room with Yvonne as she tucked Sasha in, and she'd noticed the way he'd stood back, watching her. Yvonne couldn't tell if he still felt a bit nervous about her caring for his daughter or if he was just fascinated by something she'd done. Either way, the attention he'd paid to Yvonne had only served to heighten her awareness of him.

As she rolled out of bed, she thought about the look she'd seen in his dark eyes. It could only be described as intense, though she had no idea what he'd been thinking. The professional side of her said it didn't matter because he was her boss. There was nothing more to their relationship; he'd hired her to help raise his child, and that was the extent of their association.

But the other side of her, the side that sought enjoyment over responsibility, wondered what it would be like to be the woman in his life. How would they spend the long winter nights together if they were a couple? Would he have eased up behind her in the darkness, fitting his strong body close to hers? Would he have kissed her neck or whispered endearments against her ear?

She shook herself free from those pointless fantasies. *Von, get it together, or you'll be late for work.* She drew a deep breath, exhaled slowly, and went to prepare for work.

She showered, dressed, and swept her hair back away from her face with a headband. After a quick breakfast of scrambled eggs and wheat toast in the small kitchen of her apartment, she grabbed her bag and headed over to Maxwell's house.

Arriving at the door, she was met by Tilda, Maxwell's house-keeper. Tilda, a short-statured older lady with graying hair and deep-blue eyes, had Sasha on her hip. "Good morning, Miss

Yvonne. Maxwell's gone in to work early today. He left you a note on the coffee table."

Yvonne smiled, shifting her bag higher on her shoulder and entering the house. "Thanks for letting me know."

Tilda closed the door behind her, shutting out the chilly Friday morning. Passing Sasha into Yvonne's open arms, she nodded. "No problem, dear. Now I've got to get to work. These floors aren't going to scrub themselves." With a wink, she eased through the foyer and slipped into the kitchen.

Yvonne braced the baby against her shoulder as she set her bag down on the floor in the living room. Seeing the baby's blanket spread on the floor, Yvonne gently sat Sasha in the center of the colorful fabric so she could shrug out of her coat. She ducked into the foyer to hang it, and by the time she returned, Sasha was on her belly. Yvonne sat down on the floor with her, smiling as she watched Sasha wiggle her chubby little frame, trying to get mobile.

Spying the white envelope on the table, Yvonne reached for it. Tearing it open, she opened the folded note inside and read it silently.

Yvonne,

> *I hope you won't mind staying an extra few hours tonight. I know it's Friday, so I'll be glad to compensate you for overtime. I've invited my frat brothers to the house tonight to hang out, and since you'll be playing such a big role in Sasha's life, I'd like them to meet you as well. You can expect the boys and me around seven this evening.*

Maxwell

Yvonne refolded the note and tucked it into her shirt pocket. She didn't mind working late if Maxwell needed her, though she wished he'd stuck around long enough to discuss it with her. It wasn't so much the staying late that had her feeling nervous; it was the frat brothers part. How many frat brothers did he have? And what kind of guys were they? How much time had they spent around Sasha in the past? Would she have to soothe the baby in a house full of rowdy men, or would it be a smaller, more refined gathering? She appreciated the heads-up about Maxwell's visitors. She just wished he'd given her more to go on.

She looked down at Sasha, who'd managed to gain a few inches. She raised up slightly, balancing on her hands and knees, her little body rocking back and forth. As she rocked, she made a silly little raspberry sound, drool bubbles and all.

Yvonne giggled. Without a doubt, the baby would be pulling up soon. It was only a matter of time. She guessed it would be less than a week before the little adventurer set off to explore the entire house. She thought back on the babyproofing she'd noticed when Maxwell had shown her around the place. He'd covered outlets and mounted large furniture, and he had quite a few baby gates. It was obvious he'd put some serious thought and planning into it, and it comforted her to know that all the safety issues around Maxwell's sprawling home had been addressed.

She thought of all Sasha had gone through over the past week. She was in a new situation, being with her father for such a long period of time, and she probably missed her aunt and grandmother. It was a lot of change to go through in a short period, and though Sasha likely wouldn't remember it all when she was older, Yvonne wondered what it must be like to have such a life-changing week. She reached out, lifting Sasha up and placing her onto her lap. Yes, Yvonne would look out for Sasha this evening, just in case her father's friends turned out to be too much excitement for the baby.

Throughout the day, Yvonne kept the baby entertained while moving around the designated areas of Maxwell's huge property. She read a few books to her, fed her, sat down and built a block tower with her, and played some up-tempo jazz music for her while dancing wildly around the room. If Sasha's clapping and shoulder shimmying were any indication, she enjoyed her nanny's music selections.

When nap time rolled around, Yvonne sat with Sasha in the rocker in her nursery, singing to her. She sang "Beautiful Dreamer," which seemed to be the baby's favorite lullaby.

Once she'd tucked the sleeping tot into her crib, Yvonne slipped out of the nursery and went downstairs. Though Tilda handled most of the household chores, Yvonne handled the baby's laundry. She went into the laundry room, located the basket of baby clothes she'd washed and dried, and carried them with her to the living room. There, with an episode of *American Pickers* playing on Maxwell's oversize flat-screen television, she folded the tiny articles and stacked them in neat piles.

The buzzing of her cell phone on her hip caught Yvonne's attention. Slipping it from her pocket, she answered. "Hello?"

"Hey, Sis, it's Zelda."

Yvonne smiled at the sound of her younger sister's voice. "Hey. What's up?"

"I'm on my coffee break from the spa. What are you up to?"

"I'm working, remember? I know Mommy told you about my new charge."

Zelda laughed. "Oh yeah, that's right. How's that going?"

"Pretty well. The baby is very sweet and very easy to care for." Yvonne had worked in a few infant and toddler classrooms during her career, but this was her first time taking care of a baby in this one-on-one fashion. While she'd done well in the chaos of the infant–toddler rooms, she rather enjoyed this quieter, more personal interaction with one charge. "It's a great job, and I hope to be here for a long while."

"That's not what I mean. Mommy said you're working for a single man, one who's got deep pockets." Zelda's tone conveyed her curiosity. "So what does he look like?"

Shaking her head, Yvonne asked, "Now what does that have to do with anything?"

"Oh, girl, come on. If he has a face like a billy goat, that would explain how he can be wealthy and single at the same time."

Yvonne snorted at her sister's turn of phrase. "A face like a billy goat? Honestly, Zelda. You should be writing a column for somebody's humor website."

"That may be so, but it doesn't answer my question. Besides, you know I love doing facial aesthetics." Zelda had been working as an aesthetician in a day spa for the past few years.

"If you must know"—Yvonne dropped her voice to a whisper in case Tilda happened to pass by—"he's finer than frog's hair. When I first met him, it was all I could do not to drool."

"Ooh." Zelda sighed. "Fine and rich? You'd better stake a claim on him before the other prospectors show up with their shovels, girl."

Yvonne laughed, dismissing her sister's suggestion. "Zelda, it's not like that. Yes, he's fine, and yes, he's single. But I'm here to work for him. I'm taking care of his baby, nothing more, nothing less." Even as she spoke the words, the same words she'd told herself at least a dozen times over the past week, she knew they weren't entirely true.

Apparently, Zelda wasn't buying it, either. "Yeah, right. You'd have to be a darn fool to let a handsome, wealthy brother slip through your fingers. I'm sure you're familiar with the half-assed, craptastic dating scene of today."

"Yeah. I wish I could say I wasn't, but I know how rough it is out there." Dating in the current climate sometimes felt like having dental work done without anesthetic. It was to be put off until it could no longer be avoided, and when it came around, you endured it. Hell, she'd much rather face the dental drill than have another overly casual young man ask her if they could "chill" together.

"Then you'd better get your head out of your hind parts and

work your wiles, girl." Zelda paused. "Remember what Pop always said. It's not how something starts. It's how it ends."

Yvonne did remember their grandfather's sage advice. And she could see how it applied to many things in life. "I know, Zelda. But since I just started this job, I need to settle into it first. Can you not pester me about this right now? At least let me get through the first month, okay?"

"Deal. But in exactly..." Zelda paused, as if counting. "Twenty-four days, we will revisit this topic, ma'am."

Yvonne chuckled. "Don't you have some pimples to pop?"

Zelda scoffed at her sister's teasing. "Excuse me, madam. I don't pop pimples. I perform professional extractions to remove impurities from beneath the skin's surface."

"Yeah, yeah. Either way, go back to work and quit bothering me."

Zelda laughed. "I love you, too."

After she disconnected the call and pocketed the phone again, Yvonne went back to her folding and her show. Halfway through the second episode, Yvonne heard Sasha's cries. She took a moment to tuck the neatly folded clothes into the basket, then took it upstairs with her.

The rest of the day flew by in a flurry of activity. The nap seemed to have given Sasha a second wind as well as a fresh wave of determination to perfect her crawl. Between catching the baby before she scooted off the couch, lying on the floor with her to play, and cleaning up a thousand little messes, Yvonne was good and worn out by the time she heard Maxwell's car pull up outside.

Scooping up Sasha, Yvonne went to the window and pulled the curtains slightly to the side to get a better view. Maxwell's mid-size SUV pulled into the garage, and three other cars followed him up the driveway. There was a large luxury sedan, a sports car, and another SUV, this one a little smaller than Maxwell's. To Yvonne's amusement, all the cars were jet black. *I can see why they're all friends. Their tastes are pretty similar.*

Sasha sneezed, her little body vibrating with the force of it.

"Goodness. Bless you." Yvonne turned her attention away from the scene outside the window long enough to wipe Sasha's nose. When she looked again, she saw three men emerging from the squadron of black vehicles. All three were tall, though their builds were slightly different. She couldn't make out their features beneath the winter gear of hats, scarves, trench coats, and bomber jackets. As they walked with Maxwell toward the front door, she moved to the sofa with the baby rather than be caught being nosey...uh...observing.

Moments later, she heard the key in the lock. Bouncing Sasha on her knee, she waited for the guys to enter.

CHAPTER 7

"Come on in," Maxwell said as he swung open the front door. "And wipe your feet. Don't be tracking grass on my carpet." He took a few steps back into the foyer, making room for Tyrone, Bryan, and Orion to enter, then shut the door behind them.

He took off his coat, and his boys followed suit. As he hung his trench coat next to Yvonne's wool coat, he waited for his friends to get out of their winter gear.

Tyrone spoke as he unwound his scarf. "I can't believe it's this cold outside in February. I need spring to hurry up and come on."

"I'm with you," Bryan groused. "I mean, I can't remember the last time we had this much actual winter. Usually, by mid-February, the temps have gone up."

Orion tossed his fedora up onto the top of the coatrack. "Listen, I'm fine with it as long as we don't get another ice storm like that one we had back in college."

All four men grimaced at the mention of that harrowing weather event. They'd all been trapped in the frat house on campus for days without power. Friendships had been tested by the close confinement, and while theirs had survived, others hadn't been so lucky. Maxwell knew some of the brothers who still wouldn't speak to each other, even after more than a decade.

"That's why I love my line brothers," Maxwell remarked. "We've stuck together through thick and thin." Maxwell gestured toward his living room. "After you, guys."

Bryan, Tyrone, and Orion filed into the room. Following his friends, Maxwell crossed the room toward the sofa.

Yvonne stood, turning their way. She had one arm wrapped around Sasha, who was draped over her shoulder and sucking a pacifier.

Maxwell started to make the introductions. "Yvonne, these are my fraternity line brothers, Bryan, Orion, and Tyrone. Guys, meet Yvonne Markham, my nanny."

Yvonne stuck out her free hand to each of the men in turn. "It's nice to meet you all."

Bryan observed the baby, a smile on his face. "Look at my little niece. She's getting so big. I think I can see a little of Lex in her now that she's getting older."

"That's those Devers genes shining through." Maxwell winked.

"Nah, come on, Max." Tyrone ribbed him. "We remember what you looked like in college, bro. That pretty little lady must take after her mother."

A momentary cringe came over his face at the mention of Juliana, but he forced a smile. "Since I don't want my daughter to see me kicking your butt, I'm gonna let that remark pass, Ty."

Orion, loosening the top button of his polo shirt, chuckled. "Y'all behave now. There are ladies present."

The men moved into seats then. As Bryan, Maxwell, and Orion took the leather sofa, Tyrone sat in the matching recliner. Yvonne placed Sasha on her stomach on the baby blanket spread out over the hardwood floor, then took a seat next to the baby.

"Are you sure you don't want to sit up here?" Tyrone offered his seat.

Yvonne shook her head. "Thanks, but it's better if I'm close by. Sasha's getting more and more mobile, and I need to make sure she doesn't get into any mischief."

"If she's anything like her father, good luck with that," Bryan cracked as he gave Maxwell a playful punch on the shoulder.

Maxwell groaned. His boys could be a real pain in the ass with their teasing, but at least he knew he could count on them to always keep him humble.

The room fell silent for a few moments, except for Sasha's babbling. As Maxwell watched his daughter squirming around on the floor, doggedly determined to crawl away, he wondered what other adventures she'd have in store for him. Over the months and years to come, he knew she'd be learning and growing every day, and he'd be learning right along with her and hopefully growing into everything she needed in a father.

Orion broke the silence then, his voice breaking through Maxwell's rather serious thoughts. "Man, Max. Out of all of us, I never would have thought you'd be the first to become a father."

"Me, either," Tyrone remarked. "I always thought you'd be the last holdout. The lifelong bachelor who'd never settle down."

Maxwell, aware of the female ears in the room, felt a twinge. For the sake of honesty, though, he had to agree with his buddies. He'd pictured his future self in much the same way as Tyrone had; he'd expected to go well into his fifties or sixties as a single man, with no commitments. "I was just as surprised by all this as you all are. But having Sasha is definitely a change for the better, right?"

"Of course." Tyrone smiled. "And even though we're always busting your chops, we know you love Sasha. You're a good dad, Max."

He felt the smile spread over his face. "I appreciate that."

Bryan nodded. "Children are a blessing, man. I hope to have one with Alexis when the time is right."

It hadn't been that long ago that Bryan's remark would have set Maxwell off. When his frat brother had started dating his sister, Maxwell had made his disapproval known right away. After seeing Bryan and Lex together and realizing that his friend truly loved his baby sister, Maxwell had apologized and given the pair his blessing. "Good luck getting Lex to think about a baby, man. She's always hiding out with her sketch pad."

"That's not so much of a problem since she became my wife," Bryan quipped. "I keep her plenty busy if you know what I mean."

Maxwell rolled his eyes. "Spare me."

As if sensing his discomfort with the direction of the

conversation, Yvonne asked, "So what do you gentlemen do for a living? I'd love to know a little more about Sasha's uncles."

Tyrone answered first. "I'm an attorney, and I deal mainly in family law and civil litigation."

"I'm an artists and repertoire executive for a hip-hop label out of Wilmington," Orion said. "It's called Fresh—"

Yvonne's eyes enlarged, and she cut him off midphrase. "Fresh2Deff Records?"

Orion nodded. "I'm guessing you're familiar with us."

She squealed. "Yes, I am. Two of my favorite artists are on that label. Rosie LaRock and Young-n-Wild."

Orion chuckled. "Young-n-Wild is my act. Those boys are a little out of control, but they've got a lot of talent."

"I love their album. Hip-hop nowadays is kind of garbage, but those kids hearken back to the old-school groups like Leaders of the New School and Pete Rock and CL Smooth."

"That's uncanny. Those are almost the exact words their agent used to pitch them to us before we signed them." Orion looked impressed, his brow lifting. "Wow. You've got a hell of an ear for hip-hop. When Max starts to get on your nerves, we'd love to have you at Fresh2Deff."

Maxwell cut him a look. "Stop trying to poach my nanny, O."

Bryan interjected, "Let me tell you what I do before Orion engages you in an entire conversation about the history of rap or asks for your résumé. I'm a textile marketing executive at Regal Textiles."

Yvonne nodded. "I see."

"And since I married his baby sister, Alexis, a few months ago, Maxwell and I are legit family." Bryan winked. "So now he can't shake me, no matter what."

With a laugh, Yvonne turned his way. "Maxwell, I can see why you're so close to these guys. They're hilarious."

"Please, don't encourage them." Maxwell chuckled. "One of my brothers, Xavier, isn't here. In addition to owning an accounting firm, he's a Raleigh city councilman and a youth mentor. He's out of town with some of his mentees for a couple of days."

"Sounds like a real stand-up guy." Yvonne smiled as Sasha wriggled into her lap.

"He is," Orion agreed. "He's also a persuasive one. He's been able to get every one of us to participate in at least one of his mentoring projects."

Bouncing the baby on her lap, Yvonne's smile broadened. "Well, now that I've met you all and heard such good things about Xavier, I feel very good about Sasha's future. How can she go wrong with four loving uncles and a doting father to look out for her?"

Maxwell felt his heart thudding in his chest as Yvonne's words touched him. The weight of responsibility for Sasha, both now and through all the coming stages of her life, seemed to hit him all at once. He wanted to give her everything she needed, and she could probably convince him to give her everything she wanted. He'd been at this parenting gig for less than a year, and he often wondered, would fatherhood always feel like this? The feeling in his chest, like a warm glow and growing pressure to be his best? Would his love for his daughter ever reach its peak, or would it continue to grow with every passing day?

The past few days at the office, he'd been working hard to draw up a proposal for the civic center project. But no matter how hard he tried, he'd found his focus was scattered at best and at times nonexistent. His passion for his work remained intact, as did his desire to secure the civic center project. But his mind always seemed to be on the baby. Did she need him? Was she doing something important, meeting some milestone that he should be there to witness?

"Can I hold my little niece?" Bryan's question drew Maxwell out of his thoughts. "Wanna come sit with Uncle B?"

Maxwell nodded. "Sure."

Yvonne started to get up, but Bryan stood and walked over to her spot on the floor. "Don't trouble yourself, Yvonne. Just pass her to me." He bent at the waist, and as Yvonne lifted the baby up, Bryan scooped her into his arms.

Bryan returned to his seat with Sasha in his lap. She seemed fine with her uncle, but when her other uncles started to gather around, she whined. The whine lengthened into a cry, and before anyone could react, the baby had descended into a full-on wail.

All the men in the room looked to Yvonne, whose lips were pursed in an obvious attempt to hold back laughter.

Tyrone called out over Sasha's wailing, "What are we supposed to do?"

Yvonne released a peal of pent-up laughter. When she recovered, she said, "First, stop crowding her. That's what set her off."

The guys backed away from the baby, all except Bryan, who still held her. Almost immediately, her wails dropped in volume, though the fat tears still coursed down her chubby cheeks.

Maxwell took a tissue from his pocket and dabbed her face. Seeing her cry felt like physical pain for him, and he wondered if it would always be that way.

"Now. If you want to hold her, just do it one at a time. Pass her from person to person and speak quietly so you won't scare her." Yvonne walked over to run her palm over Sasha's curls, and the move seemed to soothe her even more. "Remember, Sasha has had a pretty crazy week. She's still adjusting to things as they are."

The men followed Yvonne's instructions, speaking in quiet voices and keeping things calm as they each had a turn holding the baby. Maxwell observed them, touched by the gentle way they handled his daughter. She seemed to like them all or at least tolerate them, because there were no more tears...until Orion sat her in Maxwell's lap.

"Aw, don't you want to sit with Daddy?" Orion stepped back.

Maxwell pulled his daughter into his embrace, close to his

heart. Her little body seemed to relax, but she kept crying. It wasn't the wail she'd made earlier, but a kind of small whimpering that made him wonder what he was doing wrong. Guilt shot through him as he realized that she spent most of her time with Yvonne while he worked.

Yvonne looked nonplussed. "It's actually pretty close to her bedtime. That's probably why she's fussy."

The baby took a few deep breaths, then yawned, her little lips stretching wide.

"You're right. She looks sleepy." Maxwell looked down into his daughter's eyes, saw the way her lids drooped. Each time they closed, she forced them open again, her big brown eyes settling on his face. "She's fighting it hard, though." He felt somewhat relieved, because a moment ago, he'd been convinced he upset her. *I was overthinking it. She's just tired.*

"Okay, guys. It was nice to meet you, but I think it's time for our little princess to get some rest."

Taking a cue from the nanny, the men stood from their seats. After exchanging quick, quiet goodbyes with their host, they girded themselves in winter gear and headed out into the chilly night air.

Once they were gone, Maxwell looked down at Sasha again. She'd fallen asleep in his arms, and she was the picture of sweetness and innocence. The dark fringes of her lashes rested on her chubby cheeks, and her little tummy rose and fell in time with the deep breaths she took. He realized he could sit with her like this all night, holding her and watching her sleep. The intensity of his feelings stole his breath, and he looked away, his eyes scanning the room for Yvonne.

She was sitting in the recliner, watching him. "What is it, Maxwell?"

"Can you take her upstairs, please? I've got a few things I need to take care of before I turn in."

A look passed over Yvonne's face, but only for a moment. "No problem." She came over and gently lifted the baby's sleeping form into her arms.

Maxwell remained on the sofa, watching Yvonne as she carried Sasha away.

In the doorway, Yvonne turned to him. Fixing him with an intense stare, she said, "It's okay to love her, Maxwell. And it's impossible to love her too much." That said, she left the room.

Sitting alone in the silence, Maxwell wondered how Yvonne had managed to read his mind.

When Yvonne returned downstairs from putting the baby to bed, she found Maxwell still sitting in the same spot on the couch. His gaze was directed straight ahead, and she couldn't tell if he was staring out the front window or off into space. Either way, she could tell something was on his mind.

She'd intended to grab her purse, slip into her coat, and say her goodbyes. But now, as she caught the expression on his face, she hesitated. She was tired and ready to get some rest. In spite of her eagerness to seek her bed, leaving him sitting alone, looking so stricken, just wasn't an option. Her leisurely weekend would have to be put off for a few minutes more. Walking over to the sofa, she sat down next to him. "Maxwell, are you okay?"

He blinked, turned to look at her. "Sorry about that. Yeah, I'm fine."

She said nothing, just continued to watch him. It was her way of letting him know that she could see right past his dismissive words. He wasn't a very good liar, though she had better sense than to press him about it. He was still her employer.

After a few moments of uncomfortable silence, he sighed. "This full-time fatherhood thing is a lot to deal with. I never even thought I'd get married, let alone have a kid."

For some reason, his statement about never wanting to get married stung like a pinch on the forearm. Pushing the feeling aside, she touched his arm. "I know this has been a big change for you and that it's overwhelming."

He put up his hand, palm open. "Wait a minute. I said it was a lot. I didn't say it was overwhelming."

Yvonne noticed how he insisted on framing things a certain way. *Male pride is a hell of a drug.* To her mind, it was all the same. He was under a lot of stress and pressure and was having trouble dealing with it, as most people in this situation would. Still, she kept her expression neutral and nodded.

"I really want to lock down this civic center project. It would be the biggest job of my entire career, and the rise in my profile would lead to more work." He drew a deep breath. "When I first started out in architecture, it was about besting my rival and gaining more clients. Now that I have Sasha, I've got to make sure she's taken care of as well."

Yvonne nodded. She'd been tossing an idea around in the back of her mind ever since her first day on the job, and now seemed like a good time to bring it up. "Listen, you have a lot going on in your life right now. Why don't I just live in with you, to take some of the burdens off?"

His brow furrowed. "What made you offer?"

She searched for the right wording. "I've seen how tired and stressed you look when you come home. I'm not an expert, but it seems like balancing your job with fatherhood is difficult right now."

He was quiet for a few moments, so quiet that she started to worry she'd made him angry.

"I'm not trying to insult or offend you, Maxwell. I'm just telling you my perceptions of the situation."

More silence.

Their conversation was like a little rowboat with a hole in it.

They were taking on water fast, and she knew it. So she grabbed her imaginary bucket and started tossing the water out. "I've seen so many new parents over my career. People who have had babies, people who've adopted children or inherited them from a relative. Everyone goes through an adjustment period, and that's true for both the parents and the children. You're both doing well, considering the circumstances."

He watched her, his head tilted to one side, his lips pressed together.

"I'm here to do a job, Maxwell, and an important part of my work is to set up a routine that works for both you and the baby. All I want is to make things a little easier for you." She genuinely meant those words, and she let her sincerity come through in her tone.

His face relaxed a bit before he spoke again. "How much living in are you suggesting?"

"Five days a week. Basically, I'd come in on Monday morning and stay until Friday evening. I think it will make things easier for you if you don't have to rush home from work to let me go for the day."

He rested his chin against his crooked fingers as if thinking it through. "Are you sure you want to do this?"

She nodded, feeling as if she'd finally plugged the hole in their rowboat. "It's not really a problem. Actually, it will save me a lot of gas and time, since I won't have to drive here every morning and drive back every evening."

He appeared pleased. "How much more should I pay you to live in?"

She shook her head. "You don't need to pay me anything extra. You're already compensating me very generously." She made four figures per week, and not only was it the highest salary she'd ever been paid, it was more than enough incentive to care for a precious baby like Sasha.

"I've got to give you something for this." His gaze rose upward as if he were thinking, searching his mind for a solution. "Isn't there something else you need?"

She thought about it. With her spending more time here with Maxwell and Sasha, she'd have less time to spend at her parents' house. Her mother still got around pretty well, but her father needed a good amount of help and, occasionally, supervision. "Would you be willing to pay for a nurse or aide to help out with my parents? Someone part time should be enough."

His gaze returned to her face. "So instead of a raise, you want me to pay for nursing service for your parents? Is that right?"

She nodded. "Yes. I make enough money for what I need. But with the extra time I'll be spending here, my parents could probably use a little additional help."

He considered her words for a few moments, then said, "Done. I'll have my assistant line up some candidates for you to interview. Until someone is in place, feel free to do what you need to do for them. Take Sasha with you if you like."

Impressed and grateful, she smiled. "Thank you, Maxwell."

"You're welcome. And I'll also have your room professionally decorated." He leaned back against the sofa's pillows. "My decorator can set up the room two doors down from Sasha for you."

She thought that was a nice gesture. "Wow. I'll warn you, though. My tastes are pretty simple, and the decorator probably won't have to do very much."

"Still, I'd like to do this for you. I want you to be comfortable here."

"That's very generous. Thank you again."

"You're welcome again." He paused. "As much as I hate to admit it, I do feel overwhelmed. I want to pursue my career goals, but at the same time, I don't want to miss out on Sasha's day-to-day life. It's been hard to balance the two."

"Every parent goes through this, Maxwell. So don't be too hard on yourself. I'll be here to help you figure it all out." She genuinely wanted to see him succeed at this. Sasha deserved a great father, and she could see Maxwell's determination to fulfill that role. Beyond that, he had a loving family and close friends who cared about them both. It was a great, healthy environment for the baby, and having all those people in her corner would undoubtedly have a positive effect on her upbringing.

"So when do you want to start living in?"

"Monday. I should be able to pack up my essentials over the next two days and bring them in with me Monday morning." It wasn't how she'd planned to spend her weekend, but if she wanted to be ready to jump into this new arrangement by then, she'd have to change her plans. "I think the sooner we settle into this new schedule, the better."

He clasped his hands together. "Sounds good." He stood up. "I've kept you long enough for the day. So go on home and enjoy your weekend, Yvonne."

She stood and started toward the foyer.

"Thank you again for offering, Yvonne."

She looked back over her shoulder. "Thank you for accepting." A few moments later, after she'd bundled up and gotten her things, she let herself out, stepping into the chilly night air.

As she drove away from his house, she thought about what she'd just offered to do for him. Her motives had been pure...mostly. *Honestly, I enjoy being around Maxwell just as much as I enjoy being around Sasha.* His situation was easily the most complicated one of any parent she'd encountered in her career. On a professional level, figuring out how to best serve him and his daughter was almost like putting together a complex puzzle, and that intrigued her.

But there was more to it than that. No matter how much she tried to ignore her feelings, her attraction to him refused to go away. Setting aside his good looks, his impeccable sense of style, and his wealth, she sensed something inside him, something much deeper than any of those obvious, surface-level factors. Her instincts told her that he was far more sensitive and caring than he wanted to let on. She remembered the way he'd looked, holding his sleeping infant. His paternal instincts had risen, and he seemed to be fighting them. She couldn't be certain, but it appeared as if he thought being openly affectionate with the baby would somehow diminish his manhood. She hadn't intended to say anything about it, but she couldn't hold back. He needed to know that real men could show affection and genuine concern without it taking away from their masculinity.

Yes, she could see his flaws, his vulnerabilities. Yet she still felt drawn to him.

She sighed as she pulled into her parking spot in front of her building. *I might end up regretting this decision. But I really do think Maxwell and Sasha need me right now.*

I'll just have to do the best I can to keep my feelings from overriding my judgment.

CHAPTER 8

SATURDAY AFTERNOON, MAXWELL STEPPED INTO THE HUSKE Hardware House Restaurant and Brewery. The building, originally opened in 1904 as an actual hardware store, was a historic landmark in downtown Fayetteville and still had its original Victorian-era exterior masonry. As he waited in line behind the four people standing at the host station, he scanned the interior in search of his friends. The rich, golden wood that had been used to build the marble-topped bar, high-top tables, and booths made the place look like the inside of a honeycomb. Unzipping his green Theta Delta Theta bomber jacket, he shrugged out of it and tossed it over his arm.

Thankfully, it's a lot warmer in here than it is outside. The blast of chilly air that had hung over the Carolinas all week still persisted, and he'd be glad when it moved on.

Spotting the guys sitting on stools at the bar, he waved to Bryan to indicate his arrival. After a brief chat with the host, he walked over to where they sat. Tyrone, Orion, and Xavier were present as well, and all of them wore some type of TDT regalia. Bryan and Tyrone each had the same bomber jacket tossed over the back of their stools. Orion wore a long-sleeve green polo with silver embroidery of the fraternity letters, and Xavier had gone all out, wearing a green TDT tracksuit with a silver stripe running down each pant leg.

After greetings were exchanged, Bryan gestured to an empty stool to his right. "What's up, Max. We saved you a seat."

"Thanks." He climbed atop the stool and leaned against the backrest. "I'm just glad I could make it. A lot has changed since we made these plans a month ago."

Xavier, raising his mug, said, "You're telling me. Where is the baby today, anyway?"

"She's with my mom." He thought back on his brief interaction with her this morning. "I went over there after breakfast, and before I could even open my mouth to ask her to watch Sasha, Mom practically snatched her out of my arms. Said she needs to have some bonding time with her granddaughter."

Bryan chided, "Lucky you. This isn't exactly a suitable gathering for a baby." He took a swig from his mug.

Maxwell nodded. "You're right. I don't think I'm ready for my daughter to know about my college exploits just yet."

A chorus of agreement met that statement. They'd gathered to celebrate the anniversary of their joining the brotherhood of TDT, and each of them had war stories far too exciting for such young and delicate ears.

"I can't believe it's been ten years since our probate, man." Tyrone shook his head. "It's wild to think about it."

"Those were crazy times. When I think about the things we did to get in, man, I don't know how I made it."

Draping an arm around his shoulder, Bryan insisted, "Because you had all these upperclassmen to look out for you, bro."

"Even though we were all pledging the same year, you didn't have the benefit of previous college experience under your belt." Xavier scratched his chin. "You're welcome, Young'n.'"

With a laugh, Orion said, "Yeah, I appreciate y'all for helping a kid out."

Thinking back on those days, Maxwell remembered the shenanigans they'd pulled. The late nights, the parties, hanging out on the quad with the prophytes who'd pledged in the years before them. Those were wild times...and some of the best times of his life. He'd studied hard to get his degree, but he'd played just as hard. Some would say his desire for excitement continued for years after college, and that was true, at least when it came to his dating habits. *But now that I have Sasha to take care of, playtime is over.*

Orion gestured for the bartender. "Can I get a Nor'Easter, please?"

The Young'n's got good *taste in beer.* "Make that two Nor'Easters, my man." Maxwell visited the place often enough to be familiar with the menu, and that beer was one of the best on tap there. The India pale ale, one of the signature house brews, boasted a full-bodied yet smooth flavor. He appreciated that while low on hoppy bitterness, the beer packed a nice citrus kick on the finish.

The bartender nodded. "You got it. Any of you guys need anything?"

Maxwell knew better than to drink on an empty stomach, so he added, "Can we get a couple of baskets of fries?"

"No problem."

As the barkeep moved away, Orion said, "Hey, Max, whatever happened to that honey you got caught in the broom closet with?"

"Yeah, yeah!" Bryan chimed in, his narrowed eyes and repetitive snapping of his fingers indicating he was tapping into his memory bank. "What was her name...Donna? Darla? Something with a D..."

Letting his head drop back between his shoulder blades, Maxwell groaned. "Damn. Every time we start talking about college, one of y'all brings that story up. Am I ever gonna live that down?"

All four of his brothers answered in unison, "No!"

Shaking his head, Maxwell blew out a breath. "Dawn. Her name was Dawn. And to be honest, it was kind of a random hookup. She'd been sweating me for a few weeks prior to that, and the night of the step show, things kinda came to a head."

"In more ways than one." Bryan chuckled.

Rolling his eyes but unable to hide his smile, Maxwell continued. "That was her senior year, and I was a junior. I know she got her biology degree, but I'm not sure what happened to her after she graduated."

"Damn, bro. She was fine, smart, and a senior?" Orion shook his head, his expression conveying his awe. "No wonder you were my hero back then."

"You mean you never reached out?" Xavier's wide-eyed gaze met his.

Maxwell shook his head. "Nah. It wasn't that deep."

"Is it that deep with Yvonne?"

Maxwell's brow furrowed. *That seems like a bit of leap.* "Bryan, what does she have to do with what we're talking about?"

"Come on, Max. We all saw the way you were looking at her."

"Not me, I wasn't there." Xavier frowned. "Now I feel like I missed something."

All the guys were watching Maxwell, and he didn't care for their scrutiny at all. "B, you're way off. Yvonne is just my nanny. There's no other relationship between us. Besides, we've known each other less than a week."

"I know all that. But I also know you're attracted to her." Bryan leaned in his direction. "Admit it."

Maxwell didn't speak. *There's not really a good answer to that question.* He had only two choices: admitting his fascination with his new nanny and setting off a chain reaction of nosey questions, or lying to his best friends.

The bartender delivered their order, momentarily taking the guys' attention away from him, and Maxwell blew out a breath. The reprieve was short-lived, however.

Tyrone helped himself to a handful of fries. "Even if you don't wanna admit it, Max, it's obvious you're feeling her. We could all see it."

Maxwell felt his face tighten as everyone except Xavier nodded their heads.

"Nobody blames you for it, bro." Tyrone crunched on a fry. "She's a beautiful woman, and she's obviously very caring."

Folding his arms over his chest, Maxwell sighed. *My brothers are right about Yvonne on all counts.* "She's kind and beautiful, yes. But she's also very professional. I'm pretty sure she wouldn't even entertain the idea of a relationship with someone she works for."

Bryan snapped his fingers. "So you're admitting you like her. Now we're getting somewhere."

Maxwell rolled his eyes. "Where you're getting is on my nerves. We need to change the subject. Besides, we didn't come here to talk about my love life. We're here to reminisce about the good old days at Central."

Xavier shrugged. "I wasn't there for any of this, but I do trust my brothers' word. I'm not going to make any judgments here, but I will tell you that getting married has given me access to levels of happiness and satisfaction I never would have imagined."

"Typical Xavier. Your advice sounds like a political speech." Bryan shook his head. "He's right, even though his delivery is over the top. Marrying Alexis has enriched my life on every level. Now, I'm not saying Yvonne is the one. What I'm saying is if you have feelings for her, you might want to explore the possibilities."

Orion quipped, "Y'all are both grown and single, so conduct yourselves accordingly. But it doesn't necessarily have to lead to marriage. You and I are the last two single brothers in this group." He tilted his head. "If we're not careful, we'll end up as mushy and preachy as these three."

Maxwell chuckled on the heels of that comment. His friends were perceptive, perhaps a little more than he would have liked. *Yes, I'm attracted to Yvonne. But my situation is complicated enough without adding another layer of drama.* He had the civic center project, his regular client load, and, as of this week, full responsibility for his young daughter. His plate was so full it threatened to crack under the weight of its contents at any moment.

A couple of hours later, he was back behind the wheel of his SUV, headed to his parents' house to pick up Sasha. With the sounds of the *Black Panther* film score flowing through his speakers, he let his mind wander, thinking through all the changes in his life. While he drove, Bryan's words kept repeating in his mind.

Explore the possibilities.

If only they knew how much he'd like to do just that. This was the first time he could remember hesitating over pursuing a woman who had piqued his interest. He wasn't a man who hung back and waited to be noticed, professionally or personally. He'd take some time to assess and evaluate, but after that, he never hesitated to go after what he wanted. And he wanted Yvonne.

Thing have never been this complicated before. Before, I had only myself to consider. Now I have to consider my daughter and how my actions could affect her.

As he idled at a stoplight near his parents' neighborhood, another unsettling thought popped into his mind. Every one of his friends who'd been at his house that night had noticed his attraction to Yvonne. Hell, even the one who hadn't been present was now drinking the Maxwell-likes-Yvonne Kool-Aid.

Shit.

Yvonne seemed able to read him from the very moment she'd stepped into his presence. So if his friends could tell he was attracted to her, it stood to reason that Yvonne herself might be aware of his feelings as well.

Shit!

How in the world had he ended up in this situation? He needed someone knowledgeable and caring to take care of Sasha, but did she have to be so alluring as well? This went beyond her physical appearance; it was clear she possessed a pure, nurturing soul. Should he blame the nanny agency for sending him a woman with the most beautiful pair of big brown eyes he'd ever seen? Or should he blame fate?

He glanced in the rearview mirror, his eyes settling for a moment on Sasha's car seat. *Never thought I'd be driving around with one of those.* Yet here he was. *Life sure has a way of surprising you.*

Pulling into his parents' driveway, he drew a deep breath, doing his best to settle his mind. Resolving to keep his inconvenient yet very real feelings for his nanny to himself, he shut off the engine and went to retrieve his daughter.

Sunday afternoon, Yvonne entered Fill the Well Body Boutique around two. After spending the better part of her weekend packing and setting up for her new live-in arrangement with Maxwell, she wanted to enjoy a little pampering. Having a best friend who owned a spa made that an easy task.

As soon as Yvonne entered the lobby, she saw Athena sitting at the front desk, poring over some papers spread out in front of her. No other patrons were present; Sundays were typically a slow day at the spa, and those who did come in usually did so before noon.

Athena Jackson had been one of Yvonne's closest friends ever since their days at Hillside High School, and that hadn't changed despite the vastly different paths they'd chosen in life. Athena was Yvonne's opposite in many ways: petite, thinner, and with a fairer skin tone. Even her penchant for flashy, colorful clothes and jewelry stood in contrast to Yvonne's preference for pearls, black and gray clothing, and classic accessories. Their differences seemed to unite them, and the older Yvonne got, the more she appreciated Athena's refreshing, adventurous approach to life.

"Hey, girl," Yvonne called to get Athena's attention.

Athena looked up then, pushing her reading glasses up on top of her close-cropped hair. "Hey there, stranger! Haven't seen you in here in a good month. What's been going on?"

"I started a new job for one thing." Yvonne strolled to the

coatrack near the desk and hung up her purse. "Don't you remember me telling you I applied at the Wittenmyer Agency?"

Athena looked thoughtful for a moment as if trying to conjure up the memory. "Oh yeah, now I remember. So you got the position with them, and you've already got a client?"

Yvonne nodded. "And there's a hell of a story to go along with my new charge, too."

"You know I want to hear all about it, right?"

Yvonne chuckled. "I'm sure you do. And all will be revealed, once I'm comfy in the pedicure chair."

Standing, Athena pulled her into a hug. "It's good to see you again, girl."

"Likewise." Sometimes the busyness of adult life seemed to drain away all her free time, but Yvonne tried her best to make time for her family and friends, no matter what she had going on.

Athena led her through the clear beaded curtains to the nail spa area. Yvonne felt the calm wash over her as she took in the familiar, soothing setting. The walls were painted in muted shades of blue and beige to mimic the beach at sunrise. The floor beneath her feet mirrored both the color and texture of sand and even had a few well-placed starfish and seashells embedded in it. Shadowboxes lining the wall contained all manner of things found at the beach: pieces of coral, dried seaweed, seagull feathers. The soft recessed lighting gave the place that subtle, early-morning glow. The sleek glass manicure tables had blue leather chairs on either side, and the tan pedicure chairs boasted high-tech massage capabilities and sanitary pipeless soaking systems. "Every time I come here, I'm impressed. You really made this place feel like the beach, Athena."

Gesturing to a pedicure chair, Athena cracked, "I sure hope so. It took several months—and several thousand dollars—to get this place just right. I'm glad you appreciate my hard work."

Yvonne settled into the chair, looked around the room at all the empty ones surrounding her. They were the only people in the room, and the only sound, other than their voices, was the soundtrack of ocean waves and seagulls that played on a continuous loop. "Where's everybody else?"

"My two nail techs are both on vacation today. Since I didn't have any appointments booked, I didn't make a fuss." Athena ducked out of the room, then returned with a wicker basket filled with pedicure supplies and implements. "That means I'm doing your pedicure. Lucky you." She winked.

"Oh, I feel super special." Yvonne grinned. "What about my sister? Is she here?"

"Zelda's working today, but she's on lunch. She'll be back soon, though. She's got a client coming in for a facial at three."

Knowing she'd also see her sister today made Yvonne smile. Zelda, her only sibling, was seven years younger and an aesthetician by trade. Zelda had started working at Fill the Well fresh out of beauty school. Athena hadn't just given Zelda a job, either; she'd had to start with a trial period working under another, more experienced aesthetician, just as Athena required of all her employees. Being who she was, Zelda appreciated that she hadn't been given special treatment. Zelda worked hard and treated her clients well, and in the past four years, she had built a good-sized clientele for herself.

Athena slipped the tub insert into the chair's base and turned on the hot water. "Check the temp for me, hon."

Shifting in her seat, Yvonne kicked off her brown sandals and dipped her big toe into the water. She sighed, then slipped both feet into the rapidly filling tub. The heated water enveloped her feet as she reclined in the chair. "It's perfect." A soft purring sound escaped her throat as she turned on the chair's massage function and sank into the cushion.

Athena cocked an eyebrow as she shut off the water. Slipping into a pair of gloves, she shook her head. "It's been way too long since you've had the D, if my chair got you moaning before I even touch your feet."

Closing her eyes, Yvonne sighed again. This sound wasn't a reflection of pleasure, though. "Don't remind me, Athena. You know I haven't really dated anyone since"—she frowned as his name passed her lips—"Cornelius."

Athena shuddered. "Ooh, girl. Let's not revisit that tragedy. How long has it been now? Seven, eight months?"

"Try nine months." *And three weeks, but who's counting?* As much as she hated to think about it, Yvonne did miss being touched. Not that she'd ever let Cornelius enjoy that privilege again. He'd been a jerk of the highest order. She might be needy, but she wasn't that desperate.

"I still can't believe he had the nerve to insult your career choices, especially since he faked an entire career for himself." Athena added her special blend of salts, oils, and flower petals to the water, swirling it around with her gloved hand. "What was that line he gave you about his job?"

"That he had a very important position with the museum of history." Yvonne rolled her eyes at the memory. "Turned out he was selling key chains in the gift shop."

"Yikes. He really was bold with the lies, wasn't he?"

"It was a mess. He could have just told me he worked in the gift shop, and I wouldn't have had a problem with it. I mean, it might not be glamorous, but it's an honest day's work."

"You're telling me." Athena held up her trusty pumice stone. "I mean, I'm touching people's feet most of the day, but I love my work, and it pays the bills."

"Exactly. If he'd just been honest with me and spent less time talking shit about my work with kids, we might have had a real shot." Yvonne shook her head. The lengths men would go to in an effort to make themselves look good boggled her mind. An image of Maxwell popped into her head. *Now, there's a man who doesn't have to fake success. He's got it going on, for real.* "It's all good, though. His foolishness forced me to face reality and kept me from wasting any more of my time on him."

"You left your last job a few months after you dropped him, didn't you?"

Yvonne nodded. "It was a crazy time for me, but I think things are finally starting to settle out. New job, new possibilities."

"Yes, girl. And here's hoping Cornelius took a long walk off a short pier."

Both women laughed, the sound echoing around them.

The bell chimed then, indicated that someone had entered the lobby. Moments later, Zelda stepped into the nail suite, a clear plastic cup of red liquid in hand. Seeing her sister, she grinned. "Hey, Von." She walked over, leaned in to hug her around the shoulders with her free hand.

"Hey, girl." Yvonne quelled the urge to play in her sister's hair; Zelda hated that. Plus, it wouldn't do to have her mass of curls looking like an abandoned bird's nest when her three o'clock client came in.

"So did you tell the boss lady about your new job with Mr. Sexy Architect?" Zelda took a long draw of the drink in her cup.

Yvonne pursed her lips. "I was getting to that, Z."

"Yeah, right. I gotta get set up for my next appointment." A giggling Zelda disappeared from the room, heading back to the facial suite.

When Yvonne looked down again, she found Athena staring at her. "What?"

"Girl, don't 'what' me. You'd better spill the tea on your new job...and this fine man you work for."

Thinking of Maxwell again, Yvonne couldn't help smiling. "His name is Maxwell Devers, he's an architect, and he's a single father to the most precious little baby girl I've ever worked with. Her name is Sasha and—"

Athena shook her head. "Yeah, yeah. The baby's cute and all that. But what about the man?"

"You're just as bad as Zelda."

"Don't insult me. I'm badder." Athena lifted Yvonne's right foot out of the water and began exfoliating. "Now tell me all about Mr. Devers."

While Athena scrubbed, trimmed, and massaged, Yvonne told her about Maxwell. Knowing her friend wouldn't settle for any less, she gave as full a physical description of him as she could. Based on Athena's expression, Yvonne guessed her friend agreed with her assessment that Maxwell Devers was indeed finer than frog's hair.

By the time Athena started applying the glossy, hot-pink polish to Yvonne's toes, she was grinning from ear to ear. "Sounds like a dream job, for real. Great pay, a precious li'l one, and a boss so fine he makes your teeth hurt? And here I am scraping your crusty feet. I'm jealous." She chuckled.

Yvonne laughed at her friend's chiding words. "Athena, you know this spa is your life, and you wouldn't have it any other way."

"True, true." Applying the last bit of topcoat, Athena slid her stool back. "But here's the real question. Are you gonna move on him or wait for him to come to you?"

Yvonne's brow furrowed. "Athena, what are you talking about?"

"Come on, Von. It's obvious you're attracted to him. I can tell just by the way you describe him." Zelda walked by then, and Athena kept quiet until Zelda returned to the back with her client. "Like I was saying, you want him, and life's too short not to go after him."

"Athena, have you been inhaling nail polish remover or what? This is too good a job for me to jeopardize, no matter how I feel about him."

Athena snapped her fingers. "Aha! So you *admit* that you're attracted to him?"

Zelda poked her head around the doorway leading to the rear of the spa. "I could have told you that, boss lady." Then she disappeared as quickly as she'd appeared.

Yvonne rested her forehead in her hand. "You two are going to get me in trouble." She'd left out the part about her living in with him five days a week so she could assess Athena's reaction, and now she knew she couldn't reveal that little tidbit, at least not now. Yes, she was attracted to Maxwell, and there wasn't any getting around that as far as she could see. But she had better sense than to pursue him. She worked for him, and if anybody was going to make a move, he would have to be the one. She simply wouldn't risk looking like an idiot and losing her job, all at the same time.

Despite what she knew was for the best, she knew logic often fell by the wayside in matters of the heart. And with her best friend and her sister both egging her on, she wondered how long she'd be able to keep things strictly professional between her and Maxwell.

CHAPTER 9

MAXWELL SAT BY HIS DRAFTING TABLE, HIS EYES SWEEPING over the draft plans pinned to the surface. It was Monday morning, and the sunlight streaming through the windows of his office improved his working conditions immensely. The civic center project was one of the biggest he'd ever bid on, and he knew he would need to impress the mayor and the city council if he was going to win the job. He imagined Harold Carmichael, his self-declared "rival," doing something similar in an attempt to secure the project for himself. He chuckled.

Whatever. Let Carmichael keep participating in the world's most one-sided rivalry. I'm just going to keep doing what I do best.

"Thank goodness it's finally warming up." Carson entered the room then, carrying two steaming mugs of coffee. A black leather folio was tucked beneath his right arm. "I don't think I could have dealt with that cold snap much longer."

Taking his black ceramic mug from his intern, Maxwell quipped, "I bet. Warm weather is the whole reason you came here, right?"

Carson nodded as he grabbed a chair, pulling it near the drafting table and sitting down. "Exactly. The minute I graduated high school, I knew I was getting the heck out of Minnesota. The winters up there are just too brutal."

Maxwell took a swig from his coffee mug, enjoying the way the rich roast warmed his chest. "What's the name of your hometown again?"

"Little Falls. Famous for being the hometown of Charles Lindbergh and not much else." He sighed, leaning back in the chair. "I wanted to go to Florida State, but my parents said that was too far away. North Carolina was the compromise."

"Well, it all worked out. Your studying at State is what got you this position." Maxwell shifted on the stool, taking in the drawing from a different angle. "I normally try to hire interns from my alma mater, but your résumé was so impressive." Carson was due to graduate from the NC State College of Design with his bachelor of environmental design in architecture degree in the spring. Since Maxwell usually worked alone and contracted out work when necessary, Carson had been a great addition to his staff.

"After graduation, I'm hoping to get on with a firm in a large city. Somewhere that needs responsible redevelopment. Maybe Detroit." Carson shook his head. "There are so many places that need it, though."

"Just keep your options open. I'm sure the right job will reveal itself." Maxwell scratched his chin. "In the meantime, let's get back to the project at hand. Do you have the draft proposal?"

Carson nodded, reaching for the folio that he'd laid on the edge of Maxwell's desk, and opened it on his lap. "It's here. I just need to reconcile it with the plans you've got pegged to the table."

"Right." Maxwell stood, taking a few steps back from the drafting table. Studying the wide view of the large sheet of paper, he began to rattle off a description of his vision. "The new addition to the Crown Center is going to draw people from all over the state. The central location will make it appealing to performers and groups of all kinds."

"That's what I have. I also noted that we don't expect it to interfere with any of the other local venues because there's nothing of similar size like it within a good seventy-five miles."

"I'm picturing five unique spaces. The main auditorium will seat up to ten thousand, depending on the configuration used." Maxwell pulled the drafting pencil from behind his ear and pointed to the corresponding space on the diagram. "Then there will be the ballroom, suitable for weddings and other events of up to one thousand. We'll have a theater that seats two hundred and fifty, which will go over big with the local filmmakers who want to host premieres."

"I agree. The last two spaces are multipurpose rooms, right?"

Maxwell nodded. "They'll fit up to one hundred people each, and we're going to put in a flex wall between them so the spaces can be combined if necessary."

"I didn't have the flex wall. Let me add it." Carson pulled a pen from his shirt pocket and began marking the proposal document. "Did you come up with something for parking? That area gets a lot of traffic, and I'm not sure if the size of the lot will accommodate the amount of parking we need."

"I'm certain there won't be enough space for parking unless we do one of two things." Maxwell took another long sip of coffee, then set the mug down on the desk. "We can either build a parking deck, which I doubt is in the budget, or we can alter the footprint of the main building, leaving more space in the available parcel for parking."

Carson frowned. "Is there a good way to do that?"

Turning toward the window, Maxwell looked out at the cloudless blue sky, thinking.

As had been the case whenever he allowed his mind to wander lately, his thoughts strayed to Yvonne. She'd moved in this morning, or at least he assumed so. He'd left for the office early this morning and had only interacted with her in passing. She'd been carrying only her purse and a single duffel bag. From what he knew about women, she would probably need a lot more than that to keep her for a whole five days.

I guess she went back to the car to get the rest of her things after I left. If he hadn't been in such a hurry to get to work, he would have offered to help her move her stuff. He recalled how she'd looked, waving to him from the front door, that beautiful smile lighting up his day before it had even begun. *I wonder how she and Sasha are doing.*

"I feel like this is going to take some serious reconfiguring, Mr. D."

Carson's voice cut through Maxwell's thoughts, reminding him of the conundrum at hand. A few moments later, he turned back toward the drafting table with a snap of his fingers. "Carson, what about this. If we put the two multipurpose rooms and some restrooms in the basement, then the other spaces on the ground level, I think we can tweak the footprint just enough to do the trick."

Standing, Carson closed the folio and held it in one hand as he eased closer to the plans. "We might have to trim a bit off the lobby entrance here, but I think that might work."

"We can trim a few feet from the lobby as long as we leave the display alcoves intact. The city wants to use them to display items of significance to the town's history, and we can't remove them." The mayor and her team had left a lot of things up to the architects and designers bidding for the project, but the display alcoves had been one of the few specific requests written into the bid request document. "We'll keep the first version on hand just in case the city gives us a little wiggle room in the budget for a parking deck."

"Got it."

"I'm going to have to go back to the software and tweak the dimensions and shape of the building." Maxwell released the draft plans from the metal clips anchoring them to the drafting table. "It'll take some time, but if my instincts are right, it will be a vast improvement on what we have now, on several levels."

"Now, what should I put in the section about building materials?"

"I'm using eighty percent green materials. I've got a source for some really great reclaimed wood that we'll use for some of the interior finishes. Everything else will be sustainably sourced, recycled, or otherwise environmentally responsible."

"Sounds pretty awesome." Carson smiled, then strode toward

the door to the outer office. "I'll get to work on revising the proposal document. Need anything else from me right now?"

Maxwell shook his head. "I don't think so."

After Carson left, Maxwell sat behind his desk and booted up his computer. As he waited for his design software to load the most recent version of the plans, his phone buzzed against his hip. Slipping it from his pocket, he swiped the screen to answer the call. "Maxwell Devers."

"Good morning, Maxwell. How are your plans coming along?"

Oh, brother. It's Carmichael. Rolling his eyes, he stated dryly, "Just fine. Yours?"

"Excellent. Things are going great over here."

"Is there something you want, Harold?"

Harold sounded annoyed. "Here I am trying to do you a favor, and you're snapping at me. Anyway, I thought you should know that the deadline for the civic center proposals has been moved up."

Maxwell felt his brow furrow. *I don't trust this guy any farther than I can throw him.* "What are you talking about?"

"I just found out about an hour ago." Harold yawned. "I'm just passing the word along in case you weren't aware. It seems I was correct in assuming you didn't know."

Maxwell supposed it could be true, but thinking about his past interactions with Harold didn't instill any confidence in the man's word. "And you're telling me this why? I would have thought you'd take any opportunity to get a leg up on me."

Harold scoffed. "Oh, please. I don't need to resort to childish tricks, Maxwell. I'll simply win the bidding based on my superior design skills."

That was debatable. But Maxwell didn't have the time or desire to engage Harold in some sort of professional pissing contest. He blew out a breath. "Okay, I'll take your word. Thanks for the heads-up, and you have yourself a good day." Without waiting for a response, he disconnected the call, eager to end the unpleasantness.

Placing his phone on the desk, he minimized his design software long enough to scan through his email. To his chagrin, Harold had been telling the truth. The city's special project administrator had indeed sent out a message, and the subject line indicated the change in the deadline.

Placing his open palm against the back of his neck, Maxwell called out to his intern. "Carson? Come here, please."

A moment later, the younger man appeared in the doorway. "Need something, Mr. D?"

"Looks like the deadline has been moved up for submitting our proposals."

Carson's lips thinned and opened, revealing his teeth in a half smile. "So…how long have we got?"

"The rest of this week is it."

"Ouch." Carson passed a hand through his short brown hair. "Think we can swing it?"

Maxwell shrugged. "We don't have a choice. I'm not about to throw in the towel now." *I'm not going to give that beady-eyed Harold Carmichael the satisfaction.* He'd entered this field driven by his passion for design, determined to change the world one project at a time. He wasn't about to let a minor setback stop him from pursuing this project. Even if Harold weren't in the running, he would want to be the one to design the civic center. It was rare for an architect of color to be hired for a project of this size, and he hoped to set a precedent that would help make the road a little easier for those who'd come into the field after him.

No, this isn't about competition. This is about widening the road.

"So I'm guessing if I don't finish up the proposal before I leave today, it's homework, right?"

"Right."

"Cool. I'll keep at it." Carson disappeared again.

Maxwell sank the rest of his day into making the two versions of the draft plans: one with the parking deck and one without. Dimensions were adjusted, angles corrected, placements retooled. He ordered in for lunch and barely left his desk the whole day. At five thirty, he finally shut down the computer. Rubbing his screen-weary eyes, he stood and stretched in an attempt to release some of the kinks that had formed in his neck, back, and shoulders. Gathering his things, he walked out of the office.

"Done for the day?" Carson didn't look up from his own computer as he asked the question.

"Yes. My eyes are starting to cross." Maxwell didn't say it aloud, but there was a part of him that missed his daughter and was eager to get home to her. Other parts were missing Yvonne's smile and warmth as well, but he tamped that down as best he could.

"I'll probably be out in about twenty minutes. I'm just about done here."

"Mary Alice gone?"

Carson nodded. "She left at five on the dot."

Maxwell chuckled. She always did that, but since she was efficient at her job, he didn't make a fuss. "Okay. See you tomorrow, Carson."

"Later, Mr. D."

Car keys in hand, Maxwell turned and left.

———

"Here is big *B*. Here is little *b*. What words begin with the letter *b*?" Yvonne stifled a yawn as she flipped to the next page of the board book. The soft cushions of the sofa cradling her body seemed to exhort her to take a nap. It was late Wednesday evening, and the baby had kept her busy all day. While she was tired, a nap was out of the question at the moment. "*B* is for *ball*, *box*, and *bumblebee*." She pointed to each picture in turn.

Sasha, seated on her lap, placed her palm over the page. "Babababa."

She nodded. "That's good, Sasha. You can make the *B* sound."

Grasping the edge of the book with her tiny fingers, Sasha pulled it from Yvonne's hand and began gnawing on the edge of the page.

Knowing better than to wrest it away from her, Yvonne simply smiled. "I think I need to get up and get my blood flowing. You want down?"

"Babababa." Big, sparkling brown eyes looked back at her.

"Okay." Standing, she placed the baby on the blanket spread out on the floor. Raising her arms above her head, she stretched, bouncing on the balls of her feet to reawaken her circulation.

The front door swung open then. "I'm home."

Hearing his voice ring out through the lower level of the house made her heart skip a beat. "Welcome home," she called back.

Maxwell entered the room a few moments later. As he strode over to the baby, he asked, "Should she be eating that?"

She looked down at Sasha, who lay on her back, still contentedly mouthing the book. "It's no big deal. Babies explore with their mouths. That's why board books exist—to fill the need for reading material that can stand up to large quantities of drool."

He chuckled. "It's been a long day, but honestly, that cheesy joke has improved it."

"Glad I could help."

He stooped, scooping Sasha up into his arms. "Hi, sweetheart. Did you put Ms. Yvonne to work today?" The baby formed a small O with her lips and leaned toward him. He kissed her small forehead, and part of Yvonne's heart melted at their interaction.

"She sure did. She's very active, and her crawling has improved immensely." She ran a hand over Sasha's curly head. "She moves pretty fast now, way faster than you'd think."

Maxwell bounced Sasha against his shoulder. "I'm gonna guess you can't just put her in the crib."

She shook her head. "Not until she's already asleep. She's very active, which is common for babies her age. And when she's awake, it's better for her development if she's allowed some freedom to explore her environment."

"I get it." He moved to the couch and sat down with his daughter in his lap. "I don't smell any food. Did Tilda come in today?"

"No. Her son called the house, though. He took Tilda to urgent care this morning."

He frowned. "Is she okay?"

"I haven't heard back from him. She twisted her ankle, and it may be a sprain."

He rubbed his chin while keeping his other arm wrapped securely around the baby. "I'm sure she'll call and let me know what's going on." Glancing toward the kitchen, then back to her, he asked, "What did you eat?"

She shrugged. "I managed. The refrigerator is well stocked. I scrambled myself some eggs this morning and had a sandwich for lunch."

Tilting his head, he studied her. "Do you cook?"

"I do. Is that something you want to add to my duties?"

He shook his head. "No. Your job is looking after Sasha."

"I don't mind doing it. I'll tell you what. If Tilda has to be out for a while, I'll do the cooking, just until she comes back."

"Thanks. That would be helpful." He paused, looking down at Sasha's face. "Has she had her dinner? She looks a little sleepy."

Watching the way the baby snuggled down into her father's arms brought a smile to Yvonne's face. "She ate about a half hour ago. Strained peas, turkey, and a sippy cup of formula."

His stomach growled loudly. "Boy. That sounds pretty good right now."

"I could go whip something up."

He shook his head. "No. You look just as tired as I feel."

She didn't know how to take that, so she took it at face value. "It's been a long day for both of us, I guess."

"I've got an idea. There's a little family-owned Mexican restaurant about twenty minutes away. Nice folks, quiet atmosphere, and great food. Do you like Mexican food?"

"Sure. It's been a while since I've eaten any, though."

"Then let's go there for dinner, my treat. Sasha's half asleep, and I'm sure the car ride over there will finish the job."

She opened her mouth, then closed it without answering. She wanted to say yes, not just because of her empty stomach but because she enjoyed spending time with him. She hadn't seen very much of him since her first day of work when they'd been busy adjusting to their new roles in each other's lives. True, it was the nature of a nanny's job to spend most of their time with their charge and very little with the parents. Still, she worried it might be inappropriate to agree so quickly. She grasped at the first available excuse she could conjure. "It sounds nice, but I don't have anything nice to wear."

"You look lovely. There's no need to change."

She felt the familiar warmth rising into her cheeks. "A moment ago, you said I looked tired."

"That doesn't take away from your beauty, Yvonne." He stated it as fact, gave her a crooked half smile. "I don't want to make you uncomfortable, Yvonne. There are no strings attached. It's just a casual, friendly dinner."

What harm can come of it? We'll have the baby with us, so there's only so much trouble I can get myself into. "Okay. Let me get a warm blanket for Sasha and her baby bag, and we can go."

"Great." He stood, placing Sasha on his shoulder as she fought a losing battle to keep her eyes open.

Within a half hour, they were tucked away in a booth at Fuego y Hielo. A wooden stand placed next to the table held Sasha's car seat, and the baby slept soundly inside.

Looking over the menu, Yvonne commented, "I think I'll have a chimichanga. I haven't had one in ages." She thought about her doctor's admonitions that she should control her portions to counteract her hereditary predisposition to type 2 diabetes. "Wait. About how big are the ones they serve here?"

He made a gesture with his large hands, showing her they were roughly the size of a medium cucumber. "Not so terribly big. You get a lot of rice and beans on the side, though."

After they'd ordered and received their food, she leaned forward in her seat. "What happened at work today?"

He sighed. "We made good progress on the civic center plans and the proposal that goes along with it. Unfortunately, the deadline for bids to be submitted has been moved up. We only have until Monday to get it together."

She frowned. "Is that going to be enough time?"

"Probably. But every other project we have in the hopper has to be put aside for us to meet this new deadline." He took a sip of iced tea from his glass. "I actually found out from one of my competitors. I thought he was lying, but when I checked my email, I saw that he was telling the truth."

"Hopefully, things will go according to plan."

He set down his fork, watching her intently. "It's very fortunate that you offered to do this live-in thing. I'm going to be working late the rest of the week or at least until we can finish up this project bid."

"As I said, I wanted to make things easier for you. I'm just glad I could help."

He held her gaze. "Is that the only reason you offered this arrangement, Yvonne?"

She felt her breath stack up in her throat. *Is he...asking what I think he's asking?* She wasn't going to lie to him; it just wasn't something she did. "It was my primary reason, yes."

"And your other reason?"

He seemed to be baiting her, and she was tempted to bite. She swallowed, then reached for her water glass to quench her dry throat. Unfortunately, she was left with only ice in the glass. Raising her hand, she gestured a waitress over to the table.

"Water, ma'am?" The young woman filled her water glass from the clear pitcher she carried. "By the way, you two are such a sweet couple."

After the waitress moved away from the table, Yvonne turned her gaze to Maxwell, who wore a ghost of a smile.

"I was going to ask you a question, but I think the waitress might have answered it for me."

She swallowed again. "Maxwell, I...don't know what to say."

He shrugged. "Just be honest, Yvonne. You're a very attractive woman, and I can admit how alluring I find you." He leaned back against the padded seat of the bench. "I'd wager you already know how I feel. It seems like you've been able to read me from the first moment you walked into my office."

She dropped her gaze, studying her own reflection in the glazed tabletop. Of course she'd noticed it. The way he looked at her when he thought she wasn't paying attention, the way he smiled when he saw her. That old familiar heat was returning to her face again, and she knew it wasn't brought on by the jalapeños.

"I'm being honest with you because I respect you." He rubbed his hands together, then placed them palms up on the table. "Let me lay it out. I think you're attracted to me, too. But you need to know that I'll never push or pressure you in any way. Our association can remain just as it is, nanny and client, if that's what you want."

"That's not what I want." The words tumbled out before she could stop them. *Ugh. Why did I say that aloud?*

He looked thoughtful for a moment, then nodded. "Okay. But the depth of this relationship is up to you. And your position will never be in danger, whatever you decide. I've seen the way you care for my daughter. I'd be hard pressed to find anyone else like you."

"I appreciate that, Maxwell." She'd never done this before, and she didn't see any reason not to take him at his word. Getting involved with the parent of one of her charges was something she'd never even considered in the past. Somehow, Maxwell had become a special case. He was different from any other man she'd ever dated, in all the ways she craved. "I don't really know what to think about...what's happening between us. I just know I can't ignore the way you make me feel."

His smile deepened, the crinkles forming around his nose and eyes.

Her heart fluttered. *There's no fight left in me when it comes to my feelings. I want to see where this can go, what we can have together.*

"Then it looks like we're both on the same page."

She pushed aside her empty plate. "As long as we take things slowly...get to know each other...I think we'll be fine."

"I agree." He gestured to their dishes. "The food was good, right?"

She smiled. "It was just as excellent as you promised it would be."

He waved for the waitress, who removed their plates and left the check. Once he'd filled out the credit card slip, he asked, "Are you ready to head home?"

"Sure."

He got up from the bench, easing around Sasha's car seat, and stood next to her. Offering his hand, he helped her to her feet.

They stood there, face-to-face, with only a sliver of fragrant air between them. The sounds of the conversation and music in the restaurant faded, and the world seemed to stop as she stared into the deep brown pools of his eyes.

She let her gaze slide down to his full lips, lingering there. Feeling her emotions rise, she offered a soft entreaty. "Kiss me, Maxwell."

He leaned in, his hand guiding her chin until their lips met. Fire bloomed inside her belly, and she held back, not wanting to seem too eager. She didn't care who saw them, didn't care what people might think. She wanted this. A moment later, he pulled back, and she realized how much that brief press of his lips had affected her.

This is going to be one hell of a ride.

CHAPTER 10

Maxwell strode into his parents' garage Saturday morning, rolling up the sleeves of his green sweatshirt. Both his father's single cab pickup and his mother's compact sedan were parked in the driveway, and he assumed that was to make it easier to complete the task at hand. The weather had warmed noticeably now that they'd passed the middle of the month, so he knew he wouldn't freeze to death with the garage door left open. He'd donned a pair of old, worn jeans and sturdy boots so damage wouldn't be an issue—he fully expected his mother to put him right to work. As the only male child, he'd been assigned to handling physically demanding chores around the house since the age of ten, often acting as his father's main helper.

Looking past his father's orderly line of shelving and the carpentry workstation, he let his gaze scan over the opposite side of the space. That half of the three-car garage was where forty years of assorted junk had been piled up last year to make room for his father's custom shelving.

"I'm over here, Max."

He didn't see his mother right away, but as he walked farther into the garage, he found her sitting on a low stool near the door that led into the kitchen. "Morning, Mom."

"Good morning, Max." She wore a pair of old black sweatpants, a T-shirt, and a gray cardigan. With one hand, she held open a large black trash bag as she tossed a few small items inside. "Thanks for helping me out today."

He chuckled. *She says that as if I had a choice. I'm not going to tell her no.* "No problem. What do you want me to do first?"

She gestured toward the door. "Grab a trash bag. There's a box of them on the counter just inside the door. Then come on back out here."

Inside the warmth of the kitchen, he grabbed the bag and stood for a moment, listening. He could hear the sounds of his father and daughter interacting somewhere in the house. Smiling as he listened to her coos in response to her grandfather's voice, he opened the bag as he slipped back into the garage.

"Oh, good, you're back." She pointed to a large pile of boxes to the right of where she sat. "I'm going to keep working on this section. I want you to tackle those boxes."

He moved to the area she'd indicated. "What's in all these, anyway?"

She shrugged. "I know there are some of your and your sisters' old things in there, but beyond that, I haven't a clue."

He reached up, pulling the top box down. Setting it on the floor, he opened the flaps. As he dug his hands through the piles of pastel-colored fabric inside, the contents became clear. "This looks like Kelsey and Lex's baby clothes."

"Oh my goodness." His mother smiled, craning her neck to see around the piles. "We'd better put that box aside. I'll wash everything, and then we can see if Sasha can fit any of it."

She's always been sentimental. He set the box aside toward the middle of the cement floor in the area where his mother usually parked her car.

"Come help me up off this stool, Max."

He set aside the second box of baby clothes and went to where she sat, offering his hands. She gripped them and, with his help, pulled herself to her feet. "You good, Mom?"

She nodded. "Just remind me not to sit back down on that thing. It's way too low for these old bones." She gestured to the pile of bags between where she'd been sitting and the pile of boxes she'd assigned him. "Everything in these bags is recyclable. Glass, plastic, and cardboard. Once we get through, your dad can haul it all to recycling."

"I agree, and we're not even done going through the rest of this stuff, so there will probably be more." He walked with her back to his stack of boxes. "I found a second box of clothes."

She looked inside. "Oh, goodness, Max. These are yours." She grabbed a powder-blue sleeper, printed with dozens of tiny bluebirds. "Your little pajamas. I can still remember how sweet you looked in them."

"Mom, come on." He smiled as he placed his arms around her shoulders. "You know there's no way I can fit those things now. And since Sasha's a girl, we can probably let this whole box go."

She sighed, a wistful expression on her face as she clutched the sleeper to her chest. "I suppose. But I'm keeping this. There's no law that says she can't wear anything blue. And these are just so precious."

He chuckled as he slid the box across the floor past the first box. "There. Now I've established my 'keep' and 'donate' piles." Knowing his mother, the keep pile would soon get out of hand. She tended to hold on to things well beyond their period of usefulness.

"Here. I'll help you go through the boxes now that I'm done over there."

As they tackled the pile together, she reminisced on her days as a young mother, raising him and his sisters. "You were a pretty laid-back baby, and so was Alexis. Kelsey was the crier."

"A sign of things to come," he joked. Kelsey had always been the most outspoken and stubborn one among them, a flash of sparkle in an otherwise straitlaced family.

She shook her head as she searched through a box of old dolls. "Alexis was crazy about this one doll. I don't think it's in here…"

"The one with the pink hair and the mermaid tail?" Maxwell couldn't believe he remembered that, but somehow, an image of it had imprinted itself in his mind. "Don't you remember? She loved it so much that she already took it home with her. It's on display in her curio cabinet."

She laughed. "You kids certainly have given me plenty to smile about." She put the box of old toys in the discard pile.

"You mean you're not going to keep the girls' old toys for Sasha?"

"And deny myself the pleasure of taking her toy shopping? No way." She returned to his side, taking the box he handed her.

While his mother inspected that, he stooped down to open the very last box. Sitting on the concrete floor beneath the weight of all the other boxes had left this one misshapen and a bit crushed. Aside from that, it was the only box that was taped shut. It took some doing to get it open, and when he finally lifted off the packing tape, he looked inside, curious to see what he'd find.

His eyes widened for a moment as he marveled at all the brightly colored plastic. *Another box of toys.* In contrast to the last couple of boxes, the playthings contained in this box were made for boys. There were plastic planes and trucks, building blocks, and toy tools in bright primary colors. He dug down into the bottom, pulling up a handful of diecast metal cars.

His mother asked, "What's that? Another box of toys?"

He nodded, still staring into the box. "Yeah, but this is boy stuff."

"So it's yours. Do you want to take it home with you like your sister did her mermaid doll?"

"No, I don't want it." He couldn't tear his eyes away from the box contents. *Where did these come from? How did they get here?*

"Why not?"

He answered truthfully. "They aren't mine."

She dropped the box she'd been holding, and it hit the cement floor with a thump. "What?"

He drew a deep breath, trying to think of a good way to rephrase. "I don't recognize any of these things, Mom." He wouldn't claim to remember everything about his childhood. But his favorite childhood toys? He remembered those. His set of bright yellow Tonka trucks. His collection of Marvel action figures. His baseball signed by Hank Aaron, which was on the desk in his home office. But this box held no sentimental value for him, because these were not his things. "I think I got rid of most of my kid stuff when I left for college. Remember? I put some things in storage and donated the rest. Dad insisted I not leave a bunch of stuff behind."

Her expression hardened, her lips stretching into a thin line as she approached. "You're sure they're not yours?"

"Absolutely positive." *This is awkward.* He wasn't sure what to make of this. Could it belong to a cousin? No, he couldn't remember any of his cousins bringing that much stuff to the house, even for a weekend sleepover.

She peered into the box, and as she did, her face tightened even further. A flicker of recognition crossed her face before she turned her back with a look of distaste.

He frowned. *Does Mom know who they belong to?*

Marching to the kitchen door, she flexed the knob and pushed it open. "Humphrey! Get out here, now!"

Maxwell stood back, folded his arms over his chest. *Whatever's about to go down, I'm not getting involved. No way.* He would, however, observe. His mother looked ready to fight.

Humphrey appeared in the doorway a few moments later with Sasha propped on his shoulder. "Del, what is it? Why are you shouting?"

She narrowed her eyes. "I told you to get rid of those damn toys, Humphrey. They should have been out of here ages ago. Why in the hell are they still here?"

Patting the baby's back, Humphrey shot back, "Now who needs a chill pill? Lower your voice before you upset the baby."

She took several steps back. "Humphrey Devers. You've got some nerve telling me to lower my voice right now. You're lucky I don't do worse."

Maxwell's eyes widened as he watched the tense scene unfold.

Who did the stuff in the box belong to? And why was a box of plastic junk such a point of contention between his parents?

"I'm sorry. I never got around to it, and I guess I...forgot."

"Hmph." She shook her head. "Get that mess out of my house right now."

With a resigned sigh, Humphrey walked past his fuming wife and placed his granddaughter in his son's arms. "Max, I'll be back." Placing a soft kiss on the baby's forehead, he grabbed up the box and strode out of the garage.

Maxwell watched as his father loaded the box into the bed of his truck, climbed inside, and motored away.

"Good riddance to bad rubbish," Delphinia proclaimed, smacking her hands together. "I think I've had enough cleaning for the day. Give me my granddaughter."

Seeing the way her expression softened, he handed over the baby. "At least I got to hold her for two or three minutes."

"I'm going to ignore that comment." Cradling Sasha in her arms, she went into the house through the kitchen door.

Standing alone in the garage, Maxwell looked out at the cerulean sky. *What the hell just happened?*

—⁓—

Yvonne sat at the small kitchen table in her childhood home. The table's surface was covered with various forms and important papers pertaining to her parents' well-being. To her right sat her younger sister, Zelda. Next to Zelda was Janine, the new nursing aide Yvonne had hired to help take care of her parents.

Janine, a young woman with a short afro, bronze skin, and hazel eyes, was dressed in a set of lemon-yellow scrubs. As her eyes scanned the tabletop, she asked hesitantly, "Do you all have some kind of...filing or organization system? You know, to keep up with all the prescriptions, appointment slips, doctor's notes?"

A twinge of guilt hit Yvonne as she shook her head. "No, I can't say we do."

Her mother, tending a pot of stew at the stove, interjected, "I keep all my papers in a shoebox on the closet shelf."

Janine smiled in her direction. "Well, Mrs. Markham, you're off to a good start then." Leaning closer to Yvonne and Zelda, she lowered her voice. "I'll work on a more efficient system of organization while I'm here."

"I'm not hard of hearing, you know." Marissa tossed the words over her shoulder without taking her eyes off the contents of the large stock pot she stirred.

"I got you, Mrs. Markham." Janine released a nervous giggle. "I can see there will never be a dull moment on this job."

"You're right about that," Zelda quipped. "Mommy and Daddy are a handful, but they're also the best parents a girl could ask for."

"That's my baby." Marissa gave Zelda an exaggerated wink.

Shaking her head at the two of them, Yvonne asked, "You'll be fine with transporting them to doctor appointments and on errands, correct?"

"Sure thing. The company car is a minivan, so I should have plenty of room for your parents as well as anything they might need to bring along with them."

Yvonne nodded, satisfied with her answer. She'd pored over Janine's résumé, spoken to some of her past clients and their family members, and spoken at length with her boss at Helping Hand Home Care. *Everything checks out with her. She's young, energetic, and skilled. I think she'll be a great fit.* While she still felt a little guilty about having to hire help for her parents, she knew it was the best thing she could do for them, for Zelda, and for herself.

"I really think you're going to be a good fit for us, Janine." Zelda ran a hand over her hair. "It will be great to have someone we trust to make sure Mommy and Daddy have everything they need."

"Up until now, my daughters have always done that."

Yvonne turned toward the sound of her father's voice, noting how perturbed he sounded. "Morning, Daddy."

Clad in his blue flannel robe and pajamas, he entered the kitchen, leaning heavily on his cane. "Hmph."

Yvonne looked to Zelda, who simply shrugged.

Sighing, Yvonne stood. Placing her arm around his shoulder, she guided him to the chair she'd vacated. "Here, Daddy. Why don't you sit down and talk to Janine a little? You know, get to know her."

"I don't see why I need a babysitter. I'm a grown man." He dropped into the chair, hanging the handle of his cane on the backrest.

"Daddy!" Zelda let her head drop, appearing embarrassed on his behalf.

Yvonne remained silent. She'd had this conversation with her parents more than a week ago. Her father hadn't been happy about it, and he'd made that clear from the beginning. She doubted there was anything she or her sister could say that would change his mind about things. It was all she could do to tamp down her rising feelings of inadequacy as a daughter. *I've always taken care of Mommy and Daddy. Zelda too. I've always put their needs first. But if I'm ever going to save up enough money to open my own childcare center, I've got to get serious.* She had a dream to pursue, a goal she wanted to reach. And as much as she loved her family, it was time for her to go after it.

"You're absolutely right, Mr. Markham. You don't need a babysitter." Janine smiled in his direction.

His expression softened. "There now, see? This youngster understands where I'm coming from."

Where is she going with this? Yvonne decided not to say anything and gestured for Zelda to remain quiet as well. It was the only way they'd find out where this was leading.

"Of course I understand." Janine's expression and tone conveyed her empathy. "So it's a good thing I'm not a babysitter, isn't it?"

His brow furrowed. "What are you getting at…um…what's your name again?"

"Janine."

He folded his arms over his chest as if waiting for her to make her point.

"Mr. Markham, I bet you've worked hard most of your life."

"You'd win that bet," he replied gruffly.

"I'm just here to help you out. I'll take care of some of the chores and unfun stuff so you and your wife can spend your time the way you see fit."

Silence fell on the room for a moment, save for the sound of the stew bubbling on the stove.

"I suppose it wouldn't hurt to have someone like that around." Gordon scratched his chin. "We'll see how it goes, okay?" He reached across the table.

"Sounds good to me, Mr. Markham." Janine shook his hand.

Yvonne could only stare in disbelief. Just like that, Janine had broken through her father's ire. *Impressive. She's definitely a keeper.*

"Now since that's settled, Marissa, what you got cooking over there?"

"Brunswick stew for dinner."

He chuckled. "Sounds great. Now, how about some breakfast? I'm starved."

She shook her head as she walked over and planted a soft kiss on her husband's forehead. "Eggs and bacon, coming right up."

"*Bacon* bacon?"

She tossed the answer over her shoulder as she walked back to the stove. "Turkey bacon, Gordon. Remember we're minding our health here."

He twisted his lips into a mock pout.

His wife ignored him, instead asking her daughters, "Do you two want something to eat while I'm cooking?"

"I've already eaten." Zelda stood and stretched.

"Me, too. Stopped off on the way over here." Yvonne gestured for her sister. "Zelda, let's chat in the living room for a minute."

Once they were on the old tan couch, safely out of Janine's and their parents' earshot, Zelda asked, "What's up?"

"Plenty." Yvonne kept her eyes on the kitchen doorway in case her mother should appear there. "I've moved in with Maxwell."

Zelda's eyes bulged. "Wow, Sis. You work fast."

Yvonne shook her head, knowing exactly where her sister's mind had gone. "Let me rephrase. I'm living in with Maxwell, Monday through Friday, because it's a more convenient arrangement for him and the baby."

Zelda tossed one jean-clad leg over the other. "I'm assuming this new arrangement is the reason you decided to hire a nurse for Mommy and Daddy?"

Yvonne nodded. "I didn't want you to have to take so much time off of work."

"Isn't it expensive to have someone with them all week?"

"You bet. Luckily, Maxwell is paying for it."

Zelda's eyes grew even wider. "Geez, Von, how'd you get him to foot the bill for that?"

"It was a lot easier than you think. He offered me a raise, and I elected to have him pay for Mommy and Daddy's care instead. He agreed to it right away."

"This new gig of yours just keeps getting sweeter and sweeter." Zelda blew out a breath, leaning back against the sofa's cushions. "Wait. Why'd you bring me in here to tell me this? Do you not want Mommy and Daddy to know?"

Yvonne shook her head. "I'd rather they didn't, at least for now. So don't tell them, please."

Zelda raised her hand, placing it over her heart. "I promise, I won't spill the beans."

"Good. I'm in no mood to sit through a lecture."

"I don't blame you." Zelda stifled a yawn. "Who'd want to listen to them drone on about what's proper? We're both grown-ups now, but sometimes, I swear they forget that."

Yvonne thought back on her midtwenties when she'd decided to move in with her then-boyfriend. Her parents had hit her with a lecture tag team, going on for over a half hour about how it wasn't right to live with a man out of wedlock and how even if they weren't sharing a bed, it simply wouldn't "look right" for her to cohabitate. "I guess I'll have to tell them eventually, but I'd like to put it off as long as possible."

Zelda tapped her chin with the long, sharp purple nail of her index finger. "I wonder if they would classify this as living with a man out of wedlock. Does it count if you're doing it for your job?"

Yvonne shrugged. "I don't know. But I'd rather assume they will and just keep it to myself for now."

"I feel you. Be honest, though. Don't you think living in with him is going to make it harder to hide the fact that you're attracted to him?"

Yvonne let her head drop back, her gaze on the popcorn ceiling above. "Definitely. That's why I'm not."

Frowning, Zelda asked, "You're not what?"

Yvonne drew a deep breath, knowing once she said these words to her sister, there would be no taking them back. "I'm not hiding my attraction, and neither is he. We're just going to take things slowly and let them develop naturally."

"Oooh!" Zelda clapped her hands together, bouncing up and down on the sofa cushion. "I knew it, I knew it! I could see this coming a mile away."

"See, that's why I don't tell you things. You're so dang excitable."

Zelda giggled. "So just how far have things gone between you two?"

Yvonne didn't say anything, but she puckered her lips.

"You kissed him?"

Yvonne rolled her eyes. "Damn, Zelda. Keep it down."

"Kissed who?" Their father ambled into the room, aided by his cane.

Yvonne felt her eyes go wide. *Oh crap.*

His face folded into a frown. "Von, I know you're not talking about your boss."

She kept her mouth closed. *There's nothing I can say that won't sound disrespectful.*

"Yvonne Clair Markham. I just asked you a question, and you had better answer me." Leaning on the cane, he fixed her with a censuring fatherly stare.

CHAPTER 11

MAXWELL STRAIGHTENED HIS TIE AS HE WALKED TOWARD THE door of the Hay Street Municipal Building on Tuesday morning. It was just past ten, and he'd been asked to meet with the mayor at ten thirty. The early March day, warm and sunny, mirrored his mood and provided a welcome change from the weeks of cold dreariness that had preceded it.

The Crown Center job is in the bag. He smiled as he recalled the phone call he'd received an hour ago from the mayor's office. While the mayor's assistant hadn't revealed much, he couldn't imagine any other reason he'd be asked to come here.

The interior of the building buzzed with activity. A good number of people were inside the lobby, some standing as they held conversations and others simply moving through the space as they went about their business. The cacophony of sounds echoed off the gray marble floors and the aged wood paneling on the walls.

He stopped briefly at reception to alert the mayor to his presence. Once he'd been told where to go, he went down the hall to the elevator.

When he reached Conference Room A, he raised his hand and rapped on the partially closed door. "Good morning. Maxwell Devers here."

A moment later, the door swung fully open.

On the other side stood the smug-faced Harold Carmichael.

Maxwell kept his expression neutral. "Good morning, Harold."

"Devers." Harold didn't move aside to allow room for him to enter.

Maxwell scratched his chin. "I have a meeting here with the mayor in a few minutes, so if you could step aside, that would be great."

Harold scoffed. "Well, it looks like Madame Mayor's double-booked, then, because I've got a meeting with her as well. Same place, same time."

Maxwell felt his brow furrow. *Why in the world would she be meeting with both of us?* Maybe his celebratory mood had been premature, and the city had only narrowed down the candidates for the project as opposed to awarding it. "Whatever the case, please move so I can come in."

Finally, Harold stepped back. A few minutes later, they were sitting opposite each other, with Harold on the left side of the table and Maxwell on the right, facing the door.

From his vantage point, Maxwell saw Mayor Taylor the moment she walked in. He stood as she entered the room.

Harold, who'd spent the last few minutes looking as if he had better things to do, perked up at the mayor's entrance. He didn't stand however, at least not until after he watched Maxwell do it.

Once greetings had been exchanged, Mayor Taylor sat down at the head of the table. "Mr. Devers, Mr. Carmichael, thanks for coming in this morning on such short notice. We're in a bit of a time crunch on this project, so we need to move forward with awarding the project."

"If you don't mind my asking, what's the reason for the change in the timeline?" Maxwell posed the question, careful to keep his tone professional. As a designer, it helped him to know all the details involved in a project, no matter how minute. He wanted his designs to serve the project on every level.

"It's no problem, Mr. Devers. The city's tourism and hospitality bureau has been working hard to get the word out about the updates to the Crown, and we've been inundated with requests from performers and groups who want to book events." She smiled, clasping her hands in front of her. "If we can get this job done right and in a timely manner, it could potentially add a great deal of money to the city's coffers."

Maxwell nodded. "Thanks for the explanation." Though he lived outside the city, he worked there, and he could see many places and good causes where that extra money could be put to good use. Streets needed repair, and certain areas of the city were affected by poverty and blight. With extra funding, Maxwell could see many good things happening to the All-America City Award winner.

"I have a question as well." Harold raised his hand like a child seeking acknowledgment from his teacher. "Has a decision been made as to which architect will be awarded the project?"

"Actually, yes. That's why I've asked you two here." Her gaze shifted back and forth between their faces.

Maxwell tilted his head, waiting for whatever the mayor would say next.

"We've decided to ask the two of you to work together on this project."

Maxwell's stomach dropped, but he didn't let it show. Over the years he'd been working in the business, he'd trained himself to maintain his cool exterior, despite whatever he might be thinking or feeling on the inside. The idea of working with Harold was distasteful at best, but he wouldn't let anything stop him from completing the project to the best of his ability.

Harold's tight-lipped frown indicated he wasn't thrilled with the arrangement, either.

Mayor Taylor continued. "Your two designs were, by far, the best among the ones submitted during the bidding process. Mr. Devers, the council loved your plans for the building itself, and Mr. Carmichael, we found your plans for the exterior spaces to be quite inspired."

Maxwell and Harold looked at each other, and Maxwell swore Harold's lips got even tighter.

"We think the combination of your two designs gives us the absolute best solution for everything we're trying to accomplish with this update. That's why we're asking you to work together." She paused, watching them intently for a moment. "Gentlemen, you've been awfully quiet."

"I'm just listening to what you're saying, Mayor Taylor." Maxwell met her gaze.

Harold, on the other hand, looked away, saying nothing.

Her brow lifted. "Mr. Carmichael, are you going to have a problem working with Mr. Devers? Because if so, we'll be happy to move on to the next design on the list."

Harold sobered up then, shaking his head. "No, ma'am, that won't be necessary. I'm sure Mr. Devers and I will do fine work together." Based on the way his lips thinned even further and stretched into the fakest of smiles, he looked as if it physically hurt to say the last sentence.

She swung her attention Maxwell's way. "And will this work for you, Mr. Devers?"

"Sounds fine. Mr. Carmichael is a capable architect. I'm sure we'll be able to handle it."

Maxwell noted the change in Harold's expression at the compliment; the other man looked as if he'd swallowed a goldfish.

Despite his misgivings about working with a man who'd taken every opportunity to insult or annoy him, Maxwell wasn't going to let that interfere with his work. They were grown men after all. Why couldn't they work together? Both their businesses would see significant financial and marketing benefits from the successful completion of the job.

"Great." Mayor Taylor appeared pleased. Opening the leather case she'd brought in with her, she slid them each a small stack of stapled pages. "Here are the official contracts. Take some time to look them over, then sign them. You can turn them in downstairs in Suite B when you're done." She pushed her chair back and stood, brushing a manicured hand over the jacket of her navy skirt suit.

Both men stood as well.

"I wish I could stay and chat, gentlemen, but I've got back-to-back meetings all day. I'll be in touch with you in about a week as the project kicks off." With a smile and a wave, she exited, leaving the two men sitting across from each other.

Silence reigned for a few moments, punctuated by the sounds of them flipping through the pages of the contract. Maxwell didn't see anything out of order, so he signed the final page of the document with the pen he kept in the pocket of his suit coat.

As he tucked the pen away, he heard Harold clear his throat. "Don't think I can't see through that act, Devers."

Maxwell looked across the table, meeting his gaze. "I'm not an actor, Harold. I'm an architect."

Harold scoffed. "Whatever, man. I know you were only trying to butter up the mayor when you gave me that compliment."

Maxwell shrugged. "I meant what I said. You are a capable architect." *Not as capable as me, but that's beside the point.* "We have a job to do, Harold, and like it or not, we have to work together."

Harold's eyes narrowed as he watched Maxwell. "I don't trust you, Devers. And you should know that just because my team is working on exteriors, that doesn't mean you're in charge of me."

"Of course not. We're on equal footing as far as I'm concerned." What would be the point of a power struggle between them? Maxwell's building design had already won over the city council, so there really wasn't any need for theatrics.

That only seemed to annoy Harold more. Scrawling a hasty signature on his contract, he snatched it off the table as he stood. "This is going to be the best exterior landscaping this city has ever seen. It will be so magnificent, it may even overshadow your building design."

Maxwell got up then, keeping his eyes fixed on his new partner. "I don't doubt it. I'm sure the mayor expects both of us to do our very best work. So bring it." He didn't bother keeping the challenge out of his tone. If that was what it would take to get Harold to deliver a stellar exterior design for this project, so be it.

With a huff, Harold straightened his tie and strode from the room.

Left alone, Maxwell considered all that had transpired. When he was younger, he might have taken the bait Harold had laid for him and dished out the same level of disdain he'd been served. Now, though, he couldn't be bothered with frivolity. He had a beautiful baby girl waiting for him at home.

A smile crossed his face as he pictured those big, beautiful eyes welcoming him home. Though Sasha hadn't been in his life very long, she'd opened up a place in his heart he hadn't even known existed, bringing light to the dark corners hidden within. It amazed him how much he'd grown to love his daughter over the course of her short life, and if he were honest, it also gave him pause. How would he ever be able to let her go out with friends, or worse, on dates?

Pushing that thought aside, he let the image of Yvonne's smiling face enter his mind. She'd become just as much a part of his life as Sasha, and he looked forward to her greeting as well. Since he'd shared that sweet kiss with her and they'd agreed to explore a relationship, he'd felt a sense of contentment he'd never experienced before.

Turning toward the door, he made his way downstairs to turn in his contract.

The sooner I'm done with work, the sooner I can get home to my girls.

⸻

Yvonne inhaled deeply as she stepped outside Maxwell's house Wednesday. It was midmorning, and the air was finally warm enough to take Sasha out for a walk. After spending the last couple of weeks inside the house, she was glad that the weather had finally warmed.

She squatted in front of the stroller, checking one more time to ensure that Sasha was securely buckled into the harness. "Ready to go, sweetie?"

A series of giggles left Sasha's mouth as she bounced up and down in her seat.

Gripping the handles of the stroller, Yvonne smiled as she turned it around and guided it down the steps and onto the paved path. Just getting to the end of the driveway would constitute quite a walk, but she was determined to let the baby get some fresh air.

Once they'd left Maxwell's property, Yvonne headed to the left, moving deeper into the neighborhood. *It would be nice to take Sasha to a playground, but I wonder if a ritzy place like this even has one.* The huge homes she passed, with their manicured lawns, winding driveways, and iron gates, resembled castles. Having grown up in southern Durham, she would never have imagined even being close to such immaculate houses.

She didn't see many people out, and she assumed it was because they were at work, at whatever well-paying jobs allowed them to afford to live here. She did pass a few gardeners sculpting topiaries in one yard as well as a maintenance worker painting an address on the curb in front of another house.

A portion of her walk passed in near silence, with only the sounds of birds singing and Sasha's continuous stream of babble to punctuate the quiet. While she walked, she thought back on her days as a kid growing up in Southside. Shootings were common, as were the sounds of sirens or people arguing in the streets late at night. Her parents were adamant about always having her in their field of vision when she played outside, and they were sticklers for making sure all the doors were double deadbolted at night. She remembered the low-level nervousness she'd felt for the entire time they'd lived in that tiny duplex apartment and how relieved she'd been when they'd moved to the house on the east side of town. That little house, where her parents still lived, had been a fixer-upper in every sense of the word. But it had been theirs, and her parents took pride in restoring it to its former glory. Their father, Gordon, had done most of the repairs with his own two hands. Zelda had been born a few months after they moved in, and Yvonne had learned how much she enjoyed taking care of others as she helped her parents guide her little sister through those early milestones.

Looking down at Sasha's sweet face, she couldn't help smiling. Sasha's childhood would be a charmed one, far different from what she'd experienced growing up. There would be no frightening sounds outside her bedroom window, no endless transfers on the city bus to get around town, no empty cupboards. She'd have everything she needed and probably everything she wanted as well. Maxwell struck Yvonne as the kind of father who would spoil his daughter, doting on her at every turn. She could already see the way Sasha had begun to wrap her father around her little finger, as the old saying went. And she couldn't really blame him. Sasha was a precious little darling.

Looking ahead on the sidewalk, Yvonne saw another woman coming toward her, also pushing a stroller. Dressed in a fuchsia tank, matching sneakers, and black athletic pants, the woman had olive skin and a long black ponytail hanging down her back. The brim of a black baseball cap shaded her face.

Another nanny?

Waving, Yvonne called, "How's it going?"

The woman paused, adjusting her course a bit so their strollers wouldn't collide. "Pretty good. You?"

"Can't complain." Not wanting to waste the woman's time, Yvonne asked, "Do you know of a playground in this area?"

The woman shook her head. "No, there's not one nearby. But there is one a few miles away from the neighborhood. You'd have to drive there, but it should be pretty easy to find."

"What's it called? I'll look it up."

"Sweetwater Park."

"Thanks a lot." Yvonne waved again as the woman continued past her in the opposite direction, her long ponytail whipping around as she jogged away. "We'll go over there a little later today, Sasha. First, we'll have to take you home and grab some supplies."

She reached the end of the block, near the section of the neighborhood where Maxwell's parents lived. Sanderson River Crossing was divided into two phases. Maxwell lived in the first phase, filled with mini mansions, and his parents lived in the second phase, where the houses were even larger. Not knowing how to get to the Deverses' place on foot and not wanting to inconvenience them by showing up unannounced, she turned the stroller around, intent on heading back to Maxwell's house.

Her phone rang, the buzzing on her hip grabbing her attention. Still walking, she slipped the phone from her pocket and answered. "Hello?"

"Hi, Ms. Markham. It's me, Janine."

Why is the nurse calling me? "What's going on? Has something happened?"

"Yes, but there's no need to panic. Your father took a bit of a spill."

Yvonne stopped short when she heard those words. "He fell? Where? When?"

"He was reaching for something on the closet shelf, and…let's just say he and the footstool had a little disagreement."

Yvonne pressed her palm to her forehead. "Oh no."

"Like I said, don't worry. I'm with him at urgent care, and it's just a simple sprain of his left ankle."

Great. Daddy managed to sprain his good ankle, all because he's too stubborn to ask for help. "Listen, Janine, can I talk to him?"

"Sure thing. I'll put him on."

Yvonne listened to the muffled exchange in the background, rocking the stroller back and forth so Sasha wouldn't get too antsy.

A moment later, her father's gruff voice filled her ear. "Hello."

"Hey, Daddy. How are you feeling?"

"I'm fine. The doctor gave me some pain medicine for my ankle."

Yvonne drew a deep breath, knowing it wouldn't be appropriate to give in to her urge to lecture him. Tamping that down as much as she could, she asked, "Daddy, what was it you needed off the closet shelf?"

"My toolbox. I've been promising your mama I'd work on that rickety kitchen table leg for a while now."

"That's fair. But why didn't you just ask Janine to get it down for you? That's what she's there for."

He grumbled. "She was busy. Besides, I was already in the closet. Seemed quicker to just get it myself."

She pinched the bridge of her nose. "You know you don't have the same balance you used to have, though. It's not safe for you to be climbing stepstools."

"Oh, really? So you're telling me just because I have this fake foot, I'm relegated to sitting in the recliner all day being feeble?"

"No, of course not, Daddy. I just worry about you, that's all."

"I see," he groused. "You're so worried about me that you hired somebody to look after me rather than do it yourself."

"Daddy, please." She couldn't deal with this right now. Leaving her parents' care to someone else, no matter how skilled and caring, had already caused her major guilt. She didn't need her father making her feel any worse. "You know I'm doing the best I can to take care of you. I always have."

He sighed. "When can you come see me, Yvonne?"

Her heart squeezed in her chest. "I can come now if I bring Sasha. But it will take me about an hour and a half to get there—Maxwell lives way out in the sticks."

"Never mind. I'm sure Janine has things under control. You go on back to work."

"Daddy, wait. I can—"

Before she could finish her sentence, he hung up on her.

She took the phone from her ear, staring at the screen for a moment before she put it away. *I don't think Daddy's ever been mad enough to hang up on me.* Her shoulders drooped at the realization. In her quest to succeed at her career, she'd had to sacrifice her role as caregiver for her parents. Would her father ever be able to accept her choice, or would he go on resenting it forever?

Sasha's plaintive wail snapped her back to the present, pulling her out of the guilt spiral that threatened to consume her.

CHAPTER 12

THURSDAY EVENING, MAXWELL SAT IN THE CROWDED gymnasium of the Hiram Revels Youth Outreach Center, surrounded by screaming teens. Their vocal excitement was nearly drowned out by the booming speakers broadcasting the music throughout the space as teen hip-hop duo Young-n-Wild performed for them. A stage had been set up in the center of the basketball court, and from his vantage point on the floor to the right of the stage, Maxwell could see the slick hip-hop dance moves they performed, and due to the sound system's power, there was nowhere to go to escape the infectious rhythm of their songs.

Bopping his head in time with the music, Maxwell looked around at the audience. The kids were obviously enjoying themselves, some of them dancing in the bleachers as they sang along with the two boys on stage. The concert had been planned months ago as a reward for the young people who attended the afterschool program at the center. Through their hard work, the Revels Youth had met their ten-thousand-dollar fundraising goal and collected hundreds of items of clothing to be given to the less fortunate members of their community.

Orion, who worked with the boys as the A&R rep from their label, was somewhere in the room. Maxwell knew his friend was likely watching the show from a good vantage point, taking note of how his artists interacted with fans and how the fans reacted to the show. Orion had always been the sensible one of their group, the one who believed in letting things happen as they were meant to. *No doubt he'll be reporting back to the label everything that happens here today.*

As the show wound down, Young-n-Wild bowed through

several minutes of standing ovation before jogging off the stage under the care of their bodyguard. Xavier took the stage then and received his own, though less enthusiastic, round of applause from the kids in the bleachers.

"I hope you all enjoyed the show by Young-n-Wild tonight, and I'd like to thank Orion MacMillan, my frat brother and the group's A&R rep, for making this possible. I'd also like to thank my other frat brother, Maxwell Devers, who generously sponsored today's event."

Maxwell saw Orion stand up and wave from his seat on the bleachers, front and center to the stage. Rather than stand, Maxwell simply raised his hand. He hadn't been seeking recognition when he'd handed over the four-figure check to Xavier. He'd simply wanted to do something nice for the kids at the youth center.

After the cheers died down again, Xavier continued. "Most of all, I want to thank all of you, my Revels Youth, and the parents and family members who helped them do such phenomenal work in reaching our fundraising goal for the new building project. Your hard work will ensure that we have a state-of-the-art facility for you as well as future generations of Raleigh youth."

The room erupted in applause again, and Maxwell joined in. He'd talked at length with Xavier about the new building and all the activities the center's patrons would have access to. Sports, academics, and a workshop for carpentry were among the offerings. Seeing their exuberance made him think about his own daughter and what the future might hold for her. *I wonder what kinds of hobbies Sasha will take up when she's older.*

"You earned this reward, Revels Youth, and I'm glad you enjoyed it. Now you've all been reasonably well-behaved, and I know you're going to continue that trend as you go on over to the cafeteria for refreshments and a meet and greet with Young-n-Wild." Xavier left the stage on the heels of those words.

Not needing to be told twice, the youngsters filed out of the room with their parents and the staff members. Maxwell stood and walked over to the stage, meeting up with his frat brothers. "Wow. The kids really love these guys, huh?"

Xavier nodded. "We're a little over budget with building the new center, and the kids have been working hard to make up the difference. We asked them what they wanted as a reward if they could meet the fundraising goal, and the answer was nearly unanimous."

"I can see why. Their music definitely is catchy." Maxwell had enjoyed the show far more than he'd expected to.

"The music is a big part of it. But you've gotta remember, Young-n-Wild are from Roxboro." Xavier tapped his chin. "The kids are excited to see someone their age, from North Carolina, be so successful in the music industry."

Maxwell nodded, clapped his hands together. "So, O, what's next for them tonight?"

"They're going back home to their parents, fortunately." Orion chuckled. "They're a handful, but since they're not touring right now, I'll just send a car to take them back home to Roxboro."

"Wouldn't their manager typically be in charge of stuff like that?" Maxwell had heard Orion speak about the woman before.

"Yes, but Celeste is on vacation, so I'm stuck with them." Orion shrugged. "She's super serious, and I was shocked to hear that she'd taken a few days off, but I'm not unhappy about getting a break from Ms. By-the-Book."

Maxwell shook his head. He could see why someone like Orion, who preferred the laid-back, pragmatic approach to life, would be so annoyed by someone who insisted on rules and regulations at every turn.

Xavier cleared his throat. "Oh, guys. I've got some news. I was gonna wait until I could get all the guys together, but with everybody being so busy, who knows when that will happen?"

"What's up?" Maxwell turned toward his friend.

"Yeah," Orion added. "What's the news?"

Taking a deep breath, Xavier smiled. "Imani…is pregnant."

A grin broke over Maxwell's face. "Wow. Congratulations, man! I know you've been wanting this for a while."

"This is great news, bro." Orion bumped fists with Xavier. "Congrats. I'm happy for y'all."

The smile on Xavier's face gave away his excitement. "She's only about two months along, but we're so excited. Now, if I can just get her to cut back on her hours at the practice, we'll be golden."

Maxwell knew Xavier's wife, a dermatologist in private practice, loved her work. "I'm sure she'll take it easy. She is a doctor after all, so she should know to listen to her body."

Xavier looked wistful for a moment. "You know, our baby could end up being a playmate for Sasha one day when they're a bit older."

The thought brought warmth to Maxwell's heart. "You can bet on it."

Orion shook his head. "This is getting way too mushy for a player."

Xavier started walking toward the exit. "I need to get over to the cafeteria and make sure the kids aren't cutting up. See you guys over there."

After he left, Orion remarked, "X is gonna make a great father."

"Absolutely. Out of all of us, he loves kids the most." Maxwell knew the baby would be blessed to have parents like Xavier and Imani. He only hoped one day Sasha would speak as highly of him. "Oh, I forgot to tell you, but I got the Crown project."

"Congrats, man. I know you're happy about that."

Maxwell shrugged. "I'd be happier if I didn't have to work with Harold Carmichael."

Orion's brow hitched. "The same Harold Carmichael who went to Central with us? The one who was always announcing how great he was?"

"Same dude. Unfortunately, he hasn't changed."

Orion whistled, shaking his head. "Damn. I'm sorry you gotta work with a clown, but I'm sure you'll bring your usual level of professionalism and skill to the job."

Maxwell snapped his fingers. "You'd better believe it."

"So." Orion leaned closer, folding his arms over his chest. "What's going on with you and Miss Yvonne? Anything interesting?"

With a short nod, Maxwell admitted their new arrangement. "Yes. We're exploring a relationship right now...taking things slowly."

"I knew it. I knew y'all couldn't resist each other."

Maxwell shook his head. "I guess you were right, but don't let that go to your head, O."

"You know me. I'm always humble, man." With a chuckle, Orion turned toward the door. "Let's get over to the cafeteria. I need to make sure the boys aren't up to any shenanigans."

The two of them left the gym and walked the short distance down the hall to the cafeteria. The place was teeming with activity as the kids mingled, helped themselves to the finger foods and drinks, and stood in line to have items signed by Young-n-Wild.

"Let's grab some food," Orion shouted to be heard over the din. "I've been running with the boys all day."

At the long table, Maxwell loaded up a small paper plate with chicken nuggets, a pile of red grapes, carrot sticks, and a chocolate chip cookie. After grabbing a cup of punch ladled out by one of the center's staffers, he and Orion sat down at a table near where the boys had set up to sign autographs.

Watching the younger member of the duo give a friendly hug to a young girl who was in tears with excitement, Maxwell commented, "They certainly are good with the fans."

Munching on a celery stick, Orion nodded. "They certainly are. Especially the girls—but, you know, they're at that age. Tim, their bodyguard, makes sure they aren't alone with female fans to keep them out of trouble. But they're little charmers, you can bet."

Chewing, Maxwell remembered his own teenage days. "If they're anything like we were back in the day, they certainly need to be kept in check."

Orion chuckled. "You gotta remember, Max. In a few years, young playas just like them might be darkening your doorstep, wanting to take your daughter out on dates. Gird your loins, bro."

Maxwell cringed, knowing his friend was right. *How will I react to that? I can't imagine letting any smooth-talking young guy take my daughter anywhere.* But he knew she'd eventually become interested in boys, no matter how he felt about it. He sighed. "You're right. I'd better start preparing for that now, because it's probably going to take a good little while for me to be okay with it."

They finished up their food, then waited for the boys to sign autographs for everybody waiting in line. Tim, the tall, wide-framed bodyguard dressed in all black, stood close by, keeping a watchful eye on the proceedings.

When the last fan had left, Orion stood. "Come on, Max. It's time you met the boys."

As they approached, the two young men stood from the stools they'd been occupying.

"What's up, Mr. O?" the younger one asked.

"Got a friend I want you to meet. This is my fraternity brother, Maxwell Devers." Orion gestured toward him.

The older one extended his hand toward Maxwell. "Nice to meet you, Mr. Devers. I'm Marcus Richardson, aka Wild."

Maxwell shook his hand.

"And I'm Young—err, Malcolm." The younger one shook hands with Maxwell just as his brother had.

"Good to meet you. Any significant meaning behind your names?" Maxwell looked between the two of them.

"Our parents named us after two black revolutionaries," Marcus commented. "Marcus Garvey and Malcolm X."

"Impressive. Let's hope your lives are just as impactful as your namesakes.'" Maxwell offered a smile.

Malcolm smiled back. "That's what we want. That's why we rap about positivity and empowerment, ya know?"

Maxwell nodded. "I feel you." He wasn't sure if that was still a popular phrase among the kids, but he was pretty sure they'd know what he meant by it. All in all, he was pretty impressed with the Richardson boys. They'd come from the small town of Roxboro, just north of Durham, and were making quite a name for themselves.

As the sun began to set, Xavier and his staff rounded up the remaining youths and escorted them to the lobby. Maxwell watched as the kids left with their parents and guardians, then he and Xavier returned to the cafeteria.

Orion, who stood close by while his clients and their bodyguard gathered their things, yawned, stretching his arms above his head. "It's about time I get these boys home. Their parents will be expecting them."

"I'm headed home, too." Maxwell couldn't wait to get home to Sasha and Yvonne. He'd never experienced this sort of anticipation before. Sure, he'd had his share of long, trying days that sent him running for the quiet sanctity of his house. But knowing he was going home to them made his house a home. He took a moment to shake hands with the two young men. "I'm looking forward to great things from you two."

―⁂―

Yvonne grasped the handle of her golf club, adjusting her stance. She let her gaze trace the path from the pure-white ball resting near her feet to the hole she was aiming for. It was one of the more intimidating holes on the course, but she had an audience, and she wasn't about to back down. After a few moments of contemplation, she lifted her club and swung. *Thwack*. The ball rolled over the bright green turf and, as she watched with bated breath, fell into the hole.

"Booyah!" She pumped her fist, celebrating her victory.

Behind her, Maxwell's deep chuckle drew her attention. "I gotta admit. It was an impressive shot."

"You bet it was." She strolled over the turf, pushed aside the leaves and flowers shrouding the area, and retrieved her ball from the hole inside the lion's mouth. "I'm something of a mini golf champ, you know."

"I didn't know, but I'm finding out today." He joined her on the walk to the next hole. "Every day, I'm finding out something new about you."

She felt the smile coming over her face, and she couldn't resist asking, "And how do you feel about what you've learned so far?"

"Fascinated." He leaned down and placed a soft kiss on her cheek.

A spark of magic ignited inside her chest, spreading through her upper body and into her face. Being alone with him this way, even in such a public place, made her feel as giddy as a teen with a crush.

They walked together through the winding paths, careful to avoid the other players. The crowd was pretty thin for a Saturday, but she knew traffic would pick up in the late spring and early summer as the daytime temperatures became more reliably warm.

She watched him place his ball on the tee when they reached the last hole. The obstacles, themed as a miniature village, looked nearly impossible to conquer. There was a complex system of narrow, winding pathways for the ball to travel through as well as a drawbridge over a small moat.

"Here goes nothing." He gave the ball a hard tap with his club, and it traveled most of the way through the obstacles. For a moment, it looked like he might get the hole in one...until the ball rolled sideways off the drawbridge and splashed into the moat.

"Yikes." She shook her head. "It was a solid shot, but this hole has taken a lot of folks out of the game."

He turned her way. "Think you can do better?"

"Watch and learn." She strode up, set her ball on the tee. A few moments later, the ball rolled through the obstacles, skirted over the drawbridge, and landed in the hole inside the open castle gates. When she turned his way again, she saw the expression on his face. He looked both surprised and amused.

"Impressive, Yvonne. Very impressive."

After walking back to the main building to claim the prize for conquering all thirteen holes, they returned to his SUV. Strapping the huge teddy bear she'd picked out into the back seat, she climbed into the passenger seat with his assistance.

"Where to now?"

"There's a cupcake place downtown that I absolutely love." She'd been thinking about their cookies-and-cream-filled cupcake all day, and she couldn't wait for him to try their wares. "Pass me your phone, and I'll put the address in the GPS."

He passed her the phone, then started the engine. "Mom said not to come back until after sunset."

"I think I can keep you occupied for a few more hours."

"I don't doubt it." There was a gleam in his eye that was part wickedness, part amusement.

Her breath caught for a moment, and she swallowed. *If only he knew how much I'd like to...* But it was too soon for the physical stuff, so she halted that particular train of thought. Clearing her throat, she steered the conversation in another direction. "It's really wonderful to see how much your parents care for Sasha." She smiled at the thought. The baby couldn't have asked for a more doting set of grandparents. "They're probably going to spoil her rotten, though."

"As will I and her aunts. That's just how the Devers family gets down." He placed his phone in the rubberized holder on his dashboard and navigated the SUV out of the parking lot and onto the road.

She noted the way his voice and expression softened when he talked about his daughter. Sasha's childhood would be full of the best things that life had to offer. All the clothes, toys, and books she could ever want. Family vacations to fantastical destinations. *It will be so different from what Zelda and I experienced but in a good way.* "I have a feeling she'll never want for anything."

As if he'd read her thoughts, he asked, "What was your childhood like, Yvonne?"

Turning her head toward the familiar sights of Durham whizzing by her window, she took a breath. "It was filled with more love than you can imagine. Mommy and Daddy were always there for us, as much as their work schedules allowed. But I don't think it was anywhere near as"—she paused, searching for the right word—"comfortable as yours probably was or as Sasha's will be."

"What do you mean by that?"

"Even though my parents worked hard, sometimes holding down two jobs at a time, we never had much money. They were creative when it came to keeping us entertained when school was out. That's actually how I got into mini golf."

"I can tell you've had plenty of practice. You certainly outdid me today."

"Mini golf was our family thing. We didn't have money for trips to amusement parks or vacations at the beach. This was easy and accessible, and we played thousands of rounds as a family."

"Have you ever played regular golf?"

She shook her head.

Pulling into a parking spot on the street, he asked, "Why not?"

"Honestly? I've come to enjoy mini golf so much over the years, regular golf seems sort of stuffy and boring."

He chuckled. "I guess I can understand that. You're not going to find any castles and lions on the golf course."

He got out, coming around to her side and opening the passenger door for her. Taking his offered hand as she stepped down onto the running board, she felt the electricity shoot up her arm, radiating from his touch. Their eyes locked as he guided her to the sidewalk. When her feet were on solid ground, she maintained eye contact with him. Part of her wanted to tell him how much his touch affected her, but there was no way she could put it into words. So she leaned up, closing her eyes as she silently beseeched him to kiss her.

A moment later, his soft lips touched hers, and she leaned into him. His strong arms gathered her closer as his tongue swept into her mouth, the sensation flooding her body with warmth.

When she finally pulled back, she blinked a few times, coming back to reality. They were standing on a busy sidewalk in broad daylight, with the passenger side door still wide open. More than a few passing pedestrians quickly averted their gazes, making it obvious they'd been watching. Heat filled her face again, this time from embarrassment. "Maxwell, we have an audience."

He offered a sly smile. "Don't worry. That won't always be the case."

She touched her fingertips to her lips, still full from his kiss. "There's something about you that makes me forget myself."

He draped an arm around her waist, moving her away from the car and using his free hand to shut the door. "Let's get down to the cupcake place. Now I'm really in the mood for something sweet." The wicked gleam from earlier returned to his eyes, but only for a moment.

Inside Sweet Dreams Cupcakery, she inhaled the enticing scent filling the air. The place was so popular that the ovens were pretty much going all day, replacing the delectable confections as soon as they sold out.

"Oh. It smells like heaven in here."

She laughed. "Wait until you taste their cupcakes."

Once they'd gone through the line and sat down near the back with their plates, she dug into her cupcake. The soft chocolate cake, along with the sweet cream filling bursting with chocolate-cookie crumbs, melted in her mouth, and she groaned.

He watched her as he forked up a section of his own French vanilla cupcake. When he took a bite, his expression morphed into one of pure pleasure. "Wow. This is almost as good as my mom's baking."

Soon both of their cupcakes were devoured, and she twisted the cap off her bottled water. "So what was it like growing up in the Devers household?"

He shrugged. "Orderly. We took vacations twice a year, spring touring a city and fall at the beach. My parents never wanted to fight the crowds during summer."

"What about holiday weekends? What kinds of things did you do then?"

"Symposiums. Lectures. Museum tours." He rolled his eyes. "Something that 'enriched our minds' was their idea of fun."

She noted the annoyance in his voice. "I take it you weren't a fan of the intellectual pursuits?"

He shook his head. "None of us were. Remember, Kelsey and Lex have artsy careers just like I do."

She tapped her finger against her chin, thinking. "Maybe your parents picked up on your interests in the arts and were trying to steer you toward what they thought would be more lucrative careers?"

"Once again, you've shown yourself to be incredibly insightful. That's exactly what they were trying to do." He shrugged. "As an engineer and a librarian, their work revolved around concrete facts, measurements, and things that can be easily defined or quantified. They made it clear that they didn't see much merit in their children working in the arts."

She felt her heart squeeze in her chest. She could easily hear the tinge of pain in his voice when he spoke about his youth. "It must have been hard to know that your parents didn't have faith in your choices."

"It wasn't easy. But I'm sure you know, if you have a passion for something, there isn't much that can stop you from pursuing it." He reached across the small table, taking her hand into his. "From the first day we met, I could see your passion for your work with children. Could your parents, or anybody else for that matter, have talked you out of going after your dream?"

She didn't even have to think about her answer. "No, they couldn't have." She had an immense amount of compassion for what he'd gone through, and it opened her eyes to thinking about her own childhood in a different way. While she hadn't spent her summers on a yacht or traveling the country, she and her sister had been well-loved and encouraged to follow their own paths. And there was no price that could be put on that. She chastised herself for the earlier comparison of her own experience with her perceptions of how Maxwell had grown up. There was really no such thing as a perfect upbringing, and since she worked with children, she should know that better than anyone.

"The good news is, as the years went by, Mom and Dad have come around. They no longer complain about what any of us do for a living." He squeezed her hand. "It took time, but I think they finally understand why we do what we do, or at least they've learned to keep their opinions to themselves."

She offered him a soft smile. "Parents can be pretty stubborn. They may not say it often, but I'd be willing to bet they're proud of you and your sisters. You've all found a way to build lives for yourselves, fueled by the thing you love most. There's something really special about that, you know?"

He smiled, showing off two rows of perfect pearly white teeth. "There certainly is."

Her cheeks warmed. "That seems directed at me."

"It is. Having someone like you to take care of my daughter is more than I could have asked for." He grazed his fingertips over the sensitive skin of the back of her hand. "So you can imagine how honored I feel to be able to get to know you like this, on a personal level. You're an amazing woman, Yvonne."

She met his gaze, feeling her attraction to him rising like the tide drawn to a full moon. She never would have imagined she'd be doing this with a client, and parts of her still tried to deny what she felt. But there was no escaping the magic blossoming between them. Work was one thing that gave her a sense of fulfillment. But she knew she would never forgive herself if she passed up an opportunity to love and be loved by a man like Maxwell.

How he'd come into her life didn't matter nearly as much as how he might change it.

CHAPTER 13

MAXWELL PARKED HIS SUV ON THE DIRT PATH LEADING TO the jobsite for the Crown Center expansion project. Strolling past the line of earthmovers, graders, and pickup trucks loaded with various supplies, he moved toward the trailer housing the base of operations for the project.

It was just past eight on Friday morning, and the weather was perfect for the first day of building. Generally, jobs like this would start earlier in the week, but a paperwork error had pushed the start date back. The temperature was already around fifty degrees and was expected to climb to near seventy before day's end. He'd dressed in a pair of sturdy jeans, a maroon NCCU sweatshirt, and steel-toed work boots.

He navigated through the maze of equipment and bodies in motion, headed for the main site of what would become the new Crown Civic and Performing Arts Center. There, at the epicenter of the bustling activity of the site, men and women in bright orange construction vests and shiny yellow hard hats scurried about, carrying various tools and materials. A line of bright orange rope, supported by stakes, marked the shape of the building's footprint. The sounds of machinery, engines, and conversation were all around him, yet he barely noticed the din. Years of working on construction sites had him so accustomed to the cacophony, it was merely background noise now.

Stopping near the western edge of the rope line, he scanned the crowd for a moment before he spotted his construction supervisor. Braxton Williams was easy to spot, since his six-foot, four-inch height meant he easily towered over most people, even on a busy construction site.

Raising his hand up, Maxwell called, "Hey, Williams!"

Looking up from the clipboard in his hands, Braxton said something to the woman he'd been speaking to and shook her hand before striding over to where Maxwell stood. With an easy smile and a tip of his hard hat, he drawled, "Morning, boss man."

"How are things going?" Maxwell jerked his head in the direction of the woman he'd seen Braxton talking to. "Who was that? I've never seen her on one of your sites before."

Braxton shrugged. "She's new. Her name's Patterson, and she runs the cement company that's doing the foundation and the floors." He paused, adjusting his hard hat. "It's been a while since we were on a jobsite together. How long has it been? A year?"

Maxwell thought about it for a moment. "Yeah, about that long. I only call you in for the commercial jobs, and I've been building mostly homes lately." He had another construction manager who specialized in residential projects. "How've you been? How's the family?"

A smile spread over Braxton's face. "Amy got promoted at the bank. She's head loan officer now. And Jordan's in third grade now. Reading ahead of his grade level, though. What's new with you?"

That brought a smile to Maxwell's face. He'd often heard Braxton bragging about his son. Knowing that he now had a beautiful daughter of his own filled him with a new and wonderful sense of parental pride. "You're not going to believe it, but I'm a papa myself now."

Braxton's eyes widened, and he gave Maxwell a playful punch in the shoulder. "You're kidding me, right?"

Shaking his head, Maxwell pulled his phone from the hip pocket of his jeans. "See for yourself. Her name is Sasha, and she's almost eight months old." He scrolled through the saved photos in his gallery until he found a good one of the baby, then turned the phone around so Braxton could see.

"Wow, man. She's beautiful." Braxton's eyes darted back and forth between the screen and Maxwell's face. "She looks a lot like you. Congrats, Max."

"Thanks, Braxton."

"I'd ask about her mother, but I don't wanna get all up in your business."

Maxwell could see the questions in Braxton's gaze but appreciated that he didn't ask them. "I'd say it's complicated, but that's an understatement." Tucking the phone away again, he asked, "How have things been going out here?"

"Great. The graders have already come and gone, and the surveyor says we're good to start pouring the foundation."

"Everything good with the team? Are all the laborers in place for foundation work?" Maxwell asked these same questions at the beginning of every job they worked on together, but if Braxton was tired of hearing them, he didn't let on. Maxwell was a stickler when it came to his designs, and he expected his vision to be carried out with skill and professionalism. That was common knowledge to anyone working on one of his sites.

"Yep. We expect to get the work done by the end of the day. Framers should be able to start once it's cured."

"Sounds great." Maxwell had intended to say more, but his attention was drawn by the familiar, distinct beeping sound of a truck backing up. Looking toward the eastern border of the building footprint, he saw the cement mixer backing up toward the rope line. To his surprise, there was a familiar face behind the wheel of the large vehicle. "Isn't that Ms. Patterson driving the mixer?"

Braxton glanced in that direction, chuckled. "Yep, that's her. Her company is all ladies, and she made it clear they ain't afraid to get a little dirt under their nails."

"I can see that." Maxwell scratched his chin, impressed with Ms. Patterson and her all-female cement outfit. "As long as they do good work, they can count on working with us again. I'm heading over to the trailer. I'll swing by later to make sure everything's still on track."

When he arrived at the trailer, he paused, hearing the raised voices coming from within. As the commotion seemed to die down, he took a step. The door swung open as his boot hit the bottom step, and an angry-looking woman wearing a hard hat and a shirt bearing the Carmichael logo stormed past him.

Harold appeared in the doorway, calling after her from the top step. "Carol! Don't you walk out on me like this!"

The woman stopped, turning so fast her boots kicked up the dust from the ground. The hard set of her face betrayed her irritation. "Harold, if you think I'm working for peanuts, you're out of your mind. Good luck getting the job done without me and my crew, because I'm taking them with me." She spun and strode away without another backward glance.

A bewildered-looking Harold threw up his hands. "Women. Can't work with 'em, huh?"

Maxwell shrugged. "Women aren't the only ones who expect to be paid what they're owed, Harold." Moving up the steps to the trailer door, he stopped again. "Good morning. If you'll excuse me, I need to get inside."

Harold moved out of the way, though he didn't look happy about it.

Inside the trailer, an office had been set up with three desks and chairs. Pegboards and whiteboards on the wall displayed handwritten notes and tacked-up paperwork while a small stand holding a coffee machine, cups, and condiments occupied the far corner.

A broad-shouldered man with an orange construction vest over his bright red NC State T-shirt sat hunched at the center desk, talking on a phone. The space allotted seemed much too small for a guy his size, but he appeared to be making the best of it. His ruddy skin affirmed that he spent plenty of time in the sun, while his longish brown hair and full beard suggested he'd been too busy for a haircut as of late. He looked up when Maxwell entered, then ended his call. "Mr. Devers?"

"That's me." Maxwell walked over to the desk.

The man stood, revealing his impressive height. He was easily two inches or so taller than Maxwell. "Albert Hartsfield, project manager. You can call me Al. Pleased to meet you."

"Likewise." Maxwell shook Al's hand, trying not to lose any fingers to the larger man's kung fu grip. "Is everything set for us to start working?"

Al rolled his eyes. "It would be if Mr. Carmichael over there could get his crew in line."

Amused and annoyed, Maxwell turned to Harold, who still stood by the open door, his arms folded over his chest. "Um, what's the problem, Harold? We've got a job to do here."

"I'm aware of that," came his terse reply. "I've just lost my graders to a petty squabble over money, and—"

Maxwell's eyes went wide. "This isn't my area of specialty, Harold, but I doubt you can lay any concrete for that parking structure until the land is properly graded. That about right, Al?"

"Yeah, that's about the balance of it." The large man clasped his hands together. "And this morning, the earthmovers came to me saying they're short two drivers. That's under your jurisdiction too, isn't it, Carmichael?"

Maxwell cringed. Already the job was off to a rocky start, and they hadn't even started foundation work yet. "Come on, Harold. What the hell goes on with your outfit?"

Harold's face turned red. "I don't know! Those two were on the schedule to come in today. I don't know why they haven't shown up."

His frown deepening, Al asked, "And where is your construction manager, anyway? I've never known an architect to be this involved in a project of this type."

Harold looked uncomfortable, cleared his throat. "He...uh... quit yesterday. I'm looking to replace him soon and..."

Al shook his head. "I don't know what kind of dog and pony

show you think I'm running here, but we've got a schedule to adhere to. The city expects this job to be done on time and on budget, and I can't have incompetence mucking things up."

Harold relaxed his posture, softened his tone. "Look, Al, I just need an hour. I promise you, by ten a.m., my crew will be ready to go."

Al nodded. "I can give you that. But if you can't get it together by ten, you might as well pack up your folks and get off my jobsite. Understood?"

With a stiff nod, Harold turned and left the trailer.

Turning to Al, Maxwell shook his head. "Yikes."

"Yikes is right. Carmichael is certainly off to a bad start with his part of the project."

We both had the same amount of time to get ready for this project. Why didn't he get his people lined up and in place before now? "He talks a big game. I'm surprised he let his team get out of line like this."

"He who talks big often thinks small." Al shuffled through the pile of papers on top of his desk. "Whatever he's got planned to get things back on track, he'd better get busy." He glanced at the brown leather wristwatch on his left wrist. "He's got fifty-seven minutes."

Shaking his head, Maxwell returned to the door. "I'm headed out. See you around the worksite, Al."

Al tipped an invisible hat in his direction.

Outside in the morning sunshine, Maxwell headed back to the main building site. On the way, he noted the two earthmovers parked near the rear border of the cleared land. *I wonder if those are the ones that Harold's people are supposed to be operating.*

Back at the site where the new center would soon stand, he stood by the folding table set up on the eastern perimeter, poring over the blueprints. As an architect, he wasn't required or expected to spend very much time on the jobsite. His main goal was to create the design, then leave the actual building to the construction team. Still, he loved being present on worksites. As he watched the skilled laborers moving through the space, some carrying tools, some operating machinery and equipment, he felt the same sense of excitement he'd felt on his very first visit to a jobsite. He enjoyed watching the work of the people who would bring his vision to fruition. For him, it never seemed to get old.

He was so caught up in the goings-on of the site that he lost track of time. He felt someone tapping him on the shoulder, drawing him back to reality. Turning around, he saw Al standing there. "What's up, Al? Do you need me for something?"

His face somewhat grim, the project manager nodded. "Need you to take over the parking and landscaping aspects of the project as well. As of fifteen minutes ago, Mr. Carmichael's been kicked off my jobsite. I run a tight ship, but you seem like the type who can handle it. You in?"

"Sure." Shaking hands with Al, Maxwell watched as the man walked away.

Wow. This day certainly has taken a turn.

Around seven in the evening, Yvonne sat by the front window in the living room. With a mug of green tea in her hand, she curled up in the armchair, watching the sunset over the sprawling brick mansion across the street. Ribbons of purple, red, orange, and pale pink painted the sky, and she sighed. This was just the sort of peaceful moment she needed to end a busy day of wrangling a curious little one.

She thought of how comfortable she'd come to feel in Maxwell's home. He'd gone out of his way to make her feel welcome, including personalizing the bedroom that now belonged to her. Observing the silent street outside, she wondered how much longer it would be before he got home. True, Sasha had kept her occupied all the way up until she'd fallen asleep about twenty minutes ago. But there was no amount of busyness that could keep her mind from straying to him.

This relationship with her boss, one she never would have thought she'd have, had blossomed into something sweet and beautiful. She saw him off to work each morning during the week and anxiously awaited his return in the evenings. Whenever he left or returned, they shared soft kisses and affectionate gazes. Being in his arms had come to feel familiar, like a home she never knew she had but could now return to when the outside world became too much to bear.

She set the empty mug down on the side table, her eyes locked on the skyline. Crossing her arms over her chest and placing her open palms on her forearms, she embraced her own body. Anticipation for his return home fired her blood, and her mind began to wander. *It feels so good when he holds me. What would it be like if we did more?*

The sensible parts of her warned her to push those thoughts aside, but those desires were undeniable. She moved her palms up and down over her arms, the thin fabric of her pink chambray cardigan whispering over her skin like a lover's caress. She knew she should corral her thoughts, turn them toward something productive. Yet she couldn't do it. All she could think about was what it would feel like to let him touch her in earnest, to let his hands roam over her body. No interruptions, no pretense, and certainly no clothing to stand between them. What would happen if she stopped dousing the fires of passion she felt crackling between them? What if she let them grow until they consumed them both?

The sound of an approaching vehicle drew her gaze back to the street. Her heart did a somersault as she watched his sleek black SUV pull into the driveway. The whir of the garage door's motorized mechanism sounded once, stopped, then sounded again as the door closed behind him.

She stood, running a hand over her hair as she crossed the foyer. Just as she stepped into the kitchen, the side door swung open, and he stepped inside.

"Hey, Yvonne." He smiled as he shut the door behind him.

"Hey, yourself." The sight of him gripped her so, it was as if she hadn't seen him leaving this morning. The rugged look of jeans and construction vest suited him. He looked just as good in these casual clothes as he did in the suit and tie he normally wore to his office. "How was your day?"

He chuckled. "I'll tell you all about it…after I get my kiss." His intense gaze smoldered with heat.

She swallowed, taking a few steps to close the distance between them. His arms draped around her waist, he pulled her closer to his body. She lifted her arms, her hands coming to rest on his strong, broad shoulders. Raising her chin, she leaned up for his kiss.

His lips touched hers, and her mouth opened almost immediately. He groaned as if he sensed her feelings. Pulling her even closer to him, he grazed the tip of his tongue between her lips, teasing her before slipping it inside.

"Mmm." Her insides felt as warm and molten as lava. She could stay like this forever, with him kissing her, his tongue exploring the cavern of her mouth, driving her mad with wanting.

He finally broke the kiss, leaning back without releasing her from his embrace. "Sorry. I got a little carried away there."

Still trying to get control of her breath, she murmured, "Feel free to get carried away anytime, Maxwell."

His low chuckle vibrated through the space as he stepped back, releasing her and walking over to the fridge. "So how was your day today? Was Sasha good?"

She followed him, already missing the feeling of being wrapped in his arms. "She was just as sweet as she always is. You know, she's doing really well with her balance. She can stand on her own for a few seconds at a time now."

He shook his head, his expression wistful. "I already missed so much with her. I'm not sure I'm ready for her to be so mobile just yet."

Now it was her turn to chuckle. "Well, Maxwell, the longer you're a parent, the more you'll realize how little control you have over things like this. They're always learning, always growing."

Grabbing a soda from the fridge, he silently offered her one. When she shook her head, he closed the door.

"Nothing terribly exciting happened here today, but you just had your first day at the new jobsite. How did that go?"

His thick eyebrows lifted. "You want to hear about that?"

"Of course I do."

He studied her for another silent moment, then nodded. "Sure. I'll tell you all about it. First, I'm just going to sneak into Sasha's room and have a peek at her." He popped the tab on the soda can, took a long draw. "Don't worry. I promise not to wake her."

She tilted her head, grinning. "I doubt you could. She's sleeping hard after a whole day of playing."

Setting the can on the kitchen table, he strode across the kitchen and into the foyer, disappearing up the staircase. She stood in the doorway where the kitchen met the foyer, her gaze settled on the second-floor landing. *It's so sweet that he wants to look in on her.*

Before long, curiosity got the better of her, and she padded barefoot up the carpeted stairs. Stopping outside Sasha's room, she found Maxwell leaning over her crib. She watched as he inhaled deeply, as if taking in his daughter's scent. Then, he placed a soft kiss on her forehead, running a gentle hand over her silken curls. Mouthing the words "good night," he turned and slipped from the room.

She was leaning against the wall when he softly closed the door. "That was incredibly sweet, Maxwell."

An easy smile came over his face. "She's easy to love. What can I say?"

"I agree." *Must be a family trait. Her father isn't so bad, either.* Slipping her hand into his, she walked with him back downstairs.

As they sat on the sofa together, he removed his boots and set them aside. With that done, he cozied up to her, placing his arm over her shoulder. "Ready to hear about today's adventures?"

"Sure." She listened intently while he told her about all the things he'd encountered on the construction site that day. When he casually mentioned having shown Sasha's photo to his construction manager, she stopped him. "Wait. You mean you were bragging about her?"

"I guess I was." He smiled, his expression conveying a mixture of pride and satisfaction. "And I gotta say, it felt pretty good."

"Based on your expression, I'll bet it did." She loved the way he spoke about Sasha, the way he doted on her and displayed consistent concern for her well-being. As she'd guessed, his worries about not being a good father had been unfounded.

He continued on, telling her about how his competitor-turned-partner had lost his contract to work on the site. "I was worried about working with Harold. As it turns out, I only had to do it for a few hours."

She shook her head. "It sucks for him, but I'm glad he's out of your hair. Now you can focus on delivering exactly what the city wants."

"Exactly. See, you get me." He shifted on the sofa cushion, angling his body toward her. "You were the only one who didn't dismiss my irritation about working with him. It's like you understood how that affected my creativity."

She swallowed. "I'm...glad you feel comfortable with me, Maxwell. Your feelings were absolutely valid, by the way."

"You're so caring, Yvonne. It's one of the things I—" He stopped short.

Her heart clenched. *Was he going to say "love"? I think I heard an "L" sound. Is that where he was going?* Her mind raced. Part of her wanted him to say it. But how would she react? Everything about this man seemed to set her body and her emotions on high. She was careening full tilt toward falling in love with him, and so help her, it was a ride she never wanted to end.

His voice broke the silence, penetrating her thoughts. "You know something?"

Looking into his eyes, she asked, "What?"

"Coming home to you and Sasha every night has become the best part of my day, Yvonne."

Her mouth fell open, and her breath escaped in a *whoosh*. She didn't speak. She couldn't. Her heart pounded in her ears like an up-tempo bass line.

He ran a finger along her jawline. "I used to come home to this big empty house every day. I did that for years. But I never realized just how big and empty it was until Sasha showed up in my life." He scratched his chin. "I never thought I'd be a father. But it turned out to be the best thing that ever happened to me. She's doing more than change my lifestyle. She's changing my heart, and it's definitely a change for the better."

Yvonne nodded, feeling her throat tighten with emotion.

"And then there's you." He grabbed her hand, squeezed it. "You came in when I needed someone the most and whipped me and my big empty house into shape so Sasha could have the home she needs and deserves. I used to think I liked living alone, having my privacy, doing whatever I want, when I want. But you've shown me there's so much more."

Tears welled in her eyes now. "Maxwell, I..."

He brushed her tears away with gentle fingertips. "There's so much about you to love, Yvonne. And when I look at you, I see it all."

She wanted to speak, but a sob threatened. Instead, she drew a deep, shaky breath.

"I may be risking looking like an absolute fool by telling you this so soon." He squeezed her hand again. "But I love you, Yvonne."

Exhaling, she leaned close to him. "You're no fool. And if you are, we'll be fools together, because I love you, too, Maxwell."

Groaning, he dragged her against him, capturing her lips in a fiery kiss. She wound her arms around his neck as she slid into his lap. His tongue searched her mouth, and she leaned in all the more, wanting to give him everything he sought. Her nipples tightened, and swirling heat raced through her body, pooling at her core to remind her how much she wanted him inside her.

When she pulled away, breathless and vibrating with passion, she looked into his dark, hooded eyes. "Maxwell…"

"Yes, Yvonne?" He traced his fingertip over her kiss-swollen lips.

"Will you make love to me tonight?"

A low, rumbling sound erupted from his throat. A moment later, he said, "You wouldn't tease me about a thing like this, would you?"

She shook her head. "I've only been fantasizing about you since the first day I walked into your office."

A sharp inhale followed that, and he kissed the hollow of her neck, murmuring, "Why'd you wait so long to tell me?"

She sighed, her head falling back as he trailed sultry kisses along her collarbone. "It didn't exactly seem appropriate then." She would have elaborated on the impropriety of thinking of her charge's father in such scandalous ways, but his warm lips on her skin were turning her brain to mush.

"Oh, don't you worry. If you really want to do this, we're going to get very inappropriate here tonight."

A tingle went down her spine, and she swore her body temperature climbed by ten degrees in an instant. "Maxwell…"

"Yes, Yvonne. You remember that name, because you'll be calling it all…night…long." He punctuated each pause with another kiss and busied his hands undoing the top buttons of her blouse. "You fantasize about me, huh?"

She nodded…or something similar, since she was too busy melting to be sure.

"I think it's high time to make those fantasies a reality."

CHAPTER 14

MAXWELL HELD YVONNE'S HAND, THEIR FINGERS LACED together as they moved slowly up the staircase. Though the passion that sparked between them demanded satisfaction, it was as if they both knew that this moment, this first time, should be savored.

She walked a step behind him, and when he glanced back at her, he could see her soft smile in the dim light.

Inside his bedroom, the drawn drapes shrouded the room in darkness. He quickly turned on a bedside lamp, not wanting to disturb the groove. He kissed her on the lips, holding up his index finger. "Give me a sec."

She nodded, standing a few feet from the doorway as if awaiting his instruction.

He stepped away from her long enough to toss his construction vest, hard hat, and long-sleeved tee over the back of the armchair in the corner. He noticed the way her eyes darted from watching him to his bed, then back again. He smiled, sensing her anticipation, then sat in the chair long enough to rid himself of his socks, before returning to her.

His hands resting on her upper arms, he guided her into the circle of illumination where he stopped. Trailing his fingertips over her jawline and down the curve of her neck, he slipped his hand around to her nape. "You're sure, Yvonne?"

"I've already told you what I want..." Her voice was just above a whisper.

"Tell me again." He stroked his fingertips along her satin jawline once more.

"Yes, Maxwell. I want you."

The sexy rasp in her voice undid him, and he buried his hands in the soft recess of her hair, pulling her into his kiss. She opened her mouth right away, allowing his tongue to slip inside as she wrapped her arms around his waist. Having the lush, feminine curves of her body pressed against him hardened him almost to the point of pain.

After a few moments of kissing, he broke the kiss so he could focus on undoing her shirt buttons. Tossing the shirt aside, he removed the thin chemise beneath to expose her lacy bra. The pink fabric cradled two perfect breasts, and he kissed the brown tops above the scalloped edges. Without ceasing his kisses, he reached around her to undo the clasp, then removed the bra and tossed it aside. Gathering the luscious weight of her honey-brown breasts in his hands, he kissed and suckled each dark nipple until her back arched. Her soft sighs let him know she liked his particular brand of passion, and he planned to give her all she could stand.

He could stay there forever, but there was so much more of her to explore, so many more places to brand with his hands and mouth. He knelt, placing a trail of kisses along her belly as he undid her slacks. Pushing the fabric down until it pooled around her ankles, he backed up as she stepped out of them. The pink lace panties were cut high on her hips, exposing the expanse of her honey-brown legs. It was all he could do not to drool.

He looked up at her, told her in an awe-filled voice, "Baby, you're gorgeous."

"God, Max," she crooned, her voice soft in the dim light.

Her knees trembled, and he placed his hands on her waist to steady her. Caressing the round contours of her hips with his palms, he kissed the plane of her belly, then swirled his tongue in the hollow of her navel. "Let's get you out of these. I don't want anything between us." Her legs shook again, and he held her in place with one hand, using the other to whisk away the last scrap of pink lace.

She kicked the panties aside, and he inhaled sharply as he took in the sight of her glorious nudity. The lamp cast a glow over her sumptuous form, and his eyes lingered on the shadowy place between her thighs. He dragged his fingertip up the inside of one thigh, then down the inside of the other. "Open up for me, Von."

She did as he asked, widening her stance so that her feet were on either side of him.

He leaned forward, nuzzling against the soft curls crowning her thighs. Moments later, he swept his tongue through her folds.

Her knees buckled in time with the strangled cry that escaped her throat, and as before, he used a gentle hand on her hip to stabilize her. He followed the first lick with another, then another, and another still, enjoying the sweetness of her essence coating his tongue. She tasted of warmth and wanting, of an exotic meeting of sweetness and spice that had no name and was uniquely hers. The sounds she made only drove him to be more thorough. As her cries melted into sharp growls of pleasure, he felt the fire raging in his blood.

A single word echoed in his mind. *Mine.* And as she came, shaking and shouting his name, he knew he'd begun the process of claiming her, of truly making her his.

He eased away from her in time to keep her from collapsing beneath the weight of the magic, then gathered her into his arms, her limp legs draped over the crook of his elbow. Carrying her the short distance to the bed, he laid her down. Crawling atop her, he observed her. Her eyes were closed, her chest rising and falling in time with her rapid, shallow breaths. A light sheen of perspiration had collected around her hairline, plastering the tiny curls to her forehead, and the crimson flush of passion was all over her.

She was disheveled, flushed, nearly vibrating with pleasure.

And she was beautiful.

He lazily stroked one thigh, and her legs parted for him as she groaned.

"Ready?" He undid his pants, stepped out of them while awaiting her answer.

"Now." She hooked her lower leg around his waist and dragged him between her legs. "Please."

The tip of his dick brushed against her mound, and he winced. "Patience, baby." He said it even as the scorching heat radiating from her body turned his own patience to ash. Shifting a bit, he stretched out his arm and opened the drawer of his nightstand. Snatching out a condom, he brought his hand between their bodies and covered himself with protection. Tossing the wrapper aside, he barely had time to breathe before he felt her hand encircling him.

"Now," she murmured again, guiding him inside.

"Ahhh." He felt his entire body tense as her heat enfolded him. Slowly, he entered her, inch by tantalizing inch, letting her guide him until she'd taken him in completely. He growled, moving his hips, and those first, deep strokes nearly rendered him senseless. With her tight warmth cradling him, he felt as if his entire body were on fire, the flames consuming him from the inside out.

She moved her hips in time with his, rising to meet him each time he rocked forward. She arched for him, her head thrown back, presenting her breasts like a gift. He flicked his tongue over the taut tips, his affection climbing as she purred in response. Caught up in the wonder of her, he grasped her other ankle and brought it around so both her legs were hooked around his waist. Then he kicked up his pace, driving into her as his growing arousal demanded.

He heard his own grunts mingling with her high-pitched, staccato cries, and then it hit him. The blinding, glorious release he'd been chasing finally engulfed him, and he closed his eyes as his whole body vibrated with the force of it.

He didn't remember falling asleep, but the next sounds he heard were the baby's cries.

She stretched, her body shifting beneath his. "Sasha's fussing. Maybe she had a bad dream."

Rolling over so she could get up, he watched her walk naked across the room toward his armchair. There, she took a moment to slip into his long-sleeved tee.

Turning to face him, she asked, "Do you mind if I borrow this?"

The sight of her, hair flying around her head like a crow's nest, lips swollen from his kisses, and her neck bearing the slight redness where his lips had been, was one of the most erotic sights he'd ever seen. Hard for her all over again, he shook his head. "Not at all. But I should tell you that seeing you in my shirt is a major turn-on."

She giggled, her hand over her mouth. "Max, I have to go check on the baby."

"Go ahead. Because I'm about two seconds from dragging you back into this bed." He gestured with his hand, effectively shooing her out of the room.

With a wink, she turned and fled, shutting the door behind her.

Lying there in the quiet, he tucked a pillow behind his head and stared at the ceiling. *She's amazing.* She'd impressed him from the very moment she walked into his office. And now that they'd shared this moment, this magnificent lovemaking, he knew she'd captured him, heart and soul.

"Max?"

"Hmm?" He looked to the doorway as her voice broke into his thoughts and found her standing there with Sasha on her hip.

"I'm going to take her downstairs and try to get her settled, okay?"

He was so…enamored by the sight of her standing there, wearing his shirt and cradling his daughter, it took his breath away. He knew he should respond to what she'd said, but he couldn't. Not when he was so busy imagining a future that included her wearing a huge diamond on her left hand and holding another child in her arms, a son they'd conceive together.

She frowned. "Max, did you hear me? I'm taking Sasha downstairs."

"Sorry, I was…never mind." He smiled, nodded. "I'll be down in a minute."

Yvonne attempted to roll over in bed Saturday morning but found she couldn't move. Maxwell's arm, locked around her waist, kept her firmly in place. Lying near the center of the king-size bed with him, she took a moment to relish his hard, muscled nudity pressed against her own.

Over his shoulder, she could see the sliver of sunlight filtering between the dark drapes covering his windows. She yawned then, and as she moved to stifle it, he stirred with a low groan.

He opened his eyes, and as soon as their gazes met, a huge grin spread over his face. "Good morning, Yvonne." He gave her a squeeze, drawing her a bit closer to him.

"Good morning." She lifted her face, giving him a short peck on the lips. "Can I get up please?"

His face twisted into a mock pout. "I'm disappointed. I was really getting into holding you like this."

If only he knew. "I'm just as into it as you are. But I have to go to the potty."

He chuckled, releasing his grip on her waist. "You've been working with kids for a long time, and it shows."

"Says the man who spent all night doing all sorts of very adult things to me." She rolled over, scooting away from him before he could swat her behind. Padding over the plush carpet, she slipped into the adjoining master bathroom.

When she returned, she found him standing by the windows. He'd opened the curtains, and the resulting flood of sunlight bathed his still nude body in a bright white glow. She swallowed, taking in the sight of his male beauty. His tall, broad frame was like a sinewy statue of carved bronze, and she couldn't resist walking over to touch his chest. "I see you're giving the neighbors a free show."

He laughed. "Nope. This window faces the backyard, and with my privacy fence, nobody can see a thing."

She crossed her arms over her body, feeling the chill hit her skin now that she'd left the warmth of the bathroom with its heated floor. "I'd better get dressed. Starting to get chilly."

"I keep it pretty cool in here." He stretched, raising his arms high above his head. "I'm going to get in the shower. I'd ask you to join me, but if I did, we'd never make it to breakfast."

Her brow hitched. "What do you mean? Do you have plans for us?"

His gaze swept over her body, lingering on her chest for a moment before rising to her face again. "For this morning, I was hoping you'd join me for another family breakfast at my parents' house."

She tilted her head. "I thought y'all usually did that during the week?"

He strode across the room, flipping on the light as he entered his huge walk-in closet. "We do. But we're going out on the golf course this afternoon as a family, so we thought we'd just make a day of it."

Walking around to the side of the bed where her clothes were still piled up, she slipped into her camisole and panties. "Sure, I'm game. Just let me shower and—"

Sasha's plaintive wail cut through the silence.

"Duty calls. Come and get Sasha when you're done showering, then I'll have my turn, okay?"

"Sure thing," he called from the recesses of the closet.

She smiled. *Here we are, coordinating the baby's care like it's no big deal.* It made her thoughts stray to what it would be like to be a true member of this little family, not just Sasha's caregiver. She left the room and walked down the hall to the nursery. When she entered, she found the baby standing up, holding on to the crib railing, with fat tears standing in her eyes.

"Goodness." She picked her up, holding her close and bouncing her until she calmed down. "Somebody's hungry, huh?"

Two hours later, they were standing on the front porch of Humphrey and Delphinia's house. Sasha, dressed in a pink-and-white polka-dotted dress and solid pink leggings, bounced up and down in her father's arms as they approached the front door. He fumbled around for a moment as if trying to free a hand.

"I'll get it." Yvonne turned the knob.

Finally succeeding in freeing one of his hands, he placed it over hers to stop her. "I wanted to ask you…"

"What is it?"

"I want to tell my family that we're together today. As a couple." He watched her as if waiting to see how she'd react. "If that's okay with you."

She couldn't stop the smile from spreading over her face. Knowing he wanted to share their relationship with the people most important to him meant a lot. "I'm definitely okay with it." She sighed. "I just hope your parents approve."

"Oh, please. What's not to love about you?"

She nodded, certain he would take that as her agreement. It was more of an acquiescence; she had no way of knowing if the Deverses would approve of their son with someone like her. There wasn't anything refined about her background, and as likable as the family seemed, sometimes she felt a bit out of place in their presence.

If I remember right, though, they're all pretty eager for him to settle down with someone.

They were greeted by Kelsey as they entered the kitchen. "Morning, y'all."

Humphrey was already in his seat at the table, his face obscured by the open newspaper he held in front of him. Alexis and Delphinia were at the center island, putting the offerings on platters. Yvonne couldn't help noticing how stoic the usually cheerful Delphinia seemed; even her expression seemed flat and distant.

Greetings were exchanged, and after the food was set on the table, everyone took a seat. It was in the breakfast nook, situated in the sunny alcove on the left side of the kitchen. Yvonne sat between Maxwell and his father, while baby Sasha was seated across from them on Aunt Alexis's lap. Resting against her aunt's chest while drinking from a sippy cup of formula, she seemed as happy as the proverbial clam.

After Humphrey delivered a brief grace, the platters brimming with fluffy scrambled eggs, crisp bacon, triangles of wheat toast, and red, ripe strawberries were passed around the table until everyone had filled their plates.

Yvonne ate in silence, watching the family's interactions with one another. Alexis and Kelsey chatted easily with each other while Sasha gnawed on a strawberry she'd grabbed from her aunt's plate.

"So, Dad. When do you think we'll get out on the lake again?" Maxwell watched his father expectantly.

Humphrey shrugged. "I'll have some time maybe two weekends from now. First thing I need to do is take the boat over to Harvey's and have him take a look at it. She's been out of commission for a good couple of years now." He paused to sip from his mug of coffee. "Gotta make sure she's still fit for sailing."

"Sounds good. If things are still going well at the jobsite, I should be able to swing that." Maxwell turned Yvonne's way. "That is if Yvonne is free to look after Sasha on a weekend."

Kelsey popped her lips. "No way. Let Yvonne have her weekends. I'll be happy to take Sasha for a couple of days." She reached over and tapped the tip of her index finger against the baby's nose, eliciting a giggle. "We'll have a great time. I'm sure she'd like to try some finger-painting with Auntie Kelsey. Isn't that right?" She gave Sasha's cheek a tiny squeeze, and more giggles followed.

"Thanks, Sis." Maxwell grinned. "So where are we fishing, Dad? Lake Rim, maybe? Or do you want to go farther out?"

While the men discussed the details of their upcoming fishing trip, the sisters continued to fawn over Sasha. The baby was at peak precious today, and she'd easily turned her aunts into smiling, cooing, baby-talking enthusiasts. Yvonne couldn't help smiling at their interaction; it was entirely too cute.

Yet Delphinia, silently eating her food, her expression as blank and empty as a brand-new dry erase board, stood in stark contrast to the rest of her family. Even in the short time Yvonne had known Maxwell's mother, she'd never seen her so sullen. *I wonder what's bothering her, but I don't think it's my place to ask.*

Glancing her way, Maxwell tapped his fork against his mug. "Everybody, I want to make an announcement."

This is it. Her heart thudded in her chest, a giddy feeling growing inside her as she anticipated his next words.

He cleared his throat, draped his arm around her shoulder.

Kelsey and Alexis both looked his way for the first time since the meal began. Apparently, his impending announcement was more interesting than playing with the baby, at least for the time being.

"Yvonne and I are—"

Delphinia's fork clattered onto her empty plate, and she shoved the plate away with enough force that it crashed into one of her china platters. Kelsey swiped her hand out, her quick reflexes keeping the jostled china from crashing to the floor.

Yvonne leaned closer to Maxwell as his arm tightened around her. Glancing his way, she saw the wide-eyed stare on his face.

All eyes in the room turned toward Delphinia's face. The earlier blankness was gone, replaced by the clenched jaw and flashing eyes indicative of anger.

Maxwell frowned. "Mom, what's—"

"Hush, Maxwell." Delphinia's sharp tone split the silence like an ax blasting through a chunk of wood. She folded her arms over her chest, shifting her glare to her husband's face. "Do you know who called me this morning, Humphrey?"

His brow furrowed, Humphrey snapped, "How should I know? And why'd you interrupt Max after you've sat here not saying a word this whole time?"

Delphinia stabbed a finger in her husband's direction. "Don't try me. Not now."

Propping his clenched fists on his hips, Humphrey opened his mouth as if to speak.

Before any words could spill out, Maxwell touched his father's arm, briefly shaking his head. "Obviously, Mom has something to say."

Well, this has taken a turn. While part of her resented that their moment had been snatched away, she realized something important was happening, so she held her peace. In a situation like this, she knew better than to interfere.

"You're damn right I do." Delphinia drew a deep breath. "It was Trish. *Trish* called me this morning, Humphrey."

At the mention of the woman's name, Humphrey's posture changed, his back suddenly as straight and rigid as a board. He swallowed so hard, even Yvonne could see the bob of his Adam's apple.

Alexis, her eyes narrowed as she cradled her now drowsy niece, tilted her head. "You mean Ms. Trish who used to live three doors down from us when we were kids?"

"That's the only Trish I can think of," Kelsey remarked as she gathered and stacked the plates and platters. "But I thought you and she stopped talking years ago."

"We did." Delphinia's clipped response was delivered through clenched teeth.

"Then why would she be calling you now, out of the blue?" Maxwell's expression and tone conveyed genuine confusion.

"Jeffrey's getting married," Delphinia said. "And Trish wants us all to be there."

"That's great news, for Jeffrey." Maxwell shrugged. "But why would she call you? Y'all don't even like each other."

Looking to her husband, she said, "Why don't you tell them, Humphrey?"

"This isn't the time or place, Del."

"Everyone's here. It's as good a time as any for them to know who you really are."

Yvonne squirmed in her seat, feeling out of place. It was as if she were watching a soap opera play out in front of her. She didn't know if she was ready for such an intimate view of this family, even if they were the relatives of the man she'd grown to love. "Maybe I should leave…"

"No, Yvonne." Humphrey stood, letting his hands drop to his sides limply. "I'll leave. Because I'm not having this discussion." He walked away from the table, headed for the door to the rear of the room.

"Humphrey!" Delphinia twisted in her seat, shouting after her retreating husband. "Walking out isn't going to make it right!"

He didn't respond, and he didn't stop. Soon, he'd disappeared from the room.

And moments later, Delphinia Devers slumped forward and sobbed into her hands.

CHAPTER 15

WATCHING HIS MOTHER DISSOLVE INTO TEARS, MAXWELL'S heart clenched as if a fist were wrapped around it. His sisters rushed to her side, trying to comfort her. Kelsey, cradling Sasha on her hip, reached for the napkins, while Alexis, the baby and easily the most emotional sibling, knelt and pulled her mother into her arms as she wept.

Holy shit. I've never seen Mom like this. She'd certainly displayed irritation or dissatisfaction in the past, but never on this level. And having this happen today, in front of Yvonne and when he'd planned to share their relationship with his family, put him in possibly the most awkward situation he'd ever been in. He looked to Yvonne, whose face conveyed confusion. As their gazes locked, she gave him a small shrug and patted him on the shoulder. The small gesture settled his mood somewhat, because despite the unexpected drama unfolding before her, she hadn't left his side, hadn't bolted from the room to avoid the situation. It was as if she were showing him that she'd always be by his side, no matter what. It was a much-needed comforting thought for the tense moment at hand.

When he could no longer bear listening to her cry, he asked softly, "Mom, what's going on? What's Dad not telling us?"

"Give her a minute, Max." Kelsey dabbed at her mother's tear-streaked face with a cloth napkin.

The room fell silent while everyone waited until Delphinia felt ready to speak. He felt Yvonne lean into him, her presence salving the torrent of emotions rising inside.

Finally, Delphinia cleared her throat. Her eyes were still red-rimmed, but the tears had ceased. "I didn't want to be the one to tell you this, especially not the way it's happening. But you should know the truth. Your father…had an affair."

Alexis, who'd been kneeling by her mother's side, dropped to a sitting position on the floor.

Kelsey shrank back as if recoiling from something hideous. Her free hand flew to her mouth.

While his sisters seemed to be reacting with shock and disappointment, Maxwell felt something different: anger. It sparked inside him, red-hot and strong. Unable to hold the words back, he blurted, "How could he do something like that?" *And he had the nerve to lecture me about responsibility when I brought Yvonne here the first time.*

"So Trish called you to tell you about this other woman?" Alexis shook her head, still trying to piece it all together. "I can't see why she'd try to help since you two fell out."

Maxwell tilted his head, taking all the factors he knew into consideration. His thoughts rolled back to that Saturday he'd helped clean the garage and the box of toys that had set his mother off. His father had stormed off then, as he recalled. *The toys definitely belonged to a little boy. But they definitely weren't mine.* At the time, he couldn't fathom why something so innocuous seemed to make her so angry. *Now I get it. But that means…*

"Oh. My. God." Kelsey's eyes were as round as the china plates they'd eaten from. "It was her, wasn't it? Ms. Trish was the other woman!"

Delphinia nodded slowly.

Maxwell felt his pulse pick up, felt the hot blood rushing through his body. "Fuck. That means Jeffrey…" He couldn't even bring himself to complete the sentence.

Having observed the entire revelation in silence up to this point, Yvonne finally spoke. "But who's Jeffrey?"

Returning to her chair and sitting down, Kelsey cradled Sasha close. "Jeffrey is Trish's son. And most likely our half brother."

Yvonne turned to him, the motion slow. "Maxwell, I..."

He took a deep breath and blew it out in hopes it would cool his anger. It did, but not to the extent he'd hoped. "Trish and Jeffrey lived a few houses down from us in the old neighborhood. He's about two years younger than me—"

"And only a few weeks older than me," Kelsey ground out.

"Right," he continued. "Jeffrey and I played together as kids. We climbed trees, played football, rode bikes. He was always over to our house, but none of us were ever allowed to go to Trish's place." He looked his mother's way, taking in the quiet resignation on her face. "Now that I think of it, you never seemed to like Trish. Dad was always the one who dealt with her if anything needed to be coordinated. And you never let her into the house. She'd sit on the porch sometimes, but that was the extent of it."

"Trish used to work at the engineering firm that hired your father right out of school. She was an office manager there. I imagine he started seeing her not too long after we were married." Delphinia rubbed a hand over her face. "It was the typical things. Coming home late, claiming he'd been held up at work. I'd go to wash his clothes, and I'd smell the lingering scent of another woman's perfume...find the traces of her makeup on his shirts. One morning, I just sat on top of the washer and cried my eyes out."

"Oh, Mom." Alexis squeezed her hand.

"When your father finally came home that evening, I told him he needed to be honest with me and come clean. So he did. He admitted what they'd been doing and that Jeffrey was his son, but he didn't go into much detail. Wanted me to be 'cordial' to her. I tolerated her being around as long as I could. But by the time Kelsey was born, I'd had it."

"Mom, I..." Maxwell rubbed his temples. "I'm so sorry he put you through this. But I have to ask, why did you stay?" He couldn't imagine the pain she'd endured, the invisible daggers that had pierced her heart every time she looked at the child her husband had conceived with another woman.

"I love him." She offered a sad smile. "He promised me they weren't seeing each other anymore, except as it pertained to Jeffrey. Aside from that, when he sold that patent to the government, I knew that money could change this family's life, and it did. I wanted the best for my children, so I stayed."

He shook his head, unable to believe what he'd just heard. Growing up as the only male child in the family had been difficult at times. He'd often longed for a little brother, someone to commiserate with on the things only another young boy would understand. And while he'd done some of that with Jeffrey, it just wasn't on the same level. He'd never truly felt that level of fraternal bonding until he'd joined the ranks of Theta Delta Theta. He resented his father for denying him the brother he'd wanted...the brother he'd already had. "This is outrageous. I can't believe he stood there and lectured me about responsibility after what he's done." He held out his arms, and Kelsey passed Sasha to Yvonne, who in turn placed his daughter in his arms. Holding her sleeping form close to his heart, he inhaled the sweet scent of her baby lotion. He leaned down, kissed her warm forehead.

Alexis got up, sitting back in her chair. Touching her mother's shoulder, she said, "I'm so sorry. So, so sorry you went through this, Mom."

Delphinia nodded. "I know you are. You all are good kids and my greatest accomplishments. But you aren't responsible for what happened all those years ago. Only your father and Trish can answer for that." She sighed. "Trish told me she was sorry years ago. Just can't bring myself to be friends with her, you know?"

He nodded. *Who'd want to make friends with someone after such a betrayal?*

"Did he ever apologize, Mom?" Kelsey asked. "I mean really, sincerely apologize?"

Scooting back from the table, Delphinia shook her head. "The most I've gotten out of him is, 'Del, I have some regrets.' That man is about as stubborn as a red wine stain."

Alexis's face crumpled, and tears welled in her eyes. "I don't know how everybody else feels, but I'm definitely not in the mood for any family golf outing. Not after all this."

Maxwell stood then, unable to stay seated any longer. "I'm done. This is a lot to take in and a bit too much for me if I'm honest."

"Are you going after Dad, Max?" Kelsey gave him a questioning look.

He shook his head. "No way. He's about the last person on earth I'd want to see right now." He couldn't properly communicate the level of disgust he felt over his father's actions. Looking down at Sasha, he was amazed she'd slept through most of this ordeal. Still, her sleeping face held a tight expression, as if she'd heard the commotion in her dreams. "I just need to process all this. So I'm going to take Sasha and Yvonne home."

Yvonne got up then, taking the baby's bag from the back of her chair and slinging the strap over her shoulder. She grabbed his hand, and they crossed the room together.

Stopping to hug his mother, he asked, "Will you be all right?"

She nodded. "Go on home, Max. Enjoy her." She kissed the baby's cheek. "And her, too." She jerked her head, indicating Yvonne.

The wash of color that filled Yvonne's cheeks was both alluring and endearing. It seemed no big announcement was needed. As always, Mom simply…knew. After saying goodbye to his sisters, he and Yvonne left.

Once they were back at his house, he watched as Yvonne took Sasha out of the car seat and placed her gently on a blanket on the living room floor. While the baby crawled around, exploring the finer points of the furniture legs, Yvonne stood by as if unsure what to do next.

Seated on the sofa, he called her name. "Yvonne?"

She turned his way. "What is it?"

He didn't even know where to begin. He let his gaze pass over the regal lines of her face: the big brown eyes, the full lips he loved to kiss, the nose that wrinkled whenever she started to think too hard. "I'm...sorry. You know, about today."

She tilted her head. "Why are you apologizing? There's no way you could have anticipated so much...excitement."

He leaned back into the cushions. "Rationally, I know that. Still, I feel responsible for exposing you to it." He couldn't remember the last time in his adult life that he'd felt so embarrassed, especially over something he hadn't actually done.

She walked over then, taking a seat beside him. "Maxwell. I'm not mad, really. I'll admit I was a little disappointed at first that your thunder was stolen and you couldn't tell your family about us the way you'd planned. But it's really no big deal."

"I wish I could say the same. Part of me wants to disown my father, but I know I'm not going to do that." He shook his head. "And I don't even know what I'll say to Jeffrey the next time I see him."

"When are you planning to see him?"

"I'm definitely going to his wedding. After all, he's still one of my closest friends." *And now he's my brother. Isn't that some shit?*

"Listen. You're a levelheaded, intelligent man. I'm sure you'll be able to iron it all out...eventually." She reached for his hand, gave it a squeeze.

"What about our announcement?"

She giggled. "Don't worry. I think they know." She winked.

He laughed for the first time in what seemed like forever. This day had gone wrong in ways he couldn't even have imagined, yet she had managed to brighten his mood. "Have I told you I love you today, Yvonne?"

"You mumbled it in your sleep in the wee hours, but I think it bears repeating."

He laughed again. "I love you, Yvonne."

"I love you, too, Maxwell."

She leaned in, and as their lips met, he felt the anger and frustration melt away.

He broke the kiss a few torrid moments later. "I know you probably have things to do. Since the family outing is a huge bust, I don't want to monopolize your day."

"Yeah. I do have a few odds and ends to take care of, and I want to swing by and check in on my parents." She shifted, then stood.

"Then, go on. Enjoy the rest of the weekend. Sasha and I will be fine." He leaned over, scooping Sasha up off the floor as she crawled over his feet. Holding her little hand, he waved it side to side. "Okay, say bye-bye to Ms. Yvonne."

"Baaaaaa!" Sasha's exclamation was loud enough that he jumped.

Yvonne laughed. "I'll take it. Bye, sweetie. I'll see you Monday." She shot him a sultry look. "You, too, Maxwell."

He smiled. "I can't wait."

A few minutes later, he stood by the window with the baby, watching as Yvonne's car pulled out of the driveway. Turning to Sasha, he said, "What do you think? Ready for lunch?"

She gave him a drooly smile.

Laughing, he bounced her all the way to the kitchen.

When Yvonne pulled up to her parents' house Monday morning, she saw the curtains rustling at the front window. She smiled, knowing her mother, a dedicated member of the Neighborhood Watch, had been there. As far back as she could remember, her mother had always looked out the front windows; she'd been privy to every truck rumbling down the street, every loudly held conversation, and every new neighbor to move onto the block for the last three decades.

Glancing over her shoulder at Sasha, who was buckled in the back, she quipped, "Well, it looks like my mommy knows we're here already."

Sasha laughed, shaking the giraffe rattle that had recently become one of her favorite toys.

A short time later, Yvonne entered her parents' house, carrying Sasha on her hip. "Good morning, Mommy."

Her mother smiled and pulled her in for a hug, careful not to hurt the baby. "Morning, sweetheart." She greeted Sasha by giving her a small boop on the nose. "And how are you today, precious?"

Sasha cooed, offering her cherished rattle.

"Oh, goodness. She's such a good baby. And getting so big!" Marissa's expression turned wistful. "If only I could have a grandbaby as sweet as you."

Yvonne shook her head but knew better than to roll her eyes. To shift the conversation away from her mother's longing for grandchildren, she asked, "Is Daddy ready for his appointment?" Since Janine, the nurse, had taken the day off, Yvonne was taking on her usual duty of driving him to the hospital to see his endocrinologist.

"You know your father. Slow as cold molasses when it comes to getting ready for the doctor." Marissa shook her head. "I got him dressed over an hour ago. Since then, he's been griping about not being able to find his favorite sneakers."

"Those ratty old blue ones with the white stripes?" Yvonne shook her head, knowing the shoes were on the verge of falling apart at any moment.

"Yes. Those things are worn out and well past their use. Still, he insists on wearing them every chance he gets."

"I'd wager they're older than I am."

"You'd win that bet." Giving Yvonne a motherly pat on the shoulder, Marissa stepped back. "I'll go light a fire under him. Go ahead and sit down with that baby, take a load off."

Doing as her mother instructed, Yvonne sat down on the old

sofa, pulling Sasha onto her lap. She looked around the room, soaking in the familiarity of it. In her mind's eye, she could picture her younger self, chasing her sister Zelda around the room. She recalled a quiet childhood when she was very young, time spent taking walks with her parents, gardening with her father, and reading every book she could get her hands on. That had all changed when her parents had told her she would soon get a new baby sister. While she had fond memories of the easy pace of her early life, she loved her sister fiercely and soon came to embrace the chaotic joy she brought to the family. Zelda had been active and full of mischief from the time she took her first steps, always keeping Yvonne and their parents on their toes. A wrought iron wall shelf held her mother's collection of hand-painted statues of African deities, and at least two of them had been glued back together following one of Zelda's mad dashes through the house.

She looked to the old upright piano in the far corner, which had become something of a display piece over the last eight or ten years. A thin coating of dust had settled over the polished maple finish, and the top of the instrument was home to a grouping of family photos and various knickknacks. Looking at the claw-footed bench, she could still hear Granny Vera, her father's mother, playing hymns and warbling along to the tune. Her father had continued to play after Granny Vera's passing in the mid-1990s. After he'd lost his foot, he'd settled into a depression that had drained away the joy of making music. He'd improved so much over the last few years, with the love of his family, therapy, and meds. Still, she wondered if she'd ever hear him play again.

Sasha became restless and started to scoot off her lap. Knowing her parents' house wasn't exactly childproofed, she set the baby's wiggly form on the floor and stood up, poised to follow her wherever she roamed. They'd made a few laps between the living room, hallway, and kitchen by the time her father ambled into the living room to meet her.

"Morning, Daddy." She carried Sasha on her hip as she went to greet him with a kiss on the cheek.

"Says the one who's not getting poked and prodded today," he grumbled. Dressed in a pair of khaki slacks, a black-and-white-plaid button-down, and the aged sneakers he favored over all his other, newer shoes, his whiskered face was set firmly in a frown.

"It's just a follow-up visit, Daddy. I'm sure they won't be doing anything too major."

"You know how much I hate hospitals," he grumbled. "It's always freezing in there, they smell like disinfectant, and you can never find a good place to park the car."

She fought off the urge to chuckle. *He's always grumpy when he has doctors' visits, but this seems over the top, even for him.* "Tell you what, Daddy. I'll drop you at the door, go park the car, and then meet you in the lobby. That way, even if I have to park on the top level of the deck, you won't have to make that long walk."

"Will you do the same thing when they spring me?" His lips twisted a bit, morphing his expression into something a little less ornery.

"Sure thing." She tilted her head, studying the salt-and-pepper hair growing from his sideburns and over the lower half of his face. "Daddy, aren't you going to shave?"

"Nah." He stroked his fingers over his fuzzy chin. "Think I'm gonna grow my beard out again like I used to wear it back in the day. You remember, 'Rissa, don't you?" He looked to his wife, who was just behind him in the hallway.

"Of course I remember." She gave her husband a peck on the cheek. "You were handsome then, and you're still handsome now."

His expression relaxed considerably, allowing a ghost of a smile to peek through.

Yvonne smiled, too. *Mommy always knew how to break Daddy out of a funk.* "I like that idea, Daddy. But you gotta remember, you'll probably look younger with a beard, too. Nobody's gonna believe you've got two grown daughters."

His smile broadened. "Come on now. You're putting me on."

"No, no. Von is right." Her mother squeezed past him to the hall closet, opening the door and getting out his cane. "Now, listen. Don't you forget about me when you go out, looking all brand-new. Don't let me find out one of these younger ladies has stolen you away from me, Gordon." She handed the cane off to him, giving him her best pouty face.

He chuckled, taking the cane. "It'll never happen, 'Rissa. Can't be nothing better out there for me than you."

Yvonne watched as her mother blushed, then her father leaned over and kissed his wife softly on the lips. *Those two. Still carrying on like that after all these years.* Her thoughts turned to Maxwell, and she wondered if what they shared could ever reach that level or last that long. It was all so new, a part of her hesitated to think so far into the future.

She cleared her throat, and her parents stopped making goo-goo eyes at each other long enough to turn her way. "I have something I want to tell you."

"What is it, Yvonne?" Her father walked a few steps, coming out of the hallway and into the living room as she and her mother followed.

She hesitated, remembering the way her father had reacted when he overheard her saying she'd kissed Maxwell. She couldn't really pinpoint the cause of his ire. He'd never met Maxwell, so how could he claim not to like him? *Maybe it's one of those "no man is good enough for my daughter" things? Or is it a "don't mix business with pleasure" thing?* She blew out a breath, knowing she'd have to tell them sometime, and now was as good a time as any. "Maxwell and I are…seeing each other."

Her mother's brow hitched. "You mean as in dating?"

Yvonne nodded.

Scratching his chin again, her father crinkled his nose. "Yvonne, I don't know if I like this."

"I figured that much, Daddy. You seemed pretty upset when you overheard me and Zelda talking."

He sighed. "I didn't mean to blow up at you. But so many things are changing right now. You've got this new job, and it's taking up so much of your time that you hired us a nurse. And now you're telling me you're involved with your new boss after less than a month working for him? You've given me a lot to take in, Yvonne."

She grabbed his hand. "I understand that, Daddy. I'm not asking you to get on board right away. I'm just asking you to be patient and to give Max a chance."

"Calling him 'Max' now, huh?" Her mother clapped her hands together, then gave Sasha's nose a little tweak. "I may be closer to grandbabies than I thought."

This time, Yvonne had to close her eyes to avoid rolling them in front of her mother.

"Don't you think you're putting the buggy ahead of the team there, 'Rissa?" Gordon gave his wife a nudge. "I'm sure she's not planning on any babies, at least not until she gets married. Right, Yvonne?"

She swallowed. *Married? Is that where we're headed?* "Right, Daddy." What else could she say? She certainly wasn't about to tell her father that she and Max had already started practicing baby making. There were some things about a woman's life that her parents never, ever needed to know. "We're taking things very, very slowly." She thought back on Saturday's breakfast at the Deverses' place and the way it had quickly descended into soap opera–level drama. She'd been too shocked at first and then too sympathetic to tell him how uncomfortable she'd felt with the whole situation. She'd done her best not to be judgmental, because as Maxwell's nanny, it wasn't her place. But as his girlfriend? Now, that was another matter altogether. How could she not consider what the repercussions of getting serious with him might be, now that she knew the sorts of things going on with his closest relatives? *Even though marriage is a bit of a foreign concept for us right now, would I really want to be a part of a family with so many...issues?*

"Good girl." Her mother patted her shoulder again. "He seems like a nice fellow, based on how you've described him. And hearing about his house and all that, we know he's no pauper. So if you care for him, I'm behind you."

"Thanks, Mommy." She looked to her father, who stood by the coatrack at the door, pulling on his tan Carhartt jacket. "And you, Daddy?"

Zipping his jacket, he gave her a slow nod. "Bring him over here to meet the family, and I'll make a decision after I look him over."

Yvonne smiled, having a flashback to her teenage years when she'd had to bring her dates home to meet with her father. "Fair enough. You ready?" She jangled her keys, which Sasha immediately snatched from her.

He laughed. "I'm ready. Looks like the kid's driving, eh?"

Giggling, she strapped Sasha back into the car seat, taking back the pilfered keys as they headed out the door.

CHAPTER 16

BY MIDMORNING TUESDAY, THINGS ON THE CROWN CENTER site were in full swing. Maxwell stood next to Braxton at his workstation, looking over the now cured foundation for the main building. "This looks great, Brax."

Braxton nodded. "It does. Ms. Patterson and her crew did a bang-up job." He gestured toward the men removing the wooden slats that had formed the mold for the foundation. "It's as smooth and level as can be. Definitely a great starting point for the rest of this project."

"In other words, we'll be using their services again."

"Absolutely."

"Any word from the framers?"

"Yep. They're finishing up another job today, but they'll be on-site tomorrow."

Maxwell nodded, pleased that things were going mostly according to plan. "Now, here's our next problem. Since Carmichael and his folks got kicked off the job, we've got a lot of extra work on our hands." He jerked his head to the left, indicating the space where the parking deck would be built. "When will we be able to get the graders over there?"

"Later today. The ones who were working on this portion of the project are done with that now, so I assigned them to handle grading over there as well."

"Awesome." Maxwell glanced over there, seeing how quiet it was as opposed to the part of the site he stood on. Only a few landscapers were working on that end of the site, hauling in bushes and plants that would be used for landscaping the area. "Once I know both foundations are in, I can pull back from this project and leave everything in your capable hands."

Braxton's brow rose. "You could pull back now, but you're too much of a control freak."

Maxwell cut him a look.

"I'm just teasing you. I respect your dedication to your projects. I've worked with more than a few architects who swing by the site on the first day, and I don't see them again until the ribbon cutting." Braxton shook his head. "By the way, Max, thanks for putting in the good word for me with the city. Now that I'm overseeing the exterior landscaping and the parking structure, that's adding a nice bonus to my pay."

Maxwell waved him off. "Mine, too. I'm getting Carmichael's share of the fee on the project. But don't mention it, man. You're one of the best guys in construction management I've ever worked with. I know you're gonna deliver."

"Well, thanks to your faith in me, I'm taking the family to Disney World this summer for two whole weeks." He extended his hand, and they bumped fists. "I appreciate ya."

Braxton walked away then, leaving Maxwell to think about their conversation. What stuck out was the last thing he'd said, about the family trip. *Could that be Yvonne, Sasha, and me in a few years? It's kind of hard to picture myself in the mouse ears, pushing a stroller through the crowd and that whole deal.* Fatherhood wasn't something he'd thought would be a part of his life until he got the wonderful gift of his sweet baby girl. Still, there were so many things in his future now that hadn't been there before, so many things he worried he wouldn't know how to do.

At lunch, he headed downtown to Pierro's Italian Bistro with a few of the guys from the site. Over delicious pasta and a heap of the restaurant's famous garlic knots, they conversed and laughed. Halfway through the meal, he got a text from Orion.

Headed through the Ville on the way back to Wilmington. Want to hang?

He tapped out a quick reply.

On the jobsite today, will be free the weekend tho.

Cool. Swing by the house & bring Lil Bit.

Will do. He smiled at the thought of Sasha playing in the sand at Orion's place near the water. *I bet she'd get a big kick out of that. Did Ines and Bianca take her to the beach before? It's unlikely since she's so young.* Tucking his phone away, he used a buttery garlic knot to sweep the remainder of the spicy red sauce from his plate.

"Hey, Mr. D. What's got you thinking so hard over there?" The question came from Jimmy, one of the leads on the construction crew.

He chuckled. "Nothing. Just thinking about taking my little girl to the beach this weekend."

Jimmy smiled. "Aw, man. How old's she now?"

"Eight months."

"Great age," someone else commented. "She'll love it."

"It's too chilly to go in the water," said another man. "Make sure you dress her in long sleeves, pants, ya know? And take a jacket."

"You gotta make sure she's got the shovel and pail, Mr. D," Jimmy interjected. "And those little plastic molds for sandcastles. My sons love building 'em."

Maxwell felt his smile broaden. "Wow, looks like I've got a whole lot of fatherly wisdom at this table. How many of you have kids?"

Of the nine men at the table, seven raised their hands.

"Best thing I ever did, Mr. D. After gettin' married, o'course." Jimmy's expression matched the happiness in his voice. "My three sons are the light of my life. Love 'em something fierce."

All the other fathers nodded, murmuring their agreement, and Maxwell knew he was in great company. He'd already respected these men, who spent long hours toiling away to bring his design from the drafting table to the real world. Knowing that they were also loving fathers, working hard to support their families, only made him respect them more.

—⁂—

Yvonne spent the latter part of Tuesday afternoon touring a potential location for her day care. Located in the small Harnett County town of Lillington, the stand-alone building was just outside the downtown historic district.

Walking through the interior one last time, she swung her phone around so that Athena, who'd video-called to be a part of the tour, could see everything. "Isn't it great, Athena? There's so much good space in here."

"It looks pretty fantastic, girl. And it's nice that the building's been remodeled recently." Athena paused. "This place is how far from the spa?"

"Forty-five minutes to an hour." Yvonne shook her head, turning the screen back around so she could see her friend's face. "Don't worry. Even after I open up, I'm still gonna come over there and bug you."

"You'd better. If you don't, there's gonna be consequences and repercussions."

Yvonne laughed. "Whatever, girl."

"Meanwhile, where's the baby? It's a weekday, so I know she's with you."

"She's asleep in the stroller." Moving the phone again, she adjusted it so the camera would show Sasha's cherubic, sleeping face, then adjusted it to show her own again. "She's got a full belly from lunch, so she was knocked out as soon as I got the car rolling. I thought she'd wake up when I put her in the stroller, but she kept right on sleeping."

Athena grinned. "She really is a good baby."

"Most of the time. I fed her lunch a little late today because I got tied up with her laundry. You wouldn't believe the fit she pitched."

Athena laughed, waving her hand dismissively. "You're right, I don't believe it. So what else is on your agenda today?"

Yvonne snapped her fingers, realizing she'd lost track of time while wandering the property. "Dang, what time is it?"

"It's almost four."

"Crap." She used one hand to steer the stroller toward the door. "I gotta go, girl. I need to make it to my parents' house in time for dinner. Max is coming over to meet them."

"Oooooh." Athena's eyes gleamed with mischief. "Girl, you know your daddy is gonna roast him over an open flame, right? And I want to hear all the details after the carnage is over."

Laughing, Yvonne shook her head. "Okay, girl. I'll call you with the tea later. Now I gotta go."

After she'd disconnected the call, she had a brief chat with the real estate agent, who'd been waiting outside. Securing Sasha in the back seat, she got into her car and got on the road.

She pulled up to her parents' house a few minutes after five. She parked on the side of the road, knowing the wide body of Maxwell's SUV would be better suited for the open spot in the driveway.

Once inside, she set down Sasha's car seat on the sofa. When the baby protested, she said, "I'll be back for you in a minute, sweetie."

"Von, come help me finish up in here," her mother called from the kitchen.

Dutifully, she answered her mother's call. In the kitchen, she helped set the table with her mother's best white lace tablecloth, silver-rimmed china, and the fancy silverware Marissa's wealthy spinster aunt had given her as a wedding gift when she married Gordon.

Holding up one of the forks, Yvonne inspected the roses carved into the handle. "Mommy, when's the last time we used this silverware?"

Marissa paused, shifting her eyes up to the ceiling for a moment. "When Zelda graduated from high school, I think."

Yvonne placed the fork in the proper spot. *Daddy might not be impressed with this situation, but if Mommy has pulled out the good silver, I've at least got a leg up with her.* She ducked outside to the car, bringing in the portable high chair she'd brought for Sasha, and set it up between her seat and her mother's. "The baby's not crazy about the high chair, so I'll wait till Max gets here to buckle her in."

A knock sounded on the door just as her mother set down the pitcher of iced tea.

"I'll get it!" Her father's voice rumbled through the house, and she could hear his footsteps as he shuffled past the kitchen's swinging door.

She and her mother walked out into the living room, standing back as Gordon opened the door. Yvonne circled around the couch, unhooking the fussy baby from her car seat. "Goodness gracious," she cooed, bouncing Sasha against her shoulder. "I left you in there too long, huh? I'm sorry, sweetie."

Maxwell stood on the front porch, holding a bouquet of flowers.

He looked so handsome, Yvonne almost sighed aloud. He must have gone home and changed after coming from work. He wore black slacks and loafers, a red button-down shirt, and a red, gray, and black striped tie.

"Good evening, Mr. Markham. I'm Maxwell Devers." He stuck out his hand.

She watched her father look him up and down for a moment before shaking his hand. "Evening, Mr. Devers. Come on in."

Maxwell entered the house, shutting the door behind him. "You can call me Maxwell."

Gordon's salt-and-pepper brow rose as he quipped, "That remains to be seen."

"Now, Gordon. Go easy on our guest." With a shake of her head, Marissa stepped forward. "I'm Von's mother, Marissa. It's nice to meet you, honey."

"Likewise, Mrs. Markham." Maxwell presented the sunny armload of flowers to her. "These are for you. Thank you for your hospitality, ma'am."

Marissa smiled, taking a sniff of the bouquet. "My word. Black-eyed Susan, daisies, and buttercups. How thoughtful. Thank you, Maxwell."

"My pleasure."

Yvonne couldn't hide her smile. *So he was listening when I talked about how my mom's garden is mostly yellow and white flowers. He gets all the brownie points for that.*

Maxwell entered her space then and leaned down to kiss her… on the cheek. While she was more than a little disappointed, she understood and didn't let it show. "Hi, Max."

"Hi, Von." He grinned as he held his arms out for his daughter. Sasha, who'd been fussing for the last few minutes, went to him with a big smile. Once she was in his arms, she immediately calmed down, snuggling against her father's chest. "Da-da, Da-da."

"Hello there, little one." He spoke softly, his face close to the baby. "I'm happy to see you, too."

Yvonne felt her heart swell at the sweet sight, and she noticed the way her mother clasped her hands in front of her and exhaled. *Mommy's eating this up, but who could blame her?* "How was your day, Max?"

"Eventful. But the project is off to a great start."

Her father moved across the living room with the aid of his cane. "Let's get on in the kitchen. 'Rissa's made her famous meatloaf, and I'm ready for a nice thick slice."

"Homemade meatloaf? Sounds amazing." Maxwell winked

at Yvonne, then followed her parents through the swinging door while she followed.

Seated around the table, they made small talk as Yvonne and her mother did the serving. Sasha entertained herself by banging her bottle on the plastic table attached to her high chair.

While Marissa filled Gordon's plate and then his glass, Yvonne took care of Maxwell's.

He stayed her hand. "You don't have to do that, Von."

She shook her head, blushing. "It's no bother at all, Max. You've been working all day." Aside from that, she knew what the house rules were. None of that "new age" stuff, as her mother called it. In the Markham household, if you had a man, you fixed his plate.

"So have you, and I know my daughter keeps you plenty busy." Maxwell reached for the pitcher since she'd already filled his plate with meatloaf, mashed potatoes, and turnip greens.

She poured the drink faster than he could stop her. Then she sat the pitcher and herself down, grinning at him. "If you wanna serve yourself, you gotta be quicker than that."

He laughed, obviously picking up on her teasing tone. "You're something else."

While Yvonne alternated between eating her own food and making sure Sasha got more mashed potatoes into her mouth than into her hair, she listened to her father conversing with Maxwell. While Gordon peppered him with questions, Maxwell answered easily, without hesitation or annoyance. Even when it seemed the question was a trick one, Maxwell never got flustered; he simply asked for clarification, essentially turning Gordon's trickery back on him. She loved his confidence, loved the way he didn't shirk answering questions but didn't answer anything he deemed too pushy or unfair, either.

"So, Mr. Devers. What are your plans for my daughter?"

She sighed. "Daddy."

Maxwell shook his head, remaining unbothered. "No, it's no

problem. It's a valid question." He looked the older man in the eye. "Sir, my intentions with your daughter are whatever she wants them to be."

A shiver ran down Yvonne's back as she remembered their love-making. He'd been bent on giving her whatever she wanted that night, for certain. His words now reminded her that she longed to return to the warmth of his bed and feel the magic of his hands moving over her skin again. *Get it together, girl. Can't be thinking dirty thoughts in front of your parents.*

"Well, isn't that a conveniently vague answer." Gordon har-rumphed. "Let's try something more direct, shall we? You plan on marrying her?"

Yvonne, still feeding the baby, covered her face with her free hand. *Looks like Daddy's loaded for bear tonight.*

Maxwell only smiled. "It was a clearer answer than you think, Mr. Markham. What I mean, very plainly, is that I'm not the one who gets to decide Yvonne's future. That's up to her. If she deems me worthy to be her husband, and yes, I will certainly ask when the time is right, I'd be honored and blessed to have her in my life forever."

Yvonne's throat twitched, and she reached for her iced tea, taking a long drink to avoid going into a coughing fit. *He's thought about marriage? With me? This is an interesting development.* And with him making declarations about her future being in her own hands, she knew he'd share her excitement about the potential day care space she'd toured. *I can't wait to tell him all about it.*

Her mother smiled. "Stop harassing this nice man. Haven't you asked him enough questions?"

Her father scratched his chin repeatedly, indicating he was in deep thought. Finally, he said, "I suppose that'll suffice." He paused. "Wait, one more question."

"Sure thing."

"Who do you like in basketball? Duke or Carolina?"

Maxwell chuckled. "Actually, neither. See, I'm a Central alum, so that's my team."

"Oh, really?" Gordon narrowed his eyes. "And you wouldn't even choose between them?"

Maxwell shrugged. "I really couldn't make an informed pick, since I only follow CIAA and MEAC games if Central isn't involved."

"All right. I guess you're all right with me. For now."

"I'll take it."

Watching the two of them shake hands, Yvonne could only shake her head. *Daddy and Max make quite a pair.*

As she helped Maxwell load drowsy little Sasha and her gear into his SUV later, she said, "I hope Daddy didn't make you uncomfortable, although you handled it pretty well as far as I could tell."

He chuckled. "Your dad's a tough one. But I'm fine. Don't worry. If my trig professor in college couldn't shake me up, nothing will." Closing the hatch, he leaned against the side of the vehicle. "He's just being protective of you, and I can totally respect that."

"Thanks for coming over and for bringing flowers for Mommy."

"Not a problem." He stifled a yawn. "We'd better get Sasha home to bed. It's getting late."

"Right. But before we head back to your place, I've got some news, and I just can't wait to tell you." She could feel the joy vibrating through her body.

"What is it?"

"I went to look at a space for my day care today. It's so nice. Recently remodeled, plenty of space indoors and out, including a nice area I can fence in and use for my playground equipment. Huge windows." She gestured, showing him how large the windows were. "Lots of natural light."

He nodded. "Sounds nice. I didn't know you were out looking for property."

The buzz of joy dimmed. She frowned, noting his stunning

lack of excitement. *I didn't expect him to jump up and down, but I expected more than this.* "Well, yeah. It's gonna be a while before I can save up enough for the down payment and three months of lease payments, but I'm on the hunt."

"Hmm." He touched his chin. "So you're really serious about doing this? And soon?"

She folded her arms over her chest. "You seem surprised. I told you from the beginning what my plans were, Max."

"It's just that..." He looked flustered, as if unsure of what to say next. "Never mind. I really need to get the baby home. I'll see you there." He turned and walked around the SUV without another word.

For a moment, she stood on the edge of the lawn, wondering what had just happened. *I don't believe this. How could he sit there and make speeches about my independence, then react like that when I make a major move toward my dreams?* She didn't want to believe he was anything like her ex, who never took her career in child development seriously.

He started the engine and pulled out, driving away without a backward glance, and she shook her head as she walked to her own car. Did he really believe the things he'd said to her father? Or was he simply telling him what he thought would make him sound clever?

As she drove away from her parents' home, one question lingered in her mind, and it made her wonder if their relationship could ever get truly serious.

I've seen two Maxwells tonight. But which one is the real one?

CHAPTER 17

When Maxwell woke up Wednesday morning, he rolled over on his left side to face the window. Rubbing his eyes, he tried to adjust them to the sunlight flowing between the drapes. After a few seconds of blinking, he realized he had a problem.

If the sun's up, I've overslept. Damn it! Why didn't my alarm go off?

He shifted around in the bed, stretching to reach his phone, lying facedown on the nightstand. Flipping it up, he looked at the screen. According to the display, he had heard the alarm…and snoozed it, four times. *Oh, for fuck's sake.* He checked the time. *Ten minutes after seven. I should be on the road by now.*

Tossing the phone aside, he scrambled out of bed and rushed to the bathroom to take a quick shower. Under the hot spray of the four nozzles, he shook off the cloak of sleep that still clung to his body. What he couldn't shake, though, were thoughts of the previous day.

He'd gone from a busy day at the jobsite to the trial by fire at the Markham family's dinner table, and he couldn't believe how eventful that single twenty-four-hour period had been. He had so much to think about, so many decisions to make.

Inside his walk-in closet, he got dressed for the day, pairing charcoal-gray slacks with a black shirt, black loafers with a gray toe box and heel, and a solid red tie. Gathering his essentials, he headed down the stairs. The enticing scent of bacon cooking wafted past his nose, and his empty stomach grumbled in response. *Tilda must be here.* He jogged down the rest of the steps, hoping she'd made something he could grab and take along with him. He knew he'd missed the golden window before morning traffic started to pick up on Highway 210, so he didn't want to linger at the house much longer.

Entering the kitchen, he found Yvonne there, standing at the stove. She'd spread dishes and other necessary items on the marble countertop next to the stove top. Sasha, seated in the high chair at the table, quietly enjoyed her morning sippy cup.

He went to his daughter and kissed her on the forehead. "Morning, Sasha. Is that yummy?"

The baby didn't answer the question verbally, but her continued, enthusiastic consumption of the cup's contents made him smile.

"Good morning." He walked nearer to Yvonne, letting his eyes sweep over her frame. She wore a long-sleeved blue T-shirt with a pair of dark denim jeans that hugged the curve of her hips. Her wavy hair, pinned into a knot low on her nape, revealed the tantalizing line of her neck. More than anything, he wanted to nuzzle the soft skin, inhale her feminine fragrance. Despite his rumbling stomach, her presence tempted a different, more primal hunger.

But taking in the tense set of her shoulders, her stiffened back, and the way she focused so intensely on her task, he thought better of it. Mindful of that, he left a bit of distance between them, watching as she flipped two slices of bacon in the skillet.

"Good morning." She gestured to the oven. "Tilda left you a sausage quiche in the oven."

"So she *is* here. Where's she now?"

"She said she was going back to her car for her cleaning caddy." Yvonne didn't look away from the food she was tending.

He walked over to the oven, removing the foil-wrapped mini quiche. "Listen, I'm late for work, so I've got to go. But before I do, can we talk for a minute?"

"Sure." She removed the bacon from the skillet, cracked an egg into a small bowl, and started scrambling it with a fork. "What's up?"

He couldn't help noticing that she still hadn't looked at him. "I just wanted to let you know, I was feeling really out of sorts last night."

She picked up the pace, beating the egg a bit harder now. "Most people feel that way after my daddy takes them to the woodshed." She set the fork aside and poured the egg into the still-sizzling skillet.

He shook his head. "As I said, your dad is definitely tough. But that's not what was on my mind."

She scooped the piping hot egg onto her plate, brought it to the table and set it next to the baby cereal. "I'm listening."

While she ate, he said, "I got a text from Bianca yesterday, saying Juliana would be coming home on R & R leave soon."

"So she wanted you to know her sister was on the way home." She took Sasha's half-empty sippy cup, pouring some formula into the baby cereal and mixing it with a tiny, rubber-coated spoon. "What's odd about that?"

"Nothing. It just…threw me a little." He grabbed a paper lunch sack from the second drawer and slipped his quiche, along with a plastic fork, inside. "I don't know how Juliana is going to react to what's going on between us."

"I don't think it matters, since you two haven't been together for a long time."

He felt his brow hitch. He didn't know how he'd expected her to react to Juliana coming home, but he hadn't expected her to be so dismissive, almost flippant about it.

She looked at the baby for a long, silent moment before feeding her a spoonful of cereal. "Sasha will probably be happy to see her mommy." Using the tip of the spoon, she scraped the cereal from the corners of the baby's mouth before feeding it to her. "She misses her, I bet."

"I hope so." He could see the sadness in her eyes. Yvonne was so caring, and he knew Sasha had won her over, big time. Now that she'd probably gotten used to being the main woman in the baby's life, he imagined it would be tough for Yvonne to share her. "Anyway, I just didn't want you to think I was being dismissive about your property thing."

She frowned. "Property thing?"

"Yes. You know, the place you talked about for your day care. It's good that you found a place you like."

She nodded, though she didn't look entirely convinced by what he said. "Okay. You can go on to work. I don't want to hold you up." She shifted her full focus back to feeding the baby.

Feeling as if he were being dismissed, he gave Sasha a kiss. Then, he leaned in to kiss Yvonne, but she turned her face at the last moment, turning his intended action into a kiss on the cheek. If he'd gotten up on time, if he had a few more moments to spare, he'd put the morning on hold for a little while longer. He'd stay. He'd ask her about the lingering tension he felt rolling off her body, about the distance that seemed to stretch between them even as they occupied the same physical space.

He stood in the doorway between kitchen and foyer for a moment. *She can be so hard to read. Where's this relationship going to go if she can't—or won't—talk to me about things that are bothering her? Doesn't she trust me?*

Not knowing what else to do, he called to her softly. "Yvonne?"

"Hmm?" She glanced in his direction while dabbing Sasha's face with a napkin.

"I love you."

Her voice wavered, thick with emotion. "I love you, too."

It sounded as if she might be on the verge of tears, but he couldn't stay. Not just because he was woefully late but because he didn't think he could bear to see her cry. So he turned and left the house, his briefcase and paper sack in hand, leaving her to her day with Sasha.

He waved to Tilda, who was hauling her wheeled cleaning caddy toward the house, as he pulled out of the driveway.

At his office, he greeted Mary Alice on the way to his personal suite. Reaching the alcove where Carson's desk was situated, he found his intern hunched over his laptop. Clad in his usual checked shirt and dark slacks, Carson typed furiously. The quick movements of his hands over the keys and the focused stare behind the reflection of the screen on his eyeglass lenses indicated he was hard at work on a document.

Maxwell cleared his throat to get the young man's attention. "Morning, Carson."

Carson glanced up, then back at the screen. When he looked up again, he stopped typing and straightened in his seat. "Good morning, Mr. D."

"What are you working on over there? Looks like you're thinking pretty hard."

"Tightening up a paper for my Construction Materials and Methods class." He frowned for a moment as if realizing his faux pas. "Sorry. You know I don't normally work on schoolwork when I'm here."

"It's no big deal." Maxwell smiled. "Things have cooled off a little since we won the Civic Center project. I'm not opposed to you taking some time to keep up with your classes."

"Thanks, Mr. D."

Seated at his desk, he unwrapped Tilda's homemade quiche and dug in. He loved the combination of flavors: the spicy breakfast sausage, the mozzarella and parmesan cheeses, the crisp red peppers and savory onions. Carson popped in with his coffee, deposited it on the corner of the desk, and exited. Maxwell took a sip, enjoying the way his favorite light roast complemented Tilda's cooking.

While he ate, he contemplated what it would mean to see Juliana again. It had been almost a year since he'd laid eyes on his ex-girlfriend. She'd deployed when Sasha was about a month old. They didn't exactly part on good terms, but because they shared a child, Juliana would be a permanent part of his life, as he would of hers, whether they liked it or not.

I doubt there will be much of the typical "catching up" small talk.

With something so major for us to hash out, there would be little time. What do you say to the mother of your child when she's spent the last six months in a war zone?

It wasn't that he maintained any romantic feelings for Juliana; those had petered out long ago. And he certainly didn't hate her, though she probably wasn't too fond of him after the way they'd parted. Whatever the case, the two of them were going to have to put their issues aside and treat each other with respect. They had to act in Sasha's best interests. It was their duty as her parents.

He crumpled the foil, tossing it into the wastebasket under his desk, along with his fork and paper sack. He had a few calls to make, then he was headed to the construction site to see work begin on the Crown performing arts building. There had been some truth in Braxton's teasing; he was a bit of a control freak when it came to the execution of his designs. Since his designs were special and very personal to him, he didn't plan on changing his ways anytime soon.

Lifting his desk phone from the cradle, he set aside his worries for later and started to dial the first number on his list.

Pushing her shopping cart through the party superstore that afternoon, Yvonne glanced around at the offerings. The tall shelves, brimming with all kinds of brightly colored plastic, seemed to touch the ceilings, making her shake her head. "Why in the world do they stack the merchandise up so high? Do they just like climbing ladders all day?"

Zelda, walking beside her, slurped on the frozen fruit punch she'd carried into the store. "I don't know, girl. While we're asking questions, though, why do you have a quilt in the cart with the baby?"

Yvonne laughed, knowing what her sister referred to. "It's not a quilt, Zelda. It's a cart seat cover, and it keeps her from touching the cart itself. These things are covered in germs. That's why I always use my cleaning wipes on them."

A chuckling Zelda replied, "Okay, Mom."

Shaking her head, Yvonne looked to Sasha for some support. "You like the cart cover, don't you, sweetie? It's nice and fluffy, right? Way better than that hard plastic seat in there."

Sasha, busy gnawing on her giraffe rattle's head, giggled in response.

Yvonne took that as validation. "See? She likes it."

"Wow, Von. You were truly destined to be somebody's mama. Unlike me, who can't even keep a potted plant alive." Zelda snorted a laugh before taking another slurp of her drink.

Still looking into Sasha's sweet, slightly drool-damp face, Yvonne smiled at the thought of being "somebody's mama," as her sister had put it. The one-on-one care she'd been providing for Sasha was the closest thing to motherhood she'd ever experienced, and she loved every moment. Every messy, confusing, hilarious, exhausting moment. "I always thought I'd have kids one day. You know, after I get my day care on really solid footing. Then, I can just bring my babies in to work with me and make sure they get great care along with the rest of the kids there."

"How's that going, anyway? Athena said you looked at a building."

"I did." Yvonne whipped out her phone and scrolled through the images she'd taken of the building's interior and exterior. "It's got everything I need, except a fence around the property and a few cosmetic changes I'd need to make inside."

"Awesome." Zelda finished the drink, tossing the empty paper cup into a nearby trash can. "So are you gonna buy it?"

Yvonne shrugged. "I've toured four or five properties, and it's the most perfect one in the bunch." Blowing out a sigh, she turned the cart into the aisle stocked with solid color plates, cups, and utensils. "I'd have to save for a few more weeks before I can make a down payment."

"Does Maxwell know about it?"

She nodded, feeling a twinge as she remembered his lack of enthusiasm for her announcement. "I told him about it last night, though he didn't seem to care that much."

Frowning, Zelda turned her way. "Sis, ain't he your man now? Because that means he's supposed to be behind your dreams one hundred percent."

"I know, I know. He says he had a lot on his mind last night." Yvonne grabbed a few of the clear crystal-look platters and added them to the cart. "I just…I'm worried I'm taking this relationship more seriously than he is."

"This is a weird position for me to be in. Usually, you're the one giving me advice." Zelda grinned. "Anyway, I'll keep it short so we can get on with the preparation for Daddy's birthday party Sunday. Be careful. Focus on what he does more than what he says, and if you get a bad vibe, bail out, girl."

"That sounds exactly like something I would say to you." Yvonne scratched her chin. "Hey, wait. I think I have said that to you!"

"Sound advice is always worth repeating, Von." Grabbing a shrink-wrapped package of orange plates, Zelda tossed them into the cart. "We should definitely get these. I'm thinking orange and white for the color scheme since orange is his favorite color."

Yvonne shook her head, amazed by her sister's ability to switch topics so quickly. In many ways, Zelda hadn't changed from the rambunctious tot she'd once been. She still flitted from task to task with ease, still managing to give everything equal care and attention. "Thanks. I'll take my own sound advice, then."

She remembered her encounter with Maxwell that morning before he'd gone out to work. She'd been hurt by his apparent dismissal of her good news, and even after his explanation, she still wasn't totally convinced she had his support. She couldn't risk giving her heart to someone unwilling to stand behind the pursuit of her most cherished dream.

Sasha bounced in the seat of the cart, and Yvonne could tell the baby was getting restless. "Let's hurry up and get the rest of the party supplies. The baby is going to want out of the cart soon."

Zelda nodded, watching the baby's excited up and down motion. "I can see that."

"Let's do orange and gold. I think that'll look better together."

"Why don't you like my orange and white suggestion?" Zelda stuck out her lips in a mock pout.

"It's not that I don't like it. I just don't think it works for Daddy's party. He's turning seventy-nine, you know?" Yvonne held up a gold plastic punch bowl, putting it next to the orange plates. "See? The orange and white are more for a kid's party. It makes me think of one of those orange ice cream bars. Gold is a little more refined and age-appropriate."

Tilting her head to the side, Zelda evaluated the choices. "Okay. I get it."

They loaded up the cart with all the essentials for the party, then went to the register to check out. While they loaded the baby and their purchases into Yvonne's car, she asked, "Daddy still doesn't know anything, right?"

Zelda shook her head. "Not a thing. Nobody's better at keeping a secret than Mommy, and she's gone out of her way to keep him busy when I needed him out of the house. The nurse has been helping out, too."

"Great." Yvonne smiled at the thought of her father's reaction when he returned from church Sunday and found all his friends waiting for him. "I just need to swing by the bakery to order his favorite cake. Red velvet with white icing."

"All right. After the bakery, we can go by my place and stash this stuff." Zelda got into the passenger seat and buckled up.

Once they were on the road, Yvonne asked, "How many people are coming to the party?"

"About twelve. Not many more will fit in the house."

She nodded. Her parents' home, while filled with love, was pretty modest. "Hmm. We could probably invite a few more folks if we move it outside to the backyard."

"True, but the weather's so unpredictable this time of year." Staring out the window, Zelda asked, "What about Maxwell? Why don't you invite him and his family? I didn't get to meet him since I had to work when he came over for dinner."

Pulling to a stop at a traffic light, Yvonne shook her head. "I don't think so, Zelda. I mean, Maxwell may come. But inviting his family is...well, probably not the best idea right now."

"Why? What's going on with them?"

By the time they pulled into a parking spot at the bakery, she'd given her sister a basic rundown of what had happened when she accompanied Maxwell to his last family breakfast. "It was a mess."

"It sounds like it." Zelda's expression conveyed her curiosity. "What did you do?"

"Nothing. What could I do?" Climbing out of the car, Yvonne went around to take Sasha out. "Oh, she's asleep. I'll just hook the car seat into her stroller frame."

"Wow. That looks way too complicated." Zelda stood by the passenger side door, gawking as her sister dealt with the baby. "Anyway, you say you didn't do anything that day. So what will you do now?"

Pushing the stroller up onto the curb, Yvonne shrugged. "I don't know that there's anything for me to do. It's not really my business."

"Yes, it is. Don't you know that old saying? When you marry someone, you marry their whole family."

Yvonne furrowed her brow. "Oh, come on, Zelda. We've only been dating a little while. I don't think we're anywhere near the marriage discussion." While she'd been impressed with Maxwell's answer to her father's questions about the direction of their relationship, she knew better than to put too much stock in what he'd said. And even if she had been thinking about marriage, the past few days' events would probably have put the kibosh on that.

"I don't know, Sis. It's bound to come up eventually."

"Nah. He's got way too much going on in his life, and when you add the family drama on top of that, he doesn't have time for serious commitments right now." Even as she said it, she felt a slight pain inside.

"Well, if it ever does come up, you'd better think long and hard before you make any decisions. I know you, and I don't think you want to be involved in that kind of drama."

"Truthfully? I don't." She entered the bakery as her sister held the door open for her. "But part of me is like, how can I judge him? Every family has a few secrets."

"That's true. But the outside child secret is about as big as they come."

She had to agree with that. Everything she'd first thought about the Devers family had been turned on its head. They'd seemed so classy, so idyllic. Now, she knew too much to keep believing they were the perfect family, but she couldn't quite identify why that bothered her so much.

The short line at the counter allowed them to order the birthday cake, schedule pickup for Friday morning, and make it back to the car in under fifteen minutes.

Back at Zelda's apartment, Yvonne held on to Sasha while Zelda moved all the party supplies inside. Sitting on the pink couch in the living room, she put Sasha down on the floor to let her get some energy out.

"She's so cute." Zelda watched the baby as she scooted across the hardwood floor on her bottom. "Does she resemble her dad any?"

Yvonne nodded. "Definitely. She has his eyes and his chin. I guess the rest was contributed by her mom." She snapped her fingers. "Which reminds me. Her mother is coming home on leave in a few days."

Zelda fell back in her recliner, clutching her chest dramatically. "Girl! You can't just be springing stuff on me like that."

"Oh, quit."

"Fine. But first, tell me this. How do you feel about…what's her name?"

"Juliana."

"How do you feel about Juliana coming back?"

Yvonne shrugged. "It will be great for the baby to see her mother, I'm sure."

Throwing one leg over the other, Zelda announced, "Yeah. But that's not what I asked you. I said how do *you* feel about it?"

"I don't feel anything, really." Why should she? Juliana's return home didn't have anything to do with her, or at least that was what she told herself.

Zelda popped her lips. "You're lying. You mean to tell me you're not worried about Maxwell and ol' girl rekindling what they had? People do that a lot when there's a baby involved."

"No, no. I really can't see that happening." Yvonne kept a watchful eye on Sasha's movements as she spoke. "I've heard him talking about her. Trust me, he doesn't have feelings for her. Not anymore."

"You say that like his are the only feelings involved here." Zelda gave an exasperated sigh. "What about her feelings? You've never met her. Who's to say she's not gonna try to get back with him and do that whole happy family thing?"

Yvonne could feel her shoulders tensing. "I don't know what I'd do. I hadn't thought about it, because frankly, it seems very unlikely."

"Hmph." Zelda leaned forward in her seat. "Let me ask you this. Did he tell you she was coming home *as soon* as he knew about it?"

"No. He told me this morning."

Zelda said nothing but gave her best "I told you so" face.

Yvonne thought for a moment. *Why'd he hesitate to tell me about it? After Bianca texted him, he could have let me know what was going on.* "It's a little weird now that I'm thinking about it."

"Von, you really think he would just come out and tell you if she might still have feelings for him?"

"Yeah, I think so. Why wouldn't he?"

"I'm not trying to be funny, really. But think about it. His daddy kept a secret from the entire family for, what, thirty years? And you don't think this man could avoid a topic with you for a few weeks?"

Yvonne blinked several times but remained silent.

"I hate to tell you this, but men lie all the time. And as for Maxwell, lying is coded into the man's genes." Zelda folded her arms over her chest. "His daddy pulled off one hell of a caper."

By the time Yvonne took Sasha home, she knew she needed answers from Maxwell. *The question is, how do I get them?*

CHAPTER 18

AT THE CONSTRUCTION SITE THURSDAY MORNING, MAXWELL went straight to Braxton's workstation to view the work that was underway. Framers had already put up the first-floor walls for the arts center, and another team had laid the concrete foundation that would serve as the first level of the four-story parking deck.

"It's really coming together, isn't it?"

Braxton turned to Maxwell, wearing a broad grin. "See? I told you there was nothing to worry about. Think you can let me take over from here?"

Chuckling, Maxwell nodded. "That was the plan from the beginning. But yes, Brax. You and your crew have got things well under control here, which will free me to handle some family business, then focus on my next building project."

Braxton's eyes narrowed slightly. "Family business?"

"Yeah. My daughter's mother is an army medic, and she'll be coming home on leave tomorrow from Afghanistan."

"I see. Well, even though I complain about you being here too much, don't forget about us, okay?"

"Never. I'll be stopping by periodically, just to check on your progress." Maxwell bumped fists with the construction manager, and after one last look at the beginnings of his most complex design to date, he strolled off toward the main trailer.

Al, with the desk phone cradled between his shoulder and his ear, held up his index finger when Maxwell entered the trailer. Taking a seat in one of the guest chairs, Maxwell quietly waited for him to finish with the phone call.

After Al hung up, he said, "Well, well. Good to see you, Mr. Devers. What brings you here this morning?"

"Hey, Al. Just wanted to stop in and let you know I'm going on vacation."

"Oh, I see. How long?"

"A week. Tomorrow until the following Friday."

"I'm jealous." Al chuckled. "If I took off that many days in a row, things around this place might just fall apart. But what can I say? It's nice to be needed."

Maxwell laughed. "Anyway, I think the job is off to a great start. I've seen everything I need to see, and I'm comfortable leaving the job to you and Braxton. I'll be stopping by now and then, just to see how things are going, but that's it."

"Got it. To tell you the truth, you're way more involved than most of the other architects I've worked with. So you're welcome here whenever you wanna stop by."

"Thanks." Maxwell stood, waved. "Keep them in line for me, Al."

Al, his eyes on the computer screen, flashed him a thumbs-up.

Back outside in the sunshine, Maxwell took one more walk around the site, offering his thanks to members of the crew. Then he returned to his SUV, got in, and drove away.

Even if the foundations weren't in, I don't think I'd have stayed the whole day today. His mind had been wandering all morning, and it always seemed to take him back to thoughts of Yvonne. It seemed like ages since they'd made love, and he knew his craving for her body, for her touch, would soon get the better of him.

Back at his office, he ran through a list of things for Carson to do while he was gone. "Keep up with my messages. Keep everyone out of my office. Make sure the new blueprints for Mrs. Dartmouth's lake house are in order. And only contact me if it's a legitimate emergency."

Scribbling on a notepad, Carson asked, "Is that all you want me to do?"

"That's it. There won't be much going on around here while I'm on vacation, so I'll be okay with you catching up on your school assignments during work hours."

Carson blew out a breath. "Thanks, Mr. D. With finals coming up, you couldn't have picked a better time to take a vacation."

Maxwell laughed, shaking his head as he went into his interior office. Seated behind his desk, he spent about an hour making phone calls and answering emails, tying up loose ends so that Carson and Mary Alice wouldn't have to deal with them. As the lunch hour approached, he locked up his office.

"All right, Carson. I'm done. See you the week after next."

"Okay, Mr. D. I hope everything goes well." Carson gave him a mock salute.

Maxwell left his office, hitting up a local burger joint for a quick lunch. His stomach satiated, he headed home to satisfy his other hunger. As he pulled out of the parking lot, sipping cola from the paper cup he'd brought with him, his phone rang.

Glancing at the dashboard display, he felt his brow crease when he saw his father's number appear there. *I should just let it go to voicemail; I don't want to talk to him. But what if the old man has taken a fall or something?* With a sigh, he tapped the green button on his steering wheel. "What is it?"

"That's how you answer the phone?" Humphrey's tone indicated his disapproval. "No 'Hello, how are you?'"

"I didn't really want to talk to you, Dad. I only answered to make sure there wasn't anything wrong."

Humphrey harrumphed. "Of course there's something wrong. I've been banished from sleeping in my own bed for the first time in fifteen years or more."

Maxwell said nothing, preferring to listen rather than rail at his father. He knew that if he got started down that path and really unleashed the bitterness and anger he felt, he'd have to pull over to the side of the road. Arguing and driving just didn't mix.

"As much as I love that leather sofa in my study, that thing is hard. It was not meant to be slept on, that's for sure."

Maxwell wanted to chuckle but refrained. "Dad, I hope you're not looking to me for sympathy." He kept his eyes on the road, refusing to let himself be distracted from getting home safely. He missed his daughter, and he'd been dreaming of Yvonne's touch all day.

"Oh, I see. So you're just like your mother and Kelsey. You think I deserve to suffer for what I did."

"We're not doing this right now, Dad." Sure, he could lecture his father about how he'd disrespected his mother and betrayed their wedding vows and how his selfishness had affected so many others. But what would be the point? "Either you understand that you did something wrong, own up to it, and make it right, or we have nothing to talk about."

"And I suppose you don't think that bearing the burden of a secret for so many long years is punishment enough, Maxwell?"

He didn't hesitate. "No, Dad. I don't."

Humphrey groaned. "Son, I just want to explain—"

"Dad, have you had a real conversation with Mom about this whole thing yet?"

"No, but I—"

"Then, with all due respect, save it."

"Maxwell! How dare you…" His father's tone grew incredulous.

"Again, with all due respect, I don't want to hear it. You need to make things right with Mom before you and I can have a conversation." He couldn't begin to imagine his mother's pain, the anguish his father's self-serving actions had caused her. "She's probably suffered more than anyone else because of what you did."

"Son, I think you're speaking out of turn here." Humphrey's voice took on that deep timbre he'd used to lecture Maxwell both when he was a teenager and on the day he'd brought his baby daughter into the house.

That wasn't going to work on him now. "Dad, I don't agree. I'm not out of line now any more than you were when you lectured me about responsibility. And you didn't seem to have any problem doing that."

Humphrey grew silent, and for a few moments, Maxwell heard nothing other than the sounds of the passing traffic.

"Fine," his father snapped and hung up.

Shaking his head, Maxwell put his full focus on driving. Highway 210 had significantly less traffic this time of day, making him think he should leave work early more often. *Now that I have Sasha full-time, I'll probably have to leave early on occasion to take care of daddy duties.*

He entered the house and found Yvonne on the sofa, sitting among a huge pile of the baby's clothes. She was dressed in a yellow V-neck tee and light-wash jeans. The aroma of the laundry detergent was strong, but nothing could conceal the familiar fragrance of the woman he loved. "Hey there."

She looked up from the tiny onesie she'd been folding. "Hi, Max. You're home early. I just put Sasha down for her nap."

"I'm officially on vacation, starting now." He came near the sofa. The cushions were barely visible, and he didn't want to sit on the clean laundry, so he stood. "I haven't taken more than two days off from work in over a year, and I figured with Juliana coming home, now's the time."

"Makes sense."

He picked up a hint of something in her voice, something he couldn't quite identify. Annoyance? Jealousy, perhaps? "How has the day been going here?"

She shrugged, continued folding. "Nothing too exciting. She seemed pretty content to stay with me most of the morning instead of crawling around the house. I read her a few books, we played with the building blocks, had a snack."

He moved closer then, scooting a small pile of laundry out of the way so he could sit down next to her. "Are you all right, Yvonne? You seem a little…distant."

Raising her gaze to meet his, she sighed. "I have my reasons, Maxwell."

"Care to share them with me?"

She shook her head. "I don't think it would be productive."

He touched her shoulder, relieved that she didn't jerk away from him. "Fair enough. But I have to be honest with you. I miss you, Yvonne."

She sucked on her bottom lip, a momentary action that nearly sent him over the edge. "I haven't gone anywhere."

"I think you know what I mean." He eased into her space, nuzzling her neck.

"I have so much more folding to do." She let her head drop to the opposite side, exposing more of her skin to him.

"I know. But the laundry isn't going anywhere." He pressed his lips to the side of her throat, tugging the fabric of her top aside a bit as he placed a line of soft kisses from there to her collarbone. He thrilled at the feel of her pulse quickening beneath his lips.

She murmured weakly, "It's the…middle of the…day…"

"Doesn't matter. Baby's asleep." He flicked his tongue over the curve of her shoulder, eliciting a sexy little groan from her throat. "I want you, Yvonne. I've been thinking about making love to you all day."

"Mmm."

"Say yes, baby." He brought his kisses up the front of her throat until their lips met. Sweeping his tongue over her parted lips, he said, "Pretty please?"

"God, Maxwell." She leaned into his kiss, and as he pulled her into his lap, he knew he had his answer.

—◆—

By the time they reached his bedroom, Yvonne could feel her entire body vibrating with desire. She hadn't been expecting him to come home so early, and he'd caught her unaware. Now, as she stood near his armchair watching him undress, she licked her lips in anticipation.

Best. Distraction. Ever.

Her senses were alive, taking in every nuance of the moment. The slivers of sunlight filtering through his drapes, the thick carpet giving way beneath her feet, and the sounds of their breathing were all parts of this experience. Yet nothing was more arresting than the sight of him baring his body for her.

He was already naked from the waist up, and he held her eyes as he undid the button at his waist. She swallowed, watching him slowly tug his slacks and underwear down, only to kick them away.

"Like what you see?" He stood before her, wearing nothing more than his male confidence and the lingering scent of his woodsy cologne.

She nodded, unable to find her voice. She was too busy enjoying the visual feast of his firm, muscled body. She could remember the last time they'd made love, and recalling just what he could do with that body sent shivers racing through her. She grazed her fingertips over his flesh, wrapped her fingertips around his thickened length.

He drew a sharp breath, took a step back. "Your turn, baby." He took a seat in the armchair, never taking his eyes off her. "Let me see that beautiful body."

She drew a deep breath, lifting her shirt up and over her head. Under his intense gaze, she stripped off her bra, jeans, and panties.

He held up his index finger, making a circling motion.

Understanding what he meant, she revolved slowly, every cell in her body aware of his scrutiny. When she faced him again, his expression had taken on a darker, more sensuous appearance. "You're so perfect, Von. I want you so much."

He pointed to the nightstand, and she retrieved a condom. Bringing it over to where he sat, she held it between her index and middle fingers. "Is this what you wanted?"

"This is what I want." He slipped his hand between her thighs, his fingertips finding the tight bud of her pleasure.

Her knees buckled and she purred. She let him play for a moment, enjoying the way his touch made her blood rush. Her core warmed, flooded with the heat he generated. Finally easing his hand away, she said, "Then let's not keep you waiting."

She moved in front of him, tearing open the packet. Rolling the condom down over his hardness, she eased onto his lap, her thighs straddling his hips.

He pulled her close, closing his lips over her nipple. While he sucked, licked, and played, she crooned for him, relishing the slick heat she felt growing between her thighs. He switched to the other nipple, lavishing it with the same attention, and her core pulsed with wanting.

She lifted her body, centering herself. Then she lowered herself, simultaneously leaning forward for his kiss. His hardness slipped inside her, filling her, stretching her, touching her in all the places she craved, and she moaned into his mouth. Their tongues mated as their bodies became one.

Her heart squeezed in her chest. She loved this feeling, the moment their two souls entwined. Nothing could match this ecstasy, this glow that began low in her belly, growing until it finally consumed her.

Yes. I want this. Consume me. She pulled back from his kiss, sucking in air. "I love…you…Maxwell…" She could barely string the words together, but they simply could not go unsaid.

"I love you." He fairly growled the words as he thrust his hips up, driving himself deeper inside her.

She let her head fall back, giving in to the rhythm. Sounds escaped her throat, sharp, high-pitched cries of passion that she barely recognized as her own, mingling with the guttural growls he made with each stroke. She shivered as his palms caressed her stomach, then her waist before he gathered her hips in his hands.

Every nerve ending in her body fired, her entire being alive with pleasure. She rocked her hips, and he matched every move. Her nails dug into his shoulders as she rode him, chasing the climax that she sensed coming on. "So close...ahhh..."

He grabbed her waist, edged them both forward on the chair. Then he began pumping his hips, his wild, fast thrusts sending them both over the cliff. She shouted his name as orgasm spread through her like a burst of light and magic, leaving her shimmering and breathless.

She fell against his sweat-slicked chest, unable to move. He cradled her in his arms, and she snuggled closer as he placed a soft kiss on the crown of her head.

"You're a very naughty nanny," he whispered, his tone teasing.

She feigned offense. "Excuse me? I was diligently working when you came in and interrupted me."

"And you loved every minute of it." He stated it as fact.

She chuckled, feeling the lightness of the moment. He'd impinged upon her day, yes, but in the best possible way. "Feel free to interrupt my work anytime you like."

"I could lie here with you like this forever, Von."

Forever? It sounded both wonderful and scary at the same time. No man had ever made her feel the way Maxwell did, and she doubted anyone ever would. She loved him; her feelings couldn't be changed or denied. But what would it mean to have a real future with him? What would he ask her to sacrifice in exchange for a life with him? *Every man has an angle, something they won't budge on. What's his?*

A part of her wanted to stay there, to enjoy the feeling of being in his arms. But she knew it was only a matter of time before Sasha woke up, if she hadn't already. "I need to get up, Max."

He groaned but released her.

She extricated herself from his lap, gathering her clothes from the floor. Hoping to get a quick shower before going to get the baby, she slipped from the room.

Later, freshly dressed and with the baby in her arms, she approached his bedroom door. As she raised her hand to knock, she could hear him snoring. Not wanting to disturb him, she turned away and took Sasha downstairs.

CHAPTER 19

Friday morning, Maxwell took Sasha from Yvonne as she headed out the front door.

"My father's surprise birthday party is Sunday, and I need to pick up his cake. The bakery's closed on Sundays, and I won't have time tomorrow." She gave him a peck on the cheek. "I'm also sure you and Juliana will need privacy so you can discuss things."

Holding his daughter close, he nodded. "Thank you, Yvonne."

After she left, he took Sasha to the blanket laid out on the living room floor and sat her down among her sea of colorful plastic toys. "There you go, sweetheart." He sat down beside her, watching as she filled her little toy purse with random objects and dumped them out, over and over. Each time she dumped the contents, she laughed and clapped, and pretty soon, he joined in. He wasn't sure he understood her game, but if it brought her joy, that was enough for him.

If Von were here, she could probably tell me all the developmental reasons why she's doing this. But he knew Yvonne was right. He and Juliana had a lot to discuss, and doing it with a third party present would make things far more awkward than they already were.

When Sasha seemed to grow bored with the toy purse, he dragged out the large plastic bin holding her soft, fabric-covered blocks. "Now, this is more up my alley. Let's do our first big construction project together, okay?"

She bounced up and down, giggling as he dumped the blocks out on the floor. Watching her play with the blocks, he thought about how, one day, she really could be working with him at the architectural firm. Would that be the path she chose? Or would she follow in her mother's boot prints to a military career? Or would she choose something else altogether? There was a certain excitement in dreaming about her future. Her possibilities were boundless, and he would see to it that she had everything she needed for a happy, successful life.

He became so enthralled in their play that the ringing doorbell startled him. Climbing up from the floor, he padded barefoot to the door and checked the peephole. A moment later, he opened the door. "Come on in, Juliana."

She entered then, giving him a wry half smile. "Max. How's it going?"

"Great. You?"

"Can't complain."

She stood in the doorway for a moment, and he took in the sight of her. She was tall and slender, her athletic frame a consequence of her physically demanding career. Her attire was all black: a T-shirt with the word ARMY spelled out across her chest in bright yellow letters, slim-fit jeans, and ankle boots. Her glossy black hair, which had been long enough to touch the small of her back when he'd last seen her, was now cut into a short, blunt bob that framed her olive-skinned face. She wore lavender contacts, but he remembered the rich brown of her eyes beneath.

Realizing she was looking beyond him into the house, he stepped aside for her to enter.

She moved past him, and as he closed the door, she made a beeline for Sasha. "There's Mama's baby girl!" She scooped the baby up, nuzzling her small body against her. Tears filled her eyes. "Oh, I missed you so much, sweetie."

Sasha babbled softly as she lay against her mother's shoulder.

"I know, honey. I know." Juliana spoke in hushed tones, her voice heavy with emotion.

Watching Juliana interact with their daughter, he felt something inside him, something he couldn't name. For so long, Juliana Morales had been his ex-girlfriend, just another woman in his past. But from the moment he'd seen her give birth, then held their child, he saw her in a different light. Things would never be the same between them; he didn't feel the love and passion for her that he once had. But there was something new in his heart for her now, a different affection. He realized it was gratitude, for the gift of his child.

Her face damp with tears, she looked his way. "She's gotten so big. Is she walking yet?"

"No. She's trying, though. Sometimes she'll stand for a few seconds before she loses her balance."

Her chest contracted as she blew out a breath. "Thank goodness. I was so afraid I might miss her first steps. Mama doesn't really understand newer phones, so she probably wouldn't have recorded it."

"We think she's pretty close."

She eyed him. "We?"

"Her nanny and I." *There's more to it than that, but it's way too soon to get into the details of that.* He crossed the room, closing some of the distance between them but still giving Juliana space. "And don't worry. If she takes a step after you go back, I'll personally see to it that you get a video."

Another tear fell, and she brushed it away. "Thank you, Maxwell."

"No problem." He gestured to the sofa. "Have a seat."

He waited for her to sit with Sasha in her lap, then sat a respectful distance away. She arranged her body in her usual position, shifting a bit on the diagonal and tucking one long leg beneath her, leaving the other leg draped over the edge of the sofa, her boot resting on the floor.

Juliana smiled as she bounced Sasha on her lap. "I see a resemblance between you. It's much stronger now than before I deployed," she remarked. "She's definitely got your eyes."

"She's got my heart, too."

Juliana smiled. "I know. We may not agree on much, but I think we can concur that our baby is about as precious as they come."

"Absolutely."

"I wanted to talk to you. You know, to thank you."

His brow creased. "Thank me for what?"

"For the way you stepped up and took over Sasha's care."

He shrugged. "I don't think I did anything special. Sasha's my daughter, and she needed me."

A wistful expression came over her face. "You've grown so much as a father, Max. You really have."

He chuckled. "I'm not sure if I should take that as a compliment or an insult."

"It's definitely a compliment." She sat back, clasping her hands together. "Your actions helped me to maintain my focus on the mission. Knowing I didn't have to worry about Sasha allowed me to do my best work."

"How did you find out about what happened to your mother, anyway?"

"The Red Cross. They contact the unit if there's any family emergency back home." She leaned forward again. "They told me that Mama was in the hospital, and Sasha was with you."

"I see." He scratched his chin. Maybe now was a good time to bring it up. "I've been thinking. Since you've got at least a few more years in the military, what do you think about letting me have full custody of Sasha?"

Juliana's brow rose. "Really? When she was younger, you said you didn't think you could handle more than joint custody."

He nodded. "I remember. Things are different for me now, though. I feel far better equipped to take care of her. And if I'm ever in doubt, I'm not raising her alone. Beyond the nanny, I've also got my parents and my sisters to help out. Hell, I'm sure even my frats would step up to help if I were in a jam."

"Oh, you mean the Wild Bunch? That's comforting." She giggled. "How are those guys doing, anyway?"

"They're good. As a matter of fact, Xavier and his wife are about to have a baby of their own."

"Awesome."

"I don't want to get too far off topic. So what do you think about me having full custody of Sasha? We could always go back to joint once you retire."

She sucked in her bottom lip, the way she always did when deep in thought. After a few moments, she spoke. "I think it makes sense. To be honest, I'm not planning on getting out any time soon."

"That's what I figured. I think this might be a good way to give Sasha some stability."

She laughed wryly. "Max, I never planned on being anyone's mama. I just wanted to climb the army career ladder. Make it to first lieutenant, go to med school after I retired." She set their squirmy daughter down on the floor.

"And you know I never planned on fatherhood, either." He had to chuckle, because it was so obvious fate had had other plans for them both. "And yet here we are. The world's most unlikely parents, with this beautiful baby girl." He gestured to the baby, who was busy banging on the keys of a small toy piano.

"I hope you don't hate me for saying this, Max." Juliana folded her hands in her lap as she looked into his eyes. "But I'm absolutely not interested in getting back together."

"Don't worry. I feel the same way."

"I still think it's important for us to be able to co-parent."

He shook his head. "I don't hate you. I can't say I'm happy about being left out of this very important loop, but I could never hate you." He watched as Sasha crawled over to him, holding up her arms to be picked up. He hoisted her into his lap, snuggling his face against the crown of her soft curls. "How could I hate you when you gave me the best gift I've ever gotten?"

She sniffled, a watery smile on her face. "Damn it, Max. Don't make me cry."

"So is that a yes? To me having full custody?"

She nodded. "There's some paperwork we'll have to do, but

hopefully the process won't be too complicated." She placed a hand on his arm. "I'm trusting you. Don't let me down, Max."

"I won't. I promise." A knock on the door caught his attention. "Excuse me." Wondering who could be visiting out of the blue on a Friday afternoon, he took Sasha with him to answer the door.

When he checked the peephole, his jaw dropped.

Yvonne stood on Maxwell's porch, waiting for him to open the door. She'd passed an unfamiliar car on the way up to the door, a sleek royal-blue four-door with out-of-state plates. She could only assume the car belonged to Sasha's mother.

While he'd given her a key, she knew better than to just walk in. *He and his ex have some serious matters to discuss, and I wouldn't want to barge in on them while they're talking. Or whatever.*

She knocked again, in case he hadn't heard her the first time. Maybe they'd gone into his office to talk? Or out on the back patio? It was a nice enough day for it; the temperature had already climbed to near seventy degrees.

There were all kinds of things they *could* be doing, but she didn't want to think about that. *Get your mind right, Yvonne.*

Finally, the door swung open. He stood there, dressed in the same black sweats and green TDT tee he'd been wearing earlier, and she felt a modicum of relief. *Why am I even thinking that? I don't have any reason to think he's still attracted to her. But what if she still has feelings for him?* "Yvonne. What brings you back? I thought you were gone for the weekend?"

She smiled, hoping he couldn't read the discomfort on her face. "I did, too. But I left my dang phone. I think it's still upstairs on my bedside table."

"You could have used your key." He stepped out of the way so she could come in.

She hesitated, wishing she could see around him well enough to know what she was walking in on. "I didn't want to interrupt anything." She swallowed.

"We're just sitting in the living room, talking." He studied her for a moment, his eyes slightly narrowed. "You can come in now, Von."

She clutched her purse handle, stepping inside the house. She heard him close the door behind her as she walked into the foyer. Halfway to the staircase, she glanced into the living room. She smiled at Sasha, playing on the floor with her toy piano. Another person inhabited the space as well, her dark hair and clothing a stark contrast to Maxwell's mostly white living room.

At that moment, the visitor glanced her way. A razor-cut bob framed a beautiful, brown-skinned face. *A familiar face.*

Yvonne stopped in her tracks, her purse hitting the floor with a thud. "J-Rock? I mean...Juliana Morales?"

Juliana sat up straight, then stood. "I recognize your face." She paused, frowning as if trying to recall. "I'm sorry. I don't remember your name."

Yvonne released a dry chuckle. "There's no reason you should. But we went to high school together at DSA." Why would Juliana Morales, the tall, gorgeous track star, remember the nerdy, quiet girl who'd been more interested in reading than going to pep rallies and dances? *She's even more beautiful now. When Maxwell told me his ex was in the military, this is the last thing I expected.*

"So you two know each other?" Maxwell's wide-eyed stare communicated his surprise.

"Just barely," Yvonne replied.

"Oh, wow. It's pretty rare for me to run into anybody from high school." Juliana blinked a few times. "Nice to see you again..."

"Yvonne. Yvonne Markham."

Juliana snapped her manicured fingers. "Right, right. So... Yvonne, you're Sasha's nanny?"

Drawing a deep breath, hoping to force out the humiliation building inside, Yvonne nodded. "I am."

"Wow." Maxwell shook his head. "Small world, huh?"

"Indeed." Her throat tightened. "If you'll excuse me, I just need to get my phone." Without waiting for a response, she jogged up the staircase and hurried into her room. Closing the door behind her, she leaned against it and took several deep, cleansing breaths.

Juliana Morales...is Maxwell's ex. Juliana friggin' Morales is Sasha's mother. If ever she could be knocked over with the proverbial feather, this was that moment. Juliana hadn't bullied her or anything like that during high school. Like many of the other pretty, popular girls, she'd simply dismissed Yvonne, ignored her very existence. Yvonne could remember watching Juliana and her girl squad back then. They were the glamorous upperclassmen, athletes, and cheerleaders, already wearing makeup and the latest fashions. Juliana, nicknamed J-Rock, had one of the fastest set of legs on the entire track team and was a beast at the races. She led the pack of girls like a queen with her court.

Meanwhile, Yvonne was the awkward freshman, still wearing candy-flavored lip gloss and constantly getting lost on Durham School of the Arts' sprawling historic campus. She got a few new outfits at the beginning of school, and those had to last her through the entire year. Everything about Juliana's squad had seemed so out of reach. Seeing Juliana now, with her perfect hair, perfect body, and perfect face, brought back all those old insecurities, old feelings of inadequacy Yvonne thought she'd outgrown.

Well, if she wants him back, I'm screwed. She knew she was no slouch, but she wouldn't be taking up a second job as a swimwear model, either. Competition for a man like Maxwell didn't get any stiffer than the tall, leggy, raven-haired beauty of Juliana Morales.

She took a few more deep breaths, and once she felt a little calmer, she started moving around the room, looking for her phone. She didn't see it on the nightstand or any other visible surface. Squatting down, she found it on the floor in the narrow space between her queen-size bed and the nightstand. Pocketing it, she slipped out of the room and into the hallway.

She could hear their voices downstairs, so she stopped and listened. *I know I shouldn't be eavesdropping on them, but what's a girl to do?* She had to know what was going on down there, but she didn't want to actually *go* down there. Not yet.

So she took a seat on the top step. She could hear them going back and forth about custody arrangements.

Haven't heard her mention getting back together so far. Maybe I'm worried over nothing.

Footsteps sounded on the stairs, and she scrambled to her feet. Dashing a few steps down the hall, she ducked into the guest bathroom. Inside, she pushed the door up but didn't close it all the way and turned on the water, as if she'd been in there washing her hands. After a few seconds, she turned off the water and opened the door, returning to the hall.

Juliana stood there, carrying Sasha. Maxwell was close behind her.

"I wanted to see Sasha's room," Juliana said.

"Why don't you give Jules a tour, Von?" Maxwell walked past her to Sasha's room and pushed the door open.

"Sure."

Moments later, all four of them were inside the nursery. Juliana placed Sasha on the brightly colored rug and turned slowly as if taking in the room's decor. "Wow. This is really lovely."

Yvonne gestured to the sky-blue paint, floral-patterned curtains, and the colorful butterflies. "I painted the wall, but the butterflies are decals. And I bought those wooden letters that spell out Sasha's name at the craft store and decoupaged them myself." She paused. *Oh boy. Am I bragging about my design skills to J-Rock Morales, as if I have something to prove to her? What's the matter with me?*

"Wow. It's amazing." Juliana touched her forearm. "Thank you for giving my daughter such a beautiful space."

"It's no problem. She deserves it." Yvonne looked down at Sasha, crawling around the adults' feet. "She's one of the sweetest babies I've ever had the pleasure of caring for."

"That's good to hear. My mama and sister said the same thing, that she's a good baby." Juliana smiled down at her daughter. "I'm glad she has someone so caring to look after her."

Yvonne smiled, taking the compliment at face value. There was nothing about Juliana's expression or body language that made her think she was being insincere. *I think I've been selling Juliana too short. She wasn't mean to me, just oblivious.*

"So how are you going to be spending your leave, Jules?" Maxwell asked.

"I'll be getting a few things done around the house, making sure my bills are paid up until the end of the year when my deployment's supposed to end." Juliana shrugged. "You never know when command could hit you with an extension. But mostly, I'm looking forward to spending time with my little *mijita*." She squatted down then, giving Sasha's cheek a gentle pinch. "I just can't believe how much she's grown."

Wanting to know more about Juliana's life now, Yvonne said, "Maxwell told me you're an army medic. How long have you been in the service?"

"I joined up right out of high school, so about eighteen years. Went to college on Uncle Sam's dime, got my bachelor's degree in biochemistry. I'm a warrant officer with the 261st MMB now."

"Wow. I bet you've traveled all over." Yvonne leaned against Sasha's crib, listening. She noticed Maxwell had sat down in the rocker and appeared similarly interested in what Juliana was saying.

"Yeah. I've been to South Korea, Alaska, Germany. Always end up back at Bragg, though." Juliana rubbed her hands together.

"I'm hoping this is my last deployment. I was going to stay in for twenty-five years. But I'm so close to my twenty now, and I may go ahead and take my retirement and get my medical board certification before Sasha gets too much older."

"What would you do with your medical degree, Jules? Hospital? Private practice? What specialty?"

"Well, Max, I'd probably do private practice, since I've done pretty much all my work in a hospital setting. Specialty wise, I'm thinking about going into family practice."

Yvonne nodded, taking in all this new information. Juliana seemed like a very conscientious person, a good mother who'd taken her child into consideration while planning her future, even if that meant a departure from the path she'd originally set out on. It was a good sign, and it made Yvonne happy that both Sasha's parents were ready to make the right adjustments to ensure their daughter's well-being.

"Maxwell, would you mind if I spoke to Yvonne alone for a moment?"

He looked back and forth between the two of them. "I mean, I'm okay with it. Yvonne, are you?"

"Sure." Yvonne waved her hand dismissively as she grabbed the baby's bag from the closet doorknob. "I'll pack up some of Sasha's things while we chat."

He stood and, after one more glance between them, slipped from the room, shutting the door behind him.

Alone in the room with Juliana, Yvonne opened the dresser drawers and began sifting through the piles of neatly folded onesies. "Before you start, how long do you plan on keeping Sasha with you? That way, I'll know how much to pack for her."

"About eight days. I'll need the rest of the time for errands." Juliana sat down in the rocking chair, and Yvonne could feel the former track-star-turned-doctor's eyes on her back. "Yvonne, can I ask you a personal question?"

Yvonne could feel the knots of tension forming in her shoulders. "Sure thing," she answered in a tone far more confident than she actually felt.

"Are you and Maxwell...a thing?"

She swallowed, stuffing clothing haphazardly into the bag. Not only had Juliana asked her the very question she'd been dreading, but it was also an indication that Maxwell hadn't already told his ex that they were involved. The question was, why? Had it not come up in their conversation? Or was he simply hiding it from her? "Yes, I guess you could say we are."

"Cool." Juliana paused. "Don't be worried that I'll ask for details. I know it's not my business."

That's a relief. I'm certainly not about to go into all that with his ex-girlfriend. "Can I ask you something, too?"

"Fair enough."

Closing the top drawer and opening the second one, which held the baby's bottoms, Yvonne drew a deep breath. May as well be straight with her. "Are you interested in rekindling your relationship with Maxwell?" She turned around, wanting to see Juliana's expression when she answered.

"Oh, honey, no." Juliana chuckled for a moment, then sobered up. "I'm sorry, I don't mean to make light of this. But Max and I weren't compatible then, and that remains the same now. I'm only going to be a part of his life as it pertains to Sasha. Trust me, it's not going to go any further than that."

Whew. Yvonne nodded, exhaled that pent-up breath she'd been holding, and turned back to the dresser to load the bag up with tiny pairs of pastel leggings and socks.

"There is something I think you should be aware of though. About Maxwell."

"What's that?"

"It may not be an issue for you if you don't have any other children you look after."

Yvonne shook her head. "No, I don't have any other charges, I work for Maxwell full time. But I'm saving up to open my own child development center."

"Oh."

Yvonne frowned, hearing the change in Juliana's tone. After tossing in two pairs of Sasha's sneakers, she zipped the bag and turned around. The look she saw on Juliana's face was…concerning. She was smiling, but it was the weird, strained sort of smile a person wore after they saw someone get stuck in a revolving door or walking up a down escalator. "Um, care to elaborate?"

"Well…" Juliana pursed her lips for a moment. "Maxwell likes the woman in his life to be all about him. He was never a fan of my military career. He missed my promotion ceremony when I made first sergeant, and at the time we broke up, he'd been hinting for months that he wanted me to get out of the service."

Yvonne turned that over in her mind. "Military service is dangerous. Maybe he was just concerned for your safety?"

Juliana shrugged. "If he was, he never said so. He was always going on about how I never had time for him, never shared his interests. The night we broke up, he asked me straight out not to reenlist. When I refused, he walked."

Yvonne stood silently, her grip tightening around the strap of the baby bag. Everything Juliana recounted directly reflected his attitude when she talked about her day care center. *Is this who Maxwell is? Someone who can't support another person's dreams unless they conveniently fit into his plans?*

Juliana stood then. "Listen. I could be totally off base here, and I'm not trying to get between you two. Like I said, Max and I are not getting back together, so I don't have a dog in this fight. My main concern is that Sasha has a stable environment when she's with her father."

"I get it," Yvonne said. And she did. But this conversation had left her with so many questions, and only Maxwell could give her the answers.

"Well, let's go, baby." Juliana bent and picked up Sasha, then shouldered the baby bag as Yvonne handed it off to her. "Say bye-bye."

Sasha waved, opening and closing her fist with it facing the wrong way.

Yvonne laughed. "I'll see you later, sweetheart."

"Nice talking to you, Yvonne." Juliana opened the door.

"Same here."

As Juliana disappeared down the hall with the baby, Yvonne stood in the silence of the empty room.

What now?

CHAPTER 20

FOR THE FIRST FEW MINUTES AFTER BEING BANISHED downstairs in his own house, Maxwell didn't know what to do with himself. *My ex-girlfriend and my current girlfriend, alone in a room, talking? There isn't a man alive who could be comfortable in this situation, at least not one I know.* It was certainly not the way he'd planned on spending his Saturday.

When he got tired of wearing a trench in his hardwood floors, he went to his office. The small room, just beneath and to the left of the main staircase, was his little oasis. He'd kept the décor simple so as not to inhibit his creativity on those rare days he worked from home. The walls, painted a soft shade of gray, played host to a series of black-and-white photographs of his past projects: homes, stores, warehouses, and schools. White steel floating bookcases lined the opposing walls to the left and right, filled with a mixture of architecture books and mystery titles. His white fiberglass drafting table centered the space and could be adjusted to lie flat if he needed to use it as a desk. An ergonomically padded stool sat behind the table. There was no other furniture in the space, save for the window seat in the small window niche behind the drafting table.

Shut inside the room, he flopped down on the window seat cushion and pulled out his cell phone. *I might as well make good use of my time in exile.* He dialed, then held the phone to his ear.

"Hello?"

"Jeff, it's Max. How are you, man?"

A deep sigh met that question. "I'm doing okay, considering."

Maxwell chuckled. "Same here."

"So I guess the raccoon's out of the suitcase, huh?"

Maxwell laughed again. Nobody could bend a phrase like his old friend. "You've always had a weird sense of humor, Jeff. But yes, we all know about it now."

"It's a mess, isn't it? After a whole thirty-four years on this earth, thinking my father died in a motorcycle accident." Jeffrey scoffed. "I always looked up to Mr. D, you know? I thought he was just a kindhearted neighbor, looking out for a fatherless kid."

Maxwell could hear the pain in Jeffrey's voice, and it mirrored his own. Coming to grips with his father's selfish actions was going to take time, and he knew he wouldn't even entertain full forgiveness until his father had made things right with his mother. "I bet. I love my father, and that's not going to change. But his actions were pretty heinous, and he's gotta be accountable for what he did."

"I'm with you there," Jeffrey remarked. "He'd come around, bring me toys, take me to museums and all that jazz." He sighed. "I just hate the way I grew up, feeling that loneliness of being an only child. All I wanted in the whole world was a brother. Mr. D and my mom, they took that away from me."

Maxwell rubbed his temples. *They took that away from both of us.* "I'm truly sorry."

"It's not your apology to make, Max."

"Trust me, I know. And I would never discount what you went through. But you're not the only one who wanted a brother."

"Really?" Jeffrey sounded surprised.

"Yes. When Dad wasn't home, I was stuck in a house full of girls, you know? Now, I'm not above tea parties and dress-up. But what I really wanted was a brother. Somebody to run the streets with, somebody who didn't mind getting dirty and getting a few bruises."

"Same, man." Jeffrey paused. "But you know something? If you think about it, we had that bond with each other. I came down to your place all the time to play, at least up until y'all moved away. All that was really missing was knowing the truth, that we were really blood brothers, not just playmates."

Gazing out the window into the hazy sunshine, Maxwell reflected on those memories. "You're right, Jeff. Those Saturdays riding bikes, playing in the creek, catching frogs and bugs, they mattered. They enriched our lives. We did...the things brothers do. And we did them together."

"And if I could choose anybody to be my brother, Max, it would have been you. I'm glad it's you."

"Same here, Jeff." Maxwell's chest tightened with emotion. A childhood longing of his had just been fulfilled, in the most unlikely and unconventional way. His mother's pain was palpable, and his family had been shaken to the core. Still, he'd take this circumstance, this blessing that had bloomed in adversity. "I'm honored to call you my little brother."

"Hey, I'm only eleven months younger than you." Jeffrey feigned offense. "Plus, I'm a grown-ass man."

Maxwell chuckled. "Doesn't matter. Even if you were born a few minutes after me, and even when we're both old and shriveled up, I'm still the oldest. Therefore, the 'little' descriptor stands."

"It's all good. I figure nothing's really changed about our relationship. We're still gonna hang out, still gonna look out for each other. The only real difference is, if one of us needs a kidney or something, the other one might be able to help out."

Maxwell nodded. "True, true. Although since you're the youngest, that makes you the most likely to have to part with an organ, dude."

"Whatever, man. Hey, listen. I wanted to ask you a favor."

"Look, if you're already about to ask me for an organ, Jeff, you better pump your brakes."

Jeffrey's laughter filled his ear. "You're such a clown, Max. You know that's not what I'm about to ask you."

"In that case, shoot."

"Well, my wedding's coming up in September, and..."

Maxwell smiled at his own reflection in the window. "That's

right. I haven't seen you in a while, and I never got to meet your lady. What's her name?"

"Her name is Kiley, and I definitely want you to meet her." Jeffrey's voice held a mixture of affection and excitement. "She's the best thing to ever happen to me, and I can't wait to call her my wife."

"Well, if she's that great, I need to meet her ASAP, Bro."

"You will. I promise." There was a pause before Jeffrey spoke again. "Listen, Max. Would you consider being a groomsman at our wedding? I'd really appreciate if you could be a part of my big day."

Maxwell gripped one of the paisley pillows near him. "Jeff, for real? Are you serious?"

"Absolutely. Will you do it?"

Maxwell shook his head, his jaw hanging open for a second. "Wow. I'm just so flattered you'd ask me, but yes. I'll definitely join the festivities, Jeff."

"Great. I'll be in touch with the details about fittings and all that. Kiley wants us in cream suits."

"Cream?" Maxwell felt his lips stretch thin at the thought. *There's a reason I only wear dark suits.* "A broad-shouldered guy like me in a light-colored suit? I only end up looking like one of two things: a dyed Easter egg or a half gallon of milk."

"Oh yeah. I remember that suit you wore to your senior prom. That was definitely more on the Easter egg side." Jeffrey snorted. "Man, how did your date convince you to wear a baby-pink tux?"

Maxwell blew out a breath, shaking his head at the memories. "Let's just say she had a very convincing argument. Whew, boy. I must really love you to be agreeing to this, man."

"It's mutual, Max. I'm glad you called me."

"Thanks for talking to me. I'm in a sticky situation, and talking to you bailed me out of a bad mood."

Jeffrey's tone changed. "Really? What's happening?"

"Oh, nothing. Just my ex and my next, upstairs talking about me in my own house."

"Max, why ain't you in the room with them, trying to direct the verbal traffic?" Jeffrey cleared his throat. "The last thing you want in a situation like this is a catastrophic crash, if you know what I mean."

Maxwell ran a hand over his head, feeling the stress of the moment rise again. "I know exactly what you mean, and I would have stayed, but they kicked me out."

"Both of them?"

"No. It was Jules, my ex, who asked me to leave. Von just didn't put up much protest."

"Damn, Bro." Jeffrey laughed. "I don't mean to make light of your misfortune, but damn. I'm gonna pray for you."

"Please do." Maxwell shook his head, watching a bright red cardinal flit by the window. "I have no idea what they're talking about, so I'll take all the help I can get."

"I'll let you go, Bro. You better make sure they're not plotting your demise."

After Maxwell hung up the phone, he slid down from the window seat and crossed the room. Standing by the door, he cracked it a bit, listening. He didn't hear voices anymore, but he did hear someone's footfalls on the stairs. He smiled wryly. *If one of them is leaving, maybe it's safe to go out.*

When he entered the foyer, he saw Juliana standing there with Sasha on her hip and the baby bag over her shoulder, peering into the living room. When he approached, she turned his way.

"Oh, there you are. We're headed out."

"Okay. Do you have everything you need for her?"

She nodded. "Sure. Yvonne packed plenty of clothes, and I have bottles, bibs, formula, baby food, all that stuff at my place." She bounced the baby. "So you're looking at eight days of kid-free tomfoolery, Max."

"I've matured since you saw me last. I've come to enjoy and appreciate Sasha's little baby shenanigans." He stuck his hands in his pockets. No matter how much he'd miss his daughter, he refused to let Jules see him pouting. Instead, he walked over and kissed the baby's soft cheek. "Be good for Mama, okay? I'll see you in a few days."

Sasha smiled at him, her big brown eyes twinkling. Then she turned her little hand up and touched his face. "Da-da."

It was all he could do not to melt into a puddle of paternal goo right there in the foyer.

After Juliana and Sasha had gone, he stood at the bottom of the stairs, looking up toward the second floor. *What's Von doing up there? Is she ever coming down?* When she'd showed up at the door, she said she forgot her cell phone. But when he was upstairs with them, before Juliana kicked him out, he'd seen her phone sticking out of her pocket. *So what on earth is she still doing up there?*

As if on cue, he heard a door open. She appeared at the top of the stairs then, but she looked right past him. Jogging down the steps, she turned slightly and edged by him into the kitchen without acknowledging him at all.

He stood in the foyer, watching as she grabbed a bottle of water from the fridge. She walked out with it, looking as if she were going to pass him again without a word. This time, he lay down across the third step. "Von? What is going on?"

"Maxwell, can you move, please?"

Oh, boy. Here we go with this salty attitude again. "Why are you acting like this?"

"Like what?" She folded her arms over her chest, her lips pressed tightly together as if he were inconveniencing her.

"Like that. Closed off, having an attitude. Acting as if I'm not even in the house."

She rolled her eyes. "I'd like to go by, please."

"What did y'all talk about up there? Did Jules say something to you about me?"

"Move, Max, or I'm going over you."

He started to sit up. "Von, look..."

She blew out a breath, swung her leg up and over his body, taking her from the ground level to the fourth step. The move treated him to a view of her shapely inner thighs, but he sensed he wouldn't be enjoying them today. Without a backward glance, she jogged up to the landing and stalked away. Seconds later, he heard her door slam.

Rubbing his open hand over his face, he groaned.

If it ain't one thing, it's another. Why do women have to make love so hard?

But could he really blame her? After all, he'd given in to her charms, let himself lean into the attraction sparking between them. He'd done it willingly, even though he knew he'd end up in a situation just like this. Frustrated, confused, and wondering how he got there.

Still, he couldn't let it go. *Guess I'm a glutton for punishment.* Climbing to his feet, he trudged up the stairs.

⁓

With her gym bag open on the bed, Yvonne busied herself by tossing the contents from the dresser into it. After the conversation with Juliana and the events of the preceding week, it was clear that Maxwell lived in his own little world, and he couldn't tolerate anyone coming along to change his neatly ordered life.

How could I have let myself be drawn in? It was so stupid of me.

Her jaw stiffened when she heard him knocking on her door. At first, she ignored him.

"Yvonne, please. Let's talk about this."

Hmph. I don't wanna hear it. "Go away, Maxwell." Done with the clothes in the drawer, she went to the closet and flung the doors open. Snatching sweaters and pants off the hangers, she tossed them into a pile on the bed.

"I'm not leaving, Yvonne. I'll just sit outside the door until you open it, and you've gotta come out sometime."

He was right, and that annoyed her to no end. With a sigh, she went to the door and opened it.

He climbed up from his seat on the floor outside and entered. "Thank you."

Going back to the bed, she pulled a second bag from beneath it and tossed it down next to the pile of clothes from the closet. "Say what you have to say, Maxwell."

"So formal?"

She shrugged. "It's how you asked to be addressed when you hired me, isn't it?"

His brow furrowed. "Yes…but things have changed since then."

"Have they?" She gave him a pointed look before turning her attention back to packing.

He sighed. "I didn't just come up here to talk. I also came to listen. I want to know what's bothering you, Von."

"That's Yvonne, if you please. Or Ms. Markham."

He blew out a breath. "For fuck's sake, Von."

She could tell his hackles were up, but she didn't care. *I'm not in the wrong here. I have a right to protect myself, to self-preservation.* "I don't have anything to say, so why don't you just go ahead."

He sat in the rocking chair, glowering like a five-year-old denied a cookie. "Let's be honest here. It doesn't matter what I say, it's gonna be wrong. So why don't you just answer one question for me."

"Fine." She tucked the last pair of slacks into the second bag and zipped them both.

"What did she say to you?"

She shook her head. "What makes you think it's something Juliana said? And how is our conversation any of your business?" If Juliana had wanted to discuss his flaws in his presence, she wouldn't have asked him to leave.

"Because ever since she left, you've been closed off to me again." He rocked the chair, shaking his head. "After we made love last night, I thought we'd gotten past that. But now we're right back where we started."

"Making love doesn't magically fix everything, Maxwell." She sat down on the bed, her body slightly turned away from him.

"I know that, Yvonne. That's why I'm asking you what's wrong. I can't fix a problem I can't identify."

She looked at the bedroom door, the carpet, the ceiling. Anything to keep from looking into the dark pools of his eyes. Knowing what she knew, looking at him simply hurt too much.

"So you're not going to say anything?"

She responded with more silence.

He sighed. "Come on, Yvonne. I know she didn't sit here and tell you we're getting back together, because that sure as hell isn't going to happen."

She shook her head, still avoiding his gaze. "No, Maxwell. She doesn't want you, and she made that quite clear."

His frustration evident, he said, "Then I don't get it. Help me understand, Yvonne. Because I'm lost."

Finally, she turned his way. She looked at his mouth instead of into his eyes. "Did you ask her to get out of the military, Maxwell?"

His gaze shifted to the left, then back to center. "Yes. Right before we broke up."

He admitted it. Now let's find out the root of that request. "Why, then? Why were you so insistent that she give up her career?"

He rested his elbows on the rocker's arms, tented his fingers. "Military life is too unpredictable. Juliana was hardly ever around. There always seemed to be some work thing she had to do, training to attend, trips she had to take. It was a lot to deal with."

She felt her lips tighten, remembering Juliana's words from earlier. *If he was concerned about my safety, he never mentioned it to me.* She shook her head. *Does he have any idea how selfish he sounds right now?* "Let me ask you something else, Maxwell. Before Juliana, how many other serious girlfriends did you have?"

He rested his head in the crook of his right hand. "Oh, come on, Yvonne. What are you getting at?"

"Just answer the question, please."

He groaned. "Three. I had three serious girlfriends before her."

"And how did your relationships end?"

He closed his eyes, his chin jutting forward. "Let's see. Since you wanna go through the annotated history of my love life, Cynthia was first, and she moved to New Jersey for a promotion. We broke up because I didn't want to move with her. Next was Liz, who I broke up with when she got accepted into law school at Cambridge. Last, there was Amy. I had an important business dinner with a client, and I was expecting her to be there. Instead, she covered a shift for someone and didn't take the time to inform me. I ended up with egg on my face at the dinner, we argued, and she left."

"Where did Amy work?"

He shrugged. "At a pharmacy and as a volunteer firefighter. It was a pharmacy shift she took that night, though."

"Ugh, Maxwell." She crinkled her nose. *Forget all the elderly and sick folks who needed medication that night. He had an important social event, and she ruined it.*

"What?" He tilted his head, watching her through narrowed eyes. "I don't see what you're getting at."

"Of course you don't." She stood then, grabbing her bags, and headed for the door.

"Wait. Can you just explain it to me, since I'm obviously missing the point here?"

She blew out a breath, stopping in the doorway. "Maxwell, can you name one time, just one, where you were there for your girlfriend when it came to her career? Her professional accomplishments?"

He opened his mouth, then closed it. Tipping the rocker back, he looked up at the ceiling.

She stood there, tapping her foot on the carpet, saying nothing.

Several long, silent moments passed by before he spoke again. "Can you give me an example?"

Feeling her shoulders slump, she shook her head. Hoisting the bags, she left the room and went down the stairs. He followed her.

She ignored him.

At her car, she opened the trunk and tossed the bags inside. As she turned toward the driver's side door, he stood in front of her.

"Maxwell, trust me. You don't want to keep playing this game with me, where you block my path."

He stepped aside. "Yvonne, please. I just want—"

"That's just it, Maxwell! It's all about you and what you want. It always has been, hasn't it?"

He blinked a few times, then took a step back. "That's not true, Yvonne."

"Yes, it is." She felt the tears gathering in her eyes and cursed every one of them. She didn't want him to see her cry, didn't want him to see how much he'd hurt her. "When have you ever gone out of your way for a woman? I mean really, Maxwell, when have you ever truly supported her dreams?"

"I've…I've never stood in anyone's way, Yvonne. I wouldn't do that."

"That's not the same thing, and you know it." She opened the car door, placing it between her body and his. "Face it, Maxwell. You just can't get behind a woman's dream. Not when it doesn't fit into your own convenient little life plan."

"Yvonne, please." There was a sadness in his eyes that tugged at her heart.

"I'll keep working for you, at least until you can hire someone else to look after Sasha, but that's all I can promise you."

"Look, you've gotta listen to me. Just…"

There was nothing he could say, nothing that would change her mind. "It's over. We're not a couple anymore."

"Don't say that!"

She steeled herself against the searing pain as best she could. *I have to be strong now, strong enough to walk away before he destroys me.* Shaking her head, she got into the car and closed the door "I can't do this, Maxwell. I've already been with a man who didn't believe in my work, who stopped taking me seriously the moment my work didn't benefit him." She blinked away the tears clouding her vision as she started the car. "I won't do that to myself ever again."

His jaw was tight. "If that's really what you think of me, why am I even standing here?"

She shrugged, ignoring the tears rolling down her cheeks. "I don't know, Maxwell. But I'm sure you don't want your wealthy neighbors to witness the drama happening in your driveway. So I'm leaving." Putting the car in reverse, she backed up a bit so she could clear the curb. Then she drove off down the long, winding driveway.

Looking in the rearview mirror through the haze of her tears, she saw him still standing there.

She drove on until he was out of sight, then left his home, his neighborhood, and his selfishness behind her.

CHAPTER 21

SUNDAY, MAXWELL RECLINED ON A LOUNGE CHAIR, LETTING the midmorning sun beat down on his weary body. Wrightsville Beach had very little foot traffic today, typical of an early March day when the water was still too cold for swimming or surfing. The umbrella over his head, along with the sunglasses he wore, protected him from the glare, while a white tee and track pants protected his skin from the cool breeze coming off the water. His feet dangled off the sides of the lounger, and he could feel the chilly grains of sand that had infiltrated his closed-toe sandals but couldn't be bothered to do anything about it.

"Max!"

"Huh?" He heard his friend calling his name but didn't look toward the sound.

Orion snapped his fingers three times in quick succession. "Bro, do you want me to just dangle this beer at you, or are you gonna take it?"

Returning to reality, Maxwell took the bottle of Corona from Orion's hand. "Thanks, man." He looked at his friend, seated on a matching lounger to his left "Sorry about that, O."

Orion shook his head. "Yeah, man. I'd say 'sorry' is a pretty good descriptor of your mood. What's the matter with you?"

Maxwell cracked open the bottle, taking a long swig before answering. "I'm disappointed I didn't get to bring Sasha with me this time. I was looking forward to having a little fun with her, you know?"

Nodding, Orion looked out over the water. "Yeah, I can understand that. I'm sure li'l shorty would have had a great time playing out here."

Maxwell smiled, picturing her sitting in the sand. "I even bought her the little toys for digging in the sand and building castles, the whole nine. The guys at the Crown site told me all the stuff she'd probably like, and I've got a boatload of it in the back of my ride. I'm kinda sad she didn't get to come out here and use it."

"Yeah, I get it. But you know y'all are welcome to come down here and crash at the condo, like, whenever." Orion turned up his own bottle of beer, taking a deep swallow. "It's not like this weekend was your one and only shot to get some beach time in with her."

"I appreciate the open invite, O. And trust me, I'm definitely going to bring her down here the next chance I get."

"Good deal. And now that we established your intentions pertaining to getting the youngster some quality beach time, you can tell me what's really got your face all screwed up." Orion lifted his arms above his head and spread them wide, gesturing to their surroundings. "You're on the beach, man. It's a beautiful day. The sun is shining, the birds are singing, the waves are crashing." He swung one arm around, pointing at him. "And then there's you, sitting here looking like somebody kicked you in the shins and stole your lunch money."

Maxwell sighed. *That's the one downside to the close relationship I share with my line brothers. They might know me a little too well.* "I don't wanna talk about it, O."

Orion scoffed. "Well, tough cookies, bro. You can't come down here pouting that hard and expect me not to ask you about it." He sat sideways on his lounger, folding his arms over his chest and eyeing him pointedly. "So what's the damn problem, Max?"

Maxwell closed his eyes, inhaled. *It's obvious O ain't gonna let this go.* "It's Von. We broke up."

"Damn! You managed to fuck it up that quick? That's gotta be a new record or something."

He glared at his friend. "O, don't play with me about this."

"I'm sorry, bro." Orion held up his hands in front of him. "I was just trying to lighten your mood. Anyway, just tell me what happened."

Maxwell closed his eyes briefly, not wanting to relive the moment Von had driven off his property and turned her back on everything they'd shared. But he steeled himself and recounted the story to Orion. When he'd finished, he waited for his friend to respond.

Orion sat, blinking and staring straight ahead for a few moments before uttering his single-word reaction. "Yikes."

"You've got that right. I can't believe things between us went south so fast. We were really just getting started." Maxwell's shoulders slumped, his chest tightening with emotion. Because as much as he hated to admit it, Yvonne's declaration that they weren't a couple anymore had hurt him deeply. "I didn't even realize how invested I was in the idea of us having a future together until she told me it was over."

"You're in love with her, right?"

No use in trying to hide that now. "Yes, definitely."

"And I'm assuming you told her that?"

He nodded. "Yes. I let her know how I felt before the first time we made love."

Orion scratched his chin. "Okay, bro. I gotta ask you something else, and this is just based on what I'm hearing from you."

Maxwell leaned forward on the lounger. "Okay, ask it."

"Did you ever say anything to her about her plans to open the day care center? Like, sit down and have a real conversation about it?"

He thought for a moment, pressing his lips together. "I don't think so. At least nothing too deep."

Orion's brow arched. "Why not?"

Maxwell shrugged. "Why would I? It's not really my place to consult with her about that unless she asks for my help with it.

Like if she wanted construction advice or something, I'd help her out."

Orion blew out a breath, shaking his head. "That's not what I mean. Hasn't she been talking to you about her plans since the beginning?"

Maxwell thought back on their conversations, snippets of them passing through his mind. "Yeah, man. She's mentioned it several times in passing."

"Why do you think she keeps bringing it up, Max?"

He released a wry chuckle. "You're asking me? I'm the last person on the planet to consult about why women do anything."

"Damn straight," Orion retorted. "Because if you can't see the reasoning behind what she's been saying to you, then you really are completely fucking clueless, bro."

Feeling his brow crinkle with confusion, Maxwell snapped, "Okay then, Orion. Break it down for me."

Orion tilted his head to one side, rubbed his hands together. "Gladly, because you clearly need my help. Listen, it's like this. When y'all were arguing, she had you run down all your serious relationships and how they ended."

"Yeah, so?"

"Shut up, Max, and let me finish. She wasn't doing that for no reason, bro. She was collecting evidence to prove her theory."

"What theory would that be, oh wise one?" Maxwell's irritation grew with each passing second, warring with his pain and loneliness.

Orion rolled his eyes. "I'm gonna tell you if you stop flapping your gums. Her theory is that you don't have it in you to be a supportive partner, that she can't count on you to really get behind her dream."

Maxwell opened his mouth, ready to cuss Orion out, then snapped it shut when he realized she'd said almost exactly those same words to him before she left. "She said...that I couldn't support a woman's dreams if they didn't fit my 'convenient little plans.' That's what she said to me."

"Sweet, sweet vindication." Orion threw both hands in the air. "See what I mean?"

Maxwell cringed. "I mean, I guess."

"Let's put it another way, then. Do you support her dream, Max? Do you wanna see her open this business and be successful at it?"

"I mean, yeah. I'd be okay with it."

Orion pressed his palm to his face. "That's it right there. That's the attitude that got you in this mess. Do you hear yourself right now?"

Maxwell sat up straight, his back and shoulders tight with tension. "What so wrong with what I said?"

"If the tables were turned, and you were just getting ready to establish Devers Architectural, would you want a partner who was just okay with you pursuing your passion? Or would you want somebody who was as excited about it as you? Somebody who'd be cheering you on every step of the way? Who'd celebrate your wins and help you figure things out when shit goes to the left?" Orion gave him a pointed stare. "What would you want, Max?"

Maxwell closed his eyes against the harsh glare of reality, from which his sunglasses offered no protection. "Oh shit." When he opened them again, Orion gave him the slow blink.

"You've given her nothing in terms of concrete proof that you support her, yet you expect her to take things to the next level with you?"

Maxwell looked away from Orion's direct stare.

"I rest my case."

Falling against the backrest, Maxwell groaned aloud. "I really fucked this up, didn't I?"

"Yep. You absolutely, positively, thoroughly played yourself."

He couldn't even get annoyed this time, because he knew his friend was right. "Well, how do I fix this?"

"I don't know if you can fix it, Max. But whatever you do, you'd better made damn sure you show her you're ready to fully support her. Because just telling her ain't gonna do it at this point."

"How?" He blew out a breath. "What if I can't figure out the right way to do that?"

Orion shrugged. "It's either you figure it out or let her move on to the next man who's gonna do right by her." He steepled his fingers. "I admit I don't know her that well, but she seems like a hell of a good woman. It wouldn't be right for you to hold her back from happiness if you can't get it together."

"Ouch." Those words stung worse than sunburn, and there was no salve to soothe it, either. Nothing short of winning Yvonne back would relieve the ache Maxwell felt inside, the emptiness of losing her presence in his life. His gaze fixed on the waves rolling toward the shore, he started to formulate a plan. "Listen, I gotta try to fix this. I might need your help."

"I got your back, at least up until she tells you to kick rocks again. If that happens, I'm out."

"Understood." *But if I can get this right and really make her see what she means to me, there's no way she'll send me packing.* He needed her to know he'd be there for her, that he believed in the beauty of her dream. And the more he thought about it, the more a plan began to solidify in his mind.

~~~

"Do you know what time it is?"

Yvonne glanced down at her sister from her spot on the stepladder. "Really, Zel? Can't you see me trying to hang these last few streamers?" She shook her head, trying to tug the strip of clear tape out of the dispenser mounted to the elastic band on her wrist. "I've been doing this for a while now. We came home, and I changed clothes and went right to work on decorations." Standing four feet off the floor, she was glad she'd changed from the tan maxi dress she'd worn earlier into white jeans, a black tee, and black-and-white-striped sneakers.

Zelda, still clad in the simple white blouse and navy pencil skirt she'd worn to early service, grinned. "Yeah, I see you. I'm just trying to draw your attention to the time. Mommy and Daddy will be home from church in about thirty minutes, Sis."

"Dang it." Finally freeing the stuck tape, Yvonne affixed a few strips onto the end of the paper streamer to secure it in place, then climbed down from the stool. Taking a couple of steps back, she assessed her work. Braids formed from orange and gold streamers hung from the corners of the room and over the kitchen doorway, accented by gold paper lanterns. Bouquets of glitter-flecked orange balloons, tied to plastic weights to keep them from floating away, were anchored on either side of the old fireplace.

Zelda, holding a stack of gold plastic party hats, nodded her approval. "It looks good, Von. Nice work."

Yvonne had to agree, especially considering the total lack of concentration she'd had while completing the task. Despite her best efforts to focus on preparations for the day's festivities, her traitorous mind kept wandering back to thoughts of Maxwell. *I wish things could have turned out differently. But he's just not ready for real commitment.*

Stifling a yawn, Zelda set the party hats on the oak sofa table. "Girl, I'm already beat and the party ain't even poppin' yet. Getting up for Sunday school and early service? I'm plumb worn out, like Granny Vera used to say."

Yvonne shook her head. "Trust me, I'm not a fan of getting up at six thirty on a Sunday, either. But we had to go to early service so Daddy wouldn't ask questions about us missing regular service at eleven." She ran a hand through her hair, knowing just by touch that it looked a mess. "We needed this time, while Mommy and Daddy are in church, to finish getting the house ready."

"I know, I know." Zelda yawned again. "But I'm surely missing that extra sleep right now."

"You and me both." Yvonne sighed, knowing her sister wasn't aware of the real reason she hadn't gotten nearly enough sleep. She'd been tossing and turning most of the night until she finally gave up and went for a run on the treadmill at five in the morning. *Thank goodness my complex has a twenty-four-hour workout room. No way was I going to walk the streets at that hour.*

The sound of a car door slamming drew them to the window. "It's Quita and Ross pulling up," Zelda remarked. "And there's another car pulling up behind them. Looks like everybody's here."

Yvonne drew a deep breath, steeling herself for what was sure to be a busy day.

The party guests drove through the side yard, parking their cars out of sight behind the house. Yvonne had prearranged that to ensure that her dad knew nothing about the festivities until the last possible moment. Once that was done, Yvonne welcomed neighbors and relatives into her parents' home with hugs, kisses, and handshakes. She showed them hospitality in the manner her parents would expect, which included giving them her most genuine smile. And even though she still felt the lingering hurt from what had happened between her and Maxwell, she let the comforting presence of the people she loved soothe her wounded soul.

"I've been living across the street from this family for fifteen years." Helene Cantini smiled as she shook Yvonne's hand. "Gordon and Marissa have always been good neighbors. They've looked out for me many a time."

"It's almost three." Their cousin Quita stood near the coffee table, tapping her watch. "Service will be out by now, and they should be pulling up any minute."

"I sure hope Uncle Gordon is gonna be surprised." Ross, Marissa's nephew, a freshman at Central, grinned in Yvonne's direction.

"I think he will be," she said, then turned toward her sister. "Zel, you didn't let anything slip, did you?"

Zelda shook her head. "Nope. And besides that, Mommy's been a champ about keeping him busy and completely in the dark about our plans."

"I already got my good hiding spot." Greg, Gordon's younger brother and only sibling, chuckled as he eased to a seated position on the floor behind the sofa. "One of you youngsters will have to help me up, that's all."

Greg's wife, Aunt Shelly, joined him. "They'll have to help us both up, baby."

Yvonne couldn't help feeling wistful as she watched her relatives. *Would Maxwell and I have been like that? Still joking with each other after thirty years together?* She doubted she'd ever get the chance to find out the answer to that.

She cupped her hands around her mouth and said in a theater whisper, "Quita's right. Everybody needs to get in their hiding place."

"Dibs on the coat closet." Zelda's sneakers squeaked on the floor as she slid past her sister, pulled open the door, and slipped inside before shutting it behind her.

Yvonne snapped her fingers. "Dang. I was gonna hide in there."

"Only room for one," Zelda called from the recesses of the closet.

Shaking her head, Yvonne scanned the room for a good spot that wasn't already taken. Seeing an opening, she scooted into the narrow space between the piano and her mother's potted ficus and crouched low.

The familiar rumbling of their parents' old Buick sliced through the air. The room fell silent as they all waited for the guest of honor to appear. Next came the scratching of the key in the lock, and Yvonne covered her mouth to stifle a giggle as her mother asked her father if he knew how to work a key.

The door swung open, and Gordon lumbered in.

Yvonne and everyone else jumped from their hiding spots. "Surprise!"

Gordon stood in the doorway in his favorite brown suit and matching fedora, his mouth hanging open a moment, before he said, "What in the world?"

"Happy birthday, honey." Marissa grasped his hand in hers, leaning up to kiss him on the lips.

He smiled. "Oh my goodness."

Cheers went up among the assembled guests as the birthday boy realized what was happening.

"You girls, come here." He gestured to Yvonne and Zelda with his hand, and they dutifully went to their father's side. Embracing them along with their mother, he announced, "Thank you all so much. You didn't need to bring any gifts here today, because having these three girls and people like you who care about me is gift enough."

Yvonne felt the warmth of her father's love wash over her, and it did much to improve her mood.

"Aww." Shelly appeared on the verge of tears.

"I brought you something, though," Greg quipped.

"Well, now, if you already paid, I'll take it." Gordon laughed as he gave his wife and daughters a squeeze. "I'm not one to turn down such generosity."

Marissa shook her head. "You're such a ham. Come on in the kitchen, everybody, and eat some of this food."

The party got underway in earnest then. Zelda started up an instrumental jazz playlist on her phone, streaming it to a portable speaker to up the ambiance. Everyone ate, conversed, and laughed, celebrating the happy occasion. Yvonne stayed busy by waiting on her father and some of the other older folks in attendance, bringing them drinks and whatever other items they requested. She was glad to see to their needs, because serving others was part of her nature. Her grandmother had always declared she possessed a servant's heart.

Today, while she battled the vestiges of sadness that threatened to overcome the festive mood of the day at any moment, she needed the distraction.

I served Maxwell, too. I took care of his daughter, helped him find his identity as a father. I gave him my heart. But when it came right down to it, I was doing all the giving. He only took from me.

When everyone was settled, her melancholy finally got the better of her, and she went outside to sit on the back patio. Settling onto the floral fabric cushion on her mother's wicker settee, she gazed out over the backyard. The thicket of pine trees beyond the chain link fence hid the busy road from view, but she could still hear the faint sounds of traffic. Her mother's azalea bushes were starting to bud, indicating a possible early bloom. Thinking of the way the yard would look by April, when the bright fuchsia blooms would be as large as saucers and as numerous as the stars in the night sky, brought a bit of joy to her weary mind.

Why am I sitting out here thinking about Maxwell, anyway? I doubt he's thinking about me.

She knew the answer. He'd become a part of her, in so many ways. The fact that he'd hurt her didn't erase everything they'd shared. She couldn't simply forget his smile, his kiss, the way his hands had felt as they caressed her body. No matter how hard she tried to shake them, those memories remained. *I don't know how I'm going to move on from this. But if I have to choose between being with him and pursuing my lifelong dream, my dream wins out.*

Zelda came out of the house, plopped down beside her on the settee. "What's your malfunction, Von?"

Yvonne glanced at her sister's face. "How did you even know I was out here?"

"Mommy was in the kitchen, and she saw you through the back window."

"Ah." She didn't have to turn around to know her mother was probably still there, watching them. "It's a long story."

"Okay, then give me the shorthand version."

She pursed her lips, blew out a breath. "Let's just say now that I know who Maxwell really is—or rather, who he's not—it's over between us."

Zelda's eyes widened. "Well, that was short-lived. What happened?"

Yvonne shook her head. "I don't want to rehash all that. The gist is, he's not supportive. It seems like he's expecting me to just give up my dream so I can fit neatly into his life."

"Oh no." Zelda leaned back against the seat cushion. "You've been talking about owning a day care since forever. If he really would ask you to give that up, then you're right to move on."

"Well, he hasn't exactly asked me to give it up." Yvonne sighed. "But it's pretty clear he's not invested in my success as a business owner. Now that I work for him, I don't think he wants me to go any further with my career."

"Sounds like he's gotten comfortable with things the way they are."

Yvonne shrugged. "I guess he has." Maybe that was how Maxwell felt, but if so, his idea of comfort was the opposite of hers. "If he wants this quiet life, where I stay home and help raise his daughter and do nothing else, I can't be happy that way."

"I'm not trying to get in your business, but it seems to me you miss him."

"Is it that obvious?"

"With you sitting out here moping while there's an actual party going on inside? Yes, Sis, it's obvious."

Yvonne shook her head, raked a hand through her hair. "He just...let me leave, Zel. He didn't fight for me. He hasn't called or texted... I just don't know what to think." *If not for the passion he'd displayed in bed or when he talked about his own work, I'd think he didn't possess any.*

"I'm not gonna tell you to reach out to him. I think, based on what you've described, that he should be the one to reach out." Zelda clasped her hands together. "If he tries to make things right, let him make his case. Give him a shot, but if it doesn't feel right in the end, feel free to walk away."

Yvonne nodded. "That seems reasonable." Too bad reason rarely ruled in matters of the heart. If he were to call her right now, she wasn't sure if she'd answer. He'd hurt her deeply, and she wasn't sure she could—or should—trust him again. "At least I won't have to go to work this week. I promised I'd stay until he found a replacement, but Sasha will be with her mother all week." She was grateful for the vacation, because she'd need the time and space to clear her head.

"Listen, you know I'm with you, no matter what you decide to do." Zelda reached over, giving her hand a squeeze. "I'd advise against telling Daddy about this, though. Knowing him, he'd be ready to fight. He doesn't go for anybody hurting his daughters."

Yvonne nodded. "I know. And I appreciate it."

"Great." Zelda stood. "Now, let's get back inside before all the good snacks are gone." She held out her hand.

The gesture reminded Yvonne of when Zelda was a little girl and they'd held hands to cross the road to the ice cream truck. With a small chuckle, she took her sister's hand and headed back inside the house.

CHAPTER 22

MAXWELL PULLED INTO THE DRIVEWAY AT HIS PARENTS' house Monday, guiding his SUV into a spot behind Alexis's car and Kelsey's old pickup. Shutting off the engine, he drew a deep breath, bracing himself for what might be waiting for him.

He'd gotten a call from his father earlier, asking him to come over for dinner. "It's time for me to make things right, with your mother and with all of you," Humphrey had said. Since his father had sounded genuinely contrite, he'd agreed to make an appearance.

He got out of the car and walked around the side of the house to the back patio as he'd been instructed. The stone patio, which extended from the rear of the house by a good twenty feet, held his mother's large, L-shaped wicker sectional. The behemoth patio furniture was a deep shade of brown, had solid navy-blue all-weather cushions, and boasted enough seating for eight. A stout wicker rectangle sat near the center of the sectional, serving as both a table and a footrest for those sitting near it.

There was also an outdoor dinette table, in the same wicker as the sectional, which had a tempered glass top. The table also seated eight, and as Maxwell passed it on the way to the sectional, he observed several covered trays had been placed there.

Seated on the sectional now were his mother and sisters, all seated on the right side.

"Hey, y'all." Maxwell took a seat next to his mother, beside the center cushion. After they'd all exchanged greetings, he asked, "What's going on? Where's Dad?"

Kelsey shrugged. "Said he was going to pick something up, and he'd be right back."

He jerked his thumb in the direction of the dining table. "What's all that?"

"Dad had the caterer bring over some finger foods." Alexis shrugged. "I guess he thought it would help break the ice for his... whatever this is."

Leaning back against the cushion, he placed his arm around his mother's shoulder. "I'm only here because he claims he's ready to set things right. Mom deserves that. We all do."

Del, who'd been silently and absently flipping through an issue of *Southern Living*, nodded her head. "I just hope he's serious about this. I've been waiting so long for him to come around."

Maxwell watched his mother, taking in the tension lining her face and the way her shoulders slumped as she sat next to him. His father had wounded her, and she wore the emotional bruises he'd left behind. Wanting to comfort her, he gave his mother's shoulders a squeeze. "Don't worry, Mom. Whatever happens, I've got you."

She gave him a weak smile. "Thank you, Son."

They made small talk for a few minutes, and Maxwell felt his mood soften a bit as he listened to his mother and sisters chattering.

Then, Humphrey came walking around the side of the house. And he wasn't alone.

Maxwell didn't know which was more shocking: his father's scraggly, unshaven appearance or the two guests he'd decided to bring along.

Trish Oliver, their petite, fair-skinned former neighbor who originally hailed from the Louisiana bayou, walked a few steps behind Humphrey. Her close-trimmed brown hair, highlighted with blond, framed a round face with dark brown eyes. Maxwell hadn't seen her in more than fifteen years, and her appearance hadn't changed much in that time.

Jeffrey Oliver, tall and lanky, had a complexion that matched his mother's but facial features that mimicked his father. He seemed hesitant, his steps slow and measured, and he seemed poised to turn tail and run at a moment's notice.

Maxwell felt his jaw tighten. His mother's shoulders stiffened beneath his arm, and in a flash, she was on her feet.

"Humphrey Lee Devers. How dare you bring that tramp to my home?"

Trish's face folded into a frown, one that seemed to express more discomfort than offense.

"Del, please. We need to iron all this out, and I'm too old to manage a six-stop apology tour." He gestured for Trish and Jeffrey to sit on the left side of the sectional while he sat down in the middle. "Besides, you said never to bring her into the house. And I didn't."

Delphinia fumed. "You're an ass, Humphrey."

"I won't dispute that." He looked around at everyone present. "All I'm asking is that you give me twenty minutes. In twenty minutes, I'll take Trish and Jeff home, and they won't be on your property anymore."

"It's not Jeffrey I have a problem with, and you know it."

Trish exhaled, scooting farther away from the center of the sectional and pushing Jeffrey along with her. "Humphrey, I can't believe you'd bring me here without talking to your wife about it first."

Humphrey sighed. "I know this isn't ideal, but then again, nothing about the situation I've put us all in is."

Delphinia's brow arched. "Good Lord, Humphrey. Do I hear you finally taking some responsibility? Is that what I'm hearing?"

Kelsey winked. "Solid burn, Mom."

Maxwell could only shake his head. Why on earth did his father think this was a good idea, bringing the six of them together like this? *This is probably going to be a complete circus. But we're here now.*

Humphrey drew a deep breath. "I've been thinking a lot about my actions lately. And yes, Del, you're right. I am accepting full responsibility for what I've done and the pain and grief I've caused."

Alexis rolled her eyes. "And what brought this on, Dad?"

Maxwell could hear the anger and frustration in his sister's voice, and he didn't blame her. He was pretty upset himself. But he imagined that for Alexis, the baby of the family who'd been the ultimate daddy's girl, this whole affair was pretty difficult to accept.

"A lot of things. I've had a lot of time to reflect while I've been sleeping on that lumpy leather sofa in my study." Humphrey scratched his whiskered chin. "I thought about what's made my life as wonderful as it's been these past fifty some years. Yes, selling my patent to the government was a great accomplishment. But the only reason it really mattered is because that money gave me the freedom to make a comfortable life for you—my family." He looked around to his stoic wife, his daughters, and Maxwell. "That money would have been meaningless without you all."

Trish sighed. "Why did you bring Jeffrey and me here, Humphrey? To rub it in our faces that we aren't a part of your family?" She placed an arm around her son's shoulder. "We don't need to be reminded of that."

Humphrey shook his head. "No. That's just it, Trish. You and Jeffrey are a part of my family, and I've been wrong to deny that all these years."

A tear slid down Delphinia's face. "You'd best be making your point pretty soon, or I'm leaving."

"I want you all to know I'm listening. I want to hear from you, whatever you want to get off your chest about this." Humphrey leaned back into the cushions. "We'll go around, and each of you can just vent. Whatever you think I need to hear."

"I'll go first." Trish glared at him. "The worst thing you did to me was make all those empty promises, knowing you never intended to keep them. That's all I have to say." She folded her arms over her chest.

"You took away my chance at having a normal childhood, a stable two-parent home." Jeffrey didn't make eye contact with Humphrey. "Thank God, Mama is strong, and she raised me right. She just shouldn't have had to do it alone."

Humphrey closed his eyes, letting his head drop. "I appreciate your honesty."

"I'll go." Kelsey leaned forward in her seat. "Dad, I always looked up to you. I thought you were such a great role model, someone who would show me how I should be treated by my romantic partners. But after finding out how you treated Mom…" She shook her head. "I just don't feel that way anymore."

"Same." Alexis brushed away a tear. "I used to be such a daddy's girl. But I don't know anymore."

Humphrey cringed. "Thank you. It's hard to hear, but I need to hear it anyway."

Maxwell cleared his throat. The palpable tension all around him had begun to affect him, so he took a moment to adjust himself so he wouldn't just start yelling at his father. "Dad, I'm frustrated that you disrespected Mom. I'm angry you lied to us all these years. But most of all, I'm worried. I'm worried that I might have inherited some of your tendencies. That I might one day treat a woman as badly as you did Mom." He paused, feeling his throat tighten as he thought of the women in his past, of Yvonne. "Maybe I already have."

Humphrey nodded, swallowed. "I hear you, Son." He looked to his wife of more than three decades. "Del, I'm listening, honey."

Her eyes were damp and red-rimmed, and she spoke in a tone heavy with emotion. "Humphrey, you gutted me. You disrespected me, our vows, and this entire family with your selfishness. You denied that poor child over there the chance to have a full-time father in his life. And then you made it even worse by refusing to acknowledge what you'd done." She shook her head slowly. "That's nothing like the man I fell in love with."

By now, the old man had tears in his eyes as well. He stood, taking the cushion he'd been sitting on with him. "I'm old, and I may need help later, but I feel like this is what I need to do." Tossing the cushion down on the stone floor, he knelt. "I need you all to know I'm so, so sorry for what I've done. Everything you've said about me is true, and I don't deserve forgiveness. So I won't ask for that."

Maxwell watched his father, wide-eyed. He'd never seen the old man put himself in such a humble position.

"I'm asking you to give me a chance to show you that I've changed, a chance to earn your trust and respect again. I know I can't take away the pain, but I'm going to do my best to do right by you. All of you."

There was a long silence then. No one spoke, but all eyes remained on Humphrey. He rose, with some difficulty, from the cushion and returned it to the seat. Then he went to each person individually and whispered something to them.

When he reached Delphinia, Maxwell heard him say, "I'll sleep in the study as long as it takes. You can let me back in the bedroom when you're ready and not a minute before."

Delphinia offered a silent, solemn nod but said nothing.

Humphrey leaned to his son next. "Maxwell, can we talk in the study after this?"

"Sure." *If Dad's really had a breakthrough, maybe we can finally have a real conversation.*

Later, when Trish and Jeffrey had gone, Maxwell saw his parents embrace. It comforted him to see that, though he knew it was probably just a first step on a long road to reconciliation.

Inside Humphrey's study, Maxwell sat in the mahogany chair, listening intently to his father's words.

"Listen. I shouldn't have been so hard on you when you brought

Yvonne here. Now that everything's out in the open, I hope you can understand why I acted that way."

He nodded. "I suppose. Sitting on a secret like that is bound to put a person on edge."

"I'd say that's fair." Humphrey sat on the edge of his desk, his head slightly bowed. "I was projecting on you, Son. The reason I railed against you about being irresponsible was that I knew I'd been irresponsible myself. Everything I said to you, I've been saying to myself for years." He shook his head, looking toward the window. "I kept saying I raised you better. My parents raised me better, too."

"I get it, Dad." Maxwell could tell that his father was hurting, that it was difficult for the once-powerful engineering manager to display this level of humility, to admit he'd been wrong. "You set a pretty high bar for me, but I always tried to meet it."

"And you did, Maxwell." Humphrey looked his way. "I'm so proud of you and your sisters. You kids have turned out wonderfully. I can even say the same for Jeffrey, even though I didn't have much of a hand in his raising." He clasped his hands together. "Mainly, I just want you to know I love you, I love my granddaughter, and I want a happy life for both of you."

"I love you, too, Dad. And I appreciate that." It had been a trying day. But now that the family tension had been broken, Maxwell's mind drifted back to thoughts of what he'd lost. "Since you're feeling so fatherly right now, maybe you can give me some advice."

"I'm humbled that you'd ask me after all the ways I've screwed up."

He shrugged. "Dad, at this point, I need all the help I can get."

Humphrey got down from the desk and came to sit in the chair next to him. "What's the problem, Son?"

Maxwell explained the situation with Yvonne. "Since she left, I feel lost. Sasha's with her mother, and my house has never felt so empty. I mean, I know Sasha will be back, but Von won't unless I can make things right with her. I miss her, Dad." He clutched his chest. "I miss her so, so much."

"Have you talked to her since she left?"

He shook his head. "I wouldn't even know what to say to her. Honestly, I don't want to bother her until everything's in place for me to make a proper apology."

Humphrey nodded, tenting his fingers. "What is this grand apology going to look like?"

Maxwell shifted in his chair. "I've been thinking about it, and I've got an idea. Tell me what you think." He laid out his plans, relieved to finally be able to tell somebody about them.

When he'd finished, Humphrey smiled. "That's my boy."

⁓

Tuesday afternoon, Yvonne knocked on her parents' door. When her mother opened it, she smiled. "Mommy, are you busy today?"

"No, I'm not." Marissa folded her arms over her chest. "What are you doing here on a workday?"

"I'm on vacation, remember? Sasha's spending time with her mother, so there's no reason for me to go in to work."

"Mm-hmm." Her mother studied her. "What did you have in mind?"

"I thought we'd go out to Southpoint and hang out, do a little shopping." Yvonne pointed at her car. "I'll drive since I know how much you hate it."

Marissa glanced back and forth between her daughter and the car as if considering the offer. "Okay. Let me let Janine and your daddy know I'm leaving and change out of these house clothes."

"I'll wait for you in the car."

An hour later, they were walking through the outdoor space at the Streets at Southpoint Mall. The sprawling shopping center had opened in 2002 and was one of the most popular retail destinations in the Triangle and the state of North Carolina. This portion of the mall, designed to look like the shopping district of a downtown area, featured a mixture of specialty shops, high-end restaurants, and a movie theater.

"Remember back in the day, when we still had South Square?" Yvonne stopped in front of the Barnes & Noble, scanning the books on display in the front window. "I spent many a Saturday there with you as a kid."

"Yes, I remember." Marissa checked her reflection in the mirror, patting down a wayward gray curl. "I miss going to Dillard's. They used to have the best sales on things for the house."

Yvonne chuckled. "Yep. Daddy used to hate seeing you roll up to the house with those big Dillard's bags."

Marissa waved her hand dismissively. "Oh, child. Your daddy doesn't know a thing about fine home décor. If I'd left it up to him, the house would still have blank white walls and no curtains." She chuckled as they walked on.

They browsed through a few stores, picking up a few odds and ends. As usual, Marissa found most of the things she liked in the big department stores anchoring the mall, while Yvonne gravitated toward the more eclectic styles in the smaller boutiques. After going back to the car to stash their bags in the trunk, they headed around the corner from the mall to City Barbeque and Catering. The small restaurant, famous for their awesome ribs and potato salad, also boasted unique homemade barbeque sauces.

"Oh, good, there are some tables open." Yvonne made a beeline for a two-top in a sunny window. "You can barely get in here during the lunch rush."

"That's why I like coming here during the off hours." Marissa slid into one of the seats.

"I'll go order. What do you want, Mommy?"

"Just get a City Sampler and we'll share it. Sound good?" Yvonne nodded. "Yep."

Her mother handed her a ten-dollar bill. "Lots of Cheerwine sauce."

Yvonne smiled, tucking away the money. Fifteen minutes later, she returned with their tray. The platter they'd ordered included smoked beef brisket and turkey breast, sausage and pulled pork, along with potato salad and greens. Per her mother's request, Yvonne had added four small plastic containers of barbeque sauce made with the state's iconic soda.

While they ate, they chatted about the birthday party, the weather, the upcoming activities at church. By the time they'd finished, though, her mother just sat, watching her with narrowed eyes.

"What is it, Mommy?" She grabbed a napkin. "Do I have sauce on my face?"

Marissa shook her head. "No. You have hurt on your face, though."

Crap. "Mommy, I don't wanna talk about—"

"Oh, I know. Your sister told me what happened between you and your architect."

I see Zel dimed me out. Yvonne was annoyed, but she couldn't be mad with her sister, who'd most likely acted out of genuine concern for her. *Plus, if Mommy asks you a question, you'd better answer her if you wanna keep your teeth.*

"Don't worry, Yvonne. I'm not gonna force you to talk." Marissa leaned forward, rested her elbows on the table, and steepled her fingers. "But you are gonna listen, understand me?"

Yvonne nodded. "Yes, ma'am."

"Good. First, I'm sorry things went south and that you're in pain. But I noticed you spending money on a lot of unnecessary things today, things you don't need or ain't really gonna use."

She opened her mouth to protest.

"No, don't say anything. You only have one rear end, so you don't need five pairs of jeans. And you hate baking, so when are you going to use a stand mixer?"

She snapped her mouth closed. *As always, Mommy's making good sense. Why did I pick up that mixer? I'm likely to hurt myself trying to use it.*

"I can understand a little bit of retail therapy to break you out of a funk. But I want to make sure you're not dipping into your day care savings so you can buy these frivolities. That mixer was way overpriced."

Her mother could see right through her as if she were made of glass. Purchasing the fancy mixer had put a small dent in her savings, though she didn't want to say it out loud. *What would be the point? Mommy already knows.*

"Listen to me, child. I've always raised you to make good decisions, to really think about things before you do them. So if you think walking away from that man is the right thing to do, then I'm not going to dispute you on it. What I am going to do is remind you of something I said to you before you went off to school. I told you to be careful to separate what's temporary from what's permanent. Do you remember that?"

"Yes, ma'am, I remember."

"Good. I see you acting like you're confused about the two. You might think you want that mixer now, but when you get home and realize you can't bake, you'll see that desire as the temporary thing it is."

"Crap, you're right." Yvonne sighed, thinking of the huge box containing the powder-blue mixer, sitting in her trunk. "I should just take it back. It'd be a waste of time to take it home."

"Exactly. Now that we've established that the mixer is temporary, let's talk about the permanent." Marissa gave her a piercing look. "Do you remember the first time you decided you wanted to open your own day care?"

"Not really." Yvonne thought about it, trying to remember when she'd first had the idea. "Middle school, maybe? It just seems like the idea was always there, like it was always a part of me."

Her mother snapped her fingers. "Exactly. This dream is so much a part of you, you can't remember a time when it wasn't there. And you probably can't imagine anything else you'd want to do with your life, right?"

"Right." *I think I see where Mommy's going with this.*

"Now think about what you had with Maxwell." Her mother leaned back in her chair. "Was it meant to be temporary? Or permanent?"

She blinked a few times as she mulled that over.

"You don't need to tell me. But you do need to figure it out for yourself." Marissa stood, gathering their trash onto the red plastic tray. "It's not just about separating the two, Yvonne. It's about not letting one interfere with the other. Don't let the temporary disturb the permanent." She walked away, carrying the tray toward the trash bin.

Alone at the table, Yvonne gazed out the window. While the traffic on NC-54 whizzed by, she thought about her mother's words and how it all pertained to Maxwell. *I was so angry, so hurt when I left that day. But the truth is I miss him terribly. I miss hearing his voice, seeing his smile, feeling his touch.* He'd become a part of her, and she didn't know if she could be truly happy without him, not anymore. Still, she couldn't contact him. She couldn't take the emotional risk involved.

But if he reached out to her, and she prayed he would, she'd listen to what he had to say.

Because there was simply no forgetting a man like Maxwell.

CHAPTER 23

MAXWELL SAT IN THE COFFEE SHOP IN APEX, LOOKING OUT the window as he nursed his cup of dark roast. Today was the day he planned to make his move, to try to set things right with Yvonne. It was Wednesday, a full five days since she'd left his house, declaring that it was over. Five long, lonely, miserable days.

Here I am, in the middle of my first vacation in years, and this is what I'm doing. It wasn't the restful week he'd intended it to be, far from it. But if after it was over Yvonne gave him another chance, it would all be worth it.

He grabbed his cell phone from the tabletop, took a deep breath, and dialed her number.

She answered on the fourth ring. "Hello?"

Words tumbled out of his mouth the moment he heard her voice. "Hey, Yvonne. Are you at home? I mean, are you busy?" He stopped, took a breath, and waited for her to respond.

"No, I'm not busy, but I am at home. What is it?" Her tone was flat, unreadable.

"I'd like to talk to you if that's okay."

Sounding a bit confused, she said, "You're...talking to me right now, Maxwell."

"No, that's not what I mean." He took a sip from the ceramic mug. "What I have to say should be said in person. I was hoping you'd let me take you out for a little drive."

She was silent for a moment. "Going for the captive audience angle, I see." Her words were tinged with the tiniest bit of humor, and that gave him hope.

"I guess you could say that." He chuckled, hoping to keep the mood light. "In reality, though, it's easier for me to open up when

I'm driving. And all things considered, I think it's high time for me to lay everything out on the table with you."

"I agree." She cleared her throat. "But before I say yes, there's something I need to know."

"What's that?"

"Is this your way of getting closure? I need to know what your angle is before I agree to this."

He smiled, knowing she couldn't see it. "No, it's not. I'm not looking for closure, Yvonne. I'm hoping to show you why you should give me another chance."

The line was quiet for so long, he started to think she'd hung up on him.

Finally, she said, "I'll be ready in about thirty minutes."

"Thank you for giving me a shot."

"Don't make me regret it, Maxwell." She disconnected the call.

A few minutes later, he was behind the wheel of his SUV, headed up NC-751 toward Durham. When he arrived at her apartment complex forty minutes later, she was waiting at the bottom of the stairs.

He pulled into an empty parking spot near the building and put the vehicle in park. Watching her walk toward him nearly took his breath away. She wore a strapless maxi dress in a deep shade of green that complemented her honey-brown skin tone and a beige cardigan. She'd put her hair up in a small bun on top of her head, with a few loose pieces forming bangs in the front.

He hopped out to open the passenger door for her, and as she climbed in, he resisted the urge to touch her backside. *I lost that privilege, but I hope to earn it back today.*

Soon they were back on the road, and he asked, "How have you been? Have you done anything fun with your vacation time?"

She shrugged. "My daddy's party was fun. I've been shopping, out to eat a few times. Nothing major."

"Why not?"

"Do you really have to ask? I haven't been in a celebratory mood."

He cringed. "Neither have I. I've basically been sitting home, twiddling my thumbs. I guess that's one way to spend a vacation, but I don't think it's the best use of my time right now."

She said nothing, instead choosing to look out the window at the passing scenery.

He pulled up to a stoplight. "Okay. It's time we get into this conversation. I'll start by telling you a story." The light turned green, and he passed through the intersection.

"I'm listening."

"Here's something you don't know about me: I didn't learn to swim until I was almost nineteen."

"Really?" She sounded surprised. "Why not?"

"I was scared of water. Couldn't really tell you why. There's nothing I can point to as the thing that happened to make me afraid of water. But I was. You couldn't get me near a lake, a pool, nothing. When I was about to graduate high school, my class went on a senior trip to Miami Beach. I spent the whole weekend hiding in a cabana. Wouldn't go near the water."

"I feel like you're going somewhere with this. I just don't know where."

He chuckled. "Sorry I'm taking the long way around, but hopefully, when we reach the destination, it will have been worthwhile."

She tilted her head to the side. "Speaking of destinations, do we have one for this little drive?"

He smiled knowingly. "We do. I'm just not going to disclose it."

She crinkled her nose but didn't protest further. "Okay, then. Go on with the story."

"Right. Anyway, later that summer, we were at this swanky hotel in New York on family vacation. All five of us are out by the pool. Kelsey was sixteen, and Alexis was almost fourteen. So I walk to the pool bar to get a soda. On the way there, I passed Kelsey, and she pushed me into the pool. Boom." He turned from NC-55 onto 401 South.

"Uh-oh."

"Uh-oh is right. I could've drowned or something. But you know what? I didn't. Once I hit the water and the initial shock wore off, I found my sea legs. Started kicking, made it back to the edge of the pool. Then I grabbed Kelsey by the ankle and yanked her ass in there, too."

She covered her mouth, giggling. "Good grief."

"It's all good. We were even after that." He shook his head. "Kelsey's always been like that. Grab the bull by the horns or whatever. Anyway, after some time passed, I remembered something important about that day."

"What's that?"

"When Kelsey pushed me, she yelled, 'Sink or swim, Max!' That's what she said. She was telling me that I was in control of the situation. Even though she caught me by surprise, it was going to be my decision whether I just let myself drown or I learned how to swim."

"Sounds kind of profound."

"It wasn't when she did it, but it was after the fact." He navigated around the cars parallel-parked on the side of the road. "It was one of the most valuable lessons I've ever learned, though I can't say I've been all that good at applying it."

She turned his way then. "What do you mean?"

He pulled into a parking lot behind a bank. "We can walk the rest of the way from here."

Once they were out on the sidewalk, she said, "Okay, finish what you were saying. What did you mean when you said you haven't applied the lesson?"

"I'm glad you're so invested in my story." That very interest had served him well, because she still didn't seem to be aware of where they were going. "In my previous relationships especially, I failed to use what my sister taught me. With Amy. With Juliana. You see, when things came between us and forced me into the water, I didn't kick, didn't act. And it was my inaction that led to those relationships failing." He grasped her hand, gratified that she didn't pull away from him, and led her around the corner.

"Maxwell, I—"

"I was this close to making the same mistake with you. But I can't do that, Yvonne. I have to swim now. I have to swim harder than ever before, even if it's against the current, even if I have to swim really far. I'm gonna do it, because what we have is too special, too important, to let it sink."

Tears gathered in her eyes, accompanied by an expression of pure wonder as she started to take in the scenery around them.

He smiled, squeezed her hand. "We're here."

Her vision swimming with tears, Yvonne turned slowly, looking around the place he'd brought her to.

The very building she'd looked at, the one she'd pegged as the perfect location for her child development center. "Why would you bring me here? And how would you even know?"

"I have my ways," Maxwell remarked with a wink.

She stared at him, drinking in his handsomeness. Dressed casually in a blue polo and dark denim jeans, he grinned at her, showing that full set of sparkling teeth that had caught her eye the first day she'd met him. She took a deep breath, closed her eyes, and opened them again to be sure she wasn't dreaming. Then she walked closer to the building. In the grassy area in front of the entrance, she spotted a small red sign printed with bold block letters. LEASED.

She jerked her head around to look at him. "Oh my God, Maxwell. Somebody got it."

He reached into the pocket of his jeans, extracting a set of keys, dangling them. "I know. I'm the somebody."

A fresh rain of tears filled her eyes, and she covered her face. "You didn't."

He laughed, dangled the keys again. "I did. I hope you're okay with that."

Taking slow, deep breaths, she stood in the grass, looking back and forth between him and the building. "This is...a lot. Can you explain to me what's going on exactly?"

"Sure. I was in your room—"

"What were you doing in there?"

He shifted his gaze up and to the right. "I missed you. The room still smelled like you and..." He waved his hands. "Anyway, that's beside the point."

She smiled, feeling the glimmer of satisfaction inside. *So he did miss me.*

"So while I was in there, I saw the real estate agent's card on the nightstand. I called her up, asked to see the place you'd been raving about. I met her here, toured the place, heard her whole sales pitch. Then I rented it for you. With an option to buy later, of course."

"Just like that?"

"When you pay in cash, things tend to move along pretty quickly."

She shook her head, still processing. "When did you do all this?"

"Yesterday." He walked over to her, handed her the keys. "I wanted to make sure we didn't miss it. She had a few people interested in it."

She blinked, feeling her heart swell. *That means yesterday, probably while I was talking with Mommy about temporary versus permanent, this man was investing in my dream.* "Did you say we?"

He moved his arms, making the motion of a breaststroke. "I'm kicking hard here, Yvonne. But I just want to make it clear that I support you, one hundred percent, no matter what. So whether you decide to take me back or not, this building is yours."

She stood there, mouth agape, looking at the gleaming silver keys in her palm. "I can't believe you did this, Maxwell."

"It was time for me to show you that I believe in you and in your dream. This was the most concrete way I could think of to do it." He gestured to the door. "Let's go inside. There's one more thing I want to show you."

Not sure she could handle much more, she climbed the three steps to the entrance and unlocked the door nonetheless. Hand in hand, they walked around the space. This time, she looked at it with fresh eyes, seeing all the potential it held. *Now that it belongs to me, I have so many more ideas of what I want to do with the space.* She stopped in places, making mental notes. "This is such a great space. I'm going to put the reception desk right here." She jogged over to the spot, gesturing with her hands. "I'm going to paint the walls sky blue, do the clouds and the sun. Maybe some butterflies."

"Kind of like Sasha's nursery, huh?"

"What can I say? Painting her room was good practice for this." She spun in a slow circle, picturing the way the lobby would look when the painting was done and the furniture was in. "This is going to be great. I'm so excited to get started."

"Let's go in here really quick." He led her to the left, to a small office situated off the main room. As he pushed open the door, she gasped.

The room, which had previously been empty, now held a large, carved oak desk and a brown leather executive chair. An engraved nameplate rested on the desktop. As she approached the desk, she picked up the nameplate and read it aloud in a voice trembling with emotion. "Yvonne Markham, Center Director." She sighed as she set it back down, turning to Maxwell. Her eyes welled up all over again. "I thought I was all cried out. Maxwell, this is amazing. Thank you. Thank you so, so much."

He used the pads of his thumbs to wipe away her tears. "I'm glad you like it. I was a little worried you might be angry that I just went out and rented it, since you've been saving up for it."

She shook her head. "No. I'm not mad. Besides, I'll need the money I've saved to outfit the place."

"So I did okay, then?" The look on his face was like a kid seeking an adult's approval.

She smiled, moving closer to him. "You did amazing."

"Great." He gestured to the door. "Ready to go?"

"Yeah." With one last look around her new building, she followed him outside. After she locked the place up, they sat down on the steps outside the front entrance.

"You know, I keep a graph paper notebook in my glove box," he remarked. "If you want, I could draw you up some plans for whatever changes you want to make to the building."

"You're laying it on pretty thick, aren't you, Max?"

"Is it working?"

"Absolutely." She leaned over and gave him a kiss square on the lips.

He pulled her into his arms, and she leaned into him, letting the kiss deepen. The spring breeze swirled around them, bringing with it the smell of pollen and the blooming azaleas, caressing her skin. The sunlight filtered through the canopy of trees above them. But for that moment, all that mattered in the world was this amazing man, the man she loved.

When they finally came up for air, he said, "I've missed you, Yvonne."

"I've missed you, too." She grazed her fingertips along his strong jawline.

"It was a terrible, empty feeling. And I don't ever want to feel that way again."

"Neither do I."

"Then marry me, Yvonne." His gaze locked with hers, and

he clasped her hand to his chest. "Marry me, and I'll promise to spend the rest of my life making you happy."

She could feel the beating of his heart beneath her palm, and it almost seemed to synchronize with her own. "Maxwell, are you serious?"

"Yes. I'm absolutely serious."

She couldn't resist teasing him. "Well, I'd have to see the ring before I make a decision."

He tilted his head to one side. "You're sitting on the steps of your ring."

She looked up. "The building? I mean, it's nice, but it's not a diamond..." She made a fake pouty face. "Plus, you rented the building. You didn't buy it, so..."

He laughed. "If you say yes, I'll get you a ring. You can have both. You can have whatever you want. Just say yes, Yvonne."

She smiled, feeling the lightest and happiest she had in ages. "Yes, Maxwell."

"Hot damn!" He slapped his thigh, then dragged her close to him, planting a kiss on her that was so hot and so intense her knees melted down into her shoes.

Back in the car, she passed the set of keys back and forth between her two hands. They were light, probably made of aluminum. But the keys and everything they represented held so much weight in her life. "I can't believe I became a business owner and a fiancée in a single day. My mom will be deliriously happy when she hears about this."

He laughed. "I'm glad to hear that, Von. But what about you? Are you happy?"

She looked his way, her heart soaring. "Oh yeah."

CHAPTER 24

SITTING IN INES'S LIVING ROOM SATURDAY MORNING, Maxwell looked around the space. Things had been modified a bit since he was last there, most likely to make things easier for Ines. The throw rugs had been taken up, and the old recliner had been replaced with a lift chair that could assist her to her feet if she needed it.

Juliana entered the room with Sasha in her arms, taking a seat across from him.

Seated on the love seat, he asked, "So how much longer before you have to go back over there?"

She gave him a little half smile. "I'm flying out Wednesday evening. I've still got a bunch of stuff to take care of before then, but I'll swing by and see my baby girl once more before I head to the airport."

"We'll make sure to make time." He studied her face. "Is the tough girl getting a little misty on me?"

She rolled her eyes as she brushed a tear away. "It's never easy leaving her, you know. I cried for two days when I left the first time." She blew out a breath. "Hopefully the last half of the deployment will go by fast."

He gave her shoulder a squeeze. "Here's hoping. And I just want you to know, I do worry about you when you're doing dangerous work in dangerous places. I always did. I guess I just wasn't good at expressing it."

She nodded. "Noted. And yes, you sucked at showing it. But I'll accept your retroactive concern."

"Great."

"We can iron out more details of custody when I get back." She ran a hand over her hair. "I'm thinking she'll be with you any time duty calls me away, and then when I'm stateside, we can alternate weeks or something."

"I'll do whatever will work best for Sasha. It'll get a little more difficult after she starts school, but we'll work it out."

"Thank you for being so flexible, Max." Juliana gave the baby a kiss on the forehead. "You're a lot different now from when we were together. More...mature, I guess."

He chuckled. "Thanks for noticing my growth, Jules." *Almost losing the love of your life will do that to you.* "I'd better get her home. She'll be caterwauling for lunch before long."

Juliana laughed. "You're right. She seems to be on a pretty tight schedule."

"That's all Von. She's a natural with her."

"I'll say. I've heard Sasha babbling a lot while she's been here." She twirled one of the baby's curls around her index finger, then released it. "I'd be lying if I said I wasn't a little jealous. But I know I'll get to log more time with Sasha after I retire."

"Thinking of taking the twenty years instead of going for twenty-five?"

She nodded. "Yeah. I just don't want to miss out on any more of her growing up than I have to, you know?"

"I totally understand. Nothing changes your priorities quite like becoming a parent." He held out his arms, and Sasha crawled over to him. Standing up, he took the baby bag from Juliana. "Say see you later, Mommy."

"Adios for now, *Mijita*. Be a good girl." She stood, kissing Sasha's cheek. "Give my regards to Yvonne."

"I will," he promised as he carried Sasha to the front door and opened it.

"You know what, Max? I like Yvonne. She's good for you and for Sasha." Juliana propped her fists on her hips. "Do right by her, okay? Don't screw it up."

He shook his head, chuckling to himself. "Trust me. I won't." *She doesn't need to know how close I came.* With a wave, he and Sasha departed for home.

—⁓—

The second Saturday in July dawned with a beautiful blue, cloudless sky. And from the moment Yvonne rose that day, she wore a smile that nothing could erase.

Today's the day. It's finally here. Weeks of frenzied planning, of cake tastings and dress fittings, of phone calls and appointments, were about to come to fruition. And when it was all over, she'd be Mrs. Yvonne Markham-Devers.

A knock sounded at the door. "Von? Are you awake? It's Del."

"Good morning, Mama Del. Yes, I'm up." She'd come to love her future mother-in-law over the past few weeks, and she looked forward to joining the Devers family.

"Come on down for breakfast soon as you're ready, darling."

She popped out of bed, opening the door.

Delphinia stood in the hallway wearing a floral housecoat, bunny slippers, and a head full of pink curlers. "Well, hello, sunshine."

Pulling Delphinia in for a hug, Yvonne said, "Thank you again, for everything. For letting my mom, Zelda, and Athena stay here, and for hosting the wedding..."

Delphinia waved her off. "I'm glad to do it. Now throw on your robe and come downstairs, honey. You've got a big day ahead of you." With a smile, she walked off.

After eating a small portion of the lumberjack breakfast Humphrey and Delphinia had prepared, Yvonne and all the women retreated upstairs to get ready while Humphrey left to go over to Maxwell's, where the men were making their preparations.

In the guest room where she'd been staying, Yvonne smiled

as her mother helped her into her dress. The white chiffon gown, an A-line silhouette with a diamond-shaped back cutout and a beautiful Venice lace overlay, was a bear to get into. But when she looked at herself in the mirror, she could see all the trouble had been worth it. Her eyes were misty as her mother pulled the lace-edged veil down over her face.

Her mother brushed away tears of her own. "You look beautiful, baby. Just like an angel."

"You look really pretty, too, Mommy." She hugged her mother, careful not to wrinkle her mint-green taffeta sheath.

Zelda and Athena entered then, wearing their gold satin cocktail dresses. Pretty soon, all four of them were hugging and crying.

"Okay, quit." Yvonne dabbed at her eyes with a tissue. "I can't go out there looking like a raccoon, so y'all pull yourselves together." She turned to Athena. "Did my mascara run?"

Athena shook her head, laughing. "Nope. Looks like it's just as waterproof as the tube says. That's a first."

Yvonne looked in the mirror one more time. She touched the old, borrowed locket around her neck, a gift from her father to her mother on their first wedding anniversary. The diamond clusters in her ears were her "new," a wedding gift from Maxwell. And her Granny Vera's blue handkerchief, embroidered with music notes, was wrapped around the stems of the sterling roses and baby's breath that made up her bouquet.

Delphinia poked her head in the room. "Well, look at you. You're a vision."

"Thank you." Yvonne held it together, determined not to ruin her makeup.

"You ready, sweetheart?"

She nodded. Her forever with Maxwell was about to start, and she couldn't wait. "Yes."

Downstairs in the parlor, she stood with her father, watching as the wedding party made their way out to the pergola set up in the backyard. Rows of white chairs filled the yard, and she could see Maxwell standing there with Jeffrey, whom he'd chosen as his best man. *Maxwell looks so handsome.* The sight of him in the smart gray tuxedo trimmed with black satin made her all the more eager to become his wife.

As she and her father stood just out of sight, the procession continued. Maxwell's three married frat brothers went out first, escorting their wives. She'd gotten to know them all, and she now considered them all good friends. She nodded to Tyrone and Georgia, Xavier and Imani, and Bryan and Alexis as they passed her. Last, Orion accompanied Kelsey down the aisle, each of them holding one of Sasha's hands. Sasha, the official flower girl, was now a year old, and she drew plenty of "awws" from the guests as she toddled down the aisle with her aunt and godfather.

Finally, the doors were propped open, and she stepped out onto the patio on her father's arm. While the hired musician played Phyllis Hyman's "Meet Me on the Moon" on the acoustic guitar, Yvonne moved toward the man she loved. Her eyes met Maxwell's, and she held his gaze until she reached him. And when her father placed her hand in Maxwell's, she felt the tears rising in her throat.

She viewed his face through a sheen of tears as they exchanged vows and rings. When Reverend Emerson pronounced them husband and wife, she fell into Maxwell's arms and let him kiss her until her knees went weak.

Later, they sat at the head table beneath the big tent. The sun had set, and the interior of the tent was lit by candles and the strings of white lights hanging from the supports. Every few seconds, they leaned close to one another to steal kisses, to the delight of their guests.

"Mmm." Maxwell nipped at her ear. "Have I told you how beautiful you look today?"

She giggled. "Yes, but it never gets old."

He teased her earlobe with love-gentled teeth. "I'm about ready to get you out of here...and out of that dress."

She popped his hand. "I'm sure everybody here can tell, with the way you're carrying on."

"Well, let's dance." He stood, held out his hand. "After we dance, there's no reason we have to stay."

She cued the DJ, who started up their song, "Where Would I Be (The Question)" by Kindred the Family Soul. As he twirled her around the dance floor, she felt her very soul was at peace. A life with him was all she needed, the joy she never even knew she was missing.

As the night deepened, they escaped into a chauffeur-driven sedan under a shower of bubbles, leaving Sasha with Maxwell's parents as they headed off to their hotel for the night.

Yvonne dissolved into laughter as Maxwell lifted her up and carried her over the threshold of their honeymoon suite at a hotel near the airport. "Easy there. You don't want to be limping when we catch our flight to Turks and Caicos in the morning."

He set her down, slapping her on the butt. "Don't worry. If I hurt myself, it's gonna be in that bed. I'm about to work that body like a nine-to-five." His eyes sparkled with mischief.

The fire rose in her blood, her body demanding the satisfaction she could only get from his touch. "Well, husband, I'd say it's time to punch the clock."

He pulled her into his arms and kissed her, using his foot to kick the door shut.

"I love you, Max."

"Not half as much as I love you."

And in the darkness of their room, he stripped her out of her gown and expressed that love in many new and delightful ways.

The End

ACKNOWLEDGMENTS

Many thanks to my readers, and to my wonderful friends in the Destin Divas writing groups. You all keep me going! Also, my thanks to the folks posting on the Black Greek hashtags on social media, which provided me with a lot of inspiration. I hope the series has given people a peek into the very special traditions associated with these storied organizations, founded on the principles of brotherhood and service to the community.

ABOUT THE AUTHOR

Like any good Southern belle, Kianna Alexander wears many hats: doting mama, advice-dispensing sister, and gabbing girlfriend. She's a voracious reader, an amateur seamstress, and an occasional painter in oils. Chocolate, American history, sweet tea, and Idris Elba are a few of her favorite things. A native of the Tar Heel State, Kianna still lives there, and still maintains her collection of well-loved vintage '80s Barbie dolls.

For more about Kianna and her books, visit her website at authorkiannaalexander.com and sign up for her newsletter.

Follow Kianna at: facebook.com/KiannaWrites, twitter.com/KiannaWrites, pinterest.com/KiannaWrites, and instagram.com/KiannaAlexanderWrites.

Keep reading for an excerpt from the first book in
Kianna Alexander's **Southern Gentlemen series**

Back to Your Love

CHAPTER 1

Imani Grant stood on the balcony of her hotel room, taking in the marvelous view. The seventh-floor suite allowed her an unobstructed look at the wide, sandy band of beach below as well as the soft, rising waves of the Atlantic lapping at the shore. The late-afternoon sun steadily crept toward the horizon, and she shielded her eyes with a hand. Knowing her girlfriends would be expecting her for the rehearsal dinner, she drew in one last deep breath of the salt-tinged air, then withdrew into the room, closing the French doors behind her.

Since coming to Atlantic Beach earlier that morning, she'd been holed up in her room reading, relaxing, and girding her loins. This was the third time in fourteen months she'd been asked to serve as a bridesmaid for one of her friends. At this point, her nerves were beyond frazzled. If her mother inquired just once more about whether she was seeing anyone, she was pretty sure her head would explode.

She'd only reluctantly agreed to stay in this hotel with the wedding party. She had tired of all the pre-wedding madness, having done it twice in the last year, but she did want to be there for the bride, in case she needed anything. Georgia had been her college roommate and constant companion through four years of undergrad at Spelman. Imani was sick of weddings, but she would do anything for Georgia, so there she was. Luckily, neither the bride nor the coordinator had summoned her today, allowing her plenty of time to prepare herself to go through the motions once again.

She knew there would be questions from the well-intentioned older ladies present for the joyous event about why she was still single. She thought of Xavier, her first love, who'd crushed her heart like a bug beneath his shoe. She'd thought that was the pinnacle of pain until she'd lost her father to violence. Now, her focus was on her new business venture. She'd worked hard to reach her goal, and she didn't have time to deal with the inevitable drama relationships brought.

Adjusting the strapless, yellow maxi dress she'd chosen for the occasion, she put on a little makeup and a pair of gold, heart-shaped stud earrings. Standing in front of the full-length mirror on the wall, she pulled her hair up into a high ponytail and secured it. Satisfied with the results, she grabbed her purse, stuffed her keys inside, and left.

A brief walk through the hotel's paisley-carpeted interior took her to the private suite where the rehearsal dinner was being held. Georgia had opted to have all her events inside the hotel for the sake of convenience, which was easily accomplished due to the vast size of the property.

Waiting near the suite's open door was Georgia's mother, Diane. Seeing Imani approach, the older woman smiled, then stood to give her a big hug. "Hey, Imani. How are you doing, sweetheart?"

She returned the hug, giving the older woman a squeeze. It had been ages since she'd last seen her best friend's kindhearted mother. "I'm fine, Diane. And I'm so glad to be a part of Georgia's special day."

Diane nodded. "We're all so excited. I'll see you inside."

As Imani turned to go into the room, Diane gave her a gentle pat on the shoulder. "And don't you fret, sweetheart. We'll all be getting together for your wedding sometime soon. I just know it."

Imani stiffened a bit at the well-meaning remark but shook it off. A false smile stretched her lips as she turned back long enough to nod to Diane. Then, she strode into the large suite and looked around to get the lay of the land.

The enormous room had one long, rectangular table set up in its center. Above the table hung a beautiful crystal chandelier, the bulbs designed to look like the gas lamps of centuries past, casting a decidedly romantic glow on the whole room. Along the far wall, the buffet was so filled with silver-covered warmers and trays of food, it looked in danger of collapsing at any moment. Imani picked up one delicious scent after another, and her stomach rumbled in anticipation.

Most of Georgia's close relatives, as well as those of the groom, Tyrone Fields, were either already seated, or standing in various nooks and crannies around the room, carrying on lively conversations. She waved to the other two bridesmaids, as well as the matron of honor, Georgia's older sister, Gail. Seeing that they were all seated at the end of the table where Georgia was, Imani walked over to join them.

London and Julia, also classmates at Spelman, gestured to the empty chair between them.

"Squeeze in," London said as she slid her chair back to allow Imani room to sit down.

Georgia, sitting at the end of the table, was beaming so much Imani couldn't help smiling in her direction. "I assume from that grin that everything is going as you planned, Georgia."

Georgia nodded, still smiling. "It sure is."

At first, it had seemed that Georgia was simply staring off into the distance. Now, Imani realized that she and the other women were all looking in the same direction. Confusion and curiosity knitting her brow, Imani turned to see what had captured everyone's attention.

That was when she saw Xavier Whitted striding across the room. There was no way she could have missed him—his six-foot-three-inch height made him tower over most of the people in attendance. Her heart began pounding so loud she was sure everyone in the room could hear it. *What in the hell is he doing here?*

She tore her eyes away from the handsome man from her past and looked at Georgia with a questioning gaze. At first, Georgia didn't seem to notice, but their gazes met after Imani loudly cleared her throat.

Georgia responded this time but still watched Xavier with appreciative eyes. "Isn't he fine? He's Tyrone's best man, one of his TDT brothers. His name is—"

Imani interrupted her. "I know his name. Xavier Whitted."

All the female eyes at that end of the table turned on her. The question hung in the air for a long second before Julia all but shouted, "Where do you know him from?"

"He was my high school boyfriend." Imani stood as she answered the question, because it now seemed Xavier had spotted her and was approaching fast.

"Small world." Gail winked.

Georgia made a sound of discovery. "Oh! So that explains why he was so eager to take you out. He must still be carrying a torch for you."

Imani walked over and stood behind Georgia's chair and placed a hand on each of her shoulders. "Georgia, please tell me you didn't."

"What?" The bride-to-be feigned innocence.

"Georgia, did you set me up with him?" She uttered those words in a rushed whisper, because Xavier's long legs were bringing him closer at an alarming speed.

"I might have."

The noncommittal response was all Imani needed to know that her proverbial goose was cooked. She squeezed Georgia's shoulder. "I gave you a really nice wedding gift. I think I want it back."

It was all she had time to say before Xavier appeared next to her.

He smiled, showing off teeth so straight and white, they were almost too perfect. "Imani. It's so good to see you." He reached for her hand, capturing it in his much larger one.

It was the first touch she'd had from him in a decade, yet the shivers still danced across her skin. Aware of the four sets of nosy female eyes trained on them, she smiled, hoping to mask her nervousness. "It's good to see you again, too, Xavier."

He watched her for a few silent seconds, as if trying to read her. Then, he dipped his head and placed a soft kiss against her cheek. "I have to go sit with the boys at the other end of the table, but we'll chat later, okay?" He gave her hand a squeeze, then slipped away.

She'd been totally unprepared for the kiss, and while brief and chaste, it reminded her of other encounters they'd had, which were much the opposite. Tingles ran through her entire body, careening and colliding like a jar full of angry hornets. Recovering her senses as quickly as she could, she retook her seat and found everyone staring at her.

Glancing around at her friends, she fished around in her purse for her cell phone. "What? Why is everyone looking at me like that?"

Finally, Gail asked pointedly, "Did you bring a shawl or a jacket?"

Embarrassment heated her cheeks when she realized what Gail was referring to. She didn't have to look down to know that her nipples were standing like two pebbles inside the confines of her dress. Folding her arms over her chest, she cursed to herself.

Apparently, even after a decade apart, Xavier Whitted still held the same magical power over her body.

During the rehearsal dinner, Xavier tried to appear interested in the conversation at his end of the table while stealing glances at Imani. Tyrone Fields was his closest friend, and Xavier didn't want to shirk his duties as best man. He'd spent the better part of the last week running errands all over the Tar Heel state, taking the burden off Ty's shoulders so Ty could concentrate on getting ready to marry his dream girl. It seemed pretty slack of Xavier now to ignore his buddy's words, but Xavier couldn't help it. Seeing Imani tonight had him so off-kilter, it was all he could do not to drag her out of the room to some dark corner of the hotel, where he could kiss her full lips the way he needed so badly to do.

Around their end of the table were all the boys from Central, who'd pledged to Theta Delta Theta fraternity ten years before. This was the first time they'd all been in the same place in nearly five years, when they'd come together for the funeral of their old TDT advisor, Dr. Mitcham. Among them, Xavier was the eldest by a matter of months and had been nicknamed "the Activist," based on his passionate pursuit of community and charity work. Over the years, they'd kept in contact and seen each other whenever possible, as each brother came into his own success as an adult. Each man had lived up to his nickname in one way or another.

Between mouthfuls of food, Tyrone was going on about his latest case in family court. "This York case is getting ugly, and there are children involved. It really makes me wonder why people don't spend more time getting to know each other before they fall into bed and make a baby."

Xavier half listened, picking up on key words and nodding occasionally in a show of interest. In reality, though, his attention was on Imani. There she sat, at the opposite end of the table, looking even more beautiful than he remembered her. When they'd dated in high school, she'd been a quiet, shy teenager, and she'd owned his whole heart. Nearly ten years had passed, and he hadn't seen more than a brief glimpse of her since they'd both gone away to college.

He'd wanted to contact her so many times over the years, but he knew she would never have taken his call. After the way he'd ended things between them after their senior year of high school, he understood why. He knew he'd hurt her and still lived with the regret. His last relationship with a woman had left him with scars of his own. His ex had shown him just how conniving women could be. Imani was different, though. The Imani he knew would never do those things to him.

He could still see signs of the shy young girl he'd known all those years ago, but now she was all woman. It was hard to ignore the regal lines of her face, the glossy hair, and the yellow sundress that clung to her feminine frame in all the right places. There was nothing short of an act of God that would have made him miss his best friend's wedding, but having Imani there made this weekend even more important.

Orion MacMillan, dubbed "the Young'n" since he was the only freshman to pledge TDT that year, shook his head. "Damn, Ty. We all love you, but you are boring us to tears with all this legal talk. You don't hear me going on and on about Young-n-Wild." The popular preteen hip-hop duo was Orion's latest babysitting job as the head of A&R for Wilmington-based Fresh2Deff Records.

Bryan "the Legacy" James, grandson of one of TDT's founding members, snorted. "Actually, hearing about those little roughnecks would be way more interesting." Bryan, a marketing executive for Royal Textiles, made ass-loads of money while traveling the globe but rarely burdened his friends with the dull details of his work.

Devers Architectural Development's CEO, Maxwell Devers,

"the Bad Boy," reclined in his seat, his arms folded and tucked behind his head. "We're all suffering through Ty's monologue here, but somebody at this table isn't even pretending to be interested." Max shifted his gaze pointedly.

Xavier became aware that all eyes at that end of the table were focused on him. Loosening the top button of his light-blue shirt, he groaned. "Come on, now. How you gonna call me out like that, Max?"

Maxwell shrugged, his default reaction to a direct question he had no interest in answering.

Tyrone slugged Xavier in the shoulder. "I knew you weren't listening. I was hoping if I kept talking, you might eventually give a damn about what I was saying."

"He's only got eyes for the honey in the yellow dress." Orion made the observation as he took a draw from his mug of beer.

Bryan chuckled as he swiped his finger across the screen of his smartphone. "Who could blame him? The sister is fine."

Xavier felt a bit of jealousy creep into his mind but pushed it aside. His Theta brothers were his closest friends, and he knew none of them would pursue a woman he was so obviously interested in. "We dated in high school. I'm just admiring the woman she's become."

"What time are we supposed to meet tomorrow and where?" Maxwell effectively changed the subject.

The groom looked to his best man, deferring to him.

Xavier cleared his throat. "Four o'clock sharp, in the lobby. We'll get dressed in one of the meeting rooms and then go to the shore for the ceremony."

"By the way, I saw the tuxes. Nice touch putting us in the green and silver, bro." Orion nodded his approval of their attire while taking in the scene around them.

Tyrone grinned. "Of course. The Theta colors were the natural choice for me. I'm just glad Georgia was willing to go along with it."

Their banter was interrupted by Misty, the high-strung, blond wedding coordinator. Her pointer finger extended, she pretty much stabbed Tyrone in the shoulder. "We're wrapping things up, Mr. Fields. It'd be a good time for you and Georgia to give a quick speech. You know, expressing your gratitude and whatnot." Her words were a bit disingenuous, but in Misty's thick Southern accent, everything sounded that way.

Tyrone stood. "All right, boys. Duty calls. I guess that's it until tomorrow."

Xavier watched his friend walk away and drape his arm around Georgia's waist. He listened while the two lovebirds expressed their thanks to everyone who'd traveled in to attend the wedding or contributed in some other way. Once the speech was over and the applause and cheering died down, the crowd began to disperse.

Saying a quick good-bye to his fraternity brothers, Xavier wove his way through the crowd, intent on getting to Imani before she disappeared for the evening. He knew he would see her tomorrow at the ceremony, but he really wanted to see her tonight.

Alone.

She floated around the room for a few moments, and he got the sense she was avoiding him. But as more people left, effectively emptying the room, she had fewer places to hide.

He strode up to where she stood by the crystal punch bowl, her glass in one hand and the ladle in the other. When she saw him, her eyes widened. To his mind, she had the look of a deer facing down a set of oncoming headlights.

He stuck his hand out and repositioned her glass just in time to keep her from pouring a ladleful of bright-red punch onto the hotel's carpeted floor. "Hello again, Imani. Or should I say Dr. Grant? I heard about your new practice. Congratulations on that."

She blinked a few times, then seemed to recover her senses. Replacing the empty ladle in the bowl, she took a sip from the glass. "Thanks, but no need to be so formal. I'd prefer you call me Imani."

"Good. I prefer that as well." He felt an overwhelming urge to reach out and stroke her satin jaw but restrained himself since there were a few folks hanging around.

Still looking a little uncomfortable under his scrutiny, she asked, "So, what have you been up to since high school?"

"I'm a CPA, and I run my own little firm. It's probably not going to make me wealthy, but working for myself gives me the time I need to do community work."

The corners of her mouth turned up a bit. "I know. I've read about some of your work in the paper. I see you still have that good heart."

Honored by her acknowledgment, he gave a smile of his own. "I know this is kind of a crazy weekend, but if Georgia doesn't need you for anything else tonight, would you mind if we went somewhere to talk for a bit?"

The rapid blinking started again, her lids fluttering over those chocolate-brown eyes. She inhaled deeply, then answered, "Okay."

Pleased, he offered her the crook of his arm. She slid her delicate hand inside, and he led her out of the room.

Navigating the corridors of the hotel, Imani kept her arm looped loosely through Xavier's. Despite her attempts to avoid him tonight, he'd charmed her, and now here she was, heading off with him to "talk." She was partly annoyed at having to face the complicated array of emotions he evoked in her, but partly flattered. Apparently, in the years they'd been apart, he'd retained at least two of the qualities she'd known him for back then: persistence and handsomeness.

"Have you been here before?" She felt a need both to break the awkward silence that had fallen between them and to see if the long strides she struggled to keep up with were leading them somewhere in particular.

He nodded, not slowing his steps. "Yep. Came down here a few weeks ago with Georgia, Tyrone, and Gail to tour the hotel. Our bride and groom wanted us to be familiar with the property."

"Okay" was all she could think of to say.

"Don't worry. I know the perfect place to sit and talk. It's nice and quiet, too."

And secluded, I bet.

She let him lead her around a corner to the right, then down an interior hallway of the hotel. There were a few small meeting rooms on the left side of the hallway, but none of them seemed to be occupied. On the right side, however, she spied a section of the wall entirely made of glass. It looked out on a beautiful courtyard situated between two wings of the hotel.

Xavier stepped to the glass door and swung it open. "After you, Imani."

She stepped outside, and immediately lamented the loss of air-conditioning. Though the hour was late, the air was thick with the heat and humidity customary for early summer in North Carolina. The tart aroma of the salty waters lying just beyond the hotel property permeated the air. Lush tropical plants filled the small courtyard, some blooming with bright-colored flowers. In the center of it all, three stepping-stones led to a wrought-iron bench positioned among the leaves and vines.

By the time she finished gawking around, he had already taken a seat on the bench. He patted the empty space next to him. "Come sit with me. I won't bite unless you ask me to."

The sexy wink he threw her made her traitorous nipples pebble again beneath her dress. Ignoring her body's reaction as best she could, she eased into the spot.

Gently, he draped his arm around her bare shoulders.

The feel of his touch radiated through her, the growing warmth inside her far exceeding the temperature of the sultry June night. Being in his arms again didn't feel foreign, the way it should have after so many years. His touch felt as natural and familiar as her own heartbeat. She noticed the rapid pace of her breathing and wondered if he noticed it as well.

The low timbre of his voice broke the silence. "If I'm making you uncomfortable, just say so. That's the last thing I want to do, Imani."

So he had picked up on her nervousness. She shook her head. While her mind told her not to let him get behind her defenses, her heart didn't want him to withdraw his touch. Instead, she answered him but kept her eyes directed at her lap. "No. It's all right."

"If you say so. I brought you out here to talk, so let's talk. What have you been up to these last ten years, other than growing more beautiful?"

She felt the smile creep over her face at the smoothly delivered compliment. "Let's see. I did undergrad in biology at Spelman, then med school at Meharry, then my dermatology certification—"

"Whoa. Are you telling me all you've been doing for the last decade is being a student?"

She shrugged. "I guess so. But I had a goal in mind, and hard work and lots of school were the only ways to reach it."

That drew a low, rumbling chuckle from him. "I can't say I'm surprised. You always were intelligent and determined. I'm glad to see you're accomplishing your goals."

She took a chance and raised her gaze to his. His rich, dark eyes held the same sincerity she'd detected in his words. "Thank you, Xavier. I appreciate that."

A silent moment passed between them, their gazes connecting.

When his scrutiny became too intense, she broke the silence. "So, uh, what have you been up to? I've read in the paper, and heard from Mama, that you're doing a lot of good work in the community."

A broad smile spread across his face. "I'm glad to know Ma Alma speaks of me so highly. When I'm not in the office handling the books for my clients, I volunteer at a youth center in the old neighborhood, and I do a little work at Second Harvest Food Bank from time to time. I'm no saint, but I do what I can for the community."

"I'm really impressed, Xavier."

"Thanks." His smile broadened, dazzling her. "Then I hope I can count on your vote in the city council race. If I win, I can do even more."

Listening to him talk about his good works in such a modest way, she realized he still had a wonderful heart. In the few weeks she'd been home, her mother had gone on and on about Xavier's activism. As an all-star athlete and scholar in high school, he could have chosen any career path he'd wanted. But instead of taking some high-paying, high-profile position, he'd chosen to make a modest living so that he could give back to the community that had nurtured him as a child. Yes, Xavier Whitted was a rare bird, and if the look in his eyes was any indication, he was ready to build a nest.

There, beneath his searching gaze, she could feel her very soul opening up. Once upon a time, she'd been certain she'd marry this man. Now, she felt like an inexperienced adolescent. No matter how she tried, she couldn't look away from him.

The heartbreak she'd suffered at Xavier's hands had colored her perception of men. He'd been her first love and had shown her a first glimpse of real pain. Maybe she should thank him for that, because it had allowed her to focus on her goals, rather than be consumed by chasing after a suitable mate.

"Imani, I'm going to kiss you. Is that all right?"

She heard his soft words, and even as her brain yelled at her to back away before she lost her heart to him a second time, no words would come. All she could manage was to look into the endless pools of his eyes.

An instant later, his lips touched hers. The sweetness of his kiss and the buttery softness of his lips made her eyes shut. Her body overtook her brain once again, and she pressed herself closer to him. He pulled her close, surrounding her with his strong arms, and she loved it, God help her. The kiss deepened, and as his skilled tongue stroked against the interior of her mouth, she could feel her insides melting down into her shoes like hot wax.

When he finally broke the kiss, she sighed. It was a sound of pleasure, and by the time she covered her mouth to stop it, it was too late. Feeling the warm blood pooling in her cheeks, and in locations much farther south, she turned away from him.

His fingertips grazed her chin as he gently turned her back to face him. "It's chemistry, Imani. It can't be helped, and there's nothing to be ashamed of."

She nodded. "I wasn't ready for all of this. I just came to be here for Georgia."

"I know, and I won't interfere with that. I'm here as Ty's best man, so that's my priority now."

That made her feel somewhat relieved.

"Make no mistake, though. When this wedding is over, I intend to continue discovering the woman you've become, if you'll let me."

She drew a deep breath. "Xavier—"

He silenced her with a fleeting kiss on the cheek. "We don't have to talk about it now. It's late. Come on. I'll walk you to your room."

He got up and extended his hand to her, and she accepted it. Together, they reentered the hotel, navigating the corridors and elevators again until they stood before the door to her suite.

He squeezed her hand, then released it. "Get some rest, Imani. I'll see you tomorrow."

"Good night, Xavier."

He inclined his head, then began striding down the hall.

She slid her key card into the slot and opened the door.

But instead of going in, she stood in the doorway and watched him until he was out of sight.

Author Kianna Alexander brings enduring friendship, heartwarming romance, and true southern hospitality to life in the charming **Southern Gentlemen series**

Back to Your Love

When Xavier Whitted goes to his best friend's wedding, he's blown away to see his high school sweetheart, the only woman he's ever loved and whose heart he broke years ago. He's got a lot to make up for...

Couldn't Ask for More

Fashion designer Alexis Devers agrees to work for Bryan James's company—but there's absolutely no way she will fall for her brother's best friend...

"Worth every moment...true depth of feeling."
—*Harlequin Junkie* for *Back to Your Love*

For more info about Sourcebooks's books and authors, visit:
sourcebooks.com

RESCUE ME

In this fresh, poignant series about rescue
animals, every heart has a forever home
By Debbie Burns, award-winning debut author

A New Leash on Love

When Craig Williams arrived at the local no-kill animal shelter for
help, he didn't expect a fiery young woman to blaze into his life.
But the more time he spends with Megan, the more he realizes it's
not just animals she's adept at saving...

Sit, Stay, Love

For devoted no-kill shelter worker Kelsey Sutton, rehabbing a
group of rescue dogs is a welcome challenge. Working with a sexy
ex-military dog handler who needs some TLC himself? That's a
whole different story...

My Forever Home

There's no denying Tess Grasso has a way with animals, but when
she helps Mason Redding give a free-spirited stray a second
chance, this husky might teach them a few things about faith, love,
and forgiveness.

"Sexy and fun..."
—*RT Book Reviews* for *A New Leash on Love*,
Top Pick, 4½ Stars

For more info about Sourcebooks's books and authors, visit:
sourcebooks.com